Shad Run

Shad Run

HOWARD BRESLIN

THOMAS Y. CROWELL COMPANY · NEW YORK

For Pat
And Knowles

The shad still run up the river every Spring, and the Hudson's tides flow much as they did in 1788. All else is changed, the town on the east bank, the people, even the document so bitterly discussed, and the nation it made possible. This story is fiction set in a year of history. Except for certain, easily recognized, historical figures, all the characters are invented. For the beauty of a river beyond his invention, the author has always been thankful.

BOOK ONE: EBBTIDE

I

THAT YEAR THE ICE BROKE ON THE HUDSON RIVER IN MID-MARCH, NEI-
ther unusually late nor early. Though the time was right, there
had not been much warning. The winds of the month had carried
no hint of thaw as they swept the frozen surface, raising thin feath-
ers of spindrift. On the west bank patches of snow still clung to the
Highlands, mottling those dark cliffs like worn spots rubbed through
an old bearskin. Across the Hudson, in the town of Poughkeepsie,
other unmelted clumps made a skewbald pattern on the narrow,
brown roads. There was one huddled behind a corner of the courthouse; a sloop drawn high at Shipyard Point seemed to be resting on
a bed of dirty cotton batting.

True, the day had been clear and sunny, but it wasn't warm. If
leads, the open crevices in the ice, had widened under the feet of the
skaters who'd descended the bluff to sport on the river, a cold night
would refreeze them. Not even the most weather-wise thought that
the pale gold of the setting sun promised change. Even Lancey Quist,
who should have known better, was caught completely by surprise.

The first reports were loud, startling—a crack like a snapped tree,
a thud like a fired howitzer, the rapid splintering such as a sledge
might make as it crashed along the pickets of a fence.

Hearing, Lancey Quist stood motionless. The cold air turned her
breath of amazement to smoke. She was facing west, below a ridge
that hid the river, but she could see the rampart of the higher bank
on the far shore, and the sun starting to dip behind it. It was, Lancey
thought, a sun very like a cookie, thin, butter tinted, with an edge
of tan crisp around its rim, and the bottom already nibbled by the
ragged crest of the Highlands.

"God and Nicholas!" Lancey said, swearing.

Standing there, chin raised as she stared upward, the long skirt
alone showed her sex. Lancey was not tall, a scant three inches over
five feet. The knitted cap pulled down over her ears for warmth hid
her hair. A bulky man's coat, sailcloth dyed blue, knee length, was

3

belted over her gray homespun dress. All her clothes were worn and mended; her mittens didn't match.

Even the girl's fine features, the straight nose, the long black eyelashes, the curved brows, could have belonged to a too pretty youth. If the bone structure of cheek and jaw-line seemed delicate, the mouth, full lipped, was too broad for beauty. Her skin, faintly olive, was as smooth as polished hardwood.

It was a face that displayed every mood, every change of emotion. Now, it darkened as surprise was replaced by anger.

Her small body was tense with outrage. She knew what the sounds meant; she'd been raised on the riverfront. In all her sixteen years she had never heard those seasonal signals with such bitter feeling.

"No," she said, "no, no, no!" Her hazel eyes flashed, and she stamped her foot. The blades of the skates she was carrying clashed together, jangling.

It wasn't fair. It simply and damnably was not fair! She was four miles south of home, and she had tramped the whole way down warmed by the thought of skating back. She had lain behind a woodpile, skulked around corners, suffered agonies. Fingers and toes had grown numb while she waited her chance. They were still numb. In fact, she was chilled clean through, limbs, ribs, sit-down, everything!

If I'm that frozen, Lancey thought savagely, how can the ice be breaking?

She didn't really doubt that it was. She'd heard the river was open almost to Fishkill Landing, but that was eight miles or more farther south. Usually she'd have welcomed the sight, counted the floes joyously, as her river shook loose the frosty shackles that had locked it bank to bank. Not today!

"One more day," Lancey said, aloud. "Just one. Less. A couple or three hours!" She wasn't pleading, or praying. The words crackled as she spat them out, arguing against the louder crackling from the river.

Then, because she had to *see*, she began to run.

Raising her skirts knee high, Lancey raced for the top of the ridge. She ran well, lithely, feet drumming surely up the twisted, uneven trail. Her speed, the quick, sprinting strides, the easy balance, were all more like a boy's than a girl's, but there was nothing boyish about the legs flashing from the gathered red-and-white swirl of her petticoats. These, in spite of her height and the coarse brown knitted stockings, were long and shapely.

The skates clanged at every step, and Lancey felt an angry impulse

4

to hurl them aside. Her arm went up, but she checked the movement.

Still running she raised them to eye-level, glared at them. The pesky things had given her a deal of trouble. Then her glare softened. They were well made, pert and neat. The blades gleamed in the late sunlight, bright and sharp, hollow-ground; the wooden uppers, flat-topped hulls like toy boats, were carved to fit under the sole of a lady's shoe. There were leather thongs to tie them on, and the wood was painted the same scarlet as Lancey's wool cap. That color was what had first caught her glance.

The girl stumbled, skipped to regain balance, went on. A grin flashed as she mocked her clumsiness. Pride, she remembered, went before a fall, but she was proud of the red skates.

At the top of the ridge Lancey emerged from tree shadows full into the rays of the sunset. It bathed her in soft light, without warmth. She didn't notice it, or that the wind had died. Panting, she stared down at the river, aware only of the chill of disappointment. Her heart was pounding, her cheeks glowed, but she seemed to draw in coldness with every breath, draw it deep, down her throat, through her chest, deep into her.

"Oh, God," she said, in a whisper. "Oh, Nicholas."

The noises hadn't lied. The ice was breaking all right, and in a final fashion. Already the shingle at the foot of the opposite bank was ragged with a tumble of white boulders, tossed ice cakes. The river's surface was as cracked as a dropped stoneware platter.

While Lancey watched, the cracks widened into gaping toothless mouths that showed dark water. Here a fresh lead darted, a moving black streak that forked, and the forks split in turn; there a network of breaks suddenly spread out like the starring of a stone-hit window-pane. The sunshine made golden ripples where a wave splashed across a floe.

"Oh, *damnation!*"

Lancey's wail admitted defeat. Her shoulders slumped and she bit her lip. She knew her river; this was real thaw. Unless unseasonable weather struck there'd be no more skating in this March of 1788. The Hudson's tides, tired of winter, were in command again.

With a sigh she took a skate in each mittened hand, shaking her head over them as a younger girl might mourn a broken doll. They were such good skates! Theophilus Anthony had made them, and all Poughkeepsie knew the big blacksmith for a skilled ironworker.

Lancey was near tears. She had pictured herself skimming home, cutting fancy figures, swift as a bird, graceful and daring. She had imagined the applause of all the riverfront folk.

"Useless things now," she said, "and not worth the stealing!"

As she spoke she glanced over her shoulder. It wasn't, Lancey thought, really stealing. She'd only wanted to borrow them, try them. Maybe she was guilty of coveting her neighbor's skates, but they deserved better than prissy, silly Rachel Anthony. That one, with her airs, a fur muff to keep her hands warm, and those mincing, careful glides as if she feared she'd break if she fell! Call that skating?

Anyway, it was Rachel's own fault. If she hadn't come down from town with the skating party that very morning, showing off, she might still have her skates. Just because her father was a fine smith did she have to flaunt temptation in front of others?

Serve her right, Lancey decided, if I never returned them. Her own skates had wooden runners that no amount of honing could keep sharp. Her brother Ten Bush owned a better pair, bone beef ribs, but much too big.

Standing on one foot Lancey again measured a red skate against the sole of her square-toed, flat-heeled shoe. She nodded at the fit. What luck that Rachel had small feet, too!

Another thought cheered her. Maybe the thaw was Providence, after all. If there was no more skating this year, the Anthonys might not even miss the skates! Rachel was careless. She'd merely tossed them on a woodshed bench as she went in to supper.

Lancey was turning away, slinging the skates over her shoulder, when she heard the yell.

She whirled so fast her skirts flared from her ankles. The wordless shout, at once a cry of distress and rage, seemed to hang in the clear air. There was plenty of light from the dome-like sun on the cliff across the river. She saw the horseman at once.

He wasn't far, a quarter mile to the south, but she hadn't glanced that way. She knew instantly what had happened. Everybody used the frozen Hudson as a roadway; the drovers herded cattle across it. This rider, more reckless or unfortunate than most, had ventured to cross at just the wrong time.

Lancey judged he'd been coming from the west, and he'd almost made it before the break-up. He must have been past mid-stream when she'd heard the first reports; he was only thirty yards off the east shore now.

The horse, vivid against the ice as a scorch mark on white linen, had gone through rear first. It was tilted, haunch deep, head tossing, floundering as its front hoofs thrashed on the ice. Lancey heard the frightened whinny, saw the rider, a darker figure, slip from the saddle with a swirl of cloak.

The man stayed beside his steed, hand on bridle, trying to help. With splash and crash the ice gave beneath the pounding horseshoes, and the beast plunged in to its withers. For a moment the man stood erect, looking surprisingly tall because the black-maned neck reached only to his knees. Then he, too, broke through, dropping straight down as if pulled by the bootheels.

That shocked Lancey into movement. She started with a leap, still gripping the forgotten skates.

"Hold fast," she called, shrieking, "and don't thrash about!" After that she saved her breath for running.

Full speed, she darted down the slope toward the river's edge, feeling the angle of descent add to her momentum. There was no trace of path here, and twice she almost went headlong, but she kept her feet in spite of loose stones, and tripping brush. At that pace and distance it was a hard run even for Lancey, and she swore silently at the skirts bunched around her thighs, the skates bumping against a hip.

As she ran she searched, too busy to spare a glance for the victims trapped in the ice. This strip of shore was level shingle, looked bare of everything but rocks. With a flare of irritation she blamed the horseman for not crossing between settled places, where rescue would be easier.

"*Dumkopf*," Lancey muttered, lapsing for once into the Dutch of her fathers.

The wind was rising again. It fluttered her raised petticoats as she slowed, still searching. For all the thaw the wind had a raw sting.

Lancey's head turned as she scanned the bank for rubbish, a discarded board, an old plank, something flat, anything. When she heard thrashing, another high-pitched neigh, the girl turned riverward angrily.

A black hole circled the pair now. The horse, swimming, thrust against its edge in vain. When the man, hatless, tried to climb out the ice crumbled under the weight of his arms. He sank in a spray of slush and Lancey didn't breathe until the pale head bobbed alongside the horse.

"Don't!" Lancey screamed, winded, straining her throat. "Save your strength, you addle-pated fool!"

He shouted an answer, but she didn't listen. The remains of an old

7

campfire, a charred scar on the gray shingle drew her gaze. Then she saw the slab of driftwood that somebody had used for a bench.

It was too thick, taller than herself, but it was better than nothing. Lancey paused only to strip off her mittens, and lash the skates to the belt of her coat. She didn't mean to lose them whatever happened.

She heaved the slab upright, stooped, took its weight on her shoulder. Balancing it with both hands she carried it to the river's edge, lowered it carefully until it was flat on the ice.

Lancey calmly studied the problem; she figured the distance, judged the thickness of the ice. The man in the water was waving at her, yelling, but she was too detached to bother with his nonsense.

When she stopped panting she bent double, and put her palms on the near end of the driftwood. In that position, pushing the slab ahead of her, Lancey walked out on the ice.

It was thawing indeed, and fast. Before she'd gone a dozen steps the cold wetness seeped through the worn-thin soles of her shoes, and after that she was sloshing. Lancey didn't let the discomfort hurry her. As steadily as a lad pushing a baby on a sled she trudged forward.

She was counting on her lightness, and she covered more than half the distance before the surface changed underfoot. She could feel movement, a swaying like that of a floor under the stamp of dancers.

Lancey got down on her knees, and crawled. The slush soaked her clothes, froze her knees and shins. She knew the ice was getting dangerously thin. It shivered and trembled from the current beneath it.

It must look, Lancey thought, like eels squirming under a canvas cover. She didn't stop to look, but gazed ahead.

The hole was much nearer, and she could see them both, a blob of face, a long tan streak of muzzle. They were both staring at her. To Lancey the horse had a double set of eyes, white and rolling above, black flaring nostrils below. She shook the fancy away, and the ice snapped loudly.

"Go back! Go back, you little idiot!"

Lancey sniffed at the man's shout. Huh, she said silently, idiot your own self. Who got in this fix anyway?

She made the last few yards flat on her stomach, inching forward with careful pain. It seemed to take an hour. She kept her chin raised, but the rest of her ached from the wet, cold, and chafing. At last the jagged tip of the slab touched the rim of the ice.

"Child," said the man in the water, "are you crazy?"

His voice was so calm and exasperated, despite chattering teeth, that Lancey stared at him. Very blue eyes in a white face gazed back at her. Cold had turned his lips to a livid slash, but he tried to smile. Hair like wet straw had come loose from its queue, was plastered along one cheek.

"Grab a hold," Lancey said, annoyed. Her teeth chattered, too, and increased her annoyance.

He let go his grip on the ice edge to reach with the hand still clutching a long strand of rein. The movement brought the horse's head around, and startled Lancey.

"Let go of the horse, you duncehead!"

"Be-damned if I will!"

"We'll get him out later!"

"Her."

"What?"

"Her. Meda's a mare."

He turned to soothe the frantic horse, stroking her nose, talking.

"Just paddle, girl. Easy, now. Easy. Nothing to be afraid of. Have you out in two shakes. Good girl, Meda."

This one, Lancey decided, is stark, bedlam mad, but his prattle did seem to quiet the mare. She noticed the light was dimmer, and glanced west to find the sun gone. Fright shook her, turned to shivering. Her voice rose, an enraged howl.

"You—you weevil-brained slug! Do you plan to spend the night here?"

The man blinked. He carefully rested his chest on the slab, edged upward. He still held the rein, and his chattered reproof was as deliberate as his actions. He said: "Your parents should birch your bottom, youngun. Out of the mouths of babes!"

Lancey gasped, then flushed. She bit on a retort as the rim of ice splintered. It took all her strength to draw the slab back. She lay flat, hunched sideways, pulling. The danger, as sharp as the cold, didn't require thought. They didn't speak; this man needed no instructions. He wriggled higher, higher, tried the ice's firmness with his palms. None of his movements were hasty. Once he could use his arms it went a little faster, but they didn't dare hurry. From the hole the mare, restlessly treading water, watched them with great wide eyes.

When, several long minutes later, the man rolled off the slab onto thicker ice, he expelled a loud, shuddering breath.

"Thanks, moppet," he said and grinned.

Suddenly, for the first time, Lancey realized he was young. She didn't trust her trembling lips to manage a reply, but nodded. It

9

didn't matter. The man didn't even wait for that. He struggled to his feet, shaking the rein in his fist.

"Now, about my mare——?"

Lancey's vision blurred; she squinted at the black water. The tide, she thought, was at young ebb, but she wasn't sure. Beyond the mare the rider's tricorne bobbed on the current, its lining a white disk like the painted cockpit of a strange three-sided boat. He'd lost, or discarded, his cloak, too.

"I won't leave her!"

His voice forced Lancey to think, to outwit the aching cold that gripped her. She scanned the shoreline, frowning.

"You—you'll have to break a passage," Lancey said, "till she can find footing. It's not too far. There's a shelf bottom that juts out."

"You sound right sure."

"I am. I know this place."

The blue eyes stared, but he nodded, bent to raise the driftwood slab. He spoke over his shoulder.

"You're a bright little lass, at that. Think you can hang on to this rein?"

As she crawled to take it, Lancey noted that he wasn't extra tall himself. His height was moderate, but he stood well, slender, with wide shoulders and long horseman's thighs. Even in sodden clothes he had a neat, compact look.

As they worked shoreward, Lancey admitted that he handled himself skillfully. In spite of cold, soaked boots, teetering slipperiness underfoot, he moved lightly, on the balls of his feet, as balanced as a sailor on a heeled deck. He took his time, found a lead to widen before he began pounding. Then he swung the heavy slab with muscular ease.

She had her own troubles with Meda. The mare, skittish and frightened, shied away at the first blow, nearly upsetting Lancey. The man swore at the girl, cooed at the horse. Lancey heard him dimly through the shrill, ear-piercing whinnies.

"Hold on to her!"

"Pull your own oar!"

Their snarling added to the mare's panic, but she saw the crack spreading, and surged into it. The lead, widening itself, helped, the ice gave before her, and after that she stopped neighing. She swam frantically, head high and the long line of her back like a floating ridgepole.

Between them the man and beast hastened the action of the tide.

Twice Lancey broke through ankle deep, scrambled back just in time. The half-light of dusk helped the girl picture their task as a nightmare—the struggling horse, the treacherous ice, the man flailing like a berserk thresher.

When the mare stood firm, withers and rump clear of the water, Lancey stared in disbelief. Her voice was a croak as she called out.

"She—she's standing!"

Meda's owner turned, slab raised. A slow smile eased the haggard lines of his face. His voice, too, was strained, though his teeth no longer chattered.

"There *was* a shelf!"

"I said so."

"It's easy now. The lead's broad as a creek, and the shore's but a few yards."

The mare was walking on the bottom, dripping as each step raised her higher from the shallow water. Only a thin strip of ice separated them from the shingle, and Lancey relaxed. She couldn't stop shivering, and her gaze was shoreward. Meda didn't wait for guidance. As soon as the dark wavelets lapped below her forelegs the mare hunched, flung herself forward in a sudden hunter's leap.

Her lunge, haloed by a crescent of spray, carried her onto the white crust. The rein jerked through Lancey's fist, snapped her off her feet. Falling, she heard the crash as the shod hoofs shattered the ice.

She screamed as she tumbled sideways into the lead. Then the shock of the water drove the breath from her body. Blackness closed over her, and she knew only numb, sick despair. Her struggles seemed futile; the river gripped her with bone-chilling strength, the slimy bottom clutched at her.

Gasping, she clawed for the surface, forgetting the shallow depth even as her legs thrashed in the mud. Lancey lashed out in panic, driven by the fear that she'd be swept under the ice.

She came up, sputtering, choking, blinded by the water. Her hand closed on the edge of the lead and it crumpled in her grip. Something clamped on her shoulder, shook her, pulled at her. There was a pounding in her ears; it became a shouting voice.

"Stand up! It's not deep!"

Lancey's feet touched, but the pulling at her shoulder made her stumble. She almost went under again. The voice was as insistent as the tugging.

"Stand up, you little brat!"

Let me then, she thought with a flash of anger. She tried to shake away from that bruising clutch, struck at it. It pulled her, scraped her against the ice, dragged her. Her clothes caught, ripped as she was jerked free.

Her eyes cleared, and she saw that the man stood beside her, knee deep. He yanked her along, and she floundered after him, reeling and miserable. A moment later they were on the shore.

"You're all right now," he said.

When he let go, Lancey nearly fell. All right, she thought, swaying. She knew she'd never been so cold or soaked in her life. Skirt and petticoats clung to her legs like heavy bandages. Her belt, torn loose, dangled. She tried listlessly to knot the trailing ends, but her hands were too clumsy with cold.

The man, squatting on his heels, was peering at the mare in the last, dim light of dusk. He ran a hand up a foreleg, stroking.

"Just scratches, old girl," he said, "and nothing deep."

Shivering, the horse nickered a reply, nuzzled him. Lancey gazed at them with dull apathy. The miserable pair were only a stupid annoyance. Again she drew the belt tight, and memory stabbed her.

"My skates!" she wailed, turning.

The lovely red skates were gone, ripped away, lost somewhere under the ice, beneath the black water. It was the final blow, and Lancey blubbered.

"Child," said the man, "what is it?" He reached her with two quick strides. "Are you hurt?" He put his arms around her. "You're shaking cold, but——"

"My skates," mumbled Lancey, sobbing against his chest. "Lost."

"Is that all." He laughed, with relief. "We'll replace them, and throw in a doll to boot." He hugged the girl tightly, comforting with words and action. "The best doll I can buy. If it wasn't for you——"

His voice trailed away so strangely that Lancey checked her sobs. She drew back, gazed up at his face. He was half a head the taller, and his eyes were wide with surprise.

"Why," he said, "you—you're not a little girl at all! You're a grown wench!"

"And you," said Lancey, tartly, "are a great loon in dire need of spectacles!"

With sudden impulse she reached up to peel off her cap, shook her dark hair loose. It fell, a black, wet mass, to her shoulders; one dank strand tumbled across forehead and eyes. She brushed this away with

an impatient gesture. The stringiness of her hair, the loss of the
skates, her cold misery, the long walk home, whetted her anger to
rage. This dolt with his mare had probably made her catch her death!

"God and Nicholas!" she said, "I should have let you drown!"

2

AROUND THEM, IN THE FAST FADING LIGHT OF DUSK, WERE THE MURMURS of the March evening. The wind, still rising, made a rustling stir through the trees on the bank above the shore; the thawing river chuckled wetly through its grating ice-teeth. Overhead, a homing crow cawed for clearance as it passed in flight. The mare, restless and trembling, stamped, pawing at the shingle. Neither rescuer nor rescued heard any of these sounds.

The man laughed softly, bent low in a bow.

"My compliments, Mistress," he said, "and my apologies. Whatever your regrets, you will not find Dirck van Zandt wanting in gratitude."

Lancey wasn't mollified. She disliked his laughter, the elegant manner, the merriment in his voice. Only the wind, plastering her wet garments against her flesh, saved van Zandt a tongue lashing. It drove all thought but cold from the girl's mind. Her muscles flinched from its bite. She could not stop shivering.

"Here, now," said Dirck van Zandt, "we can't have this." His smile vanished; the blue eyes narrowed. He'd been amused at his mistake, but he didn't want the wench dying on his account. For all her language and temper the woebegone, dripping little baggage had earned his care.

No, thought Lancey, barely listening. We can't have this shaking, terrible chill. She swayed and he grabbed her arm.

"We must get you warm and dry."

"Let go," said Lancey, with stiff lips.

Before she could twist free, he swept her from her feet, cradling her against his chest. His arms were around her waist, and under her thighs, holding her. Then, as he staggered from the sudden weight, she caught at his coat in panic.

"Look out!"

"You're heavier," he said, grunting, "than you look."

"Put me down."

14

"Don't squirm or I'll drop you."

Lancey knew she wasn't squirming. She didn't wish to be carried, but she couldn't do anything about it. Her body seemed to be trying to shake itself to pieces. It was all she could do to talk, and that came in gasps.

"What're you doing?"

"I'm going to get you home."

Bundling her onto the mare's withers took all of Dirck's strength. It was the first he'd realized that his bout with the river had sapped his muscles. Fortunately, Meda stood still, and the girl, though quivering, could be handled like a soaked laundry bag.

This is too much, Lancey thought, bent double across the horse. Blood rushed to her hanging head, and brought with it shame and fury at her undignified position. She kicked, thrashed her arms, squawked.

"Let me down!"

"Steady, Meda," said Dirck. He slapped Lancey across the bottom, bent to adjust a stirrup. "You lie still!"

The slap shocked Lancey into open-mouthed amazement. How dared he! By the time her wits came back he was on the horse and hauling her upright in front of him.

"You," she said, "you——"

"Where is your home?"

"You——"

Dirck gave the girl a shake that snapped off speech. He was feeling the wind himself, and in no mood for nonsense. The sooner they reached a fire the better. Meda, moving beneath him, would need attention too. This bedraggled hussy was his rescuer, but he wouldn't let her be a problem.

"Answer me!"

His roar hurt Lancey's ears. She shut her eyes, winced. Her first reaction was subdued obedience.

"Upriver."

"Far?"

"Four miles."

"Too far. There's an inn much closer."

Dirck turned Meda's head, nudged her to a faster walk. The mare was sure-footed, but he didn't dare risk a trot. Night was closing down fast now, and the rubble underfoot made treacherous going.

The motion of the horse, the firm arms around her and the chest she leaned against, stirred a little warmth back into Lancey. She was still trembling with cold, still angry, but curiosity, stronger than both, prompted her question.

"What inn?"

"The Brick Gables."

"Oh." Lancey knew the tavern, knew its Swedish owner. She had sold him fish several times, and the choice raised her opinion of this van Zandt. The Brick Gables faced the Post Road, mostly gentry stopped there. She craned her neck for a glance at the man behind her. Did he, a stranger, know the prices the Swede asked, in hard coin or New York shinplasters only?

"Sit still," Dirck said.

"There's a path——"

"I know. That's why I crossed the river where I did."

He wasn't, then, a complete stranger. As the mare swerved and began to climb the bank, Lancey caught the mane to steady herself. Even in her misery the idea of service at such an inn pleased her. Her peddling had never taken her inside the kitchen door.

Before Meda, slowed by her double burden, reached the top of the slope dusk melted into darkness. Lancey, rocked by each step, was barely aware of nightfall; she noted how the bay mare's black mane seemed to absorb her lighter coat. The horse's bobbing head had a hypnotic effect. Lancey sighed, closed her eyes, content to let somebody else do the thinking.

"Stay awake," said Dirck, nudging her.

"Am," murmured Lancey. It was a calculated attempt to buy a moment's peace. If she could trick this fellow into silence she might steal a few winks of sleep. Her feet, dangling, felt detached, solidly packed clumps of snow.

Once over the crest of the ridge they went even more slowly. Meda, picking her way carefully downhill, set her own pace. Dirck, leaning forward to help the mare, knew that the girl was dozing. He let her alone, not wishing to tamper with Meda's balance. He had trained the horse himself, knew he could trust her to take them to the road.

"Good old Meda," he said, aloud.

Meda flattened an ear, but went on with her task. Dirck, biting his tongue to quiet his teeth, thought longingly of a fire, a hot drink, dry clothes. The girl, face muffled against his chest, whimpered in her sleep. He gave a snort of annoyance at the wordless criticism. Didn't the wench know that you couldn't hurry a horse down a steep descent in moonless dark?

16

They reached level ground, and the path straightened as it threaded inland through a wood of first growth trees. These screened them from the wind. Meda, finding the earth firm, broke into a trot without urging. The changed motion jolted Lancey out of her doze.

"What?" she asked. "What?"

"Sit still," Dirck said, holding her tight. "We've a mile or so to go." He spoke as if to a fractious child, with impatient authority.

Lancey, unused to horseback, thought her perch precarious. Sitting sideways, in front of the saddle, something jolted her with every step the mare took. It was like being punched through skirt and petticoats. Her hip would be one, great bruise.

"Do you have to hold me so tight?"

"Yes."

The wind, sweeping along the bare, cart-wide track, told them when they emerged on the Post Road. Dirck turned the mare, but again let her choose her pace. In spite of ruts, and the muddy, thaw-softened surface, Meda maintained her trot. She was as anxious as her riders to find warmth and fodder.

"Good girl," said Dirck.

"Me?" Lancey was bewildered.

"No. The mare!"

Well, the girl thought, it serves me right for asking. From the first his sole concern had been his precious horse; she vaguely remembered it had made her angry. Now even anger was too great an effort. She rode in numb lethargy, staring at the road as it slid beneath them, a moving current in the massed darkness.

They rounded a curve, and lights showed ahead. These seemed strange, yellow squares, painted high and low, upright on the black wall beside the road, flat on the roadbed itself. Then, as Lancey blinked at them, the bulk of a building took shape, and she realized she saw the candlelight in windows doubled in reflection on the ground.

"Ho, the inn!"

Dirck's cry, so close to her ear, merely annoyed Lancey. She wondered that he could still shout; she could hardly breathe.

The mare's shoes clicked on flagstones, and Dirck reined to a stop. A door, opening, sent a broader stream of light across the night; horse and riders were caught in its beam. After the dark ride the yellow-brick front of the tall, high-peaked house was like a friendly beacon.

Lancey recognized the innkeeper. Gustavus von Beck was a big man, but he pushed his aproned paunch forward with the ease of long practice. He moved with an ox-like lack of haste or clumsiness. Von Beck's bald head gleamed, smooth and pumpkin colored.

"Accident." Dirck van Zandt spoke fast, trying to explain quickly. "Broke through crossing the river. We're soaked, freezing. We need a fire, dry clothes, a——"

"Get down," interrupted the innkeeper. His deep, accented voice was unexcited. The loungers in the doorway stared, but the big man wasted no words on sympathy or greetings. A nod accepted the mishap as customary and he raised his thick arms. "I'll take the wench."

Dirck loosened his grip, nudged the girl. Lancey slid down from the mare. Von Beck caught her, but even then she seemed to go on falling. Her knees buckled; the legs that felt so stiff went limp. The inn, the lights, the innkeeper's broad face, all tilted suddenly, blurring together as if whirled.

"Hold her up!"

"I think she's fainted."

No, I haven't, said Lancey silently, but she wasn't going to argue about it. Von Beck was roaring for his help, his wife, giving commands. The girl felt herself lifted, but kept her eyes closed. It would be, she decided, a lot less trouble to be carried than to try to walk.

* * *

Swathed in a blanket, feet soaking in a tub of steaming water, Lancey Quist smiled drowsily at the flames in the bed-chamber fireplace. She was warm, delightfully warm; her skin still tingled from the brisk toweling that had rubbed her dry.

Behind her Mistress von Beck muttered in Swedish as she gathered up Lancey's discarded clothes. If the innkeeper's wife spoke English it was a well-kept secret in the town. She and her daughter had tended the shivering girl with brusque efficiency, making no mention of recognition.

Lancey sighed. It was pleasant to be coddled for a change, handled like a baby. Still she was glad that the older woman had sent the younger out before her shift was peeled off. Modesty worried Lancey little, but the shift was old and much mended.

For the first time the girl examined the room. It wasn't, she guessed, one of the best front chambers for all its fireplace. The big four-poster bed filled a good half the space, and there was a single window, shuttered now against the night. A wash stand and the stool

Lancey sat on were the only other furnishings, but the oval rag rug, though worn, was clean and the floor was scrubbed spotless.

Second best anyway, thought Lancey. What with three candles lit and the fire it was very cosy. Of course she didn't intend to stay any longer than it took for her clothes to dry.

The von Beck daughter came back, spoke to her mother, clumped toward Lancey. She held out a leather mug.

"Here's a posset. Ma said you was to drink."

Mistress von Beck nodded vigorously.

"Thank you," said Lancey. She sipped the hot milk, amply laced with spiced wine. Its tang was as new to her tongue as its fumes were to her nostrils, but she savored both. The liquid ran warmly down her throat, spread inside her, and she licked her lips.

"It's very good."

Mistress von Beck dimpled, smiling. She held out the wadded bundle of clothing, said something, and departed.

"Ma," said the daughter when the door had closed, "will dry your things in front of the big kitchen fireplace." Her voice had no accent, but a whine had replaced it. "You're Lancey Quist, ain't you?"

As you well know, thought Lancey, watching the other over the rim of the mug. They had haggled about the price of fish several times. Hilda von Beck, except for hair that was dirty blonde instead of polished pewter, was a physical copy of her mother, square and thick-set, with a big bosom and wide hips. Even the chubby pink faces were alike, but Mistress von Beck's was pleasant with dimples, this mouth was pinched.

"That's right," Lancey said.

"The fishmonger."

"That's right, too." Lancey wriggled her toes in the water, and drank. She refused to be baited.

"How'd you ever fall in with young Master van Zandt?"

"He fell in. I helped him get out."

"I've heard all that." A sniff dismissed the tale. "But what was you doing with him in the first place?"

"I just chanced to be there." Lancey hid her glee behind the mug. She knew jealousy when she saw it. And from an old spinster of twenty-five at least!

"He's stayed here before. He's a van Zandt, you know."

"So you said."

"Beekman van Zandt's younger. There's two. They live up by Rhinebeck. You'd better be careful."

"Careful? Of what?" Lancey's surprise was genuine.

"Just be careful," said the other girl, darkly, "that's all!" She flounced from the room, slamming the door.

Lancey stared after her, shrugged. She leaned forward to consider her feet, thought them too red, took them from the water. As she finished the posset, toasting her toes dry, she considered the conversation. The van Zandts must be rich, patroon Dutchy, one of the gentry families that had sided with the colony in the war. She giggled at the idea of Dirck van Zandt courting that Hilda.

The heat, the drink, the relaxing warmth after cold exertion made her sleepy. She padded over to the bed, stretched out on its featherbed softness gratefully. There was no reason why she couldn't be comfortable while she waited. If the von Becks objected Dirck van Zandt could pay the score.

"He'd gladly pay for his blasted mare," she said, aloud. It was a barely audible murmur, and she fell asleep with her next breath.

Dirck van Zandt roused her when he entered with the innkeeper. She hadn't heard his knock, but the opening door startled her.

Lancey sat up, wide-eyed. The blanket slipped from her shoulders, and she snatched at it. Her tumbled black mass of hair, the patina of sleep on her face, made her look very young. One leg was bared to the knee, and she hastily tucked it under her.

"Feeling better?" asked Dirck, grinning at her. Lud, he thought, she is a fetching little minx, disheveled like that! The realization came suddenly and unsummoned. He had not ordered the supper on the innkeeper's tray from any motive except hunger. Now, he began to have a different idea entirely.

"Much better, thank you." Lancey tried to sound composed, but her gaze was on the dishes not the man. "What's this?"

"Food," said von Beck.

"Thought you might be hungry," said Dirck. He set down the small table he was carrying. "I'm famished." As the innkeeper uncovered dishes, Dirck watched Lancey.

She counted viands in open-mouthed awe. There was enough for a feast! A roast fowl, a rib of beef, boiled potatoes, mashed turnips, pie, bread, gravy, a bottle of wine! Her mouth watered, and her stomach felt weak.

"Yes," said Lancey, "I think I can eat." She was wondering where to begin. The meals in the Quist household were filling and plentiful, but of no such variety.

"Anything else?" asked von Beck.

"Not now, mine host." Dirck waved the innkeeper away. The big man's size dwarfed Dirck's medium height, made the gesture slightly ridiculous, a trifle over-lordly.

The motion caught Lancey's eye, and, as von Beck bowed out, she regarded the man she'd rescued. His fresh clothes, his own from the fit, made her very conscious of her nakedness under the blanket. He was wearing a crisp, ruffled shirt, buff breeches, and white stockings. Soft leather slippers had replaced his boots, and the straw blonde hair was combed. She noted the black bow of his queue as he bent to pour the wine.

"I hope you like claret," Dirck said.

That, too, sounded false to Lancey. It was spoken a shade too gravely, and mocked instantly by the bright glance of his blue eyes. He wasn't sure she'd ever tasted claret. Prickles that were not caused by the coarse wool of the blanket ran down Lancey's spine.

"Oh, yes," she said.

"It's the best in the house." As Dirck moved around the table to hand her a glass, he casually pushed the door out of his way. The gentle shove left hardly a crack ajar.

Face impassive, Lancey accepted the drink. Her calm politeness mocked him. The moves were as easily followed as a beginner at draughts. Quite the rakehell, this lad, she thought.

"I can't eat like this," Lancey said.

"My dear, you look charming." Dirck raised his glass. "Let us drink to our mutual safety."

"Safety?"

"Yes. We're snug here, dry and warm."

Lancey tasted the claret, drank a good swallow. She was enjoying herself, excited and amused by the pleasant voice. Knowing gin and rum the girl considered the wine a mild beverage not to be feared.

"You're clothed, too, Master van Zandt."

"I keep a few things here. Luckily."

"You live here?"

"No, but I stay overnight occasionally. Now, we mustn't let the food get cold."

She watched him draw the stool to the table, pick up the carving knife. Smiling, he proceeded to carve the meat with neat dexterity. Lancey returned the smile. She fully intended to sup well, however things developed.

He's tumbled a wench or three in his time, Lancey decided, and willingly enough, perchance. It wasn't hard for the patroon's son to

21

coax a tenant girl behind a hay-mow. Why, the generous gentleman was even going to feed the riverfront waif before he took her to bed.

"Enough?"

The plate was piled high. With a nod, Lancey wrapped the blanket tightly, snug under her armpits, and tucked in the ends, before she reached. He could look at her bare shoulders if he wished. He did.

Dirck found the girl's manner of eating almost as fascinating. She stripped a drumstick with quick slashes of white, even teeth between spoonfuls of vegetables. She was starved, he thought with pity. Then, he gazed again at the round shoulders and poured more wine.

"Thank you, Master van Zandt."

"Dirck."

"Umm?"

"My friends call me Dirck."

"Oh."

He frowned with suspicion. She was busy eating, tearing at a slice of bread, not looking at him. Well, she was probably shy, out of her depth in these surroundings. She couldn't have meant to parry his friendly suggestion.

Your move, Lancey thought, and wondered what tack he'd try this time. She hoped they'd at least finish the meal before he tried anything. The food was very good. She gulped more wine to encourage him.

"I know your name. It's Lancey Quist."

"That's right."

"You're a fishmonger."

"My father's a fisherman. We do sell them, of course."

"And you live here in Poughkeepsie."

"No."

"No?"

"We live on the riverfront. The town's on the bluff."

"Oh, I see. You're down by the landing."

"South of it." Lancey spoke with her mouth full, trying to keep the conversation going. As long as she could keep him talking there was no need to worry. "We'll be very busy now that the river's open. We'll have to mend the nets, fix up our boat. My father's the best fisherman on the river."

"I'm sure he is."

"He is." And his daughter, Lancey told herself, has grown up among boys who could swallow this popinjay with one bite. They were more

22

abrupt about trying to raise a petticoat, but no more successful with hers. The few who had pinched her bottom long wore the marks of her nails.

"There was a Quist," said Dirck, twirling his glass, "used to peddle fish to the army around Newburgh when I was there. Short, stocky man."

The remark made Lancey stop eating to stare. "That would be Pa. You were with the army? The Continentals?"

Dirck flushed, nodded. "Only toward the end. I didn't see any fighting, worse luck. I'm no hero. Didn't even get in until after Cornwallis gave up."

"'Course not." Lancey laughed at him, pleased at his discomfort. "Six years back you were a baby."

"Not so young as all that."

"Close enough."

"I'm twenty-three!"

"Oh," said Lancey, deliberately sweet, "you don't look it."

Scowling, Dirck ate in silence. Somehow, and he couldn't figure why exactly, the conversation had gotten out of his control. The girl couldn't have done it. She was years younger than he was! He was trying to think of a remark, bantering but suggestive, that would get them back on the proper footing, when Lancey spoke.

"Times were good when the army was just downriver."

"Good for tradesmen. Dull for us."

"I often went there with Pa."

"In his arms?"

"Not so young as all that," said Lancey, laughing. Dirck laughed with her, pleased at his own question, delighted at her reply. They shared the joke, a glance, and a moment.

She can't be more than sixteen now, he judged. He glanced at the litter of empty plates, reached for the bottle. "Your glass is empty."

Lancey held it out, startled at her willingness. I will have to watch this one, she thought. He can be likeable, and, after all, I'm only clad in a blanket. A little more friendly laughter might prove my undoing.

"Did you ever see Washington?" she asked, interested.

"Often."

"I saw him three times. Close, that is. A big man, with a stern mouth. Like—like a figurehead for a ship. He made me think of that. On a horse he looked a giant."

23

"You were small. But the general's big all right. Do you remember the party he gave for the Frenchies?"

"With the fireworks?"

"You do remember."

"Of course!" Lancey, leaning forward, was flushed and animated. In her interest she forgot to be cautious. The army encampments had thrilled her as a child; the fireworks occasion had been memorable.

A tempting morsel, Dirck thought, with the wine bringing color to her cheeks, sparkle to her eyes. He was very sure of his conquest, but didn't wish to be hasty.

"Did you," asked Lancey, "ride into New York with the army?"

"Yes. Now, there *was* a party!"

"Oh, I wish I'd seen it!"

"We came in one end of the town as the British shipped out the other. As soon as we reached the houses, everybody poured out on the streets, lining the road. Flags, cheers, tears even. Maybe some of them were Tories, but they didn't show it that day. I felt a little like crying myself, and I was way toward the rear of the column. Up front with Washington and Clinton it must have been like—like Jesus on Palm Sunday."

He spoke with no irreverence. Seduction was forgotten, and he gazed past the girl as he looked into his memory. His voice was low; his tone vibrant.

Lancey liked him, liked his speech. Her own voice was pitched to match his.

"And bands? Music?"

"The fifes trilling, and the drums rattling. But the music wasn't what moved you." Dirck stared into his glass, sipped as if toasting the memory. "It was those ragged soldiers that had fought them so long, and beaten them, marching in first, with their heads up and their eyes shining, in step for once!"

Lancey nodded, moved by the description. She remembered the camps near the river, the weary, slovenly men who waited impatiently for the end of a war that was really over and done.

"They were taking back," said Dirck, "a place that they'd lost years before. A place the British had held, and used, and owned. The last big town! Our own port at the mouth of our river!"

"Our own port," said Lancey, eyes shining. "Our river." This was a language she understood, saying what riverfront folk thought, but

24

couldn't express. She felt very close to this young man from Rhine-beck.

Her repetition stirred Dirck uncomfortably. He was embarrassed by his emotional talk. One glance at the girl, the parted lips, the look on her face, rekindled his desire. Maybe, without trying, he had touched the proper spring. She was as ripe and ready as a pink-gold pear!

"The Hudson open again," said Lancey, not noticing his glance, "all the way!"

Dirck rose to replenish the fire, thinking. The length of the candles told him the hour was late. Listening, he could hear no sound from the rest of the inn. They might all be abed, or just quiet, but von Beck would honor the privacy of a purse-full guest. When he returned from the fireplace, he picked up his glass, sat on the edge of the bed.

Lancey stiffened, then relaxed. His eyes were very blue, and he was smiling. With mild surprise she found herself more excited than wary. That wine, she thought, was stronger than it tasted.

"Let us drink," said Dirck, raising his glass, "a toast to that day and that army."

Well, Lancey decided, there's no harm in that.

The glasses clinked as they touched. They drank.

Gently, Dirck took both glasses, placed them on the table. One arm curved around the girl's shoulders; the fingers of his other hand raised her chin.

He has nice hands, Lancey thought, strong but gentle.

"You're a lovely nymph, Lancey Quist."

The whisper puzzled her. She recognized a compliment, but didn't know the word.

"What's a—a nymph?"

"You are. A wood sprite, all grace and beauty."

He was bending close, bending for a kiss. Amazingly, she wanted to kiss him. Behind her something plucked at the edge of the blanket. She held one arm tightly across her breast to keep it in place.

"Sprite?"

"Yes."

Their lips met in a long, breathless kiss. Lancey's head swam with a sweet, new giddiness. She had been seldom kissed, never like this. She enjoyed it so much she forgot to be careful of the blanket. It slipped down, fell to her waist.

That warned her. So this is how it happens, she thought. The pleas-

25

ure mulls the wine in the very pit of one's stomach, sends it, heated and coursing, back up through the body like a fever. She felt very strange, and hot, and worried.

Thoroughly enjoying himself, Dirck wasn't worried. Everything was progressing as it should. The hazel eyes were very close when he raised his head. They looked large and luminous.

"Lancey."

He fairly purred the name. His palm caressed her shoulder, dropped lower to fondle her breast as he drew her closer for another kiss. Dirck was delighted with the whole situation, the soft mouth, the fallen blanket, her smooth, pliant form, her eager response. He kissed her with skillful ardor. In a moment he would ease her back on the bed, and they'd be more comfortable.

Oh, my, Lancey thought, in a moment I'll be all undone! I like this too much! Much too much! The kissing, the touching! He has me beside myself, an easy conquest.

With great effort, she reached out a leg, found the table, pushed. It went over with a tremendous crash of glassware and dishes!

The noise shook the room. Dirck, startled, jumped, relaxing his embrace. On the instant the girl was out of his arms, across the room. She had the blanket firmly back around her, and stood poised on the threshold.

"Wait," he said, thickly, "there's no need——"

"Oh, yes, there is." Lancey, breathing rapidly, sounded calmer than she looked. "That clatter should fetch the whole von Beck family. You might ask the daughter to accommodate you, Master van Zandt. *She's* willing!"

Then, she was gone. He stared at the empty doorway, heard the swift patter as she raced, barefoot, down the stairs, the gabble of voices that greeted her below.

"Well, I'm damned," said Dirck van Zandt.

3

LANCEY QUIST STOOD ON THE BLUFF OVERLOOKING THE RIVER, LISTENED to the water, thought she could smell the tang of the tide. She wrinkled her nose, sniffing, threw her arms wide in sudden exhilaration. Her river was open again, and a quickening of her blood seemed to answer the slap of the wavelets.

The late moon was a pale disk, riding high, only revealed at intervals when the drifting cloud-mass beneath it parted. No stars were visible, but the darkness had thinned enough so that the girl could see the solid range along the western bank defined against the sky. Still restlessly prowling the valley, the night wind brushed through the trees, kicked whitecaps from the black current. It had lost its power to make Lancey shiver.

Well, of course, she thought, now that I'm dry clad, or nearly. The one damp petticoat wasn't bothersome, and her soggy wool cap was in a pocket with her stockings.

She was sure her excitement came from the thaw, not claret. The long walk home had dispelled the last effects of the wine.

Now, as she counted the lights dotting the clustered shacks along the riverbank, Lancey recognized them as festive torches. The fishermen were sitting up late, greeting another season with talk. They'd be making plans for the morrow, boasting of past catches, guessing at future prices. As they did every year when the ice broke.

This was familiar! This was where she belonged! She wanted to rush down, join the family discussion around the fireplace. She stood still, reviewing her night's adventure.

"God and Nicholas," Lancey said, "but I nearly lost more than those skates!"

She laughed, but felt her cheeks burn. There were comic memories aplenty. The innkeeper's pallor at the thought of his damaged tableware. Hilda von Beck's rigid disapproval. Her own hasty dressing behind the settle in the inn's big kitchen, and the way she scampered out the door! And—funniest of all!—Dirck van Zandt's face as she last saw it. But mixed with these things was one disturbing, undeniable fact.

She had liked van Zandt's flummoxing, liked it even though she knew where he was steering! Her whole body had responded to his caresses; her skin had tingled with a strange, delightful gooseflesh!

"Like a harlot," Lancey said.

Word and judgment came from the long sermons she'd so often heard in the stone Dutch church. She might better, she admitted, have listened more and squirmed less. The dominie had thundered against such sinful practices at least twice a month. Why, then, did she feel no guilt, but only a scornful disdain for her yielding?

Considering, the girl chewed her lip. Honesty forced her to certain conclusions. There was pleasure in such dalliance even with a stranger. It had little to do with love, morals, or matrimony, was as physical as a cool swim on a sweltering day! But the careless swimmer, in strange waters, was apt to be swept away, sucked under.

That was the reason for her scorn. She, Lancey Quist, had almost let herself be cozened by the first rogue in a ruffled shirt who tried it!

Lancey knew her upbringing to be moral but not strict, rough but not slovenly. She was wise in the ways of the riverfront where raw spirits, male or liquid, gave due warning by their very crudeness. She remembered her dead mother barely, New Paltz, the place of her birth, not at all. Though she could walk the crooked lanes of Poughkeepsie blindfolded, the fishing settlement below the bluff was her true habitat, her oyster bed.

She went down to it now, trippingly in spite of the darkness. Her sureness on the path gave Lancey an added sense of security about her emotions. Dirck van Zandt had shown her that the horseplay, the snatched kisses, of earlier years was over. She was sixteen, a woman now, and fair game. An ability to run, or duck, or claw, was no longer enough because she would have to watch herself as well as the boy.

"Man," corrected Lancey, mentally reviewing her male friends. Most of the fishermen were married, or too old. Of her former playmates only Jan Elmendorf could be considered a swain. She'd had to box his ears last Independence Day when rum made him ardent, but he still came visiting. The dolt eyed her like a cow, and had about as much to say.

She dismissed Jan with the rest, wondering briefly how you decided one certain man brought love. That thought, too, disappeared as she passed the last shack before her own, saw that the square of oiled paper in the window was tinted with light.

Clouds hid the moon, but Lancey pictured her home in detail. Hendrick Quist had built carefully, and well. Several of the fisher shacks were bigger; none was more snug. The north wall and chimney were brick, and the narrow front was half-stone. It faced, south, onto a small yard that held the shed for the boat and a rack for drying nets. Lancey placed, without seeing, the two-plank pier that jutted into the river.

Drawing a breath that enjoyed the sharper tang so close to the water, Lancey felt a rush of affection for her father. Hendrick had spent years of toil on the place. Whenever he couldn't fish, he patched. Only this past winter he had re-shingled the backhouse.

Both halves of the Dutch door were hooked together, swung in as one when Lancey pulled the latch-string and pushed. Warmth, a compound of heated air, wood and tobacco smoke, visibly enveloped her as she entered.

It was a rectangular room, with fireplace opposite the door, and its one window on the landward side. The walls were bare, whitewashed to the low ceiling of unpainted planking. There was no rug, but the wide floorboards gleamed like a holystoned deck. The small space was emphasized by the massive furniture that filled it. One corner was crossed by an open cupboard; another held the ladder to the loft above. A settle, its seat a chest, was under the window. The square table alone made passage difficult on either side. There were two armchairs, a stool, a hamper. Pegs on both sides the fireplace held up shelves for cooking utensils and foodstuffs; those flanking the door were hung with coats and hats.

"It's me," said Lancey.

Three faces were turned toward her. She judged that the others— her half-brother and small half-sisters—were abed in the loft. Her father merely removed his pipe and nodded. Ten Bush, her brother, gave her a half smile. Only her stepmother greeted her with cheery question.

"You eat?"

"Yes."

As she shrugged out of her coat the girl was puzzled. She hadn't expected anxious queries about her absence until so late an hour, but complete indifference was a surprise. Besides, in spite of its normal look and crackling fire, the small room held an air of tenseness. Her entry seemed to have interrupted something.

29

Hendrick Quist, feet propped on the wood box, finished carving a tholepin, inspected it. He was a short, solid man, with a body shaped much like the high, porcelain bowl of the pipe he was smoking. Like the pipe, too, he showed the use and handling of many years. The skin of Hendrick's broad face was weathered to the color and texture of a russet apple. His bald scalp, a pink dome circled in back by a frieze of ash-gray hair, looked babyish by comparison.

Closing his clasp knife between square, corded hands, Hendrick gazed at his daughter. His eyes, a pale, watery blue, were stirred by emotion as a pool is ruffled by a breeze. As always, the sight of Lancey reminded him of her dead mother, but his voice betrayed nothing of this.

"Lancey, the river is open again."

"I know," Lancey said. She drew the stool close, sat down. Hendrick spoke as he rowed a boat, in a steady, even beat.

"Soon we will all have to be busy."

Lancey saw the blue eyes flash toward her stepmother, on toward Ten Bush. Her brother had lounged back from the candlelight, sat motionless in shadow.

"*All,*" repeated Hendrick. To emphasize the word he pointed his hooked pipe stem at each of his listeners in turn. "Even the small ones will have their tasks."

"So," Lancey murmured. Her puzzlement deepened, mixed with wonder. It was not like her father to belabor the obvious with too many sentences. Every spring opened with a few weeks of bustle and preparation.

"This year should be a good year."

Ten Bush, stirring in his corner, drew Lancey's glance. At eighteen he was a lanky lad, with a big-boned frame not yet fully fleshed. Now, as he uncrossed and recrossed his knees, the girl realized her brother was nervous.

"Depends," Lancey said, "on how the fish run."

"They will run," Hendrick said. "They always do. But this summer will bring more to eat them, buy them."

"The men for the convention, Pa?"

"Those, yes, Lancey. They come to vote on this Constitution matter. Aye or nay. To join or not. For us that is not important. But they must eat."

"June," Lancey said, "is late for shad unless——"

Hendrick raised his pipe to interrupt. He said: "How the shad run, the shad decide. What *we* do, depends on us."

For the first time his wife joined the conversation. Hester Quist was a big woman, amply curved. Her plain, pleasant face became almost handsome when the large mouth smiled, and the gray eyes twinkled. She winked at Lancey as she spoke.

"Like always, Hendrick."

It was, Lancey knew, an attempt to prod Hendrick's speech to a faster pace. The husband, unhurried, puffed smoke as he considered the remark, then nodded.

"As you say. Like always." The broad head turned as Hendrick faced his son. "You hear, Ten Bush?"

A sigh that flattened a candleflame was Ten Bush's only answer.

"Good," said Hendrick, accepting it. "Then that is settled."

"What is settled?" Lancey was completely bewildered. Nothing she had heard had posed a problem or offered a solution. Her father had returned to his pipe, and the girl's voice sharpened. "Why do you say this to Ten Bush?"

"Ten Bush," explained Hester, not waiting for her husband, "wishes to ship out with the men from Claverack Landing."

"Whaling?"

Lancey's surprised question brought the pipe from her father's lips. He leaned forward, the pale eyes troubled, and his tone quickened.

"Whaling! Shad, sturgeon, peelican, salmon—these are not any more enough! Whales Ten Bush wants to go after. A long voyage. Years, maybe! With those mad New Englanders from upriver!"

"They are not mad," Ten Bush said with quiet gravity. "There is money from whale oil cargoes. Good York State money even in these times. They have proved that these last few years. And they pay wages."

Mouth open, Lancey stared at her brother. That he spoke at such length made the discourse important, the tension understandable. Compared to Ten Bush even Hendrick was a prattling parrot. Lancey's childhood closeness with her brother had always been a silent one. She could not remember him in a single wordy argument.

"Leave the river?" she asked, disbelief in her tone.

"The river," Ten Bush said, "flows to the sea."

Why, she thought, he means it! He really wants to go voyaging. The evening's adventures were erased from her mind by the realization. Ten Bush, the reliable, the steady, was eager to leave the family!

Hendrick Quist, trying to watch both son and daughter, sighed.

These children by his first wife had his deepest affection, though he tried to be fair to all the rest. He saw Lancey, eyes narrowed, quickly adjust herself to face the new problem, and it was another reminder of her mother. So had pert Cecile Delancey looked when New Paltz was horrified by her marriage to a roving river sloop sailor.

"Ebb and flood," Lancey said. "If you must sail why not a packet to New York?"

"It is not the same," Ten Bush said.

He, too, Hendrick decided, in spite of his Dutch features, now showed his mother's French blood. For Ten Bush it was almost the first time, and Hendrick was troubled. A man liked life to follow a regular order as the tides the moon. His distress made his deep voice a trifle harsh.

"We need you here, son."

"Lancey can do anything I do."

"You are eldest."

"Old enough to choose, Pa?"

Unless you knew these two, Lancey thought as she listened, you would think both mild and reasonable. Neither spoke loudly, nor with gesture. That Ten Bush replied at all to his father's statements betrayed her brother's strong feelings.

The girl glanced at her stepmother. For all her plainness Hester had a noble forehead that swept up to braided hair which age had turned to white gold. Now it was wrinkled with a frown warning Lancey the clash was serious.

"Is it a girl's place to row?" asked Hendrick. "To go out on a night drift and cast net?"

"When have we gone out without Lancey, Pa?"

"Ten Bush, I said it was settled."

"Well," said Hester, smoothly, "suppose we see what Lancey thinks."

Lancey recognized this as a plea for peacemaking. She and her stepmother were old friends, had been since Hendrick's marriage. Hester, practical and earthy, had never tried to discipline her step-children. She had treated Lancey, at six, as another woman in a world made difficult by men.

"Lancey?"

Ten Bush made the name a question. Hendrick repeated it silently with raised eyebrows. The girl felt a stomach flutter of panic. No matter what she said she could not please them both.

"Well," Lancey said, "I—I'm not sure I know. It's so—so sudden like."

She spoke no more than truth, and she was troubled. The Nantucket whaling men had fascinated the whole valley on their arrival four years before. Together, she and Ten Bush had watched the sturdy vessels beat upriver; even Hendrick had commented on their differences from the familiar river sloops. Her brother had rowed her north to watch the Yankees hammer together the houses they'd brought in sections from the New England coast.

Since then the whaling fleet had grown to twenty-five ships, and the whalers spoke of their home port as Hudson. These things made interesting gossip, but Ten Bush had shown no desire to go awhaling.

"Would they take you, Ten Bush?" asked Lancey, still stalling.

"Yes. I have asked."

"He asked," Hendrick said, "those people. Not me."

At the hint of emotion in his father's voice Ten Bush clenched and unclenched his hands in mute apology.

"There is no harm in asking," said Hester with a quick smile. "If you don't ask, you don't find out. There was no need for Ten Bush to speak until the ice broke."

Lancey wet her lips, aware they were all waiting for her words. Ten Bush moved forward into the candlelight and the girl could see his face. His eyes were a darker blue than his father's, but he had the same square jaw. A lock of hair, fine and pale as corn silk, was tumbled over his forehead. The girl had an impulse to reach out and brush it back.

He wants me to approve, she thought, noting her brother's intent gaze. Hendrick, too, showed anxiety. The curved pipe hung from his teeth but he wasn't smoking.

"This is not an easy thing," Lancey said. "I cannot understand wishing to leave the river. It is our life and it is good. Soon it will be better, with warm days, the boat out and fish running. Truly, the convention men may bring more custom, but, even without, summer is the happiest time."

Hendrick gave a grunt of agreement. Ten Bush merely waited.

"But I am not Ten Bush," Lancey said, smiling. "He has the right to think as he pleases. Only I do not believe we need him for the fishing, Pa. I can row as well, and almost as long. If he should leave——"

33

"There is no if," said Hendrick, gazing at his daughter in pained amazement. "I said it was settled, Lancey."

"All right, Pa," Lancey said.

She knew that nothing was settled. Hendrick could forbid Ten Bush to go, but could not prevent it. Any more argument would only cement her father's decision. She needed time, to talk to Ten Bush alone, to soothe Hendrick's outraged feelings.

"I will hear no more of this," said Hendrick, glowering.

Lancey didn't dare turn her head. She dropped one hand by her side, wriggled the fingers. The table hid the motion from her father. It was a signal that she and Ten Bush had often exchanged in childhood, a warning to hold his tongue.

"All right, Pa."

Ten Bush's reply brought three sighs of relief. Hendrick coughed to muffle his, and fussed with his pipe, shaking the dottle into the fire. Lancey realized that her father, too, had dreaded more violent conflict. Smiling, she glanced at her brother, saw her smile reflected. He was willing to leave his future to her.

"I'm sleepy," Hester said, and yawned.

Hendrick, rising to stretch, said, "Let's take a last look at the weather, Ten Bush."

This was, for all its gruffness, a peace offering, an admission that the battle was over, forgotten. Ten Bush, following his father to the door, sealed the truce with an amiable question.

"We staining net tomorrow?"

"If it's coming fair."

Hester Quist waited until the door closed behind them, then grinned at her stepdaughter. The big woman shook her head.

"Men!" she said.

"Those two," Lancey said, "are too much alike. Stubborn Dutch."

"Don't I know? I was right glad to see you, Lancey. The tempest was blowing up in here before you came. It ain't a second wife's place to butt in between a man and his son."

"You favor Ten Bush's going?"

"That ain't for me to say either. Hendrick's my man, Lancey. But when you're the age of Ten Bush it's not good to want something that bad and not get it. The boy couldn't be more het up if he wanted a female instead of a whale. Only you waved him off he'd have wrecked everything."

"Whaling!" Lancey said, heavily. She was committed to her brother's cause, but her heart favored her father. Life would be lonelier without Ten Bush. "Why in the world does he want to go whaling?"

"Lancey, after two marriages I'm only sure why a man wants one thing. But, since he does, I hope you can talk my man around."

"It will take a spate of talking."

Cocking her head, Hester lowered her voice. "Well, the pickle already saved you some."

"Saved me?" Lancey stared at her stepmother. The gray eyes were twinkling. "How do you mean?"

"They was both," said Hester, nodding toward the door, "too upset to notice, and they ain't noticeable men anyway. Otherwise—not meaning to pry, Lancey—they might have wondered why you come home with a rumpled dress and bare ankles."

"Oh." Involuntarily Lancey glanced at her feet. She suddenly remembered Dirck van Zandt, felt her cheeks grow warm.

"It's all right," Hester said. "I only saw them flash for a second when you sat down." The big woman's chuckle was a throaty, ribald sound. "Figured you took your stockings off for some reason."

"To dry them!" Lancey was furious at herself for blushing. "And my dress, too! I was soaked to the skin!"

"How'd that happen?"

"There was a man on a horse crossing the river and——"

"Young man?"

"Well——"

"Thought so."

"Hester Quist, will you stop interrupting, and let me tell you?"

"I'm all ears, girl."

"This man broke through the ice about four——"

"Taking your stockings with him?"

"Hester!"

"Just asking," Hester said, laughing. "Was young myself once. If you got soaked like you said, you didn't do no drying outdoors in this weather. Means you went somewhere."

"Of course we did. He took me to Brick Gables." Lancey stamped her foot at her stepmother's broad grin. "Honestly, Hester, you're worse than a—a trollop! Mistress von Beck took care of me!"

"Then there's no need for you to take on, is there?" asked Hester. "Or to blush rosier than a baby's spanked bottom. Faces give 'way secrets, Lancey. You'd better learn that if you're making a habit of going to inns with men."

"We went there 'cause it was closest." Lancey knew she was being teased, but couldn't help sounding defensive. Hester had a bawdy streak as wide as her hips. "And absolutely nothing happened——"

"Oh, now, I wouldn't say that. I'll wager some fancy canoodling went——" Lancey's glare sent the big woman into a gale of laughter that brought tears to her eyes.

"I don't know which is worse," Lancey said, frozen to cold dignity by the close guess, "your mind or your tongue."

"I don't know either," said Hester. She gazed down at the girl with smiling affection. "But there's one thing I do know. There's nothing you'll ever want to tell me, Lancey, nothing at all, that'll upset my mind or set my tongue a-blabbing. You can rely on that, girl."

Lancey smiled back at her, letting annoyance recede with the flush. She had no intention of telling Hester anything, but she appreciated the offer. The big woman was a generous, open-hearted friend. For all her lusty banter she meant what she said.

"I know, Hester. Thank you."

The doorlatch rattled as it was raised. Hester spoke in a quick whisper.

"Just don't go throwing yourself away, Lancey. Him that gets you is a lucky man, the stinkard!"

Turning away, Hester bent to pile the fire high for the night. Lancey felt suddenly very weary. She heard her father's slow voice behind her.

"If I know weather, the morrow will be a bright one, but real blustery."

Well, Lancey thought, I don't know that I'd call this day calm.

4

FOR THE NEXT FEW DAYS THE MARCH WINDS SENT FORAYS COURSING THE length of the Hudson valley, but with diminishing bluster. The sun seemed to rise brighter and stronger each morning. It softened the earth, melted the last patches of snow, speckled tree branches with new buds.

Free from its ice the river, smiling and blue, ran between its banks, making a sport of every changing tide. Ripples and currents mixed different colors for sunshine or shadow, from azure to indigo. Even the whitecaps saluted playfully, and the eddies trimmed their coves with lace.

All along the eastern shoreline, from Wappinger's Creek to Fall-kill, were man-made signs that spring was due to arrive. Shipyard Point, recently desolate, shook to the noises of hammer and saw. At Poughkeepsie Landing there were sloops in the water with crews clambering over them, re-fitting, scraping, splicing. That ferry was the first to run, its oarblades flashing on the empty river, but the horse-ferry, farther south at Milton's, pushed its ugly, humpbacked shape across only a day later.

The fishing village below the bluff was marked by the smoke of many fires, and garlands of fishnets. Hung in yards, on piers, and between shacks, these latter looked as if an army of spiders had spun giant cobwebs overnight. Some were white, or dirty white, some yellow or tan with faded stain.

There was as much talk as there was work. The fishermen swapped tools and labor, drink, gossip and rumor. Between tasks a man ambled over to his neighbor's to see what he was doing. With the perennial optimism of their kind they considered the new season a good one before it started.

Lancey Quist enjoyed the activity, but veered between optimism and foreboding. Her frequent changes of mood surprised her. Always before she had considered these days of preparation and antic-

37

ipation the second best part of the year, bettered only by the fishing itself. Somehow, this spring was different.

The future, now bright with prospect, now heavy with portent, lay beyond her sight, like the river below the bend of the Highland gateway. Yet she recalled last year, the year before, all the others back to toddling days. Why was she, then, cheerful one minute and sad within the hour? Why was each feeling summoned and intensified by a simple, familiar action performed a hundred times before?

Lancey couldn't understand it. She would mend a tear in a net, whistling, certain her handiwork would hold the largest roe shad that had ever come upriver to spawn. Then, as she stirred the bubbling brew of oak bark tea with which they darkened the nets, she would find herself near to weeping.

One cause for her melancholy she could determine. The sight of Ten Bush, quietly doing his share of the work, brought a lump into her throat. Her brother trusted her to win their father's permission for his voyage. He would sail without it, if he had to, but wanted Hendrick's blessing.

Ten Bush had told her that the one time they'd talked. They'd been alone, standing on the pier of an evening, with the hush of twilight above them, and the murmuring river below.

"I'd feel better, Lancey. I'll be gone a long time."

"But, must you go this year?"

"Yes."

"Why, Ten Bush? Another year——"

"It's a new launched ship. Maiden voyage."

She waited, while he searched for the words of explanation.

"A fine ship, Lancey. And—well—we'll both be starting fresh like—me and her. Judah Paddock, he's the master, can teach us both together."

"You've talked to him?"

"Seven, eight times."

"I didn't know you'd been to Claverack that often."

"You was busy."

"Yes," Lancey said, biting her lip. She'd been too busy with her own affairs to notice his absence. "But now the time's so short——"

"I thought it out all winter, Lancey."

"You hanker after whales that much?"

Ten Bush stood in silence for a long minute. Then, he spoke half to himself; she had to bend close to hear.

"I don't guess it's the whales. It's—it's places, Lancey."

38

Turning, he had gazed south, downriver. With that slight movement Lancey had felt his withdrawal, her own loss. She'd ended their talk with a promise.

"I'll do my best with Pa."

That promise was another reason for her moodiness. There were many excuses why she hadn't kept it, and she seized them all. There was the work, and Hendrick's preoccupation with it; there was the gossip of visiting fishermen, and her half-brother Conrad's suddenly announced achievement.

This lad, a fox-faced miser of ten, was a puzzle to the whole Quist family. He was sandy-haired, thin-lipped and scrawny with neither Hendrick's solidity nor Hester's robust candor. Lancey, who had helped rear all of her stepmother's offspring, considered Conrad her sole failure. She could not give him affection because even in the cradle he gave nothing, smile, cry nor gurgle, that did not seem calculated to return a profit.

Hester's own opinion of her son was frankly critical.

"He ain't a by-blow, Lancey, just a throwback. Conrad's my Pa, his grandpa, all over again. A coin biter, sharp and twisty as a fish hook. I'd say Conrad was the spittin' image, but that kind's too mean to spit."

Nobody was surprised when Conrad disappeared on the first morning the river was open. He always worked grudgingly, with a suspect carelessness that made his absence more desired than his presence. The surprise came when he returned that evening to startle the supper table.

"Got me a job of work," Conrad said, smirking, "down to the Spikin-Kill ferry. Horse tender."

Hendrick lowered the dumpling impaled on his knife and stared. Hester's frown silenced the two younger children; she glanced at her husband. Lancey saw Ten Bush stop chewing as he considered how the news might affect his future.

"Who told you you could?" asked Hendrick.

"Old man Anthony himself," Conrad said. "Pay is a shilling a week. Hard coin. *And* keep."

"You ain't worth that around here," Hendrick said.

"At fourteen coppers to the shilling," Conrad said, "that's two coppers the day. 'Course I'll have to live down there, but it's only a four mile walk. Any time you want the loan of sixpence or so just send one of the younguns."

He has it all figured out, Lancey decided. With none of Ten Bush's

39

worry or shyness. The boy's cool assurance took the wind out of her father's sails. Hendrick was annoyed, but not angered. He had long since despaired ever making a fisherman out of Conrad.

"You still should have asked me first," Hendrick said. He glanced uneasily from Lancey to Ten Bush, aware that Conrad's situation was similar to his first born's. Not really, Hendrick thought, shying away from the comparison. It never occurred to him that any difference in affection was involved. Clearing his throat, he tried to explain. "Not that you can even row without catching crabs by the peck."

Lancey recognized the purpose of the remark, but Ten Bush, grim mouthed, was staring at his plate. She said, "You'll get home often, won't you, Conrad?"

"When I can," said Conrad, with a look of surprise. His sniff dismissed the question as unimportant. "But nights there's likely to be a chance to make a bit extra. When a feller crossing is thirsty maybe, or wants victuals."

"Horse tender," Hendrick said.

"What do you know about horses?" asked Hester, passing a heaped plate to her son.

"What's to know?" Conrad was aloofly superior. "You feed them, and water them, and curry them. I don't handle them on the crossings. Once they're in place on the treadmill that turns the paddlewheel, I just wait till the ferry comes back. 'Course I can go across whenever I want. Free."

"Pa," said Ten Bush, quietly, "are you going to let him?"

"Why shouldn't he?" Conrad asked. "One less mouth to feed here at home, and a store of coppers handy when he needs them. It's only common sense, Ten Bush. Fishing's Pa's trade, and yours, and even Lancey knows the ins and outs of it, but it's never been my pudding and never will be."

Ten Bush, not listening, was gazing at his father. Lancey spoke before Hendrick could answer.

"Conrad's nearly eleven, Ten Bush. And a lot older in some ways. But I wouldn't trust him rowing when I was casting net. Would you?"

Her brother turned toward her. He shook his head.

"Well, then, it doesn't matter what Pa decides. Conrad can go or stay without it bothering us one smidgeon."

"Sure," Conrad said, suddenly looking his age. His aplomb was badly shaken by Lancey's serious tone. He sensed an undercurrent that threatened his new job, and he was scared.

"That's about how," Hendrick said, "I had it figured, Ten Bush. But if you think that Conrad's being missing made it harder on anybody today——"

"No," Ten Bush said. He'd caught Lancey's wink, and he was smiling. "Let him do what he wants."

"Let your victuals stop your mouths," Hester said, ending the discussion. "Food'll be stone cold."

That was one change in status that Lancey welcomed. She thought it weakened Hendrick's position about Ten Bush, but she feared to test it too soon. This fear flourished as she grew used to the fact that her brother was leaving on a long voyage. Whether she failed or succeeded with Hendrick became of tremendous importance. She couldn't let her two men part in anger.

There were other more normal, seasonal changes, duly reported in the Quist yard. Pardon Cash had a new boat this year. Gerritt Kimmee had made himself a cow horn to hawk his fish through the township. Captain Benjamin was again staying at Jaycock's Ordinary while his sloop *Lydia* was readied for her initial trip to New York.

Other years Lancey would have been the first to learn such things, to spread them as she flitted through the settlement. Her tomboy deftness had helped lighten every fisherman's work; her speed afoot made her first choice for any errand. She'd loved it all, relishing the smell of woodsmoke, of pitch and paint, fresh shavings, tallow, oak bark dye. Soon enough these riverfront odors would be overpowered by the pervading one of fish.

This spring Lancey stayed close to home. Partly she did it to show Hendrick that she could take Ten Bush's place; partly to make sure no friction arose between father and son. Those reasons she told herself, regretting their cause without realizing that she herself had changed.

Only once, when Conrad described the ferry horses, did she think of the mare, Meda, and Dirck van Zandt. Lancey smiled at the memory. That encounter had happened to another, much younger, girl. Now, her days were busy with work, troubled with responsibility; at night her sleep was solid, and dreamless.

* * *

The morning Lancey Quist decided to paint the wooden blocks used for floats, the weather changed. Dawn had falsely promised another clear day, but the girl was finishing the third float when she noticed the river's clear blue was fading.

Lancey straightened, gazed south to where slate colored clouds gathered above the west bank.

"Pa," she called, "look at Blue Point."

Hendrick and Ten Bush, working elbow to elbow, were replacing the thongs that tied the shot weights to the bottom edge of the net. Both men turned toward the hill she'd named. Ten Bush grunted. Hendrick waited a moment before he spoke.

"The *Storm Ship's* getting ready to cast off."

Without smiling, Lancey nodded. She knew all the stories of river lore, the legends of ghosts and goblins, and still half believed most of them. This was one of the strongest. The phantom ship, lost long ago in the old Dutch days, that was moored at the foot of Blue Point, was visible only when a storm roared down from the crest, so it wasn't surprising she'd never seen it. Sailors had, or said they had. It was safer not to scoff at such things.

Her immediate problem was practical. There was little enough white paint left after the boat and oars had their fresh coats. It was hard to come by; Hendrick was already in debt to Digmus Jaycock, the tavern keeper, for this year's supply. She didn't want to risk a rainstorm spoiling the finish.

She was piling the blocks under the shed roof when Pardon Cash arrived to help her.

"Fixing to squall," Pardon said. His big hands hid the floats he raised.

"It's due." Lancey accepted his appearance without surprise. They were old friends; as a small girl she'd often ridden on the man's wide shoulders. "How's the new boat?"

"Sprightly."

His grin was one-sided to hide the gap of his missing two front teeth. Since his broken nose slanted the other way it gave his face a twisted look. But his green eyes were merry, and the result infectious.

Pardon Cash was big, the biggest fisherman along this stretch of the river. His two hundred pounds towered an inch over six feet, but he moved lightly. Pardon still rigged himself like a sailor, in leather breeches and homespun shirt, with sheath knife in his wide, brass-buckled belt, and a gold ring dangling from his left ear-lobe.

Lancey, smiling back at him, tried to guess his age. Nobody knew for certain how old Pardon was. Except for his tarred queue, another sailor's trick, his hair was as white as sun bleached linen, and his eyebrows the same. The only lines on his smooth face, burned to dusky copper, were around eyes and mouth, scored by weather and laughter.

"You try her in the water?" Lancey asked.

"Not yet," Pardon Cash said, "but only because I saw this blowing up." He finished stacking the wooden blocks, saluted Hendrick and Ten Bush with two fingers to forehead. "Need a hand, Hendrick?"

"No, thank you, Pardon. We're near through."

The big man made himself comfortable on the stacked floats. Lancey, watching the others gather, almost laughed aloud. As usual the fishermen drifted into the yard aimlessly, as if a chance breeze had blown them there, yet each gave the coming rain as a reason for loafing.

Seth Row, red faced and paunchy, squinted at the sky. "In for a spell of dirty weather, seems," he said.

Only a pace behind Seth came Gerritt Kimmee. Bandy legs beneath a thick trunk made him waddle. He said, "Brought your plane back, Hendrick. Wouldn't want it rusting."

Even the two slaves, Calico and Tanner, rolled their eyes and shook their heads. They were owned by, and fished for, one of the numerous Livingston kin. They were quiet, soft-spoken black men, dressed alike in faded nankeen clothes. Calico, gray haired and older, spoke first.

"Heavens got a mean look."

"Mighty mean," agreed Tanner. "Be a pelter."

Neither expected an answer. They squatted in the rear of the shed, attentive and silent. As skilled fishermen they were an accepted segment of the group, but they joined a discussion only when addressed.

"Anybody got credit left up to Jaycock's?" asked Seth Row.

Gerritt Kimmee cackled a laugh. Hendrick, hurrying his work, frowned over his shoulder. By the end of winter all the fishermen, except the slaves, owed a score at Jaycock's Ordinary, but Hendrick disapproved of Seth's question. A man enjoyed his gin or rum after work, or on occasions like weddings, funerals and celebrations.

Squall or not, Lancey thought noting the frown, her father's hands would not be idle. She knew he'd enjoy the talk as much as she did, but wouldn't make it an excuse for drinking.

"Credit," said Pardon Cash, "or cash, I ain't exactly welcome at the tavern."

"Why not?" asked Lancey, surprised.

"Called Captain Benjamin a snout-nosed pighead," Gerritt Kimmee explained, "and said Digmus was another."

"Pardon, you didn't!"

"Fear I did, Lancey. Digmus butted in. 'Twasn't his argument."

"It's his inn," Hendrick said, "and the captain's his best custom."

Pardon Cash said, mildly, "He is still a snout-nosed pighead. Going to cast his vote for them that's against the Constitution and he don't know one word it says."

"You know what it says?" Seth Row hitched forward eagerly.

"Well, no," Pardon said, "but then with no reading or writing I ain't got no vote anyway. If I had I'd take time to find out what everybody was yelling about."

"Now, wait," Gerritt Kimmee said, "the captain did know a thing or two. Said trade was good and getting better. Said New York money was better than anybody else's. This thing would change all that. We'd have to pay the war costs for the whole damn twelve other states!"

"They was all in it, wasn't they?"

"Talk sense, Pardon," said Seth Row. "Just 'cause you lost two teeth from scurvy in a British prison hulk is no reason I have to lose mine."

"You might get them *knocked* out, Seth." The mildness was gone from Pardon's voice. His gaze was cold and steady.

Seth's face turned even redder, and he gulped. They all knew that Pardon Cash had never forgiven the British for those teeth. In the moment of hush a breeze stirred the stretched fishnet.

Lancey put her hand on the big man's shoulder. She felt the tensed muscles relax. "Pardon," she said, "this Constitution can't be much good if George Clinton is against it."

Hendrick, Ten Bush and Gerritt Kimmee nodded as one. Seth Row, apologetically smiling, didn't dare. Calico, listening, nudged Tanner.

"Old George ain't God Almighty, Lancey," Pardon Cash said. "He makes a fair governor, maybe, but he served alongside me aboard the *Defiance* back in '58, and he was no great shakes as a sailor."

"He is a brave man," Hendrick said. "In the war he proved it."

"I ain't questioning his courage, Hendrick. I ain't even saying he's wrong. Just that he could be. Last time Lancey, here, read to me out of the *Country Journal* there was ten, twelve farms up for sale. That don't sound to me like times are good and getting better."

"Oh, farmers!" Gerritt Kimmee shrugged his shoulders.

"If you stop to think, Gerritt," said Pardon, "you'll figure that's ten, twelve less farmers might buy fish now and then."

"They weren't all from around here," Lancey said.

Pardon's lips twisted in his crooked grin. He said: "As close as Freedom Plains, and as far as Nine Partners. Unless you read the printing wrong, Lancey."

Hendrick and Ten Bush joined the others under the open shed. "Lancey don't read wrong," Hendrick said. "She learned her letters good."

"Took to it," Ten Bush said, "quicker than me." He hadn't spoken before, and his tone was proud.

Leaning against the trestle that held the inverted boat, Lancey reddened slightly as she turned away from the men's admiring glances. Few of the fishermen could read or write, none of their women-folk. She recalled her own wailed complaints when Hendrick insisted she accompany Ten Bush to the evening schooling the dominie held in the Dutch church. Her father had refused her pleas. The children of Cecile Delancey, descendant of a member of the Dusine, the twelve hereditary rulers of New Paltz, must learn their mother's accomplishments.

The river had turned lead colored, sluggish and sullen. It slapped angrily at the thin piles of the Quist pier, looked even darker than the wan, lowering sky. Above the west bank the storm clouds, swollen with rain, had moved northward. For the moment there was no wind, and sunless daylight hung across the valley, like a limp, transparent curtain, in uneasy quiet.

Hester, appearing at the open top of the Dutch door, drew Lancey's glance. Her stepmother waved to the men under the shed, swung the half-portal shut. The two little girls, Lancey judged, were safely sheltered.

Behind her, Pardon Cash was talking again, back on the main topic of the year. The girl, listening with only part of her mind, wondered in how many places men were arguing the same way about the same thing.

"It stands to reason," Pardon said, "that they didn't hold that meeting in Philadelphia for nothing. Every blessed time those high-cockalorums get together in Philadelphia something new comes out of it. For years now." He raised a big fist, snapped a finger upright as he made his points. "First off come a petition to King George, rot him. Then, come the war. Then, General Washington's appointment. Then, the Declaration. Lastly, the Confederation."

"And now, this Constitution."

"And now, like Seth says, the Constitution. Well, I been to Philadelphia, years back. It's the biggest place we got in the country,

Quaker neat and thriving. Compared to Philadelphia this here Pough-keepsie's like—like a dory next a man-o'-war!"

The group stirred in protest. Even Lancey frowned, annoyed at the comparison.

"Too big likely," said Seth Row.

Gerritt Kimmee nodded. "Ain't got no river like the Hudson."

"Go on, Pardon," Ten Bush said. His lips were parted, and his eyes shining.

He likes to hear of far-off places all right, Lancey thought, glancing at him. Her heart sank, and she gazed again at the river, not seeing it, tensed to prevent a sigh.

"It's got its own river," Pardon Cash said, with a shrug, "but that ain't here nor there. What I'm saying is this. Every blame thing plotted down there in Philadelphia has come about. Even those that seemed least likely—winning the war, being independent—happened like they planned!"

"But we all wanted those things." Hendrick spoke without glancing up from the tangled skein of fishing line he was unraveling.

"Barring the dirty Tories," said Gerritt Kimmee.

Pardon Cash laughed, spat between his teeth. "I ain't peddling nothing, one way or t'other. But maybe somebody ought to warn George Clinton. When the wind blows out of Philadelphia it don't pay to beat against it."

"I don't know," Hendrick said, prying at a tight knot with a finger-nail. He paused between sentences, but the others knew his method and waited. "Maybe Clinton's right. Maybe we should stay as we are."

Poor Pa, thought Lancey, has had enough of changes, dreads another. During the long war Hendrick, sticking doggedly to his trade, had supported the cause of the patriots, but without joy. He blamed the British for starting the trouble. Hadn't they stolen the colony from his Dutch ancestors in the first place?

She recalled his tight-lipped bitterness that September of 1777 when Vaughan's Raid brought the redcoats upriver. He had cursed the warships as they passed, their cannon thundering, on their way to burn Kingston. Those lobsterback bastards, Hendrick had said, in memorable language, spoiled several days of fine fishing weather.

Five years of peace had convinced Hendrick he was right. Left alone, not bothered by government or soldiers, a man could raise his family decently. A seasonal trade had its ups and downs, but hardship was part of living, and the river would always feed them.

Wishing, Lancey decided, didn't make things stay as they were. Ten Bush's ambition proved that. All the tiresome talk about the Constitution was another sign of change, though that outcome was important only to people like the Clintons, the Livingstons, and the Schuylers. Governor Clinton led one faction; General Schuyler's son-in-law, Hamilton, the other.

"Like as not," said Seth Row, voicing her own opinion, "it won't matter to us however the voting goes."

The rain came with a sudden hiss of wind. It drummed on the roof of the shed, lashed in charging lines across the surface of the river. One side of the shed was protected by the tarpaulin that had covered the boat, hung as a windbreak. The group drew together behind this, snug and dry, silently contemplating the storm.

In the first minute of its fury the tempest pelted the yard into mud; the narrow pier swayed, creaking in protest. From the eaves of the Quist high-peaked shanty water streamed in a steady cascade.

Then the wind slackened; the rain settled into a firm downpour, as was expected.

5

Lancey quist, waiting in the shadowed common room of jay-cock's Ordinary, gazed out through the twelve-paned window and sighed. The drizzle showed no sign of lessening. March, always a testy month, had emptied a sackful of differing rainstorms on the valley in the past week.

The girl didn't like her errand, and she didn't like the room. Jaycock's was slovenly enough when crowded, with a blaze roaring in the fireplace, and men shouting. Now, in the emptiness of early morning, the cold, wet ashes of last night's fire added their dank odor to an already thick collection—musty dampness, stale beer and tobacco smoke, the reek of rum, the clinging scents of guttered candles and badly cooked food.

Some of the tables had not been cleared, were littered with empty tankards, greasy trenchers, spilled gravy. The unswept floor was happily hidden by the day's dimness, but felt gritty underfoot. The shards of a broken jug were heaped beneath a bench.

Blurred as it was by rain streaks, and glass flaws, Lancey much preferred the view through the window. Jaycock had built his inn beside the road that sloped down from town to landing, and she could see the whole curve of the harbor.

The drizzle, drawing a haze of wetness across her vision, gave the scene a shimmering unreality. Warehouses, boathouses, the piles and planking of piers, seemed to quiver with the tremor of slick, black jelly. Flecked by raindrops the river looked tideless, stagnant, as bilious as a disease ridden swamp.

One sloop, bare mast slowly rocking, was still in her berth. Lancey knew the ship for the *Lydia*, knew too that the rest of Poughkeepsie's fleet was beating down to New York in spite of the weather. With the season's first cargo eagerly awaited, something beside his share in the shambles behind her must have delayed Captain Benjamin.

She heard a titter, and turned. Beyond the open doorway to the tavern's front hall there was a sound of scuffling, a girl's muted giggle.

A moment later a man crossed the opening, raking the room with a quick glance as he passed. Lancey had a glimpse, startlingly vivid, of sharp dark eyes, a lean, handsome face under a tilted tricorne. Even after the portal was empty it seemed to retain an impression of a tall, wide shouldered figure in black.

The front door creaked as it opened, slammed shut. That was when she realized she'd not heard the man's step. For all his height he had moved with swift silence.

Lancey was still staring at the doorway when the girl appeared. Her mob cap was awry, her hands straightening her bodice, but she was grinning. The sight of Lancey caused an instant recoil that brought her fingers up to cover the grin.

"Who's that?"

"It's all right, Nell. It's only me."

"Lancey?"

"Yes." There was neither scorn nor amusement in Lancey's voice. The ordinary's hired girl had once been a playmate. Nell Bogardus was her own age, plump and dimpled, with a too easy, nervous laugh.

"Sakes, Lancey! You gave me a turn."

"I'm waiting for Digmus."

"Oh, well, what harm?" Nell's shrug was a movement that bounced her bosom and wriggled her hips. Her rounded, pink cheeks dwarfed her tiny pointed nose and the dab of mouth beneath it. "You needn't go thinking things."

"Why should I?"

"It was just a friendly buss, Lancey. Honest. Why, that fellow ain't even staying here." Nell cast a swift look back towards the kitchen behind the common room. "That's why I jumped. Digmus don't like to catch me fooling with them that ain't spenders."

"Digmus doesn't own you, Nell."

"Might as well," Nell said, "the way he works me." Her tone was resigned, cheerless. She began to collect dirty dishes, clattering them with a deliberate loudness planned to impress a listening employer. "But there was naught happened outside there should bother him or you."

"All right, Nell."

"I know what folks say about me." Nell, scowling, spoke with whining indignation. "All of them, even Hester. Maybe even you, Lancey."

"You know me better."

"A trollop!" Nell, gripped by self-pity, wasn't listening. "Too free with my favors! No better than a common whore!"

Lancey was silent, not shocked but unwilling to encourage the tirade. She knew Nell's remarks were only too accurate. The riverfront women considered the girl's behavior scandalous and were rough tongued in their criticism.

"All I ever wanted," Nell said, sniffling, "was a bit of fun. That's all. They oughtn't to go aflogging and aflaying me just for that."

It all depended, Lancey thought, on what was meant by fun. No wife in the vicinity cherished the idea that Nell's meaning included her husband.

"If the truth was known, Lancey, there's plenty throwing stones is a lot worse than me."

Smiling, Lancey recognized Nell's statement as a hint intended to provoke questions. She refused to be drawn. The ladies of Poughkeepsie town had somewhat different standards than the riverfront women-folk, but both frowned on flagrant misconduct. Suspicion merely added spice to gossip; certainty brought horrified rebuke.

Nell's fault, she thought, is that she doesn't know how to dissemble. Others may behave worse, but carefully did so in privacy.

Footsteps signalled the end of the conversation. Nell, instantly diverted, stopped scowling to look up, simpering. Turning toward the sound, Lancey regarded the two men who entered from the inn kitchen.

They came, one behind the other, and their appearance reminded her of a skiff towing a barge. Digmus Jaycock, in front, was a small, wiry man, with a quick, shuffling step that seemed ever ready to burst into flight. He had a big nose over a wide, greasy mouth and wore spectacles whose rectangular frames looked fitted, like windows, into his eye-sockets.

Behind him lumbered Jan Elmendorf, towering over the little innkeeper. Jan was as uncompromisingly square as a granite tombstone. He carried his head lowered, chin touching the base of his throat, and gazed at Lancey from under his hat-brim.

"Morning, Lancey," Jan said.

Lancey nodded in reply. She was none too pleased by Jan's presence. His open, silent devotion irritated her. From boyhood he had tagged after her, undiscouraged by ridicule, indifference, or open insult.

"Hello, Jan," said Nell, smiling.

The greeting brought a sharp glance from Lancey. Stupid Nell, she thought, can't resist beaming at anything in breeches. Then, startled at her own vehemence, she felt a moment's wonder. Did she, at heart, consider Jan Elmendorf her own property?

"Ain't you cleaned up in here, Nell?" asked Jaycock.

"I'm doing it." Nell added a tankard to the piled tableware before her.

"You didn't waste no time with that Justin?" The innkeeper's big nose wrinkled in distaste.

"Cap'n Benjamin give him short shrift," Jan said. "The *Lydia's* got all the hands she needs."

"I was just talking to Lancey," said Nell.

"That's right," Lancey said, "to pass the time while I was waiting, Digmus." She was pleasant, but firm. He needn't think he could keep her cooling her heels as he liked.

Digmus Jaycock made no apology. He said, accusingly, "They was only eleven loaves, Lancey. I counted them three times. Ain't a full dozen."

"Then don't be so niggardly with your flour." Lancey's voice was cold and unimpressed. This was the part of her errand that she dreaded and disliked. Jaycock always found something to haggle about, the weight of a loaf, the texture of the bread.

"Niggardly? Me?"

"Hester could barely eke twelve loaves out of the last batch. It's agreed she keeps one as payment."

"If she wasn't wasteful——"

"Hester?" Lancey's interruption was mocking. The Quist bread supply depended on Jaycock's flour, but she would not be bullied. Besides, Hester always managed to keep back at least two loaves from each baking.

"I measured it out myself," Jaycock said, "and I figured on a full dozen."

Lancey drew a breath. She had reached the place where she made her dare, and she never made it without fearing it would be taken.

"Look, Digmus," she said, "if you think you can do better elsewhere, go right ahead. Hester's bread is the best fodder you have in this ordinary, and you know it."

"It is good bread," Jan Elmendorf said.

"Tasty," agreed Nell.

The comments were ignored by both contestants. Lancey serenely met Jaycock's scowl. She imagined the innkeeper was mentally computing the size of her father's score, but kept her face untroubled. At last the little man shrugged, stepped aside to show that Jan was carrying a sack.

"Well," Jaycock said, grumbling, "I'll expect you to make it up out of this supply."

"If there's enough," Lancey said. Strangely, she felt neither relief nor elation. In the past she'd regarded the beating of Jaycock as a victory. Now, it was merely a stale, familiar routine.

"I'll haul it for you," Jan said, hoisting the sack onto his shoulder. "I ain't busy."

Lancey hesitated, then shrugged. She tossed him a shawl, watched while he draped it to protect his burden. Jaycock, not bothering with farewells, whirled on Nell with an oath.

"Are you going to idle there the whole morning?"

The two voices, his scolding, the girl's protesting, followed Jan and Lancey from the common room to the front door. Outside, the drizzle was still falling with gloomy steadiness. They trudged through the slick mud of the road, passed alongside the inn, picked their way down the path behind it. When they reached the level of the riverfront Jan clumped forward until he was in step with Lancey.

"I been wanting to talk to you, Lancey."

"What about?"

"Ain't there something you'd like me to fetch from New York town?"

"No," Lancey said. Jan was a crewman on the *Lydia*, but she wouldn't entrust him with any buying even if she had the money. "I've no coin to spend."

"I was thinking of a—a present. A ribbon like. Or a comb."

"Thank you, but no." The thought of a gift was tempting, but she would not be beholden to Jan Elmendorf. He was bad enough without encouragement. Does he think, she asked herself, he can buy me with a trinket?

"They have wondrous things in the market, Lancey. There's lace, and looking glasses, and——"

"I said, *No*, Jan." She had caught the note of pleading in his voice, and her own was not as tart as she wished. Still, it did make her refusal plain. He wasn't deaf; he'd heard her. "If you go wasting your money on such things it's no fault of mine!"

Wet as it was, Jan's face brightened. He said, "Such things as what, Lancey?"

Well, she thought, if he's that stubborn in spite of all I've said, at least he can buy something I'd like. She wavered between comb and mirror, made a fast decision. "Oh, a looking glass—I mean a real, clear one with a handle—would cost much too much."

Jan's lips moved, as he silently repeated her description. "That's no matter," he said, "if I want it."

"That's up to you," Lancey said, and swiftly changed the subject. "Why hasn't the *Lydia* sailed? Usually Captain Benjamin is among the first."

"Passenger." Jan bit off the word, scowling. "Gilbert Livingston. Can't get away till later today. Cap'n wouldn't wait for anybody else but—well, lawyer Livingston."

"Of course." Lancey accepted the name as a complete explanation. No ship's captain on the river would willingly offend a Livingston, especially one that practiced law in Poughkeepsie.

They went on in silence, except for the murmur of the drizzle, the gurgle of the sullen river beside them, the squelching of their own shoes. As they neared the fishing settlement Jan tried to slow their pace. Lancey, aware of his purpose, maintained the same, steady stride.

"Lancey."

"Well?"

"Can't we talk?"

"What's stopping you?"

"It's just—well, I've been thinking——" Jan waited for prompting, any sign of encouragement. Lancey gazed straight ahead. Reddening, he blurted his next sentence. "Cap'n Benjamin, he said he might make me mate, pay me more."

"That's fine, Jan."

"You think so?" Eagerness made Jan's voice hoarse. "Would it make a—a difference to you?"

"To me?" Lancey asked with elaborate carelessness. "Now, why ever should it make any difference to me? I hope you get to be a captain, Jan."

"It ain't unlikely!"

"I'm sure it isn't." She didn't want to be coy, or tease. For all his doltishness Jan Elmendorf deserved better than cat and mouse play. Because she was sorry for him, she was deliberately cruel. "But it will never make a particle of difference to me."

Jan grunted, shook his head as if she'd slapped him. He paled, then flushed again. He said, "That's just talk, and it ain't stopping me either."

53

"Jan Elmendorf, what do I have to say that——" Vexation had Lancey shouting. Hearing herself she paused, biting her lip.

"There ain't nothing you can say," Jan said, doggedly. "I'll wait. There's no hurry."

Furious, Lancey broke into a trot. Jan's face, the stubborn chin, the grim set mouth, had made her want to hit him. To smash, and go on pummelling until she drove some sense into his thick head. Since they had reached the houses, just beyond Kimmee's and opposite Pardon Cash's, she ran ahead before she exploded.

He would probably, Lancey thought, take a blow as a sign of interest! She was not interested in Jan Elmendorf! Not as suitor, swain, or husband! Not even as an escort! His refusal to accept that as fact drove her to rage.

"It isn't pity," she said, muttering aloud, "and it isn't hate! It's just that he will *not* listen!"

She turned into the Quist yard so fast that she slipped in the mud, nearly fell. As she recovered balance, she stiffened, staring at the shed.

There, snug under the roof, was a blanket-wrapped horse! Coarse dark wool covered most of the animal, but Lancey knew that arched, sleek, reddish-tan neck, the jet-black mane. The long muzzle swung toward her, blew smoke vapor as the mare nickered.

"Meda!"

The coaly bay's ears twitched at the sound of her name. She whinnied, sounding so forlorn that Lancey hurried to stroke her nose.

Meda appreciated the attention, seemed even to appreciate the cooing noises that Lancey made. The girl was startled by Jan Elmendorf's loud astonishment.

"Whose horse?"

"Why," Lancey said, "I think that a man named——"

"Look," Jan said, pointing, "Hendrick even moved his boat to make room for him."

"Her," Lancey said, glancing to where the boat lay, bottom up, not far from the pier.

"What?"

"Her. She's a mare and her name is Meda." Lancey had a strange feeling that the conversation had happened before. She had an impulse to giggle, and, at the same time, a desire to flee. Meda's presence meant that Dirck van Zandt was near. He could only be—the boat's position showed it!—inside talking to her family.

Lancey crossed the yard with three swift strides. How dare van

Zandt come here when she was absent? What was he telling her father, Hester?

"Lancey," Jan said, "what is this——"

She flung the door open, and stood staring.

"So there I was," Dirck van Zandt was saying, "left stranded in as pretty a fix——" He stopped, turned toward Lancey, and smiled.

Oh, no, she thought, he couldn't possibly be making a story out of what happened at the inn! The whole room, and its occupants, seemed suddenly hostile.

Dirck van Zandt, in Hendrick's favorite chair, was drinking the gin Hendrick hoarded for occasions. He was wearing a snuff colored suit with a buff waistcoat, his legs, booted, were comfortably crossed, and he was smoking.

As if he owned the house, Lancey thought crossly. Hendrick held a glass and pipe, too. Even Hester and Ten Bush were drinking. The two little girls, on the floor at van Zandt's feet, were gazing at him with a rapt attention that mirrored their elders.

"Here's Lancey now," Hester said.

Dirck rose, and bowed. The blue eyes danced as he smiled across the room. Lancey flushed; she wanted to slap him.

"Lancey," Hendrick said, "why didn't you tell us?"

"Tell you what?"

"About your rescue of Dirck here."

Dirck, she thought, head swimming. He certainly didn't waste time. There was no deference on her father's face, or Hester's, or Ten Bush's. They were all smiling and friendly. She searched for, but could find no trace of smug superiority in Dirck van Zandt's smile.

"I'd have come sooner," he said, and thought it truth as he saw Lancey's flushed, rain wet, face. She was lovelier than he recalled. "I owe you my thanks. But I have been busy. Today, because Master Kent helps his partner prepare for a trip, I was free."

"Who is he?"

Jan Elmendorf's suspicious growl reached every ear. Hendrick jumped up to answer.

"Jan, Jan, come in, come in. Have a seat, a sip. Hester, fetch a mug for Jan. This is Dirck van Zandt who studies law under Master Kent. You know, Livingston and Kent. Jan Elmendorf, Dirck."

"How do you do?" Dirck made another bow. He was busily weighing the relationship between Jan and Lancey. A hulking fellow, Dirck decided, but lacking in fire. No rival.

55

Jan nodded, deposited the flour on the table. He glowered from Dirck to Lancey, but took the offered drink.

"Your health," Jan said to Dirck, making it sound like a threat.

"Yours, sir," said Dirck, and drank. "Thanks to Mistress Lancey I still have it."

"Lancey?" Jan's fingers whitened on his cup.

"Dirck broke through crossing the ice," Hester said. She rolled her eyes at Lancey, enjoying herself. "And Lancey pulled him out. Got his mare out, too."

"And never," Dirck said, quietly, "stayed for proper thanks."

Lancey let her breath out, just realizing that she'd been holding it. He'd told them of the rescue, then, and no more. She said, "I wanted no thanks."

"Lancey!"

"Now, Pa," she said, smiling, "I'm sure that Master van Zandt understands. It was not a deed that calls for thanks. Who lets a body drown, or a fine mare? Besides——" She turned the smile on Dirck van Zandt—"you had plans for the evening, I believe."

"No," said Dirck, "it seems I was mistaken about that." Her impudence delighted him; he had to struggle against laughter. She would be no easy conquest, but she was worth trouble. She actually enjoyed fencing with him in front of her family. "I can only regret that you received the wrong impression."

"I am sure you do," said Lancey. And you can go right on regretting it, she added silently.

"Perhaps, then, you will accept this token of my esteem and gratitude." Dirck reached under his coat, drew out a package. He ripped the wrappings away with one swift gesture, flipped the fan open, and laid it on the table between them.

The speed of his movements foiled Lancey's protest. She stared down at the gift.

It was delicately, beautifully made, with struts of slender ivory, and a painted pastoral scene on the silken sector. The shepherdess wore blue and gold; there was the green of hillock, the white of lamb and cloud. All the colors were vivid. Even in the unlit room, they seemed to catch the warm glow from the fireplace.

Dirck, watching the girl, reached to turn the fan. The other side held a garden fountain, its silver stream bathed in the pink of sunset, flowers about the base. It was like a piece clipped from a rainbow.

"That's nice!" said Hester.

Lancey, lips parted, could only nod. She knew the others were crowding to see—Ten Bush, Hendrick, the children, Jan. She heard the youngsters exclaim in awe, heard Jan's relieved murmur.

"Ain't a looking glass."

No, Lancey thought, it's far more lovely, but was it given with like intention? She couldn't think straight. She had never owned anything so brightly feminine, so craftily designed to catch the eye.

She picked up the fan, closed it, opened it, turned her wrist in a series of slow arcs. The colors flashed and dimmed. Holding it level and steady, she looked at Dirck van Zandt. Lancey's forehead was slightly puckered, as if she pondered a problem.

Motionless, waiting for the girl to speak, Dirck read her gaze as quizzical. She was silently asking if he expected a return for his gift. Jove, he thought, but this is a suspicious wench. Strangely, her acceptance seemed a matter of a far greater importance than the fan itself.

"You will honor me," he said, formally, "by accepting it, Mistress." Then, inspired, he added, "Although in this case, I am but Meda's agent."

Oh, thanks, Lancey cried without speaking. Because she wanted the fan, she was joyously grateful that this man had found the words to ease her choice. As the mare's gift the fan was a reward for rescue, nothing more.

"Thank you," Lancey said, "and my thanks to Meda." She spoke very softly, but her eyes were glowing and her face radiant.

Dirck van Zandt felt as if his neck-cloth had loosened. He was proud of his judgment. The girl would have been insulted by an offer of money, would have shied away from anything too personal. The fan was perfect, valuable and impractical, but not too expensive. He was glad he'd ridden Meda all the way home to Rhinebeck to beg it from his mother's collection.

"Here, Hester," Lancey said, handing the fan to her stepmother, "look at it closely." Her tone was one of proud possession.

"Real silk." Hester stroked the fabric gingerly. "Soft as down. Of course it's built more for flirting than fanning."

Dirck, laughing, said, "And it won't exactly replace those red skates."

For a moment the remark didn't penetrate Lancey's consciousness. Then, she gasped, mouth opening in swift dismay. She'd forgotten all about Rachel Anthony's skates! Now, thanks to van Zandt's rattling tongue, there'd be questions to face, explanations to invent!

"Oh, you heard," said Hendrick.

"Heard?" Dirck was politely puzzled.

Ten Bush, taking his sister's expression for bewilderment, explained. "Theophilus Anthony stopped by, Lancey. To tell Pa how Conrad was making out. Seems Rachel lost her skates."

"Stolen, she says." Hester sniffed. "More likely mislaid. That girl will misplace her groom on her wedding night."

"Now, Hester." A quick glance at his guest reassured Hendrick. He wasn't sure how gentry would take Hester's frankness, but Dirck van Zandt was grinning.

A hateful grin, decided Lancey, but it will not fluster me! She spoke with cool indifference, face bland. "Of course they're not the only red skates on the river."

"I imagine not," Dirck said.

"They were well made," said Ten Bush. "I'd hate to lose a pair like them."

"I suppose anybody would," Dirck said. "Don't you think so, Mistress Lancey?"

He was deliberately baiting her, and the girl knew it. She was annoyed that he'd leaped to the conclusion, however just, that she had stolen the skates. Borrowing was not the same as thievery. And anyway, whose fault was it that she could not return the skates?

"Why," Lancey said, "there'll be no need for skates until the ice freezes next winter. By that time I'm sure Rachel Anthony will have recovered her loss."

"'Course she will," said Hester, and turned to her husband. "Hendrick, that noggin of Dirck's looks empty."

As her father moved to pour, Lancey watched Dirck van Zandt. He settled himself in Hendrick's chair as if to stay for hours. His pipe had gone out, but he deftly raked a coal from the fire, and puffed it back to life.

"Dirck was telling a story," said Rhoda, the older of Hester's daughters.

"That's right," Hendrick said.

Hester, nodding, said, "About being stuck on an ice floe once when he was small."

Jan Elmendorf grunted. He said, "Stupid act."

"Yes," said Dirck, easily, "my only excuse is that I was too young to know better. The cake was no bigger than this table, and with my dog it was crowded." He turned toward Lancey, leaning forward as if to confide. "There was no one handy to rescue me either."

Lancey's smile was fixed; the muscles around her mouth felt stiff.

He has charmed the whole family, she thought, and even Jan is listening. Now, he knows me for a thief, but he will save that for some future date. If he thinks it will gainsay him, he is very much mistaken.

She was sure she had never disliked anyone quite so heartily.

6

As long as she could remember Lancey Quist had noted the noises from the river before she fell asleep. With the bank a scant eight yards away, the slap of the gentlest wavelet was audible in her bed under the slant of the high-peaked roof.

Storm and squall roiling the water had importance as weather omens, but the quieter, milder sounds of a calm night were even more welcome. Sometimes, as she tossed on her pallet, they penetrated Lancey's consciousness like the sudden clamor of her own heartbeats; sometimes they lulled her through drowsiness to sleep.

Tonight, as she stared wakefully into the darkness above her, the girl was only dimly aware of the river's restlessness. Her thoughts muted its splashings to a half-heard counterpoint. Like the creak of the pallet's taut ropes when she squirmed, or the sigh of her feather-bed mattress, the Hudson's familiar murmurs were accepted as normal, and dismissed.

The drizzle had stopped before Dirck van Zandt rode off on his mare. During the late afternoon the wind, buffeting along the valley, had scoured the gray clouds from the sky. By dusk, it, too, had ceased rattling against the Quist home, and the evening star had shone with the white brightness of a diamond.

Lancey, in the curtained cubbyhole that was her section of the loft, wasn't speculating about the morrow. Her concern was with the events of the day, with her family's puzzling reaction to Dirck van Zandt's visit.

Partly, she thought, it was his old Dutch name, and the gift of the fan. The girl conceded that none but herself, not even grumpy, jealous Jan Elmendorf, suspected the visitor had come for any reason but to pay a debt.

She turned her head, peering through the black void around her bed, toward the shelf where she had placed the ivory fan. It was a lovely thing, and its possession thrilled her. At least van Zandt had given it graciously, without claim. She had to admit that he had read her unspoken question aright, and answered it instantly.

"Glib as Beelzebub," muttered Lancey, aloud.

The trouble was, she decided, that the man had the Devil's own skill in assuming a pleasing shape. She hadn't dreamed that a patroon like van Zandt would be anything but patronizing to simple fisher folk. Instead, he had actually seemed to enjoy the company, had exerted himself with charm and talk.

While mocking me, she thought grimly, because of the stolen skates and what happened at Brick Gables!

That they shared a secret made her furiously angry. Dirck van Zandt had no right to presume that she had told no one of his attempted seduction!

Did he dare think, she asked herself, that she held her tongue from a feeling of guilty shame? The shame, the guilt, was all his for trying to take advantage of——

"Oh, blast him anyway," Lancey whispered. She was honest enough to confess that the occasion in question had stirred her senses to an embarrassing degree.

Feeling uncomfortably warm, she pounded the featherbed with a fist, trying to build an unheated surface. She kicked away her blankets, letting the breeze of the action soothe her naked limbs. Lancey owned no nightgown, and the air in her cubicle, moist and clammy from the day's rain, descended on her flesh like a chill dew.

It brought a momentary relief, and momentary composure. She laughed silently at her needless worrying.

What, after all, could van Zandt do to trouble her life? If he accused her of stealing Rachel Anthony's skates, she would blandly deny it. If he mentioned their supper at the inn, she would make him a laughingstock, a clumsy rake who knew nothing of women!

If, like poor Jan Elmendorf, he had intentions, honorable or otherwise, what a dance she would lead him!

God and Nicholas, Lancey thought, captivated by the prospect, then would come my turn to laugh.

Frowning, the girl recalled her stepmother's warning. Hester had liked Dirck van Zandt, and said so, but trusted no man completely at first meeting.

"That bay mare likes him, too, girl. But he has her wearing his bridle."

True enough, agreed Lancey, but I do not like him! She was merely annoyed that the reasons for her dislike had kept her sleepless for so long.

She had just settled her covers again when she heard the noise.

Lancey raised her head, listening. There was nothing but the usual night sounds of house and river. Tensely she identified Hendrick's snore as it vibrated the length of the loft. No one else seemed to be stirring, not Hester, nor the children, nor Ten Bush.

Ten Bush, she thought, and swung her legs over the side of the pallet.

Then, it came again, outside and alien, the rattle of a stone turned by a bootheel.

"Ten Bush," Lancey whispered. She was reaching for shift and petticoat as she rose. These were all she donned before she padded to her brother's closet, but she had her dress gripped in one hand.

She stood outside the curtain that guarded Ten Bush's privacy. Her father and Hester shared the only walled room in the upper half of the house, at the back, built around the stone chimney for warmth. It had a door, but the other sleeping quarters were screened by hangings. Lancey scratched her nails against the worn sailcloth stretched across her brother's corner, and raised the pitch of her whisper.

"Ten Bush?"

There was no answer, no sound of breathing or movement. Lancey brushed past the canvas; two steps and a touch confirmed her forebodings. Her brother's cot was empty!

Heart thumping, the girl moved swiftly. The loft was pitch black; no glimmer of light showed through the oiled paper that covered the single, front window. Lancey, sure of her way, didn't even pause as she drew her dress over her head. She was tugging the skirt in place about her hips before she reached the open ladder well.

Her bare feet slithered on the rungs as she descended. There was light below, the ruddy glow from the fireplace. Lancey stood for an instant, letting her eyes adjust, nimble fingers drawing and tieing the laces of her bodice.

The mound of embers behind the fire-screen was like a great red eye. As she gazed at it, calculating, the last log burned through and broke, hissing as it sent sparks flying.

Midnight at least, Lancey judged. She almost ran across the deserted room, blaming herself, feeling accusation frown from every lurking shadow. Ten Bush had grown tired of her hesitation, had decided to slip away while they slept.

She didn't know his reasons, only that she must catch and stop him.

62

If he left this way he'd regret it, and Hendrick would never forgive him. Her worry was increased by her surprise that Ten Bush would act like a thief in the night.

The wedge that held the latch bar locked was swiveled up as she'd expected. She swung the door open, peered out.

It was a clear night, starlit if moonless, and cool. Lancey could see yard and pier, the black glitter of the river. There was a figure bent by the boat, dark against the white hull.

Thank God, Lancey thought, and relaxed. She snatched a shawl from a peg, flung it around her shoulders. Anger replaced anxiety, but she tried to control the feeling. She wanted to tongue lash Ten Bush for scaring her, but what mattered was persuading him to wait.

A scrape of wood on stone startled her. Lancey closed the door carefully behind her, stood watching. She couldn't figure what Ten Bush was doing. Her brother's tall frame seemed stretched and widened by some trick of shadow and starlight.

The scraping noise sounded again, and the boat moved. Lancey's lips tightened as she realized the reason. It took two men to carry the boat easily, but Ten Bush, using a log for a roller, was inching it toward the water. He was working with slow care, sliding the gunwales a step with each lift, lest any loud report might rouse the family.

It's just good fortune, Lancey decided, that I was awake. Once the boat was launched there could be no stopping him without a shout. She was annoyed by Ten Bush's stealth, and furious at his rashness. Didn't he know his father at all? He'd send the boat back, of course, but its use in such a fashion would hurt Hendrick badly.

She moved silently toward the boat, flinching a little as her bare, winter-softened feet met the cold edges of stones. Lancey felt a flicker of amusement. It was an odd hour for her first shoeless venture of the season.

With the smugness of the undetected watcher, Lancey waited until she was only a yard away before she spoke. Ten Bush deserved to be startled, but she didn't want any outcry. She kept her voice low, smiling coldly at the crouched back before her.

"Ten Bush Quist, have you gone mad?"

The result was galvanic! As if stabbed, the figure straightened, whirling. In that instant of fluid motion Lancey's heart contracted with shock!

This man wasn't Ten Bush at all!

He was taller, bigger, moved with incredible speed. Before she could do more than gasp with stunned belief he loomed over her, grabbed her. One arm pinioned her, lifted her off her feet; a strong hand clamped over her mouth.

His swiftness had prevented speech, and Lancey hadn't thought to scream. Now, gurgling against his palm, she could only fight. Raging, she struggled to break free, writhing against his grip, kicking.

The man held her half-turned against his chest. He swayed as she twisted, but that was all. His speech stirred the girl's hair.

"One sound, wench, and I'll strangle you!"

Lancey was too furious to heed the threat. Jaws aching from the vise of his fingers she tried vainly to bite his hand. Her heels drummed futilely in the air. There was a roaring in her ears that drowned the man's menace.

"Stop that! Be still!"

He was being careful to keep his voice low, as steady as the pressure of his arms. Then, suddenly, Lancey felt the man's muscles stiffen. Through her rage and pain came the sharp rat-tat of running feet, shod feet. Rolling her eyes she saw a figure dart toward them from the shadows beside the house.

"Let her go!"

It was Ten Bush's voice, and he was shouting. Lancey made herself relax. With her brother to help she need have no fear of the stranger.

Surprisingly, the man laughed.

"Well," he said, "this spot's as crowded as a Sabbath churchyard!"

"Let her go," repeated Ten Bush. He was taut with anger, poised to rush.

"Certainly."

With the word the man tossed Lancey to one side. For an instant she seemed to hang in space, while the ground tilted to meet her. Skirts flying, she fell heavily, sprawling. Her palms and a knee burned as they scraped through the shingle. Hurt and angry she twisted instantly into a crouch and faced her assailant.

Both men were darkly clear in the blue sheen of the starlight. A low pulled hat-brim shadowed the thief's face. Ten Bush, hatless, looked so pale that his eyes and mouth were smudges. Fists raised, he charged.

The stranger stooped, plucked an oar from the ground. He used it like a bayonet-tipped musket, thrusting with a swift, sudden lunge. His forward foot stamped as he drove the oar handle at Ten Bush's middle.

"Look out!" cried Lancey.

Ten Bush checked his rush. He slapped the oar with his hand, weaved his body away from it. He snatched at the weapon, but missed.

Still leaning into his lunge, one knee bent, the man was perfectly balanced. The oarblade flashed as he whipped it through a quick arc. It was a fast maneuver, smoothly executed.

The wood cracked as it caught Ten Bush on the side of the head. Staggered by the blow he tottered sideways; his legs buckled and he collapsed in a heap.

"Too easy," said the stranger.

Lancey's horrified stare blurred with rage. Her brother was down, hurt, and her only thought was vengeance. With a wordless shout she uncoiled from her crouch in a springing leap. Fingers curved, nails ready to rake and tear, she hurled herself at the man.

Her jump stopped abruptly. The man calmly raised a stiffly extended right arm, and let her crash into it. With a jar that shook Lancey's teeth, the heel of his hand slammed against her chin. The stars suddenly jumped in the sky, flashed through her head.

She went over backwards, dazed, crashing down beside Ten Bush. Tears of pain and frustration stung her eyes, but she was too breathless to weep.

"I warned you, vixen," said the man.

"Aye," bellowed a new voice, "and I'm warning you. Drop that oar and stand still!"

The command shook through Lancey's dizziness. She sat up, aware only of rescue, and that her skirts were twisted high around her hips. As she straightened them she heard the newcomer speak again, knew him for Pardon Cash.

"Go on, drop it. This fowling piece is loaded."

"Now, it's a parade ground," said the stranger. He laughed again, shaking his head as he let the oar fall to the ground. "I might as well have blown a bugle."

Lancey glared at him. He wasn't at all bothered by what he'd done. The man stood motionless under Pardon's gun, but there was nothing frightened about his posture. The tall figure was relaxed and at ease.

"You all right, Lancey?" asked Pardon Cash.

"Yes, thanks to you." Her first concern was Ten Bush, and she turned toward him.

Her brother was lying face up. The girl swallowed nervously at sight of his paleness, the ugly bruise showing on his cheekbone.

Paper was ripped from window sash, and Hendrick Quist's question had the same staccato rasp.

"What in thunder's going on out there?"

Lancey glanced to where her father's head was thrust through the torn fragments of the upper story window. Hendrick's bald skull gleamed as he stared down at them.

"My own question," said the stranger.

"What?"

"You shut your face," Pardon Cash said. He had moved closer, and he gestured with the leveled fowling piece. It was a long-barreled gun, but Pardon's bulk dwarfed it. He answered Hendrick in a louder voice.

"Caught us a thief, Hendrick. Stole my oars and was after your boat."

"Pa," called Lancey, shakily, "Pa, come down. Ten Bush is hurt."

"Ten Bush."

Hendrick spoke the name softly. For a moment he stayed framed in the window, then he withdrew. Lancey heard the rumble of her father's voice, caught a glimpse of Hester as she peered out.

"Is he bad, Lancey?"

"I—I don't know, Pardon."

"Well, then," said the stranger, taking a step, "let somebody look who can tell."

"You stand still!"

"Oh, come. The girl's making a fuss over nothing. I only rocked him to sleep. He can't be much hurt."

"You——" Lancey tried to find an epithet bad enough to fit. "You——"

"Justin Pattison," the man said, interrupting. He took his tricorne off, bowed deeply with an elegant flourish of his arm. "At your service, sir and mistress."

Pardon Cash swore. He said, "You'll laugh out of the other——"

The sentence was never finished. Still bending from the waist in his bow, the man threw his hat with a flick of his wrist. As the tricorne sailed at Pardon's face, the other was moving. Even as Pardon Cash ducked, the stranger covered the distance between them and dove for the big fisherman's knees. He went in low, under the gun.

Lancey sat, frozen and gaping, as they went down. The tricky devil, she thought. The pair were thrashing on the ground, all flailing arms and legs. She'd never known anyone to best Pardon in a wrestle, but she saw the fowling piece snap from the tangled bodies as if slung, twirl once in the air, and splash into the river.

An instant later the stranger broke free. He was upright, and running, and she heard his hateful laugh, his panted remark.

"Time to pull foot!"

He ran toward her, away from Pardon. Now, Lancey could see his face, long and dark, with grinning white teeth. He would pass quite close, and somehow she knew exactly what to do.

She reached for the oar, raised it like a javelin, jabbed it at the man's striding, long legs. Her aim was true. The oar bucked out of her grasp as it tripped him. Calf and shin clamped against the wood, the tall body pitched headlong.

He struck the ground with a force that shook the yard. Lancey, glowing with triumph, scrambled for the oar, swung it high. Before she could strike Pardon Cash brushed past her, flung himself on the fallen man.

"I've got him, Lancey," called Pardon, breathing hard. He yanked the stranger's wrist up against his spine.

Then, Hendrick and Hester stormed out of the house, and Lancey remembered Ten Bush. She noticed that her father, in shirt and breeches, had armed himself with a boat-hook. Hester, still fastening her dress, was carrying a lighted lantern. Both were disheveled and grim.

Not listening to their excited questions, or Pardon Cash's explanations, the girl turned back to her brother. Ten Bush was breathing heavily; his head lolled when she cradled it in her lap.

He was fully clothed, and she tried to loosen his shirt. Her fingers were awkward, stiff with the same fear that chilled her breast.

"Let me see," said Hester, holding the lantern so that its beam fell on Ten Bush's face.

Lancey heard the hiss of Hendrick's indrawn breath at sight of the purple bruise. In the pale glow of the lantern it looked livid, and swollen.

"Get some water," Lancey said.

Hester thrust the lantern at her husband, tore a strip from the hem of her skirt as she hurried to the river. She came back with it dripping, dropped on her knees to bathe Ten Bush's brow. He flinched away from the cold rag when it touched the bruise.

"Ten Bush," Lancey said, "lie still."

His eyelids fluttered. He raised a hand to push away Hester's swabbing, but Lancey caught his wrist.

"Let Hester do," she said.

"I don't think his skull's cracked," said Hester. Her fingertips stroked the swelling, pressed.

Ten Bush groaned. His eyes opened, blinked glassily at the light. He shook his head, winced, tried to sit up. Lancey put a hand on his shoulder.

"Ten Bush, are you all right?"

"What happened?" he asked, foggily. His gaze focussed on Lancey, and he smiled. "What happened, Lancey?"

"Thank God," Hendrick said.

"And a thick Dutch poll," said Hester. She gave the rag to Ten Bush, and rose. "Hold that against your hurt. He hit you a real smart clout."

"Hit me?" Ten Bush rolled off Lancey's lap, struggled to his knees. With Lancey's help, and Hendrick's, he managed to rise. He said, "I'm all right."

"You were clouted with an oar," Lancey said. "When we caught——"

"The thief," Ten Bush said, his voice stronger. "The boat thief! He got away!"

"No," Hendrick said, "Pardon has him fast." He raised the lantern, waved it toward the shadows where the big fisherman held his prisoner.

The man was standing quietly. Pardon Cash had roped his wrists behind him, and gripped him by the collar. He straightened as they came toward him, and Pardon's clutch tightened.

"No more tricks, you."

"Let's have a look at him," Hendrick said. He pushed the lantern under the other's nose.

Why, Lancey thought, I've seen him before. In spite of the mud and gravel picked up in his tumble, the face was easily recognizable. It was a thin face, long in nose and jawline, darkly tanned. She remembered the eyes, almost black, that had glanced at her from a doorway in Jaycock's Ordinary. This was the man who'd been sporting with Nell Bogardus!

Closer, she could see that one of his heavy eyebrows was permanently cocked by a thin, white scar that slanted through it and across his forehead. Hatless, he looked older. There was a gray forelock in the thick brown hair, and he was grizzled at the temples.

Impassively the man met Hendrick's scrutiny. It was the fisherman who, outstared, spoke first.

"Why you want to steal my boat?"

"Who says I was stealing it?"

"I do," said Lancey, "I caught you at it."

The dark eyes flicked toward her. His wide shoulders shrugged as he said, "The girl's mistaken. I was only examining it. In the dark she startled me, and I grabbed her."

Pardon Cash said: "And what startled you into grabbing my oars?"

"Were they yours? I found them propped up against——"

"You found them," roared Pardon, "right where I left them! On pegs outside my boathouse! I wasn't expecting thieving at this time of year! Ten Bush spotted him prowling around, Hendrick."

"That's right, Pa," Ten Bush said. "I saw him sneak off with them, and roused Pardon."

Hendrick turned his head, frowning. Lancey read her father's thinking from her own. What was Ten Bush doing up at Pardon's at that hour?

"Can't we get Ten Bush inside, Pa?" said Lancey. "His head needs tending."

"I'm sorry about that," the prisoner said, "but he charged me, and I acted without thinking."

"Huh," said Lancey, "did you think he'd stand there, and let you throttle me?" She didn't wait for an answer, but pushed past him, anxious to divert her father's attention away from Ten Bush. "Bring him in, Pardon. We'll all be more comfortable inside."

She led the way into the house, insisted on putting a fresh, cold compress on her brother's cheek. Hendrick rebuilt the fire; Hester heard one of her daughters whimper and disappeared up the ladder. Only Pardon Cash and his prisoner stood and waited.

Hester returned to light the candles on the table. She'd donned petticoat and shoes, smoothed hair and dress. Without asking she took the gin from the cupboard, poured a dram for everyone but the stranger.

Strangely, when the man saw Lancey by candlelight, he pursed his lips in a soundless whistle. With the scarred eyebrow his grimace gave him a gleefully sardonic look.

"Lancey," Ten Bush said, at last, "stop fussing. I'm all right."

"You're sure, Ten Bush?" asked Hendrick.

"Yes, Pa."

"He needs rest, Pa," said Lancey. Her father's tone and frown made her sure of his next question. "He should get some sleep."

"We all could use some," Hester said.

Hendrick swallowed half his drink, and sat down. "There is something I don't understand," he said. "You went to bed with the rest of us, Ten Bush. You said good night."

"Yes, Pa."

Lancey bit her lip, watching the flush rise slowly toward the cloth Ten Bush held against his cheekbone. Oh, God, she thought, was he leaving us after all, and fetched back by this rascal's thievery?

"Then why were you at Pardon's? Why, except for your hat, are you fully dressed?"

Pardon Cash cleared his throat. "His hat fell off, Hendrick, when he ran to help Lancey."

The prisoner, legs wide, was an interested spectator. His glance moved from father to son, and back, as they spoke.

"I was just passing Pardon's, Pa."

"Where were you going?"

"I was coming back from Jaycock's."

Coming back, thought Lancey. She knew that Ten Bush wasn't lying. He was gazing at Hendrick guiltily, but he was telling the truth. Whatever his reasons for slipping from the house, he was coming back!

"What took you to the ordinary?"

"I wished to leave a message, Pa."

"So," said Hendrick. Tilting his head back he finished his drink. He set the noggin on the table. "So."

"There's nothing wrong with that," Hester said. She tried to ease tension with a laugh. "Maybe Ten Bush has a girl or——"

"No, Hester."

"No, Ten Bush?"

"No, Pa."

There are times, Lancey decided, when that slow way of talking makes a person want to scream! She had a fair idea of Ten Bush's message, but her fear of its contents was less urgent than the desire to have it stated. Tell him, she urged her brother silently, don't make him dig it out by more questions.

Ten Bush took the cloth from his face, twisted it in his hands. He gazed at it for a moment, tossed it aside, visibly braced himself.

"My message was for upriver, Pa. By post, or ship's captain, or anybody going first."

70

"For Claverack Landing, maybe?"

"Yes, Pa. To Captain Judah Paddock. To inform him that I will join his crew by next week at the latest. To help with the loading before he sails."

"And he sails?"

"The week following, Pa. For whales."

"You did this," Hendrick asked, "in spite of what I said?"

"No, Pa," said Lancey, "that's not right. Ten Bush still hoped you'd give permission. He wanted me to ask you. I promised him I'd get you to see his side."

They were all startled when the prisoner laughed. He said, "It's a dog's life, whaling, but at least it's an honest trade."

"You should talk of honesty!" said Lancey, furious at his laughter.

"Better than some. A fine gentleman's doxy, for example."

He laughed again, and Lancey stared. The man was grinning at her, mocking her. Why, she thought, he means *me!* The suddenness of the insult pinned her to her chair for a breath, then she leaped out of it with a bound.

7

"Lancey!"

Her father's gasp checked Lancey in mid-stride. Until then she hadn't realized she was crossing the room, fists clenched, muscles tensed to swing. She let her breath out, opened her hands, as she pivoted to scan the watching faces. All but one showed surprise; even Pardon Cash had his mouth open. Only the stranger, head cocked and smiling, seemed delightedly aware of her intention.

He wanted me to hit him, she thought. He taunted me in hope. She brushed her palms together as if dusting them, knees weak with relief.

"What right," she asked, voice high and shaking, "has he to laugh at us? To stick his oar into a family matter? A common thief!"

"Oh, not common," the man said. He sounded as cocksure as before. "You don't stay any length of time at Brick Gables if your purse is common."

"You live at von Beck's inn?"

"Well, I did, until a few days ago."

Lancey laughed. She saw bewilderment cloud the long face, and laughed harder. Either the man had seen her carried, limp with eyes shut, into the inn and guessed at the rest, or Hilda von Beck had been gossiping. It didn't matter. Now that she knew what was meant the insult had lost its fangs.

"What is funny?" asked Hendrick

"We are, Pa," Lancey said. She twinkled at her father, reached to pour him another drink. "Here we've been alarmed in the night, nearly lost a boat. Ten Bush and I are battered and bruised. And we spend our time talking about Ten Bush's voyage!"

Hendrick's smile flickered, faded. He said, "It must be talked about, Lancey."

"Now? In front of this—this footpad?"

"Well done," said the man in quiet admiration. "Things always look different on the morrow. Not changed, but different."

"Lancey," Ten Bush said, "this fellow can wait. My business is something that must be settled. I was willing to let you choose your time, but now it is in the open let it stay in the open."

Hendrick nodded, and said, "Your brother is right, Lancey." He rose from his chair, turned his back to the room to stare at the fire. His square figure was outlined by the dancing reflection of the flames.

Ten Bush rose, looked at Lancey. The girl nodded, opened her mouth to speak. She'd promised her brother, and was gathering her arguments. Her stepmother's gesture caught her eye.

Hester, watching her husband, raised one finger. Slowly, never shifting her gaze, she waved the finger from side to side.

Lancey waited, listening to the noise of the fire, the creak as Pardon Cash shifted his feet. Once she glanced sideways at the bound stranger. He, too, was watching Hendrick, squinting with interest.

How does he stand so motionless, Lancey thought, and why? Can he really care about anything but his own capture?

"Well," said Hendrick, turning, "I still think this whaling is foolishness, but something happened this night. Two things. It is fortune, or Providence that I found out about the first one, it is Providence alone that I do not mourn because of the second."

"I think," said the prisoner, "that I can claim a hand in both."

His calm effrontery brought tumult. Pardon Cash swore at him; Hester snorted. Brother and sister exploded into speech.

"By breaking Ten Bush's head?"

"You be quiet, you!"

Hendrick hammered on the table with his noggin. When he had their attention he sat down again, stiffly, with a sigh. "The man speaks with a pinch of truth," he said. "Maybe good comes sometimes from evil. If he had not tried to steal I would never have known that Ten Bush had left his bed to send his message."

"I had to let Captain Paddock know, Pa."

"Aye. And now I, too, know. Know that you are set. That nothing I can say will change you. Set."

"Yes, Pa."

"The other thing," Hendrick said, "is from this man also. It happened to me when Lancey called out that you were hurt. That was a bad moment, that grew no better as we came down to see. But standing over you in the yard—that was the worst moment."

Throat tight, Lancey had to nod to swallow.

"You," said Hendrick, pointing a finger at the prisoner, "I swore in my heart to kill if my son did not live."

"Of course," the man said. He sounded unafraid, and in complete agreement.

Men, thought Lancey, with a wild impulse toward hysteria.

"Struck down by a nameless thief," Hendrick said, "here on my own doorstep."

"My name is Justin Pattison."

Justin, recalled Lancey, is what they called him at Jaycock's. For all a name was easily changed, he might be stating his true one. He gave it politely, with none of the cringing air of a caught thief. His attitude puzzled her.

Concentrating on his own thoughts, Hendrick didn't hear. He paused between words, spoke very slowly. Unused to emotional expression the fisherman was finding it difficult.

"This was a lesson. My selfishness wished to keep you here, Ten Bush. With us, with me, as it has been. Yet you might have been taken from us, not for a year or two, but forever."

Justin Pattison shook his head. He noticed Lancey's glare, shrugged, and said nothing.

The girl feared an interruption that might distract Hendrick. She trembled at each pause, aching to prompt, not daring to hurry the slow speech. Her father's inner struggle touched her deeply.

Hester was smiling. Ten Bush was gnawing his lips, but his eyes were shining with hope. Pardon Cash, embarrassed, was gazing at the ceiling.

"I do not like change," Hendrick said, "but it is less bitter than death." He raised his gaze from the table top to smile at his son. "Go, then, Ten Bush, as you wish. You have my blessing, and my prayers for your safe return."

"Thank you, Pa," Ten Bush said, throat working.

Lancey wanted to shout, to clap her hands. Instead she stepped behind her father, placed her palm on his shoulder. She knew what the decision had cost him, but her sympathy was less than her joy that it had been made without friction. Father and son would part in friendship. In her gratitude she vowed to replace Ten Bush in every possible way.

Across the table her gaze met Justin Pattison's. Why, Lancey thought with shocked incredulity, we owe this peaceful settlement to that scoundrel's violence! She refused to admit such a ridiculous conclusion.

"Now," said Pardon Cash, jerking a thumb at the prisoner, "what about this barnacle, Hendrick?"

74

"Take him to the gaol," Lancey said.

"You can do that," Justin Pattison said, "though I stole nothing after all."

"Because we caught you," Ten Bush said.

"You'd have gotten the boat back. I only wanted to borrow it to cross the river to look for work."

"There are ferries!"

"True." He was unruffled by Lancey's heat. "But they are for travellers with coin, not for ex-soldiers who were paid in worthless shinplasters."

Pardon Cash grunted, leaned forward to see his captive's face. "You were a soldier?"

"From Boston to the finish. Seven years."

"Continental, then?"

"The Massachusetts Line."

"What difference does that make?" asked Lancey. "The war's been over for five years!"

"And forgotten as long," Justin Pattison said. His face darkened beneath its tan, and he spoke with cold disdain. "You needn't worry, Mistress. I beg no favors because I fought. Nor expect any at this late date! Your friend, here, asked me, and I told him."

"They call me Pardon Cash. Were you at Harlem Heights?"

"Among other places."

"It's the only victory I was in," said Pardon, wistfully. "When those blasted Hessians stormed Fort Washington, they netted the lot of us. I spent the rest of it in the hulks."

"The hulks." Justin Pattison nodded. "Then you owe nothing to anybody, Mister. Those prison ships were pest holes. Most came out as corpses."

Lancey was tapping her foot impatiently. Pardon, she thought, sounds as if he's met a lost shipmate, and the others are listening with interest. Hero or liar Pattison's tale didn't change the fact that he was a thief and a bully.

"Aren't we forgetting," she asked icily, "that he tried to kill Ten Bush when caught stealing?"

"Kill?" Justin Pattison laughed. "Begging your pardon, Mistress, there was no danger of that. With a musket butt, perhaps, but not with an oar shaft hardly thicker than my wrist. He has a sore head, yes, but I'm not unscathed myself."

"You can thank Lancey for that," said Pardon Cash. "You got away from me slick as a greased eel. Aye, and took my gun in the bargain."

The big fisherman snapped his fingers. "My gun! It's still in the river!"

"He took *your* gun?" Hendrick asked Pardon.

"Away from *you?*" Ten Bush sounded impressed.

"By a trick!" said Lancey.

"Aye," Pardon admitted with a grin, "but in fair enough fight. There's not many could do it." He clapped a big hand on Pattison's shoulder. "Next time you want a ferry ride you just come ask me."

"All right," Justin Pattison said, "I'll ask you now. I can't go back to von Beck's, or get the things I left there, until I find work. He's not a hard man for a Swede but my score adds up to pounds. If you clap me into gaol, he'll come down on me for debt, and I'll be there for months."

The coolness of the proposal outraged Lancey. She waited for Hendrick's refusal, saw with dismay he was considering it.

"Give way, Hendrick," said Pardon Cash. "After all, no harm's done. An old soldier, and all."

"How do we know he's telling the truth?"

"You don't, Mistress." Justin Pattison bowed to Lancey. "Though there are documents at von Beck's would prove it. If you care to ransom them."

"Ten Bush," said Hendrick, "you're the one was hurt the most."

Even before her brother spoke, Lancey knew what he'd say. Ten Bush was so happy to have his father's blessing that he'd forgive anything.

"I bear no ill will, Pa."

That leaves me, Lancey thought. The attempted theft was easily forgotten. They were fisher folk and understood that a man who needed a boat might borrow it without asking the owner. It was a fisherman's task to protect his gear, and nobody went screaming to the watch over a foiled filching. But what of her sore knee and scraped hands, Ten Bush's great bruise?

"What do you say, Lancey?"

Lancey's mouth twitched as she fought a smile. Somehow the rogue had managed to turn the tables, to put her at a disadvantage. He stood there daring her to judge him, and she had to admire his audacity.

"Oh," she said, with barbed sweetness, "let the poor beggar go. Didn't he fight for God and country?"

The flush and quick glare that brought delighted her. For all his proud, reckless air this Pattison had his tender spots. Well, he'd called her a doxy, hadn't he, and probably still thought the term apt? He needn't think she'd let him off scot free after that.

Pardon was already undoing the captive's bonds. The big fisherman looped the rope through his belt, reached for the stone bottle.

"Have a swig of this, lad," he said.

Justin Pattison chafed each wrist in turn, nodded. Then as he accepted the offered drink, he swayed. The muscles about his mouth paled, and he put a hand on the table to steady himself.

He had stood motionless for so long that the change startled the company. Lancey frowned with quick suspicion, but her stepmother forestalled comment.

"Young man," said Hester, "when did you have your last decent meal?"

"I'm all right, ma'am," said Justin Pattison. He took a gulp of the liquor.

"Sit down there," Hester said, up and bustling. "It's pot luck indeed at this hour, but there's bread and cheese and some cold beans."

"Scraps." Lancey made the word a taunt.

Pattison looked ready to hurl his noggin at her, but the rebuke came from her father.

"Lancey!" he said. "Haven't we always shared what we had in this house?"

"Yes, Pa." Lancey was meek, but not contrite. There was no denying that the Quists had fed light-fingered scamps before, but this one was special. She was content to know that he nursed a hatred for his present condition, and could be hurt through it.

"I don't want to be any trouble," he said, gruffly. Lancey's laugh, genuinely merry, brought his head up. With a smile he said, "Any *more* trouble."

"It *has* been a night of hurly-burly," Lancey said. Watching Hester set dishes before him, she realized the man was really hungry. He tried to hide it, face impassive and hands still, but his eyes betrayed him.

Pardon Cash, fidgeting on his stool, was obviously itching to ask questions. He said, "You know the river?"

"I should," Justin Pattison said, "after being camped both sides of it more times than I can count. I was with an invalid regiment outside Newburgh for more than a year."

"You were wounded then?"

"Yes."

"Eat," said Hester.

With them all watching, Lancey noted, he was careful to eat slowly. Every movement of his spoon was controlled; no mouthful was bolted. She liked that in him.

In fact there was much about him that was likeable. For all its long jaw, his face was well made, strong, clear skinned, and very male. His dark complexion made the white streak in his hair, the scar-quirked eyebrow, strangely attractive.

He had long-fingered, big hands that looked capable, and he used them with a minimum of waste motion. The way he fights, Lancey thought. Something about his worn, patched coat puzzled her, and then memory solved the problem. It was an old uniform, re-cut and dyed black.

Pardon Cash barely waited until the meal was finished. "What's your trade, Justin?" he asked.

"I was 'prenticed to a boat builder on the Connecticut River. But I went off soldiering before my time was up."

"Hear that, Hendrick? River raised."

"I hear, Pardon. They say it's good sized that Connecticut."

"Fair to middling," agreed Justin Pattison, "but you notice I've come back to the Hudson."

That, Lancey decided, was the right thing to say. Even Ten Bush, who was planning to leave the river, beamed at the compliment.

"You come at the right time," Hendrick said. "The river's open her whole length, the packets are sailing, and there'll be work."

"If you really want it," Lancey said.

Justin Pattison looked at her. "I'm not saying I'd take anything," he said, "not even for a crust and a cot when I need both. The day when a man can't choose his labor he becomes a slave."

"There are several whalers," Ten Bush said, "making ready to sail. Upriver at Claverack. Some call it Hudson. I don't know if they lack hands or not, but——"

"Thank you," Justin Pattison interrupted, "but that is not for me. Cooped up inside a vessel month after month with the same people, hearing the same talk. Besides those ships are owned and skippered by New Englanders. I've had enough of that breed to last me for a time!"

"You hear, Ten Bush?"

Ten Bush merely smiled at his father's question, but Lancey glowered at the stranger. Who was he to be criticizing her brother's chosen trade?

She said, tartly, "Seems to me you're mighty finicky about what you will or won't do!"

"Maybe," said Justin Pattison, nodding, "but it's not for fear of hardship. Or of hunger."

"I guess not." Pardon Cash laughed. "Not for a man who spent that winter at Valley Forge. I take it you were there, Justin?"

"I was there."

It was a flat statement and Lancey believed it. She saw her own sudden interest reflected on every face. In the decade that had passed since the then rebel army had suffered in that camp, its plight and fortitude had become a legend. The stay-at-homes had felt the severity of that same winter, understood the hardships related by the soldiers.

Hester and Hendrick exchanged a glance; Ten Bush moved his stool a trifle closer. Pardon Cash's big head bobbed in a series of slow nods.

More than some of the great battles, Lancey thought, we are proud of those months at Valley Forge. Folks like us especially, fishermen and farmers, the hewers and drawers, the poor, the landless, the riff-raff.

"You know," said Pardon, "I guess most everybody in Poughkeepsie, 'cept me, has heard all about that time. From the troops quartered downriver." He sounded both apologetic and eager. "But me, I was their prisoner till the war was over."

"You came back here like a skeleton," Hester said.

"I managed." Pardon laid a crooked finger on his lips as if to hide the gap in his teeth. "But I never did hear, first hand that is, about Valley Forge. If you wouldn't mind talking about it, Justin——"

For the space of his quick frown Lancey was sure that the ex-soldier would refuse the unfinished request. He glanced at each of them in turn, but his gaze rested longest on Pardon Cash. The frown slackened, returned. She spoke to that indecision, very softly.

"He was in the hulks."

The dark eyes swung toward her, hooded beneath lowered eyelids. "I know," said Justin Pattison. Then, he smiled and turned to the big fisherman.

"What do you want to know?"

"What it was like."

"You're asking the wrong man," Justin Pattison said. His voice was bitter and vibrant. "There's plenty could give you chapter and verse about the Forge. If half of them had been there we'd have moved out and taken Philadelphia!"

Cold prickles ran down Lancey's spine at his hard, relentless tone. This man was not telling a story. He was a zealot cursing the unbelievers, a soldier talking to civilians.

"Those who lived through it want to forget it. From the general down. It was bad, bad. Hovels to live in, rags to wear. Little fire and less food. And, Christ knows, it was cold. Cold that never let up on you, never let you sleep much, or thaw. I can't even tell you how many days it lasted. I lost count. Because it didn't seem like it would ever end.

"Some died, and some ran, and some stuck. You got sick and you died or stayed sick. You froze, and you died or stayed frozen. There was no reason why this one lived, and that one didn't.

"Maybe the general put it down different in some report. He could tell it best. He saw the whole camp. I saw it smaller. One hut that was crowded even after four burying parties. One campfire that was never big enough. A couple or three paths—to muster, to the burying ground, to the captain's for rations. Paths to Calvary all of them, and the last was the worst.

"I was eighteen that winter, but missed the day being out of my head with ague and fever.

"So they made me a sergeant for living through it because too many sergeants hadn't. Old von Steuben's drilling helped some toward the end, and warmer weather helped more. But telling it now you can't make it like it happened. You had to be there."

He stopped so abruptly that they were still waiting for him to continue while he drank. He set down his noggin with a finality that broke the spell.

"That's all?" asked Pardon.

"That's all."

Lancey didn't share the others' disappointment. She wanted him to go on talking for another reason. While he spoke she'd felt an attraction, a magnetism, as strong as it was exciting.

"Justin," she said, using the name without thought, "the dominie, our preacher, said that General Washington prayed."

"Maybe he did," said Justin Pattison. "He had reason. Don't think I'm running down the general. He was the best we had at all times, and he was never better than that winter."

"How do you mean?"

"He was always *there,* somehow. At your elbow, going past the campfire, taking a salute. We didn't have a war, nor powder, nor food. God, counting noses we didn't have an army! But we had him.

I'm no officer boot-licker, but the man was good. You didn't even envy him his boots, or his warm cloak. He was *that* good!"

"A great man," Hendrick said.

Pardon Cash said, "You think he's right wanting this Constitution passed?"

"Of course he's right," said Justin Pattison, with a harsh laugh, "according to his lights. He's a rich man, isn't he? Oh, he risked it, and his neck with it. He put it all up for hazard like a gentleman, I'll give him that. But now he's won the gamble."

They stared at him, disturbed by his vehemence. Even Pardon Cash had seen Washington, held him in awe.

"He won the war!" Lancey's protest was sharp.

"Granted," Justin Pattison said. "But some of us at Valley Forge, quick and dead, thought we were fighting for liberty. Not for any lousy piece of paper that says the rich get richer, and the poor man keeps his place!"

Lancey, involuntarily, had a mental picture of Dirck van Zandt, compared him to the speaker. Silk and steel, she thought. Ivory fan and iron hammer. This Pattison was older, tougher, tempered by war and trouble. She knew van Zandt was rich, well-born, sure of place and position. The other was a rascal and a rogue, ready to steal, fight or conspire to get what he wanted. She recognized his spirit as akin to her own.

I would like to see them together, she decided. The idea amused her.

"I'm sleepy," Hester said, yawning. "Are we going to sit here talking until dawn?"

8

LIKE MOST OF THE MARRIED RIVERFRONT FOLK THE QUISTS WERE A churchgoing family, slightly more irregular than their neighbors, especially in the fine weather of fishing season. Hendrick was religious, but not fanatical. He wasn't bothered that Ten Bush courted ill luck by departing on the Sabbath, but he insisted they must all attend services first.

"That old talk," Hendrick said, "about the oarsman who still rows the river because he broke the Sabbath is a grandmother's tale. But it is better that Ten Bush take no chances before a long voyage."

Lancey didn't mind. She'd long since adopted her stepmother's attitude toward Sunday services. Hester went to please her husband, to see people, to note new bonnets and dresses. She'd been a seamstress before marriage and never lost interest. Sometimes there was gossip to exchange, and occasionally the preacher's sermon stirred fresh curiosity about certain sins of the flesh.

Only Conrad, summoned from the horse-ferry, complained. The boy bemoaned his loss of revenue, but submitted when Hendrick threatened to forbid his working at all.

Scrubbed and shining, dressed in their best, the family assembled before the first peal of the church bell. Ten Bush, chin propped high by a starched white stock, seemed more uncomfortable than pleased. He kept gazing around the room as if trying to imprint every detail on his memory.

"You're sure you have everything?" Lancey said, for the tenth time. She was trying to mask sadness with brisk efficiency.

"Yes, Lancey."

"He must have," said Conrad, hefting his half-brother's bundle.

"I'll carry that." Hendrick inspected the knots that fastened the blanket wrapping, swung the parcel onto his shoulder. It was a goodwill gesture, an assurance that he didn't regret his grant of approval.

Hester fastened her cloak at the throat, took a small daughter by each hand. Cocking her head, she examined her tall stepson from

82

boots to hat crown. "You'll pass," she said, "but save that jacket for the belles in foreign ports."

"I don't think we make any ports," Ten Bush said, reddening.

"There's the bell," Lancey said. She tied her bonnet ribbons as she stepped outside. Automatically her glance checked the weather, but without real interest. It was a warm morning, but damp. Mist rose from the river like steam; haze wrapped the sun in gauze. The girl felt depressed. Her brother's departure meant the end of the life she'd known.

I've too much of Pa in me, she thought, to like change. The melancholy of the moment convinced her this was true. Actually, she was enjoying her sorrowful reflections.

Strung out along the path, they took the short cut to the Post Road. Hendrick led, Conrad on his heels; Hester herded her charges in the rear.

Lancey, walking behind Ten Bush, believed she quivered at each stroke of the church bell. She was wearing her best dress, a year-old sprigged dimity Hester had made, now faded to soft yellow, and she considered it too gay for the occasion. Her step was subdued and stately, befitting a funeral.

"Lancey." Ten Bush spoke over his shoulder.

"Yes?"

"I just thought. I'm leaving one kind of country, and liable to come back to another."

His cheerfulness irritated Lancey. Didn't he realize that he was breaking up the family? She had wanted Ten Bush to get his wish, but the reality was unpleasant. It's all the fault of that Justin Pattison, she decided illogically.

"You're coming back here," she said.

"Oh, sure. But it'll be changed if they set up this Constitution."

"It won't pass. Not in New York."

"You know," Ten Bush said, "I'm sorry I'm going to miss that meeting. This town'll be jam packed."

A snort ended Lancey's sobriety. He was, in typical man fashion, worrying about missing a stupid convention, while her heart mourned his coming absence! Her toe shot out to trip him, but she remembered his good clothes in time.

"I'll tell you all about it," she said with heavy sarcasm, "when you get back. Who spoke and how they voted. I wouldn't want it bothering you while you were playing tag with those whales!"

They reached the wider road, and were able to walk abreast. Ten

Bush waited for Lancey. His expression was one of baffled concern.

"You mad about something, Lancey?"

"No. Of course not."

"You sound mad."

"I'm not." She couldn't spoil their last morning with a fit of temper. They were not demonstrative with each other, but now she took his arm. "I'm glad for you, Ten Bush. That you're doing what you want. I just wish I was going with you."

"You're a girl."

"I know." It was the remark that settled the question. Girls did not go awhaling. She had no real desire to leave the river, but she was nettled. Why, she thought rebelliously, do men always bring *that* up, when you're just trying to say you'll miss their company?

"Likely you'll get married within the year."

"Married?" Lancey glared at her brother. "Me?"

"You're of age. I'm surprised it ain't happened before this."

"You needn't be! It's not going to happen in any hurry, believe me!" Even to her own ears she sounded too violent, so she laughed. "You'll find your whales a lot easier to catch than this miss!"

Hester called a warning, and they drew aside to let a chaise rattle past. They were close to the crossroads now, and Hendrick was waiting in front of the old Dutch graveyard. Conrad was watching the people gathered in the doorway of the English church opposite.

Probably, Lancey thought, estimating their wealth as compared to our own congregation. She had no qualms about gazing that way herself. The English church was fashionable, but no more so than the older Dutch establishment.

There on the steps, talking to a tall, smiling young lady, was Dirck van Zandt. He had his hat in his hand, and he was laughing.

Lancey didn't stare, but she gathered every detail of the other girl's costume. She was wearing a dress of blue brocade that shimmered as she moved, with matching bonnet. Her cloak was trimmed with fur. Both were cut in the latest fashion, looked new.

I'll wager, Lancey thought savagely, he hasn't tried any of his fancy tricks with her! She shifted her gaze to the girl's face, noting a cool and handsome beauty, as pale and finely carved as a cameo.

As tall as he is, Lancey noted, and rich. Well, water sought its own level, and who cared!

Hester came up to wink at Lancey, nod toward Dirck. Lancey's smile was cool, unflustered. She turned away, not hurrying, glad that he was too busy to notice them. She didn't fear a snub but a year old dimity could not match blue brocade.

Together, the family crossed the Filkintown Road to the Dutch church. The bell had stopped tolling, but churchgoers were still moving toward the entrance. Wagons were ranked along the edges of both roads; a few horses were even hitched in front of the new courthouse that faced the church across the junction of Post and Filkintown Roads.

Lancey gave the courthouse an affectionate inspection. The burning of the previous one had been one of the town's great fires, the best in her experience. The new structure had barely been finished in time for the legislature's meeting in January. Lancey had personally, if unofficially, supervised every stage of its construction.

It was a large stone building, almost square, with two stories of glassed windows below its peaked roof, and a chimney at both ends. A strange-looking, open-sided cupola crowned the edifice.

Frowning at the cupola, which she had never approved, Lancey wondered again that it had withstood the winds of March. It looked flimsy, less sturdy than the Quist boatshed.

"Come on," Hendrick said, "come on. Reverend Livingston's waiting." He stowed Ten Bush's bundle beside the doorway as they entered, left Conrad to guard it.

The church was crowded, heavy with the mixed odor of massed humanity and damp clothing. Lancey's depression returned. Everything was all too familiar, the same faces, the same hymns, the same routine. She recognized Nell Bogardus peering from a rear corner, Digmus Jaycock forcing his way into a pew. Down front a trio of stalwart backs could only be the von Becks.

There was a clatter as they sat for the sermon. John Livingston, another of the ubiquitous clan so prominent in the county, had studied and taken his degree in Holland, but no longer gave alternate sermons in Dutch and English. The practice had outlived British rule, but died out with the war's end.

The minister read his text.

"He shall return no more to his house, neither shall his place know him any more."

Startled, Lancey heard Hendrick grunt beside her, turned to see Ten Bush's mouth drop open. Even Hester wore a worried frown. The girl had been depressed because the service held nothing special for her brother's leave taking, but this was too close for comfort!

Listening, she discovered that Reverend Livingston wasn't talking about Ten Bush, but of those who left the house of righteousness for the palaces of sin. It was both a relief and a disappointment.

The preacher droned on, not unpleasantly, but Lancey lost the thread of the discourse. Hendrick had relaxed into dutiful solemnity; Ten Bush, restless, was fingering his starched neckpiece. Hester smiled at her stepdaughter, sharing a relief that the text had been a meaningless coincidence.

After a prayer and another hymn, it was over. Lancey recited the words without thinking of their meaning. She was praying mentally for her brother's safety, a fair voyage and a quick return. The muttering voices around her did give comfort, a sense of unity.

God, she said inaudibly, take care of him.

Outside, she felt better, sure that her prayer had been heard. The Quists did not stop for greetings, for the social gatherings that always followed the services. Hendrick, again shouldering the bundle, led the way to the Filkintown Road.

As they went down it, toward the river, Lancey walked in step with Ten Bush. She thought he looked grave, troubled, and wondered if the preacher's text had upset him. Most fishermen were superstitious.

"The sermon wasn't aimed at you, Ten Bush."

"Huh?" He was puzzled, then grinned. "I didn't think it was, Lancey. I ain't exactly heading for any palaces of sin."

Hendrick, overhearing, glanced back. He said, "That gave me a bad turn for a second there." He frowned, shaking his head. "Good thing he never mentioned the sea. Stands to reason you can't luck the sea without naming it."

"I had my fingers crossed anyway," Ten Bush said.

The statement brought them all to a standstill, clustered about Ten Bush. Even the two little girls stared their disbelief.

"Had your fingers crossed?" said Hendrick slowly. "In church?"

"It just happened to be, Pa. You see, I was holding my copper that way. So's to have it ready."

Pleasure chased the frown from Hendrick's face. Conrad chuckled, clapped fist in palm. They were all worried, Lancey thought, but this simple thing has relieved them.

"That's all right, then," Hendrick said. "You hear, Hester. He had his fingers crossed."

Hester crowed an approving laugh. "I guess we don't have to worry about you, boy."

They trudged on toward the landing in high spirits. Lancey didn't

86

share their cheerfulness, but had no wish to dampen it. You'd think, she decided, that by crossing his fingers Ten Bush had diminished the hazards of the journey and cut its time in half. She was a fisherman's daughter, knew the belief placed in a lucky hat, a special charm, a favorite bit of gear.

Her own depression was deepening as the moment for farewells approached. It took considerable effort to keep smiling.

The pinnace was moored to the ferry landing. They all knew it; its owner used it for short hauls along the river. The roads, though passable, were muddy and slow. Ten Bush, like all his kind, considered the river the quickest, most comfortable highway.

Lancey, judging wind and water, found that the mist had burned off, above and below. The river was a clear, sparkling blue; the sky, lighter in hue, unrippled, was crossed by lazily moving clouds, bleached white by a bright sun.

It should not be, she thought, such a smiling day.

The barge ferry was in, too, its four oarsmen loafing in the sunshine. They watched the Quists with idle curiosity.

"Well," Ten Bush said.

"Well." Hendrick gripped his son's hand. "Good voyage." He turned away, handed the bundle down into the pinnace.

Hester kissed her stepson; he bent to each of the children, shook hands with Conrad.

"Lancey."

"Ten Bush," she said, feeling the stinging rush of tears. Oh, God, no, she swore silently, I am not going to cry! She said, "That's a nice breeze from the south. On your quarter all the way."

Their hands touched, fell apart. They didn't kiss.

Ten Bush climbed down into the boat. Conrad cast off the line; the pinnace owner shoved off from the pier. Ten Bush stood tall against the mast as he helped scull the little vessel out into the stream.

The sail rattled up, caught wind and bellied. They began to move faster.

"Goodbye, goodbye, Ten Bush." The children were calling and waving. Hester fluttered a handkerchief; Hendrick raised an arm.

White plumes blossomed at the pinnace's bow, spumed along its sides, dissolved into wake.

"That's a fair wind," Conrad said.

Goodbye, Lancey said, without speaking. Goodbye, my brother. Goodbye, Ten Bush.

They stood there watching until the white sail was no bigger than a speck.

*   *   *

The walk home, on the path below the bluff, alongside the river, was a subdued procession for the three Quist adults. Conrad, in a hurry to return to work, disappeared; the two small girls ran ahead, scampering in gay release.

Hendrick Quist, hands clasped behind his back, walked with head bent, gaze on the ground. His pace was slow but steady; the set of his shoulders discouraged talk. Obviously thinking of his departed son, he seemed oblivious to his surroundings.

Shoulder to shoulder, a yard in the rear, came Hendrick's wife and daughter. Neither spoke. Twice Hester turned toward her stepdaughter, saw the frozen scowl on Lancey's face, shrugged and held her tongue.

Ten Bush is gone, thought Lancey, matching her steps to the words. Ten Bush is gone!

The sun beat down with surprising warmth. Without thinking Lancey opened her cloak, accepting this new discomfort as a part of her misery. There was a gloomy satisfaction in the rhythm of their march, in the drumbeat cadence of her father's bootheels as they struck the shingle.

She wanted to weep, but knew she mustn't. Forgetting all the days when she'd not seen Ten Bush from sunrise to supper, she pictured a future without him as dreary loneliness. Grief was a new emotion to Lancey, and she let it control her, fascinated by its powerful sweep.

They had almost reached the fishing settlement when Hester nudged Lancey. Her whisper was sharper than her elbow.

"Lancey, look at the river!"

You couldn't expect, Lancey conceded with sad generosity, that Hester would share the same deep feelings as Ten Bush's father and sister. She raised her head in patient obedience.

The white clouds were still drifting from the south. Under them, far downriver, a sloop's jib, foreshortened by distance to fingernail height, flashed in the sunshine. There was a scent of spring in the air at last; there was a gentleness in the breeze that touched her cheek. Then, as she lowered her gaze to the nearer stretch of broad river, Lancey stiffened.

88

She stared, blinked, and stared again. Ten Bush vanished from her mind as if erased from a slate.

"Pa!" she called, "Pa, look! They're afishing!"

"Three of them!" cried Hester.

Hendrick swung around, jerked from his reverie by their outburst. He saw Lancey's arm raised in a rigid point, turned his head to follow her indication. At once his voice rose in a roar.

"Lancey, they're afishing!"

"I know!"

"Kimmee's boat!" Hendrick started to run.

Hester and Lancey were running, too. The girl drew away from her stepmother immediately.

"And Cash!" bellowed Hendrick as Lancey flashed past him. "That's Pardon's new dory!" His thick body swayed, short legs pumping, as he tried to strip off his coat as he ran.

"The slaves too!" Lancey called back over her shoulder. Then, she hoisted her skirts and really sprinted! She would have to change clothes before they put their own boat in the water.

Anger as well as exercise set her blood tingling. The season was too early, the day too bright, the river itself too cold for decent fishing! Yet local custom always made a contest of the first casting of nets. There was no prize but the boat with the biggest catch was considered lucky by the rest.

She wondered which fisherman had picked this day to start. Pardon Cash, probably, beguiled by the fair weather and anxious to try his new made craft. Hendrick's absence was surely an extra inducement. One less feared rival meant less competition.

A scurvy trick, she thought, but typical. Fishermen had no scruples about besting each other. Hendrick would have done the same.

As she tore through the village, she watched the flow of water through the gaps between the shacks. The tide was at flood peak, almost ready to change. They still had time to fish in the flood and float on the ebb!

She was turning into the Quist yard when she saw Seth Row's boat move out from shore toward mid-stream. Seth, then, was a late starter, too! He and his eldest were rowing hard, stroking in perfect unison. Four oarblades scattered seed pearl droplets as they lifted, splashed creamy foam when they dug.

Lancey didn't wait to watch. Her cloak was off before she reached the threshold of her front door; it was flung aside as she crossed. The dimity dress was unfastened and yanked over her head in three strides. Something caught, ripped as she tugged it loose.

Her bonnet came off in the folds of the dress. She twisted out from under the crumpled cloth, let it drop to the floor. Scrambling up the ladder to the loft she was fumbling at the laces of her petticoats.

The fanciest, her best, fell half-way to her cubicle. Lancey leaped free of the puddle of lawn, kicked her second petticoat into a corner. Now, she was down to two, her everyday sturdiest of flannel and wool.

Hopping on one foot, and then the other, she pried off each shoe in turn, peeled the knitted stockings from her legs. She was half into her homespun dress when she heard Hendrick below.

"Lancey! Fetch my other coat!"

She shook the house as she raced across the loft to her father's room. Swiftly, from pegs, she grabbed Hendrick's fishing garb, shirt, coat, breeches. Flinging them ahead of her, she practically slid down the ladder.

"I'm ready, Pa."

"Good." Hendrick's voice was muffled in his shirt. He pulled his head free, continued, "Take a pair of oars. Be with you in two shakes."

Lancey snatched a battered tricorne from behind the door, swept her hair high, crammed the hat on her head. She didn't want a breeze-swept strand blinding her at the wrong moment. Then, quickly, but carefully, she selected a pair of oars from the half dozen standing in their corner. She tilted them forward onto her shoulder, raised them, and went out.

Red-faced and winded, Hester was busy in the yard. She'd already turned the boat, was sticking the tholepins in the gunwale. Her eyes were bright with excitement.

"Those snakes," she said, panting. "They knew we were busy saying goodbye to Ten Bush!"

"We're not skunked yet!"

"Well, I hope not. Give me those oars. Fetch the gear."

By the time Lancey brought the wooden box with its carefully folded layers of net from the shed, and stowed it in the square stern of the boat, Hendrick joined them. He gave the gear a quick inspection, straightened to gaze out over the river.

"You've naught to eat," Hester said.

"No need," Hendrick said, "we're only going to make a short drift."

"And you're wearing your best breeches!" This time Hester's complaint was wailed.

"Look," said Hendrick, "I know this is a lot of tomfool nonsense. But they ain't going to be able to say they caught me with a dry net first thing."

Lancey was checking the positions of the other fishermen. Seth Row's brown boat was still moving upstream, blades now as thin as toothpicks. The others were strung out, drifting beside their nets. The Kimmee boat was black; it was almost in mid-river. Closest to the near bank bobbed the slaves' faded green skiff. Farthest away and hardest to see, Pardon Cash's new dory made a gray scar against the blue current.

"Pa," she said, "they're not moving much. Tide hasn't changed yet." Hendrick said, "We've time."

With Hester's help they ran the boat into the water. Hendrick embarked from the pier, but Lancey waded heedlessly through the shallows, gasping as the cold ripples lapped around her ankles.

They shoved off, laying the oars between the tholepins. Hester raised voice and arm in farewell.

"Best the lot," she called.

Sitting behind her father, Lancey took her beat from his. Hendrick rowed with a steady, unhurried rhythm, glancing over his shoulder to set the course.

"We'll go up almost to the landing, Lancey. There's plenty of time. They didn't expect us back soon as this."

It was good, Lancey decided, to feel a boat moving beneath her again, to sniff the cool breeze rising from the river. Her hands, arms, and body adapted to the rowing as if she had never been landlocked.

Lift, feather, stretch, dip, *pull.*

All the tricks returned to her, as familiar as the gurgle of the water rushing past, the creak of the tholepins. She had complete faith in her father's judgment, and was content to let him decide their speed. Racing might raise blisters on her palms, but not this easy, swinging stroke.

Lift, feather, stretch, dip, *pull.*

A hail floated across the waves, soft and unintelligible. Lancey didn't bother to turn her head. Hendrick glanced and grunted.

"Calico," he said, "cheering us on."

Nice of him, Lancey thought. The sun was warm on her face and arms; the exercise had her glowing. She was suddenly aware that she could see the gray dory from the corner of her eye. There were two figures waving.

A moment later the Kimmee boat was abreast of them. She heard Gerritt Kimmee's raucous jeer.

"Almost caught you napping, Hendrick!"

Hendrick saved his breath for rowing. Ten strokes later the Kimmees were well astern, faces turned to watch them pull away. Lancey could see the floats of the other boat's net; she swung her gaze along the line, but none appeared to be dipping under the surface.

No fish yet, she judged, and smiled grimly.

Lift, feather, stretch, dip, *pull*.

They changed course slightly, slanting toward the western bank. Hendrick told her the reason.

"Seth's casting net. Let's get out of his way."

She glanced back, then. The closeness of Seth Row's boat surprised her, a feeling replaced by satisfaction. They'd made excellent speed. Not far beyond Seth, bending and straightening as he tossed net, she could see the ferry barge.

Watching the filmy gray veiling billow, and splash, billow, and splash, behind Seth's boat, Lancey frowned. He never did manage to stain his nets dark enough.

"All right, Lancey. Let her run."

Shipping oars, Lancey mopped her face. Her first glance was for the tide.

"On the turn," she said, happily.

"Just." Hendrick, always serious in a boat, allowed himself a grin. He drew in his oars, laid them aside, moved to the stern. Crouching over the net box, his head turned in one sweeping survey. "Good," he said, "swing her around and keep her steady."

Using each oar as needed, Lancey jockeyed the boat into position. Hendrick nodded; he bent, straightened, flung out both arms, casting the first foot of net well away from him. The weight hit the water with a solid smack; the white painted wooden buoy slapped, skipped on the surface.

Lancey began to row with careful steadiness as her father dipped back into the box. Again, he came up smoothly, jerked as he cast net. Weight and float splashed white scars from the blue water.

Down, up and out, Lancey thought, down, up and out. With never an unbalanced moment, a hitch or a tangle. It was really a graceful skill, this fisherman sowing of the river. She drew in a deep breath, very proud of her father.

When the whole line of white blocks was bobbing behind them, they rowed back along it to make sure it wasn't tangled. By that time the net was floating gently downriver with the ebb tide.

"So," said Hendrick, "now we wait."

They drifted, silently pleased with their work, not talking. Lancey stretched in the bow, her feet propped on a thwart; Hendrick studied the net.

The girl watched the sky rock gently above her, shut her eyes. Sunshine seemed to press warmth and peace deep into her. For the first time since she'd noticed the fishermen, she thought of her brother.

He should be there with them, waiting for the changing tide, watching for the first telltale ducking of a float that signalled a fish in the net. It was too early for even the craziest herring to be running, but there were always perch. Not that the catch mattered too much on such a lovely day.

Poor Ten Bush, she thought, there's no better life than this anywhere.

9

AFTER THE DAY OF THE FIRST CASTING THE LIFE OF THE FISHING VIL-
lage settled into its seasonal routine. There were always nets to be
washed, hung to dry; threadbare gear was given its final mending.

Each boat owner had his favorite hours for making a drift, but
these varied according to weather, tides, the luck of another boat. It
was still too early for luck to be much of a factor, but the men
watched each other.

Every haul was carefully scanned for a telltale herring, the fore-
runner of the shad. The shad would come upriver to spawn in their
own time, when the water was warm enough, but the herring came
first.

Lancey Quist would have been more surprised at sight of a herring than she was to discover that Justin Pattison was the helper in
Pardon Cash's dory. Somehow it seemed a natural result of the wrestle between the two men, foreshadowed by Pardon's admiration for
a soldier who'd avoided capture.

The girl asked her father about it.

"Pardon feeling his years, that he's taken a partner?"

"They ain't rightly partners," Hendrick explained, with slow deliberation. "Seems Pardon went bond for the fellow over to von Beck's.
Got his things back on a promise to pay the score. Justin's working
for keep till then."

"Or till he steals something else, and skedaddles!"

Hendrick blinked at his daughter's tone. "He's not just an ordinary
thief, Lancey."

"No. He's a clumsy one."

"Well, that's Pardon's watchout, not ours. Besides, the man knows a
thwart from the gunwale. He's a good helper."

Lancey had to admit that her father was right. Justin Pattison
showed himself to be a skilled boatman. She was a little annoyed by
the man's adaptability, by his powerful rowing, his deft handling of

94

a net. It made her own efforts as Hendrick's helper seem of less importance.

They met with mutual hostility concealed behind politeness. Lancey was guarded, wary of every glance and smile. She had not forgotten his insult, nor did she believe that he had changed his opinion. Justin's bow of greeting, his deferential address, his very tone mocked her. She waited only for the overt act or remark that would break their truce.

Strangely, the other fishermen, usually suspicious of outlanders, accepted him from the first. Pardon Cash sponsored him and the man had genuine fishing ability. They welcomed his talk as fresh and interesting.

No boat returned from a drift without an audience. The fishermen ashore gathered to comment, to weigh the haul mentally, to count the netted fish. That was why the Livingston pier was crowded with loungers watching the slaves approach the day the sloops came back upriver.

Lancey saw them first, and the sight brought her to her feet. She felt a familiar thrill of excitement as her breathing quickened, and her smile came unbidden. Later, she knew, the flotilla would be familiar and everyday, a hazard even to the nets. But, always, the sloops' initial return visibly brought spring, seemed to emphasize the beauty of the river.

They came in a long line, and the white shields of their jibs, gleaming in the sunshine, had the gallant bravery of an untried, but confident, army. There was a fair wind behind them, out of the south straight up the valley, and they sailed in the order set by the way they had jostled through the Highland gateway.

"Ah, lovely," Lancey said.

Justin Pattison, standing behind her, said, "Yes."

The one word brought her head around. He was looking past her, staring at the ships. Admiration showed in the glow of his dark eyes, in the parted lips. It was genuine, unmasked, and it stirred the girl.

He's as moved as I am, she thought. He was, at once, less an enemy.

The other men bunched together to gaze downriver. Even the slaves, a few yards off shore, rested on their oars and regarded the spectacle.

"Ain't that the *Lydia* running third?" asked Gerritt Kimmee.

"Aye." Seth Row sounded definite.

Pardon Cash glanced at Hendrick, shrugged. He said, "A mite far to be certain sure, I'd say."

Lancey noticed that Justin Pattison didn't seem to hear the remarks. He was still watching the sloops, and he spoke musingly, more to himself than to anyone else.

"They're strung out like charging cavalry."

Although the comparison was beyond her experience Lancey thought she saw what he meant. The sloops formed a ragged wedge across the width of the river; the leading ship at the point of the triangle, the others scattered behind. There was movement and speed in the advancing line.

For herself, the beauty of the sight came more from its colors. The snow-white sails against the gray-green cliffs, on the shining-blue water. The creamy furrows that each prow carved from the river, dancing horn-shaped plumes that seemed to decorate every bow. From a bright sky the sun laid a fresh sparkle on the whole fleet.

They were closer now, and the girl could see the different paint on the hulls, flashing green here, gray there, there a yellow stripe on black, catching the sunlight like so many brilliants. Every sloop was heeled over, canvas tautly curved in that arc that seemed to contain both grace and power.

When they changed course, Lancey caught her breath. The booms whipped across in turn as each riverwise helmsman tried to catch the valley's crosscurrent of air at just the right moment.

"Squads left oblique," murmured Justin Pattison.

Not squads, thought Lancey, but sloops. No horses had the beauty of ships moving before the wind. Horses had their own beauty, probably, but only the flight of birds could compare with a sailing vessel!

Then, they straightened out again, and were sliding past, no longer a wedge, but a row of heavy laden sloops that covered a mile of river.

"The *Lydia* is fifth," said Pardon Cash.

"Aye," Seth Row said, "now."

"They ain't all Poughkeepsie sloops," Gerritt Kimmee said. "Some's bound for Rhinebeck, or Kingston."

"Albany even," Hendrick said. "That yellow striper is the *Prince Orange*, out of Albany. I saw her when she passed down."

They stood watching while the local sloops swung out of line, veering for Poughkeepsie Landing. All had seen the movement before, but not this year, and they didn't want any local skipper to blunder in front of upriver captains. Lancey was more concerned because Justin was a spectator. Her worry was needless. The *Lydia* and the others peeled toward their berths as gracefully as ducks banking out of formation.

The northbound sloops went on, but the fishermen relaxed. As one they turned back to their trade.

"Calico," called Gerritt Kimmee, "any herring?"

Teeth flashed as Calico grinned, shook his head. Tanner bent to his oars, called back over his shoulder.

"No, sir. Water too cold."

Hendrick moved to the edge of the pier to help the slaves come alongside, but the others didn't bother. Lancey, turning away, paused. Justin Pattison was still gazing after the sloops.

He looks, she thought, like somebody in a dream. She had a sudden impulse to shield him from an abrupt awakening. The feeling startled her.

Pardon Cash stretched, spat through the gap in his teeth.

"Well," he said, "old Cap'n Benjamin got back in time to vote anyway."

Justin Pattison's head turned. His eyes were narrowed, sharpened. He said, "Vote?"

"Aye," Seth Row said, "for delegates to the convention. The fellows that will decide on the Constitution."

"How's he voting?"

Lancey caught the intense note in the question. For some reason the answer was important to Justin. She bit her lip, puzzled. This man had as many moods as scales on a tommy cod.

"Why," Pardon said, "I guess the town's way. The county's way. George Clinton's way."

"For them that's against," added Gerritt Kimmee.

"Your way?"

Pardon Cash laughed. "You asking *me*, Justin? I ain't got a way."

"Why not?"

"Well, I've never had a vote."

"Why not? You've a boat, a trade. That's property. Even if only the propertied can vote——"

"I think," said Seth Row, "you got to have a certain amount."

"Don't you know?"

Lancey saw that the repeated questions were bothering the fishermen. Even Pardon shifted his big shoulders uneasily. They didn't like Justin's insistence.

"No," Seth Row said, "I never bothered to find out. *I* mind my own business."

The slur darkened Justin's tan, but he smiled. He said: "So do I. This is *your* business. And mine!"

"Voting?"

Lancey heard the jeer in Gerritt Kimmee's voice, but kept her gaze on Justin's face. He was unruffled, poised and motionless. Something in his stance reminded her of his figure awaiting Ten Bush's rush. The memory brought instant recognition. He was ready and eager for combat.

His glance, gay and reckless, brought added conviction. She expected violence, was relieved to have it come in the vibrant passion of the man's voice.

"That's right. Voting. How else do we get a voice in things? Isn't that what the war was about? Because King George wouldn't give us a voice? Well, there's plenty nearer home feel the same way. They won their own votes from King George but they don't intend to let the likes of you and me have any say at all."

The fishermen looked at each other. Hendrick, helping the slaves empty their catch onto the pier, paused to listen. Tanner nudged Calico, received a head shake in reply, went on with his work.

"Who do you mean?" asked Seth Row.

"Hamilton, for one. And all the others that are bent on getting this Constitution passed. Things are bad enough now, but they'll be worse if that happens. The idea that every man—every grown-up man—should have a vote sticks in their craw!"

"Well it might," said Seth Row.

Gerrit Kimmee nodded. "That's a New England notion anyway."

They're annoyed at his criticism, Lancey decided, and reminding him he's a stranger. She didn't think it would bother Justin. She hoped he'd go on talking. When he talked this way she could listen the livelong day.

"And New England," said Justin, "was better off when they followed it. When everybody stood up in town meeting before the rich taxed the poor out of their votes. I don't understand you York Staters. You knuckled under to the patroons from the first."

"How's that?" asked Pardon Cash. His voice was mild.

Pardon, thought Lancey, has something up his sleeve. She knew that deceptive mildness. The big fisherman baited his hook with it.

"You know how," Justin said. "Most of the people had to work for the patroons, pay rent, do as they were told. They couldn't even own their own farms! No wonder you think voting is outlandish. You never had a chance to try it out."

"Well, now," said Pardon Cash, "I wouldn't exactly say that. You see, I can't talk for anyone else, but there's a reason behind my not voting. Wasn't healthy for a while."

"Wasn't healthy?" Justin sounded puzzled.

"Aye, that's right. 'Twas better, and safer, to steer clear of the authorities. I was out with Prendergast, son."

"Who?"

"William Prendergast. I'm not surprised you never heard of him. This was over twenty years ago. But it's a name still remembered around here."

"This side of the river," said Hendrick. The other fishermen nodded, watching Pardon Cash with the grave attention of those hearing a familiar tale.

Lancey could see that interest had replaced Justin Pattison's vehemence. His glance raked the group, returned to Pardon. He spoke with less confidence.

"I'm afraid I know nothing about him."

"Well," Pardon Cash said, "maybe it's time you learned. You New Englander fellows seem to think the Revolution was mostly your idea. Or at least that you started it. You had some real smart talkers over that way, especially around Boston, and they carried on at a great rate whenever anything happened."

"Now, wait——"

"You wait, son. I'm not taking any credit away from Massachusetts. But in '66—nine years before Lexington and Concord Bridge—some of us poor, downtrodden, patroon ridden Dutchess County boys stood up to redcoat regulars. Aye, we burned a few grains of gunpowder, and shed some blood."

"You mean you rebelled?"

"Aye. At least the royal governor called us rebels. And Levelers. We didn't see it that way. Will Prendergast—he lived over near Quaker Hill on the Philipse Grant, paid his rent to that damned old Tory—he thought the way you do. That it wasn't fair for the patroons to hold all the choice land, and make the farmers stay tenants."

"He was right."

"Quite a few people thought so. Farmers especially. He was a big man, Will was, with Irish in him. He tried to do something about it. He raised an army—over a thousand muskets came down off their hooks. I was ashore at the time, and no farmer but I went along with the rest. 'Honest debts but no rent,' Will told us. And we marched south toward New York."

"A thousand men?"

"More joined us every day. But we wanted redress not rebellion. We sent word to the governor, to the landlords. Either meet our just demands or we'd start tearing down manor houses. The landlords screamed, and wrote letters to the governor. But we went nearly all the way to Kingsbridge. I heard later that the New York folk were shaking in their boots.

"Gage was in command down there, then," Pardon Cash said. "The same fellow you New Englanders later threw out of Boston town. And Sir Henry Moore was governor. But our quarrel was with the landlords, not them. We sent half a dozen men in to parley. Maybe it was a mistake because Gage said he'd have to fight, and paraded his Grenadiers, and what with one thing and another, our army turned back this side the Harlem River."

"But you said you fought."

"So we did, later, but it was coming on summer, fine haying weather, and a lot of farmers went home. General Gage didn't have that trouble. He did have the Twenty Eighth British Grenadiers sailing downriver from Albany, and he ordered them to land at Poughkeepsie. I saw them come off the sloops myself, and their aim was to capture Will Prendergast, so I got me a horse and rode east to warn him. I didn't know just where he was, and I wasted some time alooking, and some other fellows joined me until there was about thirty of us."

"Armed?"

"Aye, we had muskets. We decided that Will was probably to home, so we rode for Quaker Hill. The regulars were marching for the same place, and between Fredericksburg and Quaker Hill we sort of stumbled into each other. There was a bridge over a little river, and a field of tall corn, tasseled but green, beside the road. We got in among that corn and looked out at them."

Pardon Cash shook his head, smiled his crooked smile. His voice was mocking, but held a hint of pride.

"Thirty young fools against a regiment of British Grenadiers. They filled the road like a windrow of fallen sumac leaves. I don't know what we were thinking of—stopping them, giving Will Prendergast more time, or what. Maybe we were too riled to do much thinking. Anyway, when they swung 'round to face the cornfield, we fired.

"Two of them fell at that first volley. Then, they charged, and that glittering line of bayonets made a man's stomach turn over. Colder and brighter and more deadly than any surf rolling at you. There

was no time to reload. We got out of that corn fast. The soldie
made a shambles of that stand, but caught nary a one of us."

"And this Prendergast?"

"Well, they didn't exactly catch him either. But his wife, Mehitabel,
was a peaceable woman, a Quaker. A few days later she persuaded
him to give himself up. The redcoats took him to New York, and
then back here to Poughkeepsie for trial. That came in August, and
the charge was high treason. He was found guilty and sentenced to
be hanged."

"Ah," said Justin Pattison.

"We couldn't let that happen, of course, and a bunch of us made
plans. His wife had other ideas. She rode down to New York and
talked to the governor. She came back with a promise of pardon and
a reprieve. She was a fine-talking woman, Mehitabel Prendergast,
and her husband listened to her. She'd hardly rode in before we surrounded the gaol house, ready to split it open like a rotted beer keg.
We had enough boarders to get Will Prendergast out the minute
he said the word. He refused, preferring to do it the legal way.

"And that's the way it ended. We lost, and you fellows over to
Massachusetts did a better job some nine years later. Some of us were
marked men, and I shipped out on the first vessel I could sign on.
Didn't come back for five years or more.

"But we was the first to fight redcoats, Justin, no matter what they
tell you anywhere else."

"All right," said Justin Pattison, "I'll not belittle what you did. Losing doesn't even matter. We all did our share of losing before we
did much winning. You've just proved what I was saying. When they
won't give you legal means to fix things, by vote for example, you've
got to rise up and demand them at musket muzzle."

Hendrick stirred, frowning. He said, "All we want is to be let
alone."

"That's right," said Gerritt Kimmee.

Seth Row bobbed his head in a nod. "What's fishermen got to do
with farmers and such-like? Even in '66 Pardon here only joined
Prendergast for sport."

"Never could pass up a fracas," admitted Pardon.

Lancey saw Justin flush with annoyance. He started to speak,
checked himself with a shrug. The movement seemed to dismiss the
argument, but the girl felt he had merely postponed it, decided to
bide his time. She wasn't certain she could read his moods, but
thought she was learning.

Pardon Cash stretched, linking his fingers above his head and raising his big body onto his toes. "Hendrick," he asked, "you aiming to try dark flood tonight?"

"No." Hendrick shook his head. "Not for several days yet."

"Can we borrow a lantern then? Justin's got a hankering for a night drift."

The fishermen looked at Justin. He met their regard with a nod. Seth Row's lip curled. Hendrick's face was blank. Gerritt Kimmee tried to swallow a chuckle, failed. Even the slaves, though politely grave, widened their eyes.

What's the matter with Pardon, thought Lancey. She was annoyed at the big fisherman for letting Justin make such a mistake before the others. Pardon knew the river, knew it was too early for night fishing. Her opinion of Justin's capability lessened, but she felt protective, not superior.

"It's hardly worth the row," she said, "because——"

"Oh," said Justin, "we didn't figure to catch much. I'd just like to get the feel of the river at night."

The other faces cleared; Lancey's reddened with anger. Justin's cool interruption made her solicitude ridiculous. His tone mocked and rejected her advice. Pardon Cash's grin did not make her any calmer.

Why, the oaf, she thought, glaring at Justin. He was so damnably, irritatingly smug!

"You're welcome to the lantern," Hendrick said. "Lancey will show you where it is."

Lancey's skirt swirled as she turned on her heel. She left the group without bothering with farewells. As she stepped from pier to shingle she heard a footfall behind her, but she didn't glance back to see who followed. It was either Pardon or Justin, and she was angry with both men.

They mounted to the path in silence. The day's brightness had passed its peak; the sun, moving westward, had drawn some color from the sky, faded it to a milder blue. A line of shadow covered the shallows where the river lapped at the foot of its west bank.

Justin's voice identified him, brought her head around. He said, "You don't have to rush, Mistress."

The title stressed the mockery in his speech. It refueled the girl's anger. So did his ambling stride, the long legs easily keeping pace with her own brisk walk. Hat on the back of his head, jacket slung over one shoulder, Justin was the picture of a casual stroller. He

102

wore a collared waistcoat, buttoned high to the throat, and the rolled back shirtsleeves displayed the dark hair on his forearms.

Lancey noticed these things with a single swift glance. She bit her tongue until the heat was drained from her reply, spoke to the landscape.

"Sooner done, sooner over."

"You find my company so trying?"

"Why," said Lancey, casually, "I hadn't thought about it one way or the other. I'm just surprised you bothered to ask for the lantern. It's more your custom to *borrow* when no one's looking, isn't it?"

She was conscious that Justin drew alongside, was grinning down at her, but she gazed straight ahead.

"You don't forgive quickly, do you? Or forget?"

"No," she said, "why should I?"

"It might be more—charitable," Justin chuckled, destroying the gravity of his voice. "Live and let live. Throw not the first stone. We are all children of iniquity, and each sins in his—or her—own manner."

"What do you mean by that?" Lancey faced him, hands clenched, as she asked. She knew what he meant. He was hinting that she had sinned at the Brick Gables inn with Dirck van Zandt. She had been waiting for him to mention it again, welcomed the chance to scotch his wrong impression.

"Why, nothing. I was merely quoting the preachers of my boyhood."

The dancing dark eyes belied his assumed innocence. He was teasing, sure of himself and of her. Lancey lowered her eyelids, forced herself to stay unflustered. She wanted to find out how much he knew before she shouted a denial.

"Preachers long ignored," she said.

"We listen," Justin agreed, "but we do not hear."

He thinks me a girl of easy morals, Lancey decided, but he is more interested than shocked or disgusted. It gave her a feeling of power. If she could provoke a flat statement, a flagrant remark, she would not mince words. Justin's ears would sting for weeks!

"Lancey!"

The hail came from behind them. Turning, Lancey instantly recognized the stolid figure lumbering along the path. Oh, no, she wailed inwardly, not Jan Elmendorf! Not now!

"Wait a minute, Lancey!"

Jan sounded breathless. His hurry was more a scamper than a run, but it covered ground. Lancey was very conscious of Justin's amused interest. He was standing at her elbow, head cocked as he watched the approaching sailor.

"Ah, yes." Justin's murmur was critically aloof. "Elmendorf from the *Lydia*. Another victim, Mistress?"

Lancey had time only to glare before Jan reached them. He was panting and red-faced, but beamed with pleasure.

"Lancey," he said, "what luck to catch you! I only have a moment. Got to get back to help unload the sloop. But, I wanted you to have it first off. Here!"

He thrust a paper wrapped parcel into Lancey's hands. She was still so annoyed by his appearance that she stared at the package in bewildered silence. In size and shape it seemed to resemble a small skillet.

"What is it?" she asked.

"Open it." Jan, gasping, choked on a laugh, apologized. "I ran all the way from the landing. Go on, unwrap it!"

The paper rasped under Lancey's fingers as she tore away the wrappings. Sunlight was caught suddenly by glass, turned it to a golden oval. For an instant the reflection dazzled and blinded her, then she knew the gift for a hand mirror. It was pewter backed with a plain wooden handle, but the glass was flawless.

"Oh, Jan."

"Is it what you wanted?"

"Of course!" Justin's nearness laid a constraint on her pleasure. If only Jan had picked another time for his presentation! She knew it wasn't his fault, and yet she blamed him. She tried to sound gracious. "It's perfect. But—you shouldn't—I mean——"

Jan's grin made his face even broader. He said, "My pleasure, Lancey."

"Aptly put," said Justin Pattison.

For the first time Jan seemed conscious of an onlooker. His head swiveled toward Justin; his mouth dropped open, closed with a click. Scowling, his voice dropped to a surly growl.

"What's *he* doing here?"

"Pardon Cash," said Justin easily, "proved more amiable than your Captain Benjamin. I'm a fisherman now, Master Elmendorf."

"Lancey?"

"That's right," Lancey said. "He's helper in Pardon's boat."

Jan's scowl deepened. He glanced suspiciously from girl to man, and back. He said, "He ain't been bothering you, Lancey?"

The attitude was familiar and unwelcome. Jan is a fool, Lancey decided, if he thinks I like his glowering at every man who talks to me! Justin's smile added to the sharpness of her answer.

"Of course not! Mind your manners, Jan!"

"Yes," said Justin.

Tensed muscles tightened the sleeves of Jan's coat. He took a step toward the other man. Head lowered, he said, "Do you tell me this?"

"That will do," Lancey said. She was furious with Jan. His mulish obstinacy always irritated her; this behavior in front of Justin was unpardonable. Light flashed, glittering, as she shook the mirror under Jan's chin. "Another word, Jan Elmendorf, and you can take this mirror back!"

"Lancey——"

"I mean it. You needn't think it gives you any right to question my acts! It's a nice gift, and you have my thanks, but I'll talk to whoever I please, whenever I please!"

"I just thought——"

"Do you want me to have this mirror?"

"You know I do." Jan was sullen, but cowed.

"All right, then. Thank you." Lancey wished the scene ended. She only hoped that Justin would hold his tongue, not goad Jan into further antics. As grandly as possible, she said, "Now, you'd better not keep Captain Benjamin waiting."

"Oh." Jan blinked as he remembered his duty.

"Come visit when you're free. Hester will want to add her thanks to mine." Lancey thought the invitation inspired. It would lead Justin to think that Jan's gift was for the Quist household.

"Soon as I can," said Jan, at last aware that she found the stranger's presence awkward. Not all pleased he glared at Justin, was turning away when he swung back. "Oh, I nearly forgot."

What now, Lancey thought, exasperated.

"We spoke the *Aunt Namina*, Lancey. Downriver in the Tappan Zee."

"The *Aunt Namina?*"

"Judah Paddock's whaler."

"Ten Bush," Lancey said, heart leaping. "Downriver, Jan?"

"Aye. They passed here in the night. But I talked to Ten Bush. He's fine. Said he wrote you about sailing."

"We never got it." Lancey shook her head dolefully. She'd kept constant lookout for Ten Bush's ship, but it had sailed past while they slept. Now her brother was gone, probably already out to sea, and they'd been robbed of a final glimpse.

"It'll come. You know the post." Jan guessed at her feelings, tried to ease them. "Ten Bush is fine, Lancey."

"Thank you, Jan."

"Well." Jan's wriggling fingers tried to express his thought, failed. "I'd better get back." He went reluctantly, gazing over his shoulder.

Justin watched the girl. The mirror hung unnoticed from her grip as she stared moodily at the river. She really was fond of her brother, he thought. Then, he smiled cynically, deciding she was fond of many males.

"He'll come back," he said. "And bearing gifts, too."

"Too?" Lancey's eyes flashed; she raised the mirror. "You mean like Jan?"

"Not exactly. Your Jan's a swain."

"He is not!"

"Sticks out like a carbuncle. Poor dolt." Justin shook his head in exaggerated sorrow. "How can a simple sailor vie with a rich van Zandt?"

There it was at last, Lancey thought, out in the open. She looked Justin straight in the face, irrelevantly aware once more of the white forelock, the quizzical, scarred eyebrow, the sardonic glee.

"Listen," she said, "I don't know what you've heard, or what you think." Her voice was cold and flat. "But nothing besides a shared supper passed between Dirck van Zandt and me at the Brick Gables."

"Nothing?" Justin drawled the word, saw the quick color rise in her cheeks. "While I watched your clothes dry in the kitchen?"

"The clothes were soaked." She gave the reason, disdained from explaining more fully. If he wished to think she supped naked, he was welcome. She gazed at him with cold dignity, neither outraged nor intense, putting him to the test.

"Either you are a liar," said Justin, impressed, "or young van Zandt is a fool."

"It could be that I am chaste." Lancey did not emphasize the statement. With a shrug, she dismissed the subject. She had told the truth; let him believe or disbelieve. She could only judge that by his future attitude.

"Come along," she said, "and get that lantern."

10

Saint Nicholas, my dear good friend,
To serve you always was my end;
If you now me something will give,
Serve you I will as long as I live.

LANCEY QUIST, MENDING THE SECOND BEST NET, CHANTED THE OLD
Dutch Christmas song as happily as she had ever piped it in childhood. She wasn't conscious of words or language, but fitted the movements of her needle to the rhythm of the familiar tune.

It was, she thought, an April morning made for singing, clear and
warm after a night of gentle showers. The early sunshine felt good,
baking pleasantly through the back of her dress as she sat, tailor fashion, facing the river. Across the Hudson the tree covered cliffs looked
freshly washed; the foliage displayed its deep, cool greenery with
gay pride. The water itself showed the changing shimmer of blue
brocade as the sunken channel in mid-stream imposed its deeper
hue on the tide.

Sing a song of old Kris Kringle
While the sleigh-bells loudly jingle;
If he now something will give
Serve him I will as long as I live.

The hammering behind her stopped, and the quiet hushed Lancey. She glanced over her shoulder to meet her father's broad grin.
Hendrick had been smashing bluestone fragments in a burlap bag;
he dropped his mallet, slung the bag over his arm. His slow voice was
amused.

"You have the seasons mixed, yes, Lancey?"

"Yes and no," said Lancey, laughing. "The weather is spring, but
the feeling is Christmasy. A day like this gives promise of carnival,
of something happening, *anything!* Can't you just feel it, Pa?"

"It is a nice day."

Hendrick carried the bag of bluestone to a vat of water. He dipped it, began to swish it around to make the solution used for cleaning the nets. Lancey smiled at his bent figure, aware that with fisherman superstition he would never comment on coming hours.

"And getting nicer, Pa."

"Meanwhile," said Hendrick, gruffly, "how are you coming with the breading of that net?" He used the technical term for the intricate needlework that formed and knotted the mesh.

"Nearly finished." Lancey flattened the patch with a palm, watched the needle glint as it flashed in and out. She recalled the wild tossings of the floats when the net was torn. "What do you suppose ripped such a hole, Pa?"

"Sturgeon, mayhap. Or peelican."

"Must have been a big one."

"Big enough. But if the mesh hadn't been worn at that spot it might have held."

They heard the whistling before they saw the whistler. Lancey, recognizing *Yankee Doodle*, was not surprised when Justin Pattison swaggered into the yard. Coatless, he was swinging the borrowed lantern from one hand, and twirling his tricorne around the other. He interrupted his trilling to call a greeting.

"Morning, Hendrick."

"Morning, Justin."

"Brought your lantern back. We owe you for a fresh candle."

Lancey finished her work, biting the last knot tight, cutting the needle free with a deft slash of knifeblade. She was too happy, too sun drenched, to be wary of Justin. There was no reason for her cheerfulness except the day's glory, but that was enough. Her question was loudly gay, friendly.

"You didn't go out in the rain?"

"No," Justin said, "we didn't. It stopped long enough for a short drift just before dawn."

"How'd you like our river at night?"

"I liked it."

"It's the best time." Lancey, arms filled with billowing folds of net, struggled to her feet. "So still and hushed you can hear every tiny ripple. Lights blue on the water, and stars dancing overhead." She laughed at her own enthusiasm. "Not that you saw any stars last night."

"Overcast," said Hendrick.

"It didn't matter," Justin said. "There'll be other nights. It was cold, and damp, and we didn't catch anything, but it still didn't matter." He sounded serious, frowned at Lancey as he spoke. "There was something about just drifting in the darkness. Pardon and me and the dory."

"And the river," Lancey said.

"And the river." Justin's smile mirrored the girl's as he reached to help her. "Where do you want this, Hendrick?"

"Lancey knows."

"In the shed." Lancey tried to be casual. She was delighted that Justin seemed to share her own feeling about night fishing. For all his practical approach to life, his bitter outlook, he had been impressed. She, too, had been unable to express that experience adequately. It isn't because it's Justin, she told herself, it's anybody who really appreciates the river.

They worked together in comradely silence, storing the net in its box. Lancey accepted Justin's deftness without comment. He was a fisherman, and ought to know the tricks of the trade. Somehow, this morning, she did not think of him as either ex-soldier, or newcomer.

Hendrick's grunt drew their attention. They came out from under the shed to find him standing rigid, listening. Lancey, holding her breath, managed to hear sounds that cut across the familiar riverfront noises—a steady, muffled beat; the clink of metal. Justin identified them at once.

"That's a horse. Walking."

"Aye," said Hendrick, "but here? Who——?" Puzzlement left face and voice as he nodded. "Ah, of course! Dirck."

"Dirck?"

"Must be, Lancey." Hendrick turned to Justin. "He's a young friend of ours, Dirck van Zandt."

"I have seen the gentleman."

Lancey nearly hooted at Justin's polite tone. She was suddenly sure that her father was right. Mischief seemed to bubble inside her, race along her veins. I knew, she thought, that this day had a reason for raising my spirits! She had wanted these two men to meet, awaited the encounter with relish!

"You must meet him, Justin," she said, and dared him with her eyes.

"I don't mind," Justin said.

The coaly bay mare walked sedately into the Quist yard, and Dirck van Zandt saluted from the saddle. They were both, Lancey saw with satisfaction, looking their best. Meda's coat had the gloss of polished cedar; mane, tail and stockings were as black as her master's boots. Dirck, in a bottle green riding coat, and buff breeches, fairly shimmered in the sunlight. He glanced at Justin Pattison, but he addressed father and daughter.

"Greetings, Hendrick. Compliments, Mistress Lancey."

"Hello, Dirck," said Hendrick, "it is good to see you again."

"Master van Zandt," said Lancey, "may I introduce Master Pattison." Her casual tone lessened the formality of the polite formula.

Hendrick, with a snort, said, "Dirck meet Justin. Is this the courthouse?"

Both young men bowed. Justin, straightening, kept his face impassive. This van Zandt was even more of a popinjay than he'd expected. Not Solomon in all his glory, he thought. He'd seen the man at von Beck's tavern, but never so finely bedecked.

Dirck's thoughts were masked behind a courteous smile. Justin Pattison was a new factor in the problem of Lancey Quist. The fellow was tall, well built, not ill favored for all his dark visage. A girl might find that showy silver coxcomb in his hair attractive.

"Honored," murmured Dirck.

Justin said, "Pleasure."

Nothing could have pleased Lancey more than their strict adherence to proper etiquette. Hendrick's presence made it obligatory; she hoped her own made it difficult. Justin stood beside her, and she could sense his hostility. Dirck, mounted, was a trifle harder to fathom.

"No law today, Master Dirck?" she asked.

"Blame this fine April weather," Dirck said. "Even Master Kent could not withstand it. He took to his garden and the study of Greek, but I doubt he construes three lines."

"The law," said Justin, "sounds like an easy taskmaster." He made the remark with careful lightness. The horseman represented everything he disliked—inherited wealth, entrenched position, *patroon* manners—but he was not unaware of Lancey's watchful nearness. I'll be damned, Justin decided, if I'll perform for her like a trained bear!

"You do not know James Kent." Dirck dismounted with reluctance. He judged Pattison to be inches taller, and hated to yield the advantage. "He holds the law a sacred testament, and knows more of it at twenty-four than many of his elders. He couldn't be a sterner teacher if he was sixty."

"A smart man," agreed Hendrick.

Lancey walked forward to stroke Meda's nose. The mare was restless, but submitted. Dirck smiled at the girl, turned to her father.

"Are you busy, Hendrick? Or could you ferry me across the river?"

"Ferry you?"

"And Meda?" Lancey echoed Hendrick's surprise.

"She'll swim, of course. She's done it before without trouble."

Justin gave the mare a quick inspection. He didn't question Dirck's statement, but resented its calm assurance. Let the master ride, Justin thought, and the beast swim. Since the decision was Hendrick's, he said nothing.

"Well," Hendrick said, frowning, "I don't know, Dirck. We're not busy, but——"

"Why didn't you go to the landing?" asked Lancey. "They'd get you across quicker."

"I've been there," Dirck said. "The barge is on the other side, and there are five or six wagons lined up waiting. I don't want Meda swimming in a crowd, and I'd like to get to Newburgh by lunch time."

"What about Anthony's below?"

"If I have to pay horse-ferry prices, I'd rather pay them to you, Hendrick." Dirck glanced at Lancey, nodded. "Besides, that's a four mile ride."

He sounded coolly practical, but Lancey wasn't fooled. This was Dirck's method of adding to the Quist income. He had put it on a footing that removed all taint of charity, but she knew he'd normally take the regular ferries. It was a nice gesture; any of the fishermen would jump at a chance to earn hard coin.

"Why not, Pa? He has to cross somewhere."

Hendrick's gaze shifted from Dirck to his daughter. He rubbed his chin, thinking.

"I'll give you a hand," Justin said, suddenly, "if you have an extra pair of oars." He saw no reason why Hendrick should refuse. Young van Zandt might be showing off before Lancey, but cash was cash. With himself, a stranger, in the boat it became straight business.

"An excellent idea," said Dirck, instantly recognizing the other's motive. The fellow wasn't stupid, and had his uses. Hendrick mustn't get the idea that he was being helped, or patronized.

"All right," Hendrick said. "Fetch the oars, Lancey."

With a nod, Lancey skipped away. Dirck turned to the mare. He undid the girth, removed saddle and blanket. He led the horse down to the water's edge, and waited.

The boat was tied to the pier. Hester came from the house with Lancey. She greeted Dirck with candid pleasure.

"Glad to see you, boy. Glad you're in a hurry, too."

"That makes it unanimous," Dirck said, laughing. "I'd be stuck this side for at least an hour if I hadn't thought of Hendrick." He patted the mare, murmured to her, while the others prepared the boat.

Lancey arranged the positions. "You set the stroke, Pa," she said. "I'm used to you. I'll take the bow. That puts you in the middle, Justin, and our passenger in the stern." She didn't want Justin where a deliberate crab would drench Dirck.

"As you wish," said Justin. His half-grin acknowledged the reason behind her instructions. A little water wouldn't shrink that green coat, he thought, but it's too crude a jest. He climbed into the boat, held it close to the pier for Dirck.

"Steady, girl. Steady." Dirck handed Hendrick the saddle, walked, sideways, along the pier, guiding the horse into the shallow water. Meda stepped gingerly, snorted as she flicked a foreleg, but gave no trouble.

"Get in, Dirck," said Hendrick. He held out a supporting hand. "Don't step on the gunwale."

"I'm not that much a lubber," Dirck said. He was watching Justin Pattison from the corner of one eye. The fellow would like nothing better than to see him go in up to his knees. Dirck clucked to the mare, slid down into the boat with swift grace. "All set. You can shove off now."

They pushed away from the pier, paddling cautiously while Meda followed. Hester, on the shore, raised her hand, but didn't call for fear of distracting the horse.

"Come on, Meda." Dirck's voice was calm and coaxing. "This is nothing new. Come on. That's my girl." Without turning to them, he waved to the rowers. "Give way."

Hendrick bent, pulled back. Justin joined him on the next stroke. Lancey, gazing past the backs in front of her, saw that the mare was breast deep. A moment later Meda tossed her head, began to swim. Then, Lancey, too, swung into the tempo of the stroke.

The six oarblades rose from the water as one, dripped as they swept back, dipped down together.

"Good Meda," Dirck said. He grinned at the boat's crew over his shoulder. "She's all right now. She'll stay with us all the way."

They rowed on in silence, with a steady, even beat. The thole-pins creaked in a single sound, as regularly as a clock's ticking. Hen-

112

drick kept them carefully ahead of the horse, just enough to lead and help without pulling.

Lancey glanced past the others at the receding shoreline. They were, she noted, angling south to move with the ebb tide. The movement as Dirck removed his hat drew her attention. His smile vanished when Justin spoke.

"Now, I know you. The brevet cornet."

Dirck flushed, glared. Lancey knew instantly that Justin had touched a raw spot.

"What's that, Justin?" she asked.

"We used to call him the brevet cornet." There was laughter in Justin's voice. The effort of rowing didn't quicken his breath or speech.

"But what's it mean?"

"It's army talk," Dirck said, thickly. He cleared his throat, explained. "Brevet's a nominal rank higher than one's regular commission. Honorary, mostly. And without extra pay. Cornet——"

"Cornet," said Justin, "is a cavalry flag carrier. The lowest form of horse riding officer."

Nobody's stroke wavered, but Lancey knew from the set of Hendrick's head that he, too, was listening. She was puzzled by the angry flash of Dirck's eyes, the suddenly tight mouth. Justin had said nothing insulting.

"Well," she said, looking at Dirck, "if you were an officer——"

"I wasn't!" He snapped the denial. "I was only a courier, and he knows it. Without any rank at all. They let me carry messages because I was handy and had a horse!"

"You messed with the officers."

"By invitation."

"That's what I mean."

Both voices were hard now. Justin's was low, but tinged with contempt. Dirck spoke more loudly, with bitter indignation. Lancey, distressed and uneasy, shook her head at the man in the stern.

"Where was this?" she asked.

"Newburgh," said Justin.

Dirck nodded, visibly trying to regain composure. He drew a breath, said, "I don't remember you."

"I didn't you, till the hat came off. And, of course, you're older."

"What regiment were you——"

"Nicola's!"

To Lancey's amazement Justin's interruption sounded defensive, brought a grin to Dirck's face. She was completely beyond her depth, a little annoyed that the animosity between the two had nothing to do with her. I might just as well not be in the boat, she thought.

"Oh, lud," said Dirck, laughing. He glanced at his mare, chirruped to her, swung back. "The invalids. No wonder you called me names. But they never gave me a chance to be wounded, Pattison."

"It wasn't that, blast you!" Justin was coldly angry, but his oar never hesitated. "I blame no man for not getting hurt. It was the way you strutted with the rest of the epaulet crowd."

"While you were in the Kingmaker's Own Rifles!"

"No choice of mine, van Zandt. Believe me. The men didn't back Nicola. He got that plan from the officers, not us! Hamilton, most likely, and a few others."

"Hamilton wasn't even there."

"So you say. I've heard differently. He was there in spirit anyway. The voice was the voice of Nicola, but the hands——"

Exasperated, not understanding the argument, Lancey gazed aft at Meda. The mare had swung a bit wide of the boat's stern, but she was swimming strongly, head high. Dirck kept turning to check her position, but it was a mechanical movement. His interest was in the talk with Justin.

"That's just campfire hogwash," he said.

"How else did we learn about it?" Justin said. "Maybe you were told, but it leaked down through the ranks."

"Whatever in the world are you talking about?" Lancey's question was sharper than intended. She was pleased that they seemed to have forgotten their enmity, but curiosity made her irritable. "It sounds like a great riddle!"

"Aye," said Hendrick.

Dirck's laugh drowned Justin's chuckle. Lancey could only see the former's face, but she was sure that they exchanged a glance. Again she felt shut out, ignored. This meeting, she thought resentfully, certainly wasn't going the way she had planned.

"Of course they wouldn't know," Justin said. "It was kept a deep, dark secret, remember."

"Some secret when we both——" Dirck noticed Lancey's glare, broke his remark with a laugh. He leaned forward, reins bunched in one hand, the saddle at his feet. "All right, Lancey, we'll explain."

It was the first time since the inn that he had called her by name without any title. Lancey wondered if Justin noticed. Probably, like

Dirck, he was too interested in the conversation to worry about niceties.

"This was after Yorktown," Dirck said, "while the army was camped down around Newburgh. There was a colonel named Nicola. Lewis Nicola. A Frenchman."

"Wait a minute," said Justin. "Don't give them the wrong idea. He'd come over here ten years before the war, and he'd done most of his soldiering in Ireland. He wasn't one of the Johnnies who'd come running to take a fresh stab at the British. Nicola was in our army from the beginning."

"True enough." Dirck accepted the correction with a nod. "He wasn't like Lafayette. He was a Continental colonel, and at Newburgh he was in command of an invalid regiment. Mostly men recovering from wounds or sickness, and some recruits in training." He snickered, twinkling at Justin. "Later called the Kingmaker's Own."

"Tell it right or let me," said Justin, growling. "They never called us that to our faces!"

"Well," Dirck said, "it was pretty dull in that camp. The fighting was over, but the war wasn't. Congress was far from prompt with the soldiers' pay, but didn't want them going home. Colonel Nicola got a bee in his bonnet."

Justin said: "Or had it put there, van Zandt. If you ask me, old Nicola was just spokesman for the crew. I'd wager that half the Society of Cincinnati was in on it."

"Mayhap." Dirck nodded as he glanced back at the mare. "He was important in the Society's Pennsylvania branch after the peace. But, anyway, spokesman or not he wrote the letter and he signed it. You know, Pattison, I think I delivered that letter."

"You?"

"Well, I'm not sure. But all I did in those days was deliver letters. And there was one from Nicola to Washington that the general opened in my presence." Dirck shook his head, remembering. "Lud, he looked at me as if I was a night crawler. You know how he was when he lost his temper. But he didn't swear or anything, just waved me out. I was glad to go."

"What was in the letter?" asked Lancey.

"Aye," Hendrick said.

"Nothing much," Justin said. "It just proposed that General Washington set himself up as king, that's all."

Lancey gaped, open mouthed. She heard her father's grunt.

115

"That's right," said Dirck. "It wasn't such a hare-brained scheme at that. The general had the army, and the army had the guns."

Justin nodded as he pulled on his oar. He said: "That was the devilish part of it. We'd followed him so long we might have supported him out of habit. Congress had been no friend to the common soldier. Slack with pay and provision. I don't say everybody felt that way—*I* didn't for one—but I'm glad it wasn't put to the test."

"General Washington refused," Lancey said.

"Yes," said Dirck, "and in no uncertain terms. They say the letter he sent Colonel Nicola almost scorched the paper. After that, the general called a meeting of all his officers, and told them to hush up about the military taking charge of the government."

"That I know about," Justin said. "Friend of mine was sentry outside the meeting. Of course they closed the doors, but he listened. The general made it plain what his feelings were. He held his command by grant of Congress, and so did they."

"Pattison," asked Dirck, "is it true he said something about going blind in his country's service?"

"Yes. He took out his spectacles before he read what he'd written, and mentioned he'd grown gray *and* blind." Justin chuckled. "Though he could still spot a dirty musket at fifty yards!"

"A great man," Hendrick said.

Lancey, rowing automatically, said, "To reject the offer of a crown!" She was thinking of the temptation, the power, the general's reputation. He could have been king, she decided, recalling a small girl who felt safer whenever she heard that Washington was encamped on the river.

"Too bad," said Justin, with sudden bitterness, "that he changed his mind!"

"Changed his mind?"

"The general?"

"General Washington?"

"Are you blind?" Justin asked. "Who presided in Philadelphia when they made up this Constitution? Who'll be president if it's passed?"

"That's not the same as king, Pattison!"

"A different name. Maybe he won't be able to hand it down in the family like in Europe, but he'll be president for the rest of his life!"

"I've read the document," Dirck said, "and——"

"So have I." Justin sounded insulted. "It says four years the term, but nothing about how many terms!"

The Quists, father and daughter, listened in silence. Lancey was impressed that both these young men had read the text of the proposed Constitution. Her own knowledge was based on newspaper comment, and hearsay.

"It's still no monarchy," Dirck insisted. "There's to be a parliament, a Congress, a Senate and a lower house."

"There was a Senate in Rome," Justin said, "when the Caesars strutted as emperors. And I seem to recall a war against unjust acts passed by another parliament."

"Because we weren't represented there!"

"Look, van Zandt. Tell me one place where this Constitution says the government can't pass any law it wants. Any law at all. Good or bad. Represented, my elbow! Some places won't even *hear* about a law for weeks. Suppose they don't like it when they do hear?"

"They can protest and——"

"And your president—the general—stops that just the way the king tried to, with powder, ball, musket and bayonet!"

"You can't have a country without law, Pattison!"

"There speaks the budding lawyer. How about some laws that say what the government *can't* do! Like throw a man in gaol for debt. Or tax him right off his land. Or shoot the beggar down because he tells his neighbors they're being cheated!"

"Nobody says this document is perfect," Dirck said. "It merely provides a workable plan of government better than the present Confederation. If you'd read some of the essays Master Kent's shown me, instead of only what George Clinton writes——"

Justin interrupted with a snort that was a wordless expletive. "I've read the thing itself! I don't need Clinton *or* Alexander Hamilton to tell me what it means!"

"Ship your oars, Lancey," called Hendrick.

Lancey, startled, obeyed the command jerkily. She'd been listening avidly, rowing with an ease of habit that required no thought. Now she saw that they were close to the shingle under the river's western cliff.

The mare, swimming more strongly as the shoreline neared, drew alongside the boat.

"Steady, girl," cried Dirck, half rising. "Almost there." He stretched his arm full length to give the horse slack reins.

Hendrick and Justin slowed their stroke, but Meda was standing in the shallows before the boat's keel grated on the bottom. The mare, puffing but unwinded, stalked ashore without even glancing at the human beings. Dirck, laughing, dropped the reins and let them trail through the water after her.

"Meda's a true female," he said. "She's in a pique."

"You would be, too," said Lancey, "if somebody made you swim across." She stepped onto the beach, held the bow steady. "Won't she run?"

"Not Meda." Dirck, carrying the saddle, edged past Hendrick, stepped warily over the thwart where Justin gave him room. He didn't trust the argumentative stranger not to upset him deliberately. If he does, Dirck thought, I'll heave the saddle at him.

Justin, grinning up at Dirck, wasn't even tempted. A bargain was a bargain, and the passenger was paying to be ferried across. If it had been his own boat, not Hendrick's, things might have been different.

"Thanks, Hendrick," said Dirck. He jumped ashore, set down the saddle, ran to dry Meda with the blanket.

The others watched in silence while he patted the mare, talked to her. Lancey, amused, was reminded of their first meeting. She'd grown fond of the mare since then, but Dirck van Zandt was like a small boy with a pet. The horse was his first concern; it never occurred to him that he was keeping them waiting. Turning, she read the same thought in Justin's scowl.

Dirck came back, counted coins into Lancey's palm. She stared at the money, shook her head.

"Three shillings!" She glanced at Hendrick.

"Too much, Dirck," he called.

"Nonsense. Three rowers at a shilling apiece." Dirck was brusque and definite. "Fair rate."

"Thank you—cornet," said Lancey, unable to resist teasing. She gurgled happily at Dirck's glare.

"Brevet only," Justin said, and chuckled.

"When the Constitution is passed," Dirck said, solemnly, "you will both be hung by the thumbs." He picked up the saddle, and walked toward Meda.

The boat was well off shore when Dirck rode away. Lancey watched him disappear with mixed feelings. He and Justin had met, and argued, and the honors were about even.

Too even, Lancey decided, with a muffled sigh.

II

THE NEW DRESS WAS WHOLLY HESTER QUIST'S IDEA. SHE PRODUCED THE material, re-cut and altered it. She even persuaded a dazzled Lancey to stand still for fittings.

From the first moment that Hester poured the heavy folds of the skirt across the table Lancey had been entranced by texture and color. The russet velvet was old, reeked of camphor, showed the wear of rubbed-off nap and tattered hem, but it wasn't faded. By firelight it had the sheen of bronze; in sunshine it looked of an even deeper richness. The girl was too stunned by its beauty to cry out as Hester's two little daughters did.

"Look, Hannah! Look!"

"Ma, is it yours? Is it, Ma?"

"Yes, Hannah," said Hester, critically examining the worn spots. "Every stitch in it is mine, and in the end the gown was given to me. But it's going to be Lancey's."

"Mine?" Lancey reached to stroke the smooth nap. "Mine, Hester?"

"When it's cut down some. You can see it was made for a taller girl than you."

"But—wherever did you get it?"

"Trunk," said Hester. She shook the dress, held it up against Lancey, already mentally figuring size and design. "But it was made for a young lady right here in Poughkeepsie. That was before I even met your Pa, but I always thought it was the nicest material I ever worked on."

"You've saved it all these years?" Lancey knew her stepmother's ability as a seamstress. Hester made, re-made, and patched most of the garments in the Quist household from small Hannah's aprons to Hendrick's shirts.

"Yes. You see, it was payment for my work, Lancey. The girl belonged to a wealthy family, my best custom. They were Tory, though, and when they fled needed what cash they had. I took the dress as settlement and gladly."

119

"Then you wanted it for yourself, Hester. I can't let you give it to me!"

"Fiddlesticks!" Hester snorted; the broad face brightened with a grin. "What need have I for fancy frills? You're the one has the young men flocking around like foxes at a hen coop." She tapped a finger on her elder daughter's head. "Rhoda, fetch my sewing basket."

Lancey, blushing, argued halfheartedly. She wanted the russet velvet so badly that her calves trembled. "Any young man who doesn't like me the way I am——"

"They do. But when I'm finished their eyes'll pop!"

"Dirck," said Hannah, wisely.

Her sister set the sewing basket on the table, sniffed. "And Justin, too, Hannah, and Jan Elmendorf."

"Little pitchers," said Hester, and laughed. "Get out of your things, Lancey, and let's try this on. It needs airing, but it's clean."

"I ought to help Pa." Lancey was undoing the buttons of her homespun. She was so excited that her fingers fumbled.

"Your Pa can do without. He knows I planned this. It's time you had a real fine dress, Lancey. Homespun's all right for fishing, and your dimity for church-going, but for courting——"

"Nobody's courting me!"

"Well, I wouldn't say that, but if it's true you really *need* a new dress!"

The gown was much too large for Lancey. It made her look about the age of Hester's daughters, a little girl playing in her mother's clothing. The feel of the velvet, the glow from its color, had her bemused.

"Rhoda," she said, "my mirror. It's upstairs in the loft." She danced impatiently, as the child scampered away. "Be careful not to drop it!"

"Stand still," said Hester. She was on her knees, tugging and pulling at the skirt. "We can flounce it on each hip, and in back." She rummaged in her basket, drew out a pin cushion bristling with wood slivers, and a few real pins. "You'll need to wear at least five petticoats, but I can take in a couple of mine."

"Hester, be careful!" Lancey cried out in anguish as her stepmother's scissors cut through the material.

"I know what I'm doing. The hem is threadbare anyway."

Hendrick, coming in for his dinner at noon, found the entire distaff side of his family clustered around the table. There was no sign of food. The board was covered with what looked like an assortment of red velvet rags. His wife was ripping seams, snipping threads. The little girls, kneeling on stools, were watching with rapt concentration.

In petticoats and shift, Lancey hovered at Hester's shoulder. She stared, blankly, at her father, blinked and gave him a vague smile. The wreckage on the table was such a tangled jumble that she was afraid to speak. In her mind she was already wearing the gown.

"It's mid-day," said Hendrick, amused.

"Shh, Pa," Rhoda said.

Hester was startled into dismay. "It can't be!" She gaped at her husband, glanced from the litter before her to the potless fire.

"Sun's overhead."

"Oh, Pa!" Lancey felt guilty, remembering her promise to take Ten Bush's place as his helper. "And I haven't done a lick all morning. Why didn't you call out?"

"Why?" Hendrick thought his daughter had never looked better. He was glad Hester had decided to fix the gown. He wasn't quite sure why his wife had slashed it to ribbons as a starter, but that was her business. "There are things besides fish," he said, "I will tell you when I need you, Lancey."

Hester began to gather up the velvet. "I'm sorry, Hendrick," she said. "I lost all track of time. Cut a slice of bread to stay you until I can——"

"Today," said Hendrick, "I will eat with Pardon and Justin. I would not like your handiwork upset. This house is no place for a man."

All four females gazed at him with abashed but silent agreement. Hester's chuckle broke the hush, proved infectious. The little girls giggled, and Lancey laughed.

"Have they enough?" asked Hester.

"And to spare. I will have, perhaps, a nice bit of grilled herring." Hendrick kept his face blank, peeped sideways at Lancey.

Stooping to pick an empty velvet sleeve from the floor, the girl only half heard his remark. "That will be nice," she said, smoothing the remnant against her breast. Then, the import penetrated, and she whirled.

"Aye," Hendrick answered the question in her face, "that is what I said."

"Herring!"

"So you see there is cause to hurry your seamstressing. For the shad will be running soon."

"Pa, wait. If you're going to make a drift——"

"You will know. There is a time for everything, Lancey. Now, I want you to be Hester's helper. To do as she says. I, too, wish to see the new dress."

He bowed, and went out humming, evidently pleased with himself. The quartette stared after him.

"He means it, Lancey," said Hester. "He has something up his sleeve, too. Always when he hums like that." She gazed around distractedly, spoke with resignation. "I guess we'd better eat a bite ourselves."

The thing up Hendrick's sleeve proved to be a pair of cut-steel shoe buckles. He unwrapped them that evening, placed them in front of Lancey.

"For the fancy gown, fancy shoes," he said. "These will brighten your good ones, Lancey."

"Oh, Pa. Hester, look."

"I see." Hester beamed at her husband. "So that was why you went up to the landing. It was a good thought, Hendrick."

"They were a bargain," Hendrick said, with hasty gruffness. "An attempt to get my meals on time."

Lancey breathed on a buckle, rubbed it, gazed her thanks. They must have cost, she thought, both of Dirck van Zandt's shillings. She was suddenly shy, confused by the favors of both father and step-mother. A russet velvet gown, and buckled shoes!

They missed no more meals, and Lancey made sure she was ready whenever Hendrick wanted to launch the boat, conscious as ever that she was Ten Bush's substitute. There were long hours when Hester sewed; the fittings were frequent, but brief. Rhoda and Hannah soon tired of watching their mother at work, but Lancey thought her needle magical.

Then, at last, the dress was finished. Hester helped her stepdaughter into the gown, gave her a professionally critical regard, nodded. She handed Lancey the mirror and stepped back.

The small oval glass barely reflected the low, square neckline. Lancey kept shifting it for different views. She admired the way the russet framed her flesh.

"I wish," she said, "we had a mirror would show all of me."

"Don't worry," Hester said, with proud approval. "You look real fine. Watch the faces of the men folk when they gander at you. And, of course, the women. They're going to hate you in that dress, Lancey."

Lancey Quist, well pleased with herself, was returning from church when she heard the shouting. The tumult that shattered the Sunday morning calm ended a very enjoyable reverie.

Her new gown was already a proven success. It had caused a stir among the congregation, brought whispers from the women, stares from the men. As was seemly the girl had pretended to ignore these reactions, but she had not missed a glance. As she strolled homeward she was reviewing, with relish, the gaping admiration of Nell Bogardus, and Hilda von Beck's envious glare. The sunshine was bright, the day fair; it was warm enough to let her cloak hang open. Head bent, skirts carefully hoisted out of the dust, Lancey was delighted by the twinkle of a new shoe buckle at every step.

The uproar that halted her seemed to bounce from the surface of the water. Listening, she tried to locate its source. She was alone on the river path. Hester had stayed behind, with her daughters, to reap compliments to her needlework; Hendrick hadn't gone to the services.

Then, the men swept from behind Jaycock's Ordinary in a hurrying, stumbling, noisy crowd.

They were yelling in high pitched excitement, a continuous, unintelligible sound that rose and fell, punctuated by the sharper notes of barking dogs. For a moment, as the men milled in their own dust, the animal yelps led Lancey to believe that the occasion was a dog fight. The throng jostled and pushed, constantly changed positions, in the manner of spectators following such a moving battle. A couple of riverfront mongrels were cavorting on the outskirts of the mob, but she saw at once that their shrill frenzy was inspired by their masters.

Lancey hesitated, torn between curiosity and caution. She wanted to see what was happening, but feared to risk her precious gown in such a press. Hitching her skirts higher she began to run, toward the shouters but veering up the slope of the bluff to a spot where she could look down over their heads.

As she drew near she could recognize individuals. There was Digmus Jaycock jumping up and down as he sought to peer past taller shoulders. Seth Row, scarlet cheeked and bawling, was waving his hat. She knew some of the others, sailors from the sloops, two ferrymen, a stableman.

It was a good-sized gathering for a Sabbath morning. Thirst had probably assembled them all in Jaycock's common room.

Suddenly, the crowd burst apart like an exploded firework torpedo. The rank nearest her thinned, opened, as men scurried sideways. Through the gap a stocky figure tottered backwards, arms flailing the air. The man's heels drummed the earth in a weird jig that fought to keep him upright.

A deeper roar shook from the watchers' throats as he sat down with a bone shaking jar!

Lancey had only a glimpse before the shifting throng hid him again. Yelling men sprinted to close the circle, to form a fresh arena with themselves in the front row. Through the dust and the hurrying legs, the girl saw the blurred figure scramble to its feet.

She sprinted herself, bounding up the bank. The glimpse had been enough. With the realization that men fought, had come recognition of the staggered fighter.

It was Jan Elmendorf! His shirt was torn and his face bloody, but she couldn't be mistaken.

Remembering Jan's surly belligerence in the past, Lancey thought she knew his opponent. He had bullied and chivvied all her schoolboy playmates, scared away all other riverfront youths. A Dirck van Zandt, moneyed gentry, might awe Jan into sullen respect, but he would feel himself on equal footing with a fisherman's helper like Justin Pattison.

"Poor Jan," she muttered, as she ran. "He never saw Justin fight." Her memory of the ex-soldier's deadly competence was vividly fresh. He had handled Ten Bush with ease, and proved an agile match for Pardon Cash.

Reaching her chosen perch she turned, panting, to gaze down on the restless, bellowing mass of men. She was well above the crowd, able to see most of the circle it enclosed. Almost at once she spotted Pardon by his height. He stood on the far side of the ragged ring, holding someone's coat and hat. The garments increased her certainty that Justin was involved.

The fighters were hidden behind the nearer spectators, and Lancey stamped a foot impatiently. As if summoned by the movement they instantly stepped into her view.

Justin Pattison, erect and poised, was retreating before Jan's crouched advance. Amazingly, even as Jan shuffled forward, it was the taller man who seemed to be the stalker. His fists were raised, coiled to strike; he gave ground with a deliberate, slow ease that permitted no awkward unreadiness.

A hovering hawk, Lancey thought, or a human slingshot, loaded and aimed. The sun was directly overhead, and she shaded her eyes with a palm.

One sleeve hung flapping from Justin's shoulder, and his shirt showed dark specks. She couldn't tell at that distance if he was marked, but the white streak in his hair looked unmussed. Certainly, he was less tattered and dusty than Jan.

She could hear the crowd more clearly, now, distinguish voices through the wordless, pulsing shouts. The majority, of course, cried encouragement to the native, destruction to the outlander.

"Rush him, Jan!"

"Grapple the varmint, Jan!"

"Kill the beggar!"

"Jump him!"

"Jan, Jan, *Jan!*"

Any cries for Justin were smothered by the senseless, blood-thirsty chorus that supported his opponent. Lancey doubted that this bothered him, that he even heard. There was something calm and contained in the way he stood, moved, waited for the next encounter.

The shouting did not disturb her, either. Lancey knew her neighbors. They were expressing local loyalty, not hatred. Jan had been down, and risen; his fellow citizens were saluting his courage.

Behind Justin, the line of the circle swayed, surged back to give him more room. It was a signal for renewed violence.

Lowering his head Jan Elmendorf charged.

As he came in Justin hit him twice, left and right. They were short, vicious punches, thrown from the shoulders, hammered in the way a carpenter drove nails. Jan was rocked, but not stopped; his churning legs had already flung him forward in a dive. The blows twisted him so that he hit Justin with his side instead of his shoulder. They crashed down together.

Lancey sucked in a deep, shuddering breath. The crowd's din forced her to cover her ears. Any semblance of circle or arena vanished in wild disorder as men struggled for a closer look. They hid the fighters from the girl. She could see only dust, bobbing hats, the heaving shoulders of a mob in the grip of an invisible whirlpool. In the center of this human vortex, to judge by the noise, was a raging battle.

Again the throng, giving the contestants room, changed shape, deflating itself from circle to ellipse. This opened at one end to disgorge a single, rolling figure.

Justin and Jan, locked together, heaved and wrestled, turning over and over on the ground as each fought to end on top. Their struggle was a blur of movement, kicking legs, punching arms, hands that slipped, pried, clawed for the hold that would punish.

From her ledge Lancey couldn't separate the quick motions into individual acts, but she knew this savage form of fighting. It had no rules, no standards; even weapons were not barred if the fighters were equally armed. The towns in the valley had been settled for a hundred years, but on the riverfront men fought frontier style.

Down there in the dust the grapplers were gouging, biting, butting. Every grip was intended to break a bone; every kick was meant to cripple. To maim or scar was an accepted method of obtaining victory.

Lancey had watched such fights before. No child reared among the riverfolk failed to witness drunken brawls. She tried to recall whether she had cheered or gaped, could not honestly remember horror. This contest was different. She felt squeamish and revolted. Nausea flooded her mouth with salt saliva.

Maybe, she thought, it's because I know them both. The picture of Justin minus an eye, or Jan with a twisted, useless arm, made her shudder. Yet she could not turn her gaze from the fight.

She blamed Jan for letting his jealousy flare into violence, but Justin too was far from guiltless. He, at least, had no cause to fight over her, was intelligent enough to realize that Jan's claim was worthless. She was Lancey Quist, belonged to no one, resented being made a reason for a quarrel!

The grappled figures stopped rolling, lay still. They seemed to quiver; there were no abrupt movements. Lancey wondered if they were exhausted. She was suddenly aware that a hush had come over the watching men. They were no longer shoving and jostling. The barking dogs made the only noise.

Slowly, very slowly, the joined wrestlers came to their knees, to their feet. Even at a distance Lancey could sense the tenseness of that struggle. A moment later she saw the reason.

Justin held Jan's head locked in the crook of his left arm, was exerting all his strength to keep the other bent double. Jan, with a pulling grip on Justin's hair, pawed with his free hand to break the hold. They swayed, stiffened.

Then, Justin let go of his left wrist, swung his right arm back. Three times, with the swift, chopping sweep of a farmer using a sickle, he smashed his fist into Jan's face.

As the crowd's bellow roared like thunder, Justin changed his tactics. With a movement too quick for Lancey to follow, he gripped, crouched, and flipped Jan over his shoulder. It was a tremendous heave, that flung the man through the air.

For an instant the stocky body seemed to hang by its heels. Then, Jan crashed down on his back with a force that shook the ground.

He was stunned. The fingers of one hand groped in the dust; his feet twitched. Justin took no chances. He was beside Jan in two leaps; his leg swung back.

Lancey shut her eyes. Justin was within his rights, but she couldn't bear to see that final kick. She heard the shouting reach a new peak, fade from roar to a buzz of talk.

When she looked again, the fight was over. Justin, with Pardon Cash and the other fishermen around him, was walking away. Digmus Jaycock was in the group clustered around Jan. The rest of the crowd had separated, were standing in knots, chattering, gesticulating. One man, laughing, threw an imaginary opponent over his shoulder. Another, downcast, had his purse out and was evidently paying a wager.

They liked it, she thought scornfully, they'll talk about this fight for days. The strength of her feeling surprised her. A year ago she would have enjoyed it herself. Now she almost felt hatred for the whole stupid male sex!

The men were drifting away, most of them heading back to Jaycock's. Digmus rose hastily from beside Jan, and hurried to tend to business, slapping dust from his breeches as he skipped along. Justin had led the fishermen to the river's edge where they screened his washing. Lancey stayed where she was.

She was waiting for Jan to rise. Her relief when he did betrayed the fact she'd been numb with fear. Jan moved painfully, but he pushed aside helping hands. He held a handkerchief to his face, and swayed, but he walked without assistance. Defeat showed in the slumped shoulders, the hanging head.

At least, Lancey thought, there was no permanent damage. Suddenly furious, she hoped Jan had learned a lesson. She intended to berate him at the first opportunity, to settle forever his ridiculous dreams. After that she would never speak to him again!

Conscious of a few curious glances from the last of the spectators, Lancey turned to leave. As she picked her way down the slope, she wondered if they recognized her. It was nothing new for men to fight over a girl, but it always made a nice morsel of scandal. Her presence might well make the morsel a mouthful. The men would tell their women; they, in turn, would be catty, envious, or shocked, but ready to believe the worst. Well, let them!

Justin's victory did not impress her. She had expected it. By fighting he had helped Jan place her in the false position of prize for the winner.

"Like stags over a doe," said Lancey, aloud.

She had almost reached the fishing village when a shout from behind named her. Turning, she saw it was Pardon Cash. The big fisherman was alone, jogging along the river path. He called out as he approached.

"Lancey, you got any liniment up to the house?"

"Who's hurt?" asked Lancey, as if she didn't know.

"Justin's got a sprained thumb." Pardon gazed down at the girl, grinned crookedly. "And assorted bruises. 'Twas a real pert scrap, wasn't it?"

"So you saw me."

"Aye. Couldn't miss that dress against the bluff. That's a mighty nice outfit, Lancey, but the wrong color for hide-and-seek."

"Pardon, why did they fight?"

"Because Jan's a thick Dutchman with no more sense than a mule. He prodded Justin into it. Finally threw a mug of ale in Justin's face. But I guess you know the real reason."

"You mean me."

"You wasn't mentioned. They was both careful about that."

"Well! Small thanks for small favors."

"Now, back water, Lancey. It ain't a secret how Jan feels about you. Nobody's gonna blame you. After Jan tossed that ale Justin had no choice. He couldn't take that in front of folks."

"I suppose not," Lancey said, grudgingly, "but why did he let it come to that?"

"He couldn't help it. Digmus had word that mostly Clinton men were elected to the convention. We were all talking about that practically scuttling any chance of the Constitution passing in this state. Jan started to argue with Justin——"

"Jan? He takes his politics from Captain Benjamin. He's against passing the same as Justin is!"

"Not this morning," Pardon said. "Alexander Hamilton hisself was less pro than Jan this morning. He took exception to everything Justin said."

"But, the Constitution of all things!" Lancey started to laugh. "Nobody's going to believe they came to blows over that!"

128

"Any excuse suited Jan. He was set on fighting. In the end, I guess he got his fill of it."

"If you ask me," Lancey said, "they both played the fool. And so did the rest of you cheering them on." She tossed her head, and walked on. When Pardon Cash fell into step beside her, she refused to look at him.

12

THE LITTLE SAILBOAT SEEMED NO BIGGER THAN A TOY AS IT TACKED across the river. Lancey watched it idly, noted that the skiff carried a single spritsail. She was standing in the doorway of her home, lazily somnolent after the mid-day meal. She could hear the children playing on the other side of the house, and her father and stepmother talking behind her. Hester and Hendrick were still discussing the fight.

Lancey hadn't changed from her new gown. The sun was too high and bright for good fishing, and she enjoyed the feeling of looking her best. She felt, too, vaguely disappointed that the afternoon afforded no further opportunity to display herself.

So light that it seemed to skim across the water the sailboat angled upstream. Lancey straightened, frowning.

"Pa," she called, "there's a skiff making for here."

Hendrick and Hester joined her. All three stepped out into the yard for a clearer view. There was no doubt that the skiff, with the prevailing wind from the south, was heading for the Quist pier.

"Who is it?" asked Hester.

Hendrick shook his head. "Nice, trim little craft, but I don't recall her. Some feller out for a Sunday sail."

They saw the canvas spill breeze as the sprit, the diagonal strut that held it open, was removed. The sail rattled down to reveal the helmsman. He shipped his rudder, stood up to scull the skiff closer to the shore.

"Why," said Hester, "it's Dirck van Zandt!"

Aware of mounting excitement Lancey forced herself to walk sedately down to the pier with the others. She was very pleased that Dirck, for once, would find her attired in finery instead of barefoot and grimy. The russet velvet, she thought, was her armor against his usual light attitude. At last he would be forced to consider the wench a lady.

"Ahoy, the skiff," cried Lancey, "and where did you get that cockle shell?"

Dirck van Zandt paused in his sculling to wave. The boat was only a few yards from the pier, drifting lightly. His answer sounded gay, and proud.

"She's mine. Owned her since I was fifteen. Haven't had a chance to use her much these past years, but our boatman kept her in shape."

"Boatman," murmured Hester. "La, di, da."

"Hush," said Hendrick. He raised his voice. "Come alongside and tie up, Dirck, You're welcome."

"Thanks, Hendrick." Dirck was staring at Lancey. He worked his oar to bring the boat closer, then managed a bow. "My compliments, Mistress Lancey. You honor the day."

Lancey dipped in a curtsy. For all that they both mocked the elaborate etiquette of a formal occasion, the girl warmed with pleasure. He was, she thought, rather elegantly dressed himself, in nankeen suiting that was almost as white as the sail. Dirck had discarded his jacket, and his shirt was open at the throat. He was bareheaded, but the hat lying on a thwart was a wide brimmed straw instead of a tricorne.

"Where's Meda?" asked Lancey. The fact that he wore brown stockings and soft leather shoes instead of boots prompted the question.

"She's a little big for the *Argo*."

"The which?" Hester said.

"My skiff." Dirck seemed a trifle embarrassed. "I was only fifteen, and well—I named her that."

Hendrick knelt on the pier, fended the skiff from the piling, held it steady. He said, "She is a neat-made boat, Dirck, though she wouldn't hold many fish."

"It's a perfect day for sailing," Dirck said. "Even against the wind I came down from Rhinebeck in record time. I thought maybe Mistress Lancey might like a ride."

"Why," said Lancey, eyes dancing, "if Pa doesn't need me——"

"No, Lancey. Not till dark anyway. We will make a night drift then, maybe."

"I'll get your cloak," said Hester, already hurrying away. "It's always chill on the river."

For the first time in her life Lancey let a man hand her down into a boat. Somehow, the gesture befitted her velvet gown. Dirck's grip was firm and steady. He even made sure that there was a cushion for her to sit on. Aware that the plush would show every crease, Lancey carefully arranged her skirt, raising it in back to sit on her petticoats.

This artfully displayed her shoe buckles, but not too much ankle.

Hester tossed down the cloak; Hendrick shoved off the skiff. Dirck sculled them out into the river, raised the sail. It caught the wind at once. The tiny *Argo* seemed to shake herself like a frisky puppy, and dart forward. They sailed north, upriver.

For the first few minutes the pure pleasure of sailing kept them silent. Dirck watched sail and steering. Lancey, enjoying the wind in her hair, the warmth of the sun, gazed at the shore, the water tumbling past, the tide, the helmsman. When their glances locked they laughed in sheer exuberance.

"This *is* nice!" Lancey said, enthusiasm taking all primness from the speech.

"Better than rowing."

"Much better. I've sailed before of course, but not too often. Our own boat's pretty clumsy with a mast up."

"There's a line if you'd care to troll."

"Troll? For what?"

"Well, the shad might have started to run. A few venturesome bucks anyway."

"You can't hook shad! It's a net fish!"

"Is that so?"

"They won't take bait."

"Is that so?"

"What are you grinning about?" Lancey was nettled.

"I've hooked shad, and boated them, and eaten them. They're a good game fish, and they'll give you a battle."

Lancey stared, open mouthed. "I never heard of such a thing!"

"I'm not lying, Lancey. I know it's against the rules, but I did it. Using a piece of red flannel for bait, too. I'm not saying they'll all take it, but some will. I was pretty surprised by the first one. That was the year the British came up the river."

"I remember. Did you see them?"

"Too much of them. I saw them sack Kingston."

"You saw them?"

Dirck nodded, face grave. "That's right. We had word they were coming of course. Could even hear the cannon below us. My father was taking the family inland, but young Dirck had other ideas. With a farm lad a year or so older—old enough to have more sense—we put a couple of fowling pieces in the *Argo*, and sailed across."

Lancey could picture the expedition. Two lads in a tiny boat, out to beard the British fleet. She said, softly, "The brevet cornet."

"Yes, even then." Dirck gave her a rueful smile. "I was a fierce, fire-eating rebel at fifteen, Lancey. 'Course we were just underfoot at Kingston. We wanted to join the army and fight the invaders. There wasn't any army, and everybody was packing to get out. You never saw such panic."

"Cowards?"

"No, they were just being sensible. They didn't have any force that could stand up to Vaughan's regulars, and you can't meet bayonets with rocks. But at the time I was pretty disgusted. My friend and I hid on a wooded hill. We could look down on most of the town, and we swore we'd get us at least one redcoat."

"You might have been killed."

"Not us." Dirck showed his teeth in a grin. "Because when the redcoats came neither one of us so much as stirred. We could see the smoke from the ships they burned, and the empty town below us. Just the houses, some with their doors standing open, and a broken-down wagon by the side of the road. It looked like the loneliest place on earth."

"Until the British entered."

"Until then. One minute there was nobody, the next there was this red wave. They came in at a trot, with a fan of bayonets out in front. Then, of course, they got their torches going, and the rest was an inferno. Flames leaping from windows, thick black smoke, the noise of burning, and roofs falling in."

Dirck stopped talking, to glance at the shoreline. He gauged the skiff's speed, nodded his head.

"We're making fine time, Lancey."

"Are we going somewhere?"

"Rhinebeck. My home. My mother's having a party."

Lancey stared at him, found her mouth open, shut it. "But—but, Dirck—I wasn't invited to——"

"You are now," Dirck said.

* * *

The van Zandt house topped a knoll that sloped gently to the river. Like other east-bank manor houses it faced the water, and had its own landing, but it lacked the size and pretensions of the great patroon estates.

Lancey Quist, on trips upriver, had seen the place too often to be overly impressed. She knew that it was pleasantly situated, a few miles south of Rhinebeck, but this was Livingston territory where even distant cousins found higher eminences on which to build more stately mansions. Dirck's home was merely a rather tall, Dutch style, two storied structure with a row of flat-roofed dormers squinting above the eave. It was built of local bluestone, and though it was trim and neat the land that stretched before it was meadow, not lawn or formal gardens. Except for the tiny boathouse the outbuildings were hidden behind the crest of the hill.

No, Lancey's nervousness came from the people in view, strolling the grounds or gathered into groups. God and Nicholas, she thought as Dirck maneuvered the skiff toward the landing, there must be a score of women and even more men. She managed to keep her voice calm.

"Dirck, are you truly certain it's all right?"

"Of course," Dirck said, smiling. "I'd not have asked you otherwise. It's no great occasion, Lancey. Merely our turn to hold a gathering of friends and neighbors."

The girl frowned, not sure of his motives. She was fairly certain the invitation had been impulsive, inspired by her appearance, but she didn't blame him for that. Certainly, in any other clothes, she'd have refused it. Did he plan this meeting as a test, measuring the fisherman's daughter against the yardstick of his own family?

Dirck noticed the frown, guessed at her thoughts. He felt a flash of impatience at her qualms. Couldn't the girl realize that his gesture was a compliment?

"There's nothing to worry about, Lancey."

"Then we needn't worry."

"I want you to meet my mother and father, my brother. As I've met Hendrick and Hester. That's all."

"Thank you," Lancey said, knowing it was not all. He was a man, and he met people with an easy masculine friendliness made confident by his background. A girl, suddenly thrust among strange women, faced a different problem. However friendly the company she would be judged with a female thoroughness that was ready to turn hostile.

The mechanics of landing gave her a short respite. Conscious of the watchers on the slope Lancey stayed on her cushion as they drew alongside the van Zandt pier. She did lean to fend the boat from the pilings, and hold it close while Dirck tied fast, but these were the natural actions of any boat-wise girl.

"Well," Dirck said, "here we are." He shrugged into his coat, offered his hand.

134

Taking it, Lancey stepped from the skiff with practiced ease. It was, she decided, a good beginning, but a little like leaving safety for danger. She knew how to handle herself on the river, the walk up the slope would be much more trying.

Two young men hurried down the gravel path to greet them. With a start Lancey realized that she knew both by name and sight. The way these two raced their horses through Poughkeepsie was a scandal among more sedate householders.

"Dirck," cried the shorter man, a grin crinkling his florid, pug-nosed face, "where in thunder have you been?"

"We can see why," the other said.

"Mistress Lancey," said Dirck, "may I present Tappen Platt and Schuyler Davis? Gentlemen, Mistress Lancey Quist."

"Honored," said tall Schuyler Davis.

"Enchanted," Tappen Platt said. His bow was the more elegant leg, the flourish of his hat was exuberant. "A pleasure as welcome as 'tis unexpected."

Lancey dipped a curtsy, smiling. Neither man showed recognition of her name, nor anything but gay interest. Their manner gave her confidence; it was added assurance that she looked her best. She was glad they had greeted her first, aware she might need all her poise under the scrutiny still to come.

"Gentlemen," she said, with a sideways glance at Dirck van Zandt, "you must blame Master van Zandt for the unexpectedness."

"Oh, we do," said Tappen Platt. "We do!"

Schuyler Davis had a grave air, stressed by slow speech and an impassive expression. He said, "A deliberate prevaricator who left word he had gone fishing."

"A legal quibble only," Dirck said, "since I did not say for what." He was pleased by his friends' reception of Lancey. They were a madcap pair, but they had breeding and taste.

"Now there's a speech," said Lancey, "with more law than politeness. To liken a lady to a fish——" She spoke with exaggerated disapproval, in a mincing tone mocked by her dancing eyes.

"Barbarous," agreed Schuyler Davis.

"Unforgivable," Tappen Platt said.

Dirck chuckled, bowed low. "*Peccavi*, Mistress. These two always get me into scrapes. Let us seek other, more circumspect company."

The banter continued as they climbed the path. Lancey's laughter and retorts covered a mounting uneasiness. She saw heads turn as they approached, heard the chatter diminish to whispers. The men gazed with open interest; the women were more polite, shot guarded glances, and pretended indifference. Lancey, watchful and worried, decided it was pleasant to have three escorts to thaw the stiffness from her arrival, but it could arouse jealousy.

Even before Dirck led her toward his family, the girl separated them from the others. Beekman van Zandt was a big man who wore his hair powdered in the old-fashioned mode, but his face was an inflated version of Dirck's. His elder son, heir, and namesake, was as tall but not quite as corpulent as the father. Between her men, the ruffles of her mob-cap no higher than their biceps, stood the mother, plump and sleek as a well-fed pigeon.

As Dirck made the introductions Lancey realized that it was the woman, no taller than herself, who ruled this household. The two big men bowed, murmuring their compliments, but even as they bent both pair of eyes slid, in unison, toward the face under the mob-cap.

It was, Lancey thought, a pleasant face, its prettiness blurred by the softness of rounded cheeks and double chin. The mouth was thin, but red and smiling. Only the deep blue eyes showed shrewdness; they had the hard glaze of delft.

"Mistress Quist," said Mrs. van Zandt, "of Poughkeepsie." Her voice was soft and polite, with the assurance that comes from long authority.

"Yes, ma'am," Lancey said.

"Quist." The name was repeated musingly. "You are visiting perhaps?"

"No, ma'am. I live there."

"That's right, Mother," Dirck said. He spoke with easy confidence. "And since I have been a guest at the Quist table, I thought it time to repay the courtesy."

"Of course. You are welcome, my dear." Mrs. van Zandt's gaze shifted to her son. "I cannot recall when you last brought a fresh young face to one of our afternoons, Dirck."

Dirck blinked, then grinned. He said: "That is a complaint, Mistress Lancey. Mother thinks she sees too little of me these days."

A smile was Lancey's only reply. She could not blame Dirck's mother for being curious about a stranger, yet she sensed hostility behind the politeness. If asked about my family, she thought, I shall tell the truth.

"At least," said Mrs. van Zandt, "you have not been idle, Dirck. We were very pleased with Master Kent's account of your progress." She turned back to Lancey. "We have great hopes for Dirck, Mistress Quist."

Beekman van Zandt cleared his throat. He said, "Master Kent thinks there'll be even more demand for lawyers under the Constitution."

"If it's adopted," Lancey said.

Mrs. van Zandt's smile stiffened; young Beekman raised his eyebrows. The father stared for an instant before he spoke.

"It must be, Mistress. For once, George Clinton and his cronies will have to yield to the sentiments of others. Now that six of the states have ratified—including our neighbors of Massachusetts and Connecticut—we must do the same."

"Governor Clinton's faction," said Lancey, "seems to have the majority of the delegates." She knew it was imprudent, even unladylike, to argue the topic in such company. The landed gentry were anti-Clinton, shared Hamilton's views favoring a strong government.

"In numbers, mayhap," said Beekman van Zandt. "Not in influence. The older river families, the real, solid backbone of the state, will have a strong voice in the convention. You shall see that it will prevail."

"After all," agreed his wife, "position and culture should count for something." Her steady gaze seemed in contrast to her mild tone. "Don't you agree, Mistress Quist?"

Dirck said, "It may be more difficult, Mother, to get the Clintonians to agree."

He was, Lancey thought, trying to save her from a direct answer. His pleasant remark failed to fool his mother. The girl saw that lady's brow pucker for a frowning instant. Then, blandly, Mrs. van Zandt changed subject and tactics.

"True, Dirck. A while ago Master Kent was saying much the same thing to Eunice Wynbridge."

"Oh," Dirck said, "is Eunice here?"

"For some time."

Lancey, amused, believed the mention of the name deliberate, and Dirck's casual question overdone. There was an undercurrent of rebuke in Mrs. van Zandt's quiet speech. This·was emphasized by the manner in which her husband plucked at the ornate fob dangling from his waistcoat, produced a heavy gold watch.

"For an hour," he said, squinting at the timepiece, "and fourteen minutes."

"By Hasius," Dirck said, and chuckled.

To Lancey's amazement all the van Zandts grinned. An instant before there had been disapproval under the polite formality; this vanished as if thawed by Dirck's exclamation. Glancing at each in turn she realized they shared some hidden family joke. It made them more natural and more likeable.

"By who?" she asked.

Beekman van Zandt guffawed, held out his watch. "Hasius of Haarlem," he said, "who made this for my father."

"As boys," said the younger Beekman, "both Dirck and I were ruled by Hasius."

"Ruled, indeed," Mrs. van Zandt said, sounding younger and less distant. "A more unruly pair never existed." She gazed fondly at her three men, turned to Lancey. "My husband swears by that watch, Mistress Quist, and my sons *at* it."

"Never loses a minute," cried the father.

"When found and wound," said Dirck.

"Or unless," his brother said, beaming, "set back by the goblins in the night."

"Goblins named Dirck and Beekman." Mrs. van Zandt shook her head. "They paid dear for that stolen hour later."

The whole family was laughing now, and it gave them a unity more striking than similar features. Lancey recognized that real affection bound them together, and felt herself an outsider. The sun told fishermen the time, but the van Zandts had Roman numerals and golden hands that cost a score of pounds.

"It's a lovely watch," she said, without envy.

"Thank you, my dear," said Beekman van Zandt, tucking it away.

Mrs. van Zandt tapped Dirck's arm. "You had better take Mistress Quist about. I'm sure she'll enjoy meeting our guests." The humor invoked by Hasius was still in her voice, but she didn't neglect her purpose. "Oh, and please remind Eunice that I've something for her to take home."

Eunice again, thought Lancey as she dipped in a farewell curtsy. The woman might just as well hang a sign on Dirck: keep off, spoken for. Grimly, the girl looked forward to meeting Mistress Eunice Wynbridge. Dirck was nothing more than a pleasant companion, but no girl liked to be challenged!

"I knew they'd like you," whispered Dirck after they turned away.

Men, Lancey said silently, are certainly stone blind and tone deaf. Didn't he even listen? She had no chance to reply because Tappen

Platt and Schuyler Davis, who had been hovering, joined them immediately.

They made the ordeal of introductions less trying. Lancey found herself smiling politely, making small talk, among groups of people whose names she didn't catch. They were all dressed in their Sunday best, the men's vari-colored waistcoats much more colorful than the women's clothes. Wealth was displayed by the cloth and cut of suitings and dresses, by the crispness of lawn neckpiece and lace-trimmed bodice. If some of the male calves were covered by stockings finer than her own, nobody could see hers.

No gown outshone the russet velvet. Her lack of jewelry could be deliberate and her cloak was certainly suitable for sailing.

Satisfied about such details Lancey found only half her brain necessary to exchange pleasantries, accept compliments, answer queries. Some of the older women were prying, some of the younger cool. With polite diffidence she ignored any attitude latent with trouble.

It was, she decided, a lot easier than dealing with outspoken riverfront folk. These people were hobbled by convention, bridled by formality. She had three escorts, all quick-tongued and popular, and their presence gave her freedom to inspect her surroundings.

The van Zandts, Lancey noted, clung to the old Dutch tradition of hospitality, food before frolic and drink with both. A long trestle table had been set up outdoors, to enjoy the fine April weather, at the side of the house under a great wine-glass elm. There were benches drawn up to the cloth covered board, and these were kept filled by ever-changing rows of hungry guests.

Many of the older folk had apparently already eaten, but there was still enough food for a feast. Two buxom serving girls shuttled between table and kitchen, refilling bowls and pitchers, carrying away dirty but empty dishes.

The fare was both ample and varied, hot and cold. There was a ham, a roast of beef, a huge *hoof kaas* or head cheese; all showed the inroads of carvers but were still substantial. There were plates of *zult* and *worst*, the latter links of sausage surrounding the forearm-size *zult* like a nestling litter. Cabbage hot with pod-peas steamed as *en poetyes;* cold and shredded it was *kool slaa.* Bread was present in great round loaves, or in the small rolls called *roltetje.*

In the center of the table was a giant bowl of claret punch for the ladies; the men had pitchers of beer. Anything stronger, like Holland gin or rum, was quaffed by gentlemen indoors on the invitation of the host.

"Hungry, Mistress Lancey?" asked Dirck as they neared the bustle beneath the elm.

She glanced at him, saw the twinkle that remembered her trencherwork at the Brick Gables. Lancey colored faintly at the memory. This was no place to be thinking of that evening at the inn! She was still nervously aware that she was under scrutiny, but too honest to be delicate.

"Yes," she said, "I am. The sailing gave me an appetite."

Tappen Platt uttered a chortle of joy, hurried to find them places. A stout matron sitting alone at the end of the near bench giggled at his whisper, slid sideways to make room.

As Lancey sat down, between Dirck and Schuyler Davis, a male voice spoke.

"Mistress Quist, I believe. Good afternoon."

The man across the table met her startled gaze with judicial calm. He was young, wide shouldered, with a keen, intelligent face. She knew him at once, and the smiling young wife at his shoulder.

"Master Kent," said Lancey, bowing. "Mistress."

"You know my mentor?" asked Dirck, delighted.

"By sight only."

"Yes," James Kent said, "paths cross in Poughkeepsie. Though I did not know Mistress Quist had noticed me, I could not fail to notice *her*."

Fishmongering, Lancey thought, and her stomach fluttered as she waited for the lawyer's next speech.

"James notices everything," said Mrs. Kent, with a laugh, "and especially pretty girls."

Kent smiled at his wife. "The evidence bears you out, Elizabeth. We are wed. Q.E.D." He raised a forkful of cole slaw, glanced across the table. "You must bring Mistress Quist to visit us sometime, Dirck."

"With pleasure, sir."

Lancey glowed with gratitude as the tension within her loosened. She had passed the lawyer's little cottage a hundred times in the three years since the Kents had married. If he knew her name, he knew all about her, and probably his wife did, too. Yet he found nothing unseemly in her presence at the van Zandts'.

No more was said that did not concern the serious business of eating. The three men vied with each other in piling Lancey's plate until she begged for mercy. She attacked the meal with zest, but found the punch rather sweet and insipid. It had been doctored beyond any semblance to the last claret she had tasted, but she sipped it warily.

The Kents left before Lancey was half finished. She bowed her farewells, returned to her plate. Her mouth was full of sausage when the men beside her suddenly rose to their feet. Startled, she raised her head.

Edging into position across the table was the tall, chestnut-haired girl she'd seen chatting with Dirck on the steps of the English church.

This time Dirck was making the introduction for which Lancey had waited, the one she wished to hear.

"Mistress Eunice Wynbridge. Mistress Lancey Quist."

She would catch me, thought Lancey savagely, with mouth full and jaw bulging! Almost choking, she tried to swallow and smile at the same time. The other girl's brown eyes showed cool appraisal, but she inclined her head. When she spoke her voice was low but lilting.

"Lancey. What an interesting name!"

"It's a family name," Lancey said.

"Oh, like yours, Tappen. And yours, Schuyler. *Our* parents lacked imagination, Dirck." She sat down, her cameo loveliness smiling in chiseled perfection, without warmth. "Eunice has meaning but no connections."

"What's it mean?" asked Tappen Platt.

"Happy victory," Eunice said.

Well it might, thought Lancey. It only took her three sentences to link herself with Dirck and me with Tappen and Schuyler. The tall girl was wearing yellow brocade this time, spanking new. Lancey admitted it was a becoming shade that gave the pale skin above the square bodice a warm tint of ivory.

Schuyler Davis said: "My compliments, Eunice. You look the personification of it today."

"Why, thank you, Schuyler. I thought you'd been too busy to notice." The musical speech continued without pause. "When did you launch the *Argo*, Dirck?"

"This morning."

"It's a pert little craft," Lancey said, determined to join the conversation. This Eunice, knowing the three men longer, could easily steer the talk as she wished. "We fairly flew upriver."

"You seem partial to boating, Mistress Quist."

"Nearly everyone along the river is, Mistress Wynbridge."

"You must sail on one of my sloops some day."

"That would be pleasant." Lancey noted the plural, but refused to express surprise. The men's acceptance of the statement proved the girl really did own ships.

"Eunice's father," Dirck said, "started the Blue-Hull Line out of Newburgh Bay." He was aware that the girls were fencing, didn't want Lancey patronized.

Schuyler Davis said, "Quite the heiress, our Eunice."

"Acreage," said Tappen Platt, "as well as sloops. Cows, horses, hens, and what not. All handled for her by lawyers and guardians." He was teasing; his head turned as he glanced from Eunice to Dirck.

"Now, Tappen, you exaggerate." Eunice sounded more pleased than protesting. "The war ruined Papa's affairs as well as his health. Things are only now recovering from those wretched years."

Lancey finished eating, but the food had lost its savor. She was less impressed by Eunice's wealth than by the way Tappen and Schuyler referred to it. Both men were gently mocking; their raillery left the girl unruffled. She was, Lancey decided, so sure of herself that she accepted the pair merely as Dirck's friends.

"By the way," Dirck said, "Mother mentioned that she has something for you, Eunice."

"Oh, yes." The grave brown eyes regarded Lancey. "It's that quilt I much admired. She's too kind, but she insisted. Her handiwork is exquisite, Mistress Quist."

The implication was plain and intended. Quiltmaking was a prized art, and skillful mothers gave such gifts only to intimates, daughters real or potential. Even the men looked startled. Dirck's smile slowly melted into thin-lipped tightness.

"I am sure it is," Lancey said. Her handiwork and yours, she thought. Warned beforehand of her coming, Mrs. van Zandt and Eunice had taken this means of announcing their alliance. No wonder the older woman hadn't been very curious about her background. Whoever Lancey Quist might be, the van Zandts had already decided their younger son's future.

Politeness had the men tongue-tied. Dirck, mentally swearing, couldn't think of anything to say. His friends waited for him to speak first. Eunice let the silence stretch to uncomfortable seconds before she broke it.

"Dirck, would you carve me a slice of that ham, please?"

That, Lancey thought, is gaffing a dead fish. She wanted to laugh in spite of her anger at the unnecessary intrigue. These highborn ladies were afraid of shadows! She had no real interest in Dirck van Zandt. He was gay, rich, different; after an accidental meeting he had cultivated her.

"Schuyler's the better carver." Dirck was easily casual, but Schuyler Davis rose at once.

Why, bless their hearts, Lancey thought, but men do know how to stick together. She gave Eunice Wynbridge a quick, mischievous smile. Just for a lark she decided to support Dirck, and give Mistress Happy Victory a lesson.

"You mustn't think Dirck discourteous, Mistress Wynbridge." Placing a possessive hand on Dirck's wrist, Lancey tilted her head for a look at the sun. "I'm afraid the hour prevents us from lingering."

"But it's early," protested Tappen Platt.

"After four," Lancey said, "and it's a long sail back to Poughkeepsie against the wind."

"I had to plead with Lancey to come." Following her lead, Dirck dropped the more formal title from her name. He didn't know what the girl planned, but Eunice had provoked this.

"Then, of course, we mustn't detain you," Eunice said.

"We simply must get back by night tide," Lancey said. "You see I promised my father I'd help him make a night drift."

"Night drift?"

The question was Tappen Platt's. Neither Schuyler Davis nor Eunice Wynbridge glanced at the ham slice he forked onto her plate. Both watched Lancey.

As she rose, Lancey let her cloak slide from her shoulders. It gave her a chance to show the russet velvet in full glory, and Dirck the chance for a gesture.

Grave-faced, Dirck seized the opportunity, swept up the cloak as it tumbled past the bench.

"Allow me," he said, replacing the garment with careful solicitude. He managed to keep laughter from his voice, but didn't dare look at Eunice Wynbridge.

"Thank you, Dirck." Lancey tossed the remark with a twist of her head. Then, she turned to Tappen Platt. "If it stays mild tonight, after such a nice, warm day, the shad may be running."

"Shad?" Bewilderment made Tappen plaintive.

"That's a fish," Dirck said, solemnly.

"I know it, but——"

"My father's a fisherman," said Lancey. It seemed strange to state the truth deliberately after avoiding it all afternoon.

"The best on the river," Dirck said.

"A—fisherman?" In the pause between the two words disbelief replaced astonishment in Eunice's face. The sound of her own voice brought a pink tint to the pale cheeks.

"Mistress Wynbridge thinks we jest, Dirck. You must tell her sometime how I fished you from the river, mare and all." Lancey turned toward the other girl, flipped her palms in a gesture. "I couldn't very well throw him back, could I?"

"Not Meda anyway," Dirck said.

Schuyler Davis started to laugh.

Eunice glared at him, at the couple across the table. She wasn't convinced, but the small, dark-haired girl had shaken her. Dirck van Zandt wouldn't bring a riverfront trollop to meet his mother. But he might bring a fisherman's daughter who could dress like Lancey Quist.

"Quist." Tappen Platt snapped his fingers. "Hendrick and Ten Bush. Knew I'd heard the name."

"Ten Bush has gone awhaling," Dirck said. He bowed to Eunice, offered Lancey his arm. "Will you tell my mother that I took Lancey home, Eunice?"

"It's been very pleasant," said Lancey Quist, "meeting all of you."

13

As the Argo slid south through the Hudson, silver now in the late afternoon, Lancey Quist, for once, forgot to pay attention to the weather.

There were reasons. The breeze had shifted, died down to a gentle breath of warm, light air. It barely stirred the trees on the east bank as it passed through from the north, and it dipped onto the river with a feathery touch that made no ripples on the flowing water. The tide was at ebb; the little spritsail caught what wind there was; the skiff moved, steadily if not speedily, downriver. Lancey, lulled by food and sunshine, was content to let Dirck handle the sailing.

The girl was thinking of her brother. How Ten Bush would have enjoyed the sail, her account of the party! He had, Lancey recalled, liked Dirck and would have been pleased by her success among the van Zandts and their friends. She wondered how many watery miles now stretched between the *Argo* and Ten Bush's whaler, feeling a touch of loneliness that she now lacked a confidant close to her own age.

For a long while they sailed in silence. Dirck, the tiller between his knees, glanced at his course, but gazed at the girl. She had her eyes closed, face raised to the sun, and he thought she had never looked more attractive. He felt a mixture of emotions—tenderness, affection, protectiveness, admiration. Strangely, at the moment, there was no desire. Dirck vaguely realized that the afternoon had changed his attitude about Lancey.

It wasn't, he decided, that she was less desirable or bedable. He was honest enough to admit that he still wanted her in that final, physical way, but the status had shifted. Lancey was no longer a wench to be lightly wooed, easily left when won. Her surrender was worth more than the false coin of seduction.

Dirck swung his leg over the tiller, sank, cross-legged, beside the girl. He could hold the rudder steady with one hand, and it didn't occur to him to glance back to where the sky darkened over distant mountains.

"Lancey."

Dozing, back to the gunwale, Lancey opened her eyes. The sunshine made everything blurry for an instant, then she saw Dirck seated at her elbow. She gave him an apologetic smile contorted by a yawn.

"I'm sorry," she said, "I must have dropped off."

"I've the more reason to be sorry." Dirck watched the sail, not the girl. "My apologies for this afternoon."

"Apologies?" Lancey straightened, shook away the last drowsiness. "Why? I enjoyed the party, Dirck."

"I told my mother only that I might bring back a friend. She guessed your sex from my manner." He turned his head, smiled. "I have never needed permission to bring a man friend home, and I never before brought a girl."

"I guessed that much myself."

"That gave your visit a swollen, puffed-up importance for which I blame myself. Both mother and—Eunice—get their backs up when things go contrary to their wishes."

So he knows that, Lancey thought. She was more pleased than annoyed at her reception. It made the outing a complete success. Given the proper clothes she, Lancey Quist, was acceptable in any company, fit to rival Eunice Wynbridge.

"Are you engaged to Mistress Wynbridge?"

"No!" The negative was vehement. Dirck hesitated, continued. "Oh, I'll admit I know the family favors the match. Father only hems and hints, but Mother is openly for it."

"So, methinks, is the lady."

"Well, they needn't take so damn much for granted!"

Lancey laughed softly at his flare of anger. Added to his apology it gave her a feeling of closer intimacy. She said, "Of course you've given them no reason."

"Not that much!" Dirck's glare faded into sheepishness when she laughed again. "We've known each other for years. When her father was alive he'd bring her to play with Beekman and me. We know the same people, attend the same parties." He ended with a lame admission. "Eunice is all right."

"All right?" Lancey stifled a quick curiosity about the gentry's kissing customs. "Well, I guess! A rich heiress, beautiful, more than willing to wed."

146

"You think she's beautiful?"

"I have eyes, Dirck."

"There are others."

"Yes," said Lancey, delighted by the statement, "but not many along this stretch of the river. None that own a fleet of sloops."

"Four, that's all. Just four."

"That's a fleet."

"That doesn't give her the right to act as if she owns *me!* She as good as told you that you were trespassing."

"You can't blame her for that," Lancey said, slowly. "The poor girl made a mistake."

"She certainly did!"

"Well, she knows better now." Lancey gazed over the side, half-noted the skiff was almost drifting. "The dress had her fooled, but——"

"What dress?"

"Dirck." Lancey faced him squarely. "Would you have asked me to that party if I'd been clad as usual?"

"What makes you think——?"

"Be honest."

"I sailed down to ask you." Dirck flushed under her steady gaze. "*All right!* To ask you to go for a sail! I wasn't sure about the party till I saw you. I might have taken you anyway!"

"You never mentioned it till we were half-way there."

"I—I wasn't sure you'd want to go."

"I wasn't sure myself," said Lancey, nodding, "but the gown and the day made an adventure of it. It was—well, like playing at grown-up in your mother's clothes. Pretending. I knew your friends would wonder who I was, and I was afraid someone would recognize me, and tell them."

"Master Kent recognized you."

"And said nothing. That's when I began to feel ashamed." She saw him start to protest, fluttered her fingers at him. "Please, Dirck. Let me finish. Up till then it had been a game. Tappen and Schuyler helped make it so. Even meeting your family was exciting. There was the risk of being found out; the task of behaving properly. Could I do it, or not?"

Dirck, listening, nodded. He said, "But you told Eunice yourself."

"That was for fun." Lancey chuckled at the memory. "I couldn't resist pulling her off her high horse. She'll not quickly forget that she considered a riverfront fisher girl an equal."

"What makes you think you're not?"

"The fact that I sailed under false colors. If I belonged there at all it was as the real Lancey Quist. Not the way you introduced me."

"I was playing the game, too, Lancey."

"But why did we feel we had to?"

"Well," Dirck said, frowning as he thought, "for my part, it was an impulse. The hoax was amusing, but somehow fairer." He was choosing his words with care, judging their importance by the girl's attitude. "Fairer to you, Lancey. They met you without prejudice."

"What does that mean?"

"Look, Lancey. Don't think too lowly of my friends and family. If I had taken you there barefoot, straight out of Hendrick's boat——"

"Smelling of fish?"

"Don't interrupt. If I'd done that, people would have been kind. Kind and polite. Oh, they'd wonder why you were there, and Mother might draw me aside to ask, but you'd have been treated with great courtesy."

"Because I was your guest."

"I suppose so, yes. But you were that today, and there was no need to explain. You looked like what you are. A very pretty girl, whom it was my good fortune to know, and who honored me by her attendance."

He sounded, Lancey thought, completely sincere, and the compliments were pleasing. Still, she could never tell when Dirck was using compliments to weaken her defenses. The party had proved there was a far greater distance between them than the few miles of river between Rhinebeck and Poughkeepsie.

"Mistress Lancey Quist," she said, "of Poughkeepsie. She had a short life, but a merry one."

"Lancey——"

"Oh, come, Dirck. We fooled everybody, and we enjoyed it, but the jest is over. By this time your Eunice has spread the tale."

"She's not my Eunice!"

"She will be again," said Lancey. A shrug dismissed the afternoon; her mood changed to gaiety. She had acquitted herself well, and she could not resist teasing Dirck. "Once you tell her the truth. That you felt obligated to give the poor fisher maid a holiday from the nets."

"You make me sound like King what's-his-name and the beggar girl."

Lancey didn't know the allusion, but she nodded wisely. He looked, she thought, very boyish, bareheaded, with the straw colored hair awry. Almost, she envied Eunice Wynbridge. His blue eyes sparkled at her, merrily unclouded by her teasing.

"Any obligation," said Dirck, with a bow made comical by his tailor-fashion position, "has long since disappeared between you and me. Erased, wiped out, vanished."

"So?" Lancey tried to place the new note in his voice. It was bantering, amused, but with undertones of reckless purpose.

"Just so," he said, "because the girl I'm looking at bears no resemblance to the waif that pushed a plank over thin ice toward a struggling mare and her master."

"No resemblance? You flatter me, but——"

"If you mention your velvet gown again, I'll throw you overboard. I saw that other girl in naught but a blanket, remember! She was deucedly fetching, too."

The girl blushed hotly, spoke tartly. "I hope that, too, Master van Zandt, is erased, wiped out, vanished."

"Completely."

"Oh." In her surprise she gaped, then laughed.

"I mean it."

"Thank you for the lie."

"We start afresh, Lancey."

Before she could speak Dirck slid closer. He slipped his free arm around her shoulders, drew her against his chest. Lancey's muscles tensed; her fingers coiled ready to rake. She glared up at Dirck's laughing face.

"Velvet claws," he said.

"But——"

"Sit still. I have to hold the tiller with one hand. Aren't you more comfortable this way?"

Drawn slightly off the cushion, Lancey noted that her ankles were exposed. She'd been sitting with her skirt carefully hiked in back. The arm holding her was firm, but not too tight. Her fingers relaxed, but she didn't smile.

"I was comfortable before, Dirck."

"But not as comfortable, I'm sure. This is the only proper way for a courting couple to go sailing."

"Courting couple!" Lancey punctuated the words with a snort.

"Swain and damsel. I told you we were starting afresh."

She searched his face, trying to pierce through the mask of laughter. He couldn't be serious! Her body felt the warmth of contact, and she tried to quell a stir of excitement. God and Nicholas, she thought, this damned man always gets me fussed.

"Dirck——"

"Ah, my deepest thanks. May I reciprocate by using your Christian name, too, Mistress Quist?"

His exaggerated bashfulness, spoken with husky gravity, made her laugh. Lancey's amusement was genuine; his pretending appealed to her own love of play. Her reproof sounded almost gay.

"You are as mad as Bedlam."

"You're not the first to think so, Lancey."

"No," she said, gazing up at him, "I'll wager I'm not. There's Eunice for one, and——"

Suddenly serious, Dirck interrupted. He said, "Eunice has never been on board the *Argo*."

Lancey was surprised by her glow of pleasure. He had stopped grinning, but his eyes seemed even brighter.

"Nor has any other girl, Lancey."

She didn't quite believe that, but it was pleasant listening. The moment had an unreal quality that made a fitting climax to the afternoon. She had walked among the gentry, joined the world of fashion in a manner beyond her dreams. Now, the barely moving boat, the sultry air, the feel of his linen against her cheek, seemed equally fantastic.

"Should I be flattered?" she asked.

"Yes."

Warned by the tightening fingers on her shoulder, Lancey was ready when he bent his head. She merely raised her chin, and waited. Dirck didn't hurry; he found her lips with skillful ease, kissed her slowly and thoroughly.

Lancey, enjoying it, sat very still. Her fingers were locked in her lap, gripping hard to hold control. Only her mouth responded, answering pressure with pressure, savoring the sweet warmth of the kiss.

Yes, she thought, it's as I remembered, arousing and weakening, joyous excitement. It was hard to think clearly with her senses quickening. She was glad that Dirck was practiced in the art. When she was breathless, she drew her head back.

"Lancey."

Dirck's face was very close; she felt the breath of his whisper. Her own breast rose as she drew in air. Her eyes, opening, blinked at the light. It seemed unreal, too, strangely livid.

"Well," she said, with a false coolness, "I suppose a passenger must always pay the fare."

"Lancey!" Dirck stiffened as if he'd been slapped.

"But this one is a gift." She took his face between her hands, held it an instant, smiling as she watched anger give way to delight. "You'll please accept it as such."

"I am honored."

She wanted to kiss him again, but he mustn't think she invited liberties. She said, "This much, and no more, Dirck."

"Yes, Lancey."

"All right, then."

This time, as they kissed, Dirck let go of the tiller to put both arms around her. Lancey clasped her hands behind his neck. They held each other in a fierce embrace, crushed chest to chest. Lancey felt a caressing palm on her back, scarcely heard his murmur above the tumult of her pounding heart.

"Lancey, Lancey."

"No, Dirck. Stop."

"But——"

"Oh, please."

At that moment the squall hit them.

It struck with scant warning. A few big raindrops spattered the boat; one slapped on Lancey's knuckles. The others, rattling against the sail, made noise enough to penetrate their passion. They sat upright, staring at each other, puzzled and confused.

"What?" said Lancey, thick-tongued. "What?"

Dirck glanced wildly around, blanched. Even as the blood drained from his cheeks the rain-filled wind roared down on them.

The *Argo* pitched, shivering, before that quick, slashing attack. An instant brought the river to a boil; waves leaped above the gunwale in sudden, white-fanged fury. The rain was heavy and drenching, but the wind was savage, berserk power.

"Get the sail down!" screamed Lancey. "The sail!" The storm whipped the words from her mouth. She knew the danger of a northern-bred river squall.

"Take the tiller!"

Shouting, Dirck leaped for the spritsail. He was too late. He was reaching for the strut that held the canvas spread when a line snapped, flicked past his ear. The sail, taut as a drumhead, seemed to float away from his outstretched fingers. Then, as the mast jumped in its socket, the little skiff twisted and reared like a frightened pony.

Lancey, gripping the useless tiller, was sure that the *Argo* was going. The gale plucked her cloak from the boat, flipped it, whirling, through space. Skirts fluttering, half-blinded by the rain, the girl felt the boards beneath her knees heave as if pushed from below. Turning, she had a glimpse of Dirck tilting one way as the mast tilted another.

Some kiss, she thought, raging because the squall had caught them unprepared. They'd behaved like a pair of dolts who'd never seen a river!

Helpless in the grip of the wind, the tiny *Argo* capsized. Lancey, in that insecure second while the skiff hung, heeled over, between balance and upset, heard the crack of the toppling mast. She waited no longer, rose from her knees with thrusting legs, left the doomed boat in a flat, shallow dive.

She hit the roiling water, face down, with a skilled smoothness that barely knifed under the surface. The river was more chill than she'd expected after the sun-baked day, but she'd known it colder.

Lancey was still angry, unafraid. The mishap was their own fault, but there was no reason to panic. She was a strong swimmer, self-taught in this very stream. Maybe it wasn't a lady-like practice, but it was mighty handy on the riverfront.

As she turned, raising her head among the angry whitecaps, skirt and petticoats wrapped themselves around her legs. The hampering feel of the sodden garments gave Lancey her first shock. She remembered her russet velvet gown.

"Oh, God!" she wailed, aloud. "Ruined!"

"Lancey!"

Dirck's voice, muted by the swish of wind and rain, sounded frightened. Through the gray haze of storm-darkened day Lancey could see the overturned skiff, keel gleaming wetly on the water.

"*Lancey!*"

"I'm all right! Stay there!"

She paddled toward the wreck, fighting the clinging weight of her clothes. Calmly she considered and rejected stopping to remove her shoes. Not yet, she thought. The water heavy velvet made her grimly determined. She could not afford to lose both the dress and her best footwear.

Dirck came thrashing toward her, and she yelled at him.

"Go back! Hang on to the skiff!"

Open mouthed, treading water, he gaped at her.

"You can swim!"

"Of course, I can swim!"

Not for long, she thought, nor far, encumbered like this. She noted that Dirck, turning beside her, swam with steady, powerful strokes. It was only a few yards to the boat, but she found it a struggle. At last she touched the smooth wood, leaned against it gratefully.

"All right?" asked Dirck.

"Yes," she said, panting, "it isn't the swimming, it's my clothes."

He shook water from his eyes, gazed at the sail floating beside them. His voice was sorrowful. "Poor *Argo*. She never had a chance. It took less than a minute."

"Where are we?" Lancey had an arm draped over the skiff's round bottom, resting. The wind still lashed the river, dashed spray over them, but she judged the worst of the squall had passed. They always struck like lightning, never lasted long.

"I don't know," Dirck said, ruefully. "I wasn't watching."

"North of Poughkeepsie, anyway." Lancey raised herself, peered toward the west bank. The rain drew a misty curtain in front of the shoreline; it was impossible to find a landmark. "About mid-river, I think."

"We were about the middle." Dirck gauged the drift of the skiff on the ebbing tide. "And we're not going to get to shore this way. We'll have to swim for it."

Lancey looked at him. They were both clinging to the wreck with a hand hooked under the submerged gunwale, and an arm hugging the curve of the hull. He had less trouble hanging on because he was lighter clad. She saw that his jacket was gone, and guessed he'd discarded his shoes.

Dirck mistook her silence for apprehension. He said, "If it's too far for you, Lancey, we'll stay right here."

"It's not the distance."

"Well, then, why——"

"I can't swim dressed like this!" She was impatient with his obtuseness.

"Take things off."

"No."

Dirck stared, puzzled by her cold tone. His own impatience was kindled by hers. He blamed himself for the accident, but it wasn't the first craft upset by a river squall. After all, the *Argo* was his loss, and the girl could at least cooperate to save her own neck.

"Lancey, use your common sense. We could drift like this for hours. Sooner or later we'll have to swim."

"Later, then." Lancey realized she was being stubborn. Dirck was right; it was senseless to postpone the inevitable. Yet she couldn't bring herself to a decision.

"Why wait? We'll just get colder."

"I don't care." She bit her tongue after she spoke. The statement sounded so foolish. Feeling the leaden drag of her soaked dress she wanted to weep for its lost beauty.

"Lancey," said Dirck, as if humoring a child, "this is no time for proprieties, for modesty. I promise I won't even look if that's what——"

"It's not that, blast you!"

"Oh." Frowning at her vehemence, he sought the reason behind it. It wasn't like Lancey to act skittish in an emergency. His voice quickened, stirred by a fresh idea. "Look, if—if it's your laces or something—getting out of your clothes, petticoats, I mean, if you need help, why, I'll do what I can."

She laid her forehead against the keel, and her shoulders shook. Laughter, tinged with bitterness, flavored her speech.

"Haven't you done enough, Dirck?"

"For God's sake," he said, angrily, "I'm not just trying to undress you!"

That brought her head up. The wind had lessened; the rain had slackened to a steady drizzle. Lancey spoke quietly, almost wearily, but her tone cut through the hissing murmur of the storm.

"I'm not being a prissy idiot, Dirck. Whatever you may think. These clothes, this dress, they're my best, and the dress was *new!* It's not easy to—to give them up, to let the river have them."

"You needn't. We'll lash them to the skiff. I mean to recover the *Argo.*"

"The *Argo* can be fixed. The dress——" Lancey's shrug was a gesture of despair.

"Then why risk your life for it?"

"I'm not," she said. "I know I can strip it off, and easily make shore in my shift. It's *doing it,* that's hard!" She saw the impatient toss of his head, flared into anger. "First and last you've brought me naught but ill luck!"

"Me?"

"You! You're my goblin, Dirck, an evil spirit that lures me into the river!" All her mixture of Dutch lore and fisherman superstition was fertilized by her resentment. "Somehow you're a Jonah!"

"Now wait, Lancey. I'll admit I was careless, but——"

"Careless!" Lancey knew she was being unreasonable, but she

154

didn't care. Emotions pent-up by the etiquette of the afternoon, heated by kisses, dampened by her ducking, came boiling from deep within her. "'Twas wantonness upset us, and well you know it!"

"Maybe," said Dirck, grimly, "you think that was all my doing, too!"

"You started it!" Honesty checked her bitterness, changed her tone. "Ah, no. Fair's fair. It takes two, and my guilt's as great as yours!"

"Guilt," he said, with a laugh, "is a harsh term for a couple of harmless kisses."

"Dirck," Lancey said, "Dirck." She beat her palm on the side of the skiff as if physically tapping her thoughts into shape. "Together, we —we curdle everything we do—like vinegar in milk. There is a curse, a hex, on our meetings. On the ice with Meda, at the inn, now here—"

"Lancey, that's nonsense."

"Is it?" She cast a glance northward into the mist toward the Catskills, and shivered. "Or is it that the bowlers in the mountains think we should each stay in our proper place?"

"Well," said Dirck, "you can't call this river a proper place for anybody."

His calmness stopped her torrent of words. He doesn't understand, she thought, but without irritation. The ridiculousness of arguing while chest deep in a rain swept river brought a fleeting smile.

"You're right, of course," she said. "But so am I," she cried silently. The wetness of her face tasted salty; she wasn't sure whether from tears or tide. "We'd best swim."

The drizzle hung around them like gray vapor, hardly stirred by wind that had dwindled to a breeze. Lancey let go with one hand, reached into the river, twisting as she tried to raise a foot against the clinging weight of sodden skirts.

Dirck, startled, grabbed her as her chin dipped under. "What's the matter? You weakening?"

"No. My shoes. They're a tight fit." Her fingers had touched a steel buckle before it slid away. Those, too, she thought, must be sacrificed. Her surrender was complete, but she would not forget who made it necessary. "I'll have to pry them off."

"Wait," said Dirck, nodding, "and hold tight." He doubled suddenly in the water, diving.

Lancey watched his hips break the surface, sink. She felt his hands fold her skirts along her calf, fumble lower, clamp around her shoe. Her knuckles were white as she gripped the gunwale to offset Dirck's added weight. Her foot slipped loose with colder bouyancy.

"One gone," she whispered.

A moment later Dirck rose out of the river beside her. His impetus carried him waist deep from the water, then he fell back in his own splashing. He blew out breath, sucked air.

"You're a crazy sturgeon," Lancey said. "Get your breath."

"I—I'll go down for the other shoe in a second," Dirck said, panting.

Then, Lancey heard the voices, and waved him to silence.

"What is it, Lancey?"

"Hush! Listen!"

They both were still, tense, listening. Through the misty drizzle, flat across the water, came the sound of talk. They could not distinguish words, but they heard two men. There was the creak of a tholepin, the slap-splash of an oarblade.

"Ahoy, there!" shouted Dirck. "Help!"

"Help!" Lancey's scream left her breathless.

"All right, all right." The unseen caller sounded annoyed. "Keep your hatch battened. We'll find you." He said something unintelligible, and someone else laughed.

"I know that voice," Lancey said. "That's Pardon Cash." She hailed again, joyful with recognition. "Pardon, it's me! Lancey! Lancey Quist!"

"Lancey!" Pardon seemed closer. The man with him swore a round oath.

Dirck said, "That's your friend Justin."

Nodding, Lancey thought it fitting that they should be rescued by fishermen. It seemed to prove the point she'd been arguing; she belonged with her own kind.

The rowboat nosed its way through the drizzle. Pardon Cash was rowing; Justin Pattison scowled down at them from the bow. His glare shifted from Lancey to Dirck.

"Let her run, Pardon," said Justin, and spat. He leaned over the gunwale, arm extended.

Lancey grabbed his hand, reached for the gunwale. She heard Justin's surprised grunt as he took her water-logged weight. They were both straining when Dirck's shoulder boosted her from behind. She tumbled into the boat, lay panting on the bottom.

"We ought to leave *you*," Justin said as he helped Dirck clamber over the side.

"Well, thanks," said Dirck.

"Don't get uppity," Pardon Cash said. "You both deserve that and more. I never seed such half-assed sailing in my life. Couldn't hardly believe it. There was that squall getting blacker and closer, and there, smack in its path, is a dinky, carpenter's chip of a coracle with a kerchief sized sail! Lancey, you know better than——"

"Don't blame Lancey," said Dirck, face scarlet. "We noticed the squall too late to lower sail."

"You should stick to horse riding," Justin said.

"You saw us, Pardon?" asked Lancey.

"Aye. *We'd* pulled in to tie snug, but you stood out like a boil on a wench's nose. Only Justin and me decided to make a drift this far north of the landing——"

Lancey realized she was lying among a catch of fish. She shifted, pushed one from under her. Its silvery color caught her glance, and she scooped it into her hands.

"Pardon!" Her voice rang with excitement. "This—this is *shad!*"

"Aye," said Pardon Cash. "Buck. They're starting to run, Lancey."

BOOK TWO: FLOODTIDE

14

OUT OF THE UNCHARTED EXPANSE OF THE SOUTHERN OCEAN, WHERE their presence was inconspicuous, the shad came north with spring. Each year the great schools of fish turned with the season, separated into regiments, swam in the same direction like a vast and purposeful army.

All along the eastern coast of the North American continent, from Spanish Florida to English Canada, on the serrated shores of the newly independent states between, the phenomena occurred. As the rivers that flowed into the Atlantic grew warm the shad entered their mouths. Their appearance was decided by no calendar date, but by the temperature of the streams. Unerringly, men believed, the shad knew this, as they knew which entrance to select. Drawn to the fresh water of their own spawning, they pushed upriver to fulfill their natural cycle, deposit their eggs, replenish their kind.

It was a series of successive invasions that increased in numbers as it progressed northward. The more southerly rivers knew the forays of the shad, but the major movements—the great runs that counted shad in thousands—started in the waters of Chesapeake Bay. Returning fish turned through that wide gateway in a mighty column, fought their way into and up the Indian named rivers: the Potomac, the Patuxent, the Susquehanna. Almost immediately another run started in the Delaware. Then, with a time lapse that varied as the weather, shad arrived in the Hudson.

This was not the final magnet to draw countless spawners from the migrating silverbacks. The Connecticut received its share, and other coastal rivers as far north as the cliff-banked St. Lawrence. These runs, however, came later, especially where the water stayed cold until mid-summer.

In the Hudson, as elsewhere, the buck shad, the male, appeared first, a numerous vanguard that seemed to test the dangers of passage for the following roe.

The greatest danger was man. Centuries before the white men

sailed cautiously up its unexplored channels, the redskinned tribes along the river's banks had noted the annual return of the shad. They hailed it as a fresh, ever-renewed, source of food, a change of diet, an occasion that supplied reason and dish for a feast. The warriors fished with every primitive implement they could contrive—spear, barbed hook of bone, rush-woven seines. No matter how many they caught and gorged upon, the shad still ran in myriad plenty.

More resourceful, the white men used nets. If their method was old, brought from Europe, the prize it entangled was new—new in shape and taste. The hauls from the nets exceeded the Indians' wildest dreams, but the running shad seemed undiminished.

A hundred and three-score years had passed since the Europeans first settled on the Hudson. Much had happened in that time; the river had witnessed many changes. On both banks Indian villages and lodges had vanished, been replaced by towns of sturdier houses. Ships of trade and war had sailed these waters; cannon fired in anger had mocked the thunder from the mountains. Men had died, and shed blood, as they made history.

The Dutch had vanquished the savages, and, in turn, had been vanquished by the English. These had ruled the land longest, only to be driven out at last by a rebellious people after a bloody struggle. The victors were a new, mixed breed, native born and immigrant, who called themselves Americans, New Yorkers, York Staters. They were part of a loose alliance of similar free states that were not yet a nation.

But the shad ran upriver to spawn in the year 1788, as always.

*　*　*

Lancey Quist, rowing behind her father, bent to the oars with grim purpose. She considered it her fault that Hendrick had yet to cast net in this year's run.

Her foolish accident with Dirck van Zandt had hobbled her father, given the other fishermen a head start. Hester, who had peeled off the soaked velvet gown in tight-lipped silence, had insisted on foot baths, rest, doses of steaming brews intended to ward off the ague.

"You look like a drowned cat," Hester said, "but you ain't gonna be a sick one!"

"But Pa needs me, Hester!"

"He can wait. The shad'll be coming for some time."

She'd never, Lancey thought, known her stepmother to be so adamant. A night and a full day passed before she allowed the girl to go outdoors. All that time the russet dress had hung, drying, before the fire.

As the boat slid along the darkening river, Lancey recalled another conversation. She was glad that no one could see her face now. Night was gathering around them, draining all color from earth, water, and sky. Already the high west bank was a dark bulk against a shadow streaked tapestry from which the last sunless daylight faded. It was an hour of depressing hush that suited Lancey's mood, made the remembered words tragic.

"You might as well face it, girl. That dress won't be the same."

"Hester, I only wore it once!"

"I know. But velvet don't take to drenching lightly. It'll dry, sure, but getting its looks back will take a deal of doing."

"I've seen you hold a velvet ribbon over the kettle spout and——"

"A ribbon's handy small. A full sized dress is something else again." The woebegone expression on Lancey's face had softened Hester. "I'll try, girl, but I can't promise success."

"At least Dirck saved my shoe."

"Uh-huh. Right smart of him to tuck it in his belt that way. But how'd it happen that neither of you noticed that squall amaking? River bred and reared, the pair of you."

"We were—talking."

"Talking, eh? Well, I guess that's close enough to the truth. Pigeons coo, and bullfrogs——"

"Now, Hester!"

"You needn't glare at me, girl. There's sharp talk and sweet talk. But any kind that could make *you* ignore a gathering storm is the kind that can loose the knots in a garter."

In a way, Lancey decided, Hester was right. Of course it hadn't come to garters or anything like that, but she had let Dirck's kisses befuddle her judgment.

As always the rhythmic motion of rowing, smoothly repetitive, helped her thinking. She could trust Hendrick to set stroke and course, let her muscles work at the familiar task while she thought about something else. You couldn't day dream and handle oars, but they seemed to quicken your mind for the solving of a problem.

Lancey's problem revolved around Dirck van Zandt. She felt that she'd settled it, but couldn't refrain from another last review of the arguments. They made her decision right and inevitable. No one, she felt, could help her reach that decision, and even Dirck would have to admit its correctness.

163

They were, Lancey thought, ill matched for anything but casual friendship. She had never considered Dirck as a suitor, a prospective husband, a devoted swain. The gap between their lives was too great for that, as unbridgeable as the wide Hudson itself. A Lancey Quist did not, could not, swim in the same school as the van Zandts. Men like George Clinton and Justin Pattison could prate of rights, and being born equal, but women knew better. Patroons were not fisher folk. Like should mate with like.

Oh, nonsense, said Lancey silently, who wants to marry him anyway? The fact that Dirck's touch could make her stomach flutter, his kisses heat her blood to boiling, was beside the point.

He was nice looking, clean, had wit and charm. The girl was proud of the way she coolly listed Dirck's assets. He was, mostly, fun to be with, could make a stone laugh, turned even sinful dalliance into a pleasant romp. All the more reason for her to make sure that he kept his distance. Such pleasures, repeated, could lead to but one ending. She knew, guiltily, that in a moment of desire she might easily welcome such an ending, but she considered this a bodily craving that had nothing to do with love.

You're a wanton, Lancey told herself, and no better than Nell Bogardus, or any trollop. She'd been lucky to discover this in time; she was determined to take no more chances.

Once more, the girl wished her older brother had not gone awhaling. She might not, she admitted, have sought his advice, but his presence would be reassuring. Ten Bush, after all, was a young man like any other. His quiet answers to a few careful questions might supply just the knowledge his sister needed.

"This is far enough. Let her run."

Hendrick's voice jerked her back to the present. Lancey shipped her oars, and they drifted. Sky and water were almost black now; the evening star was winking a welcome to a scattering of newly apparent fellows. From the boat the lights in the windows of Poughkeepsie houses looked like yellow flags strung haphazardly on the crest of the bluff. As yet there was no moon, and the only sound was the river current gurgling against the hull.

"Where's the lantern?" asked Hendrick.

"Here." Lancey passed it. Her father's face was a featureless blur. When he bent to shield the candle it was hard to detach his figure from the surrounding blackness.

Steel clicked on flint, clicked again to throw out a spray of blue and white sparks. The third try caught on the tinder, glowed orange, spread.

Lancey could hear her father's breathing, saw it made visible as the tinder turned cherry red, puffed into flame. The tiny triangle of fire, poked into the lantern, swelled over the candle wick; the flame split in two as the tinder was removed.

Hendrick quenched the lighter, shut the lantern's door. The candle's beam, diffused by the lamp's horn side-panels, gave his face a liverish tinge. He held the light over the side for a few moments, gaze searching the river.

Head turning, Lancey scanned the surface. There was nothing but the movement of the tide.

"Here, Lancey. Hang it."

She took the lantern, draped it on the peg at the boat's bow. There was small need for the marker on a fair night, but Hendrick was always careful. The light showed his net's position to barge ferryman or sloop helmsman as well as other fishermen.

In silence, Lancey rowing and Hendrick casting, they went through the routine of placing the net. The white floats slapped on the water in regular cadence, bobbed behind them like blossoms of foam in a wake.

As they drifted, waiting for the flood, Lancey noted that they seemed to be alone on the river. The other fishermen had made their drifts by daylight. Her father had reported the results at the supper table. Shad in every net; Pardon Cash and Justin were high boat.

Hendrick loaded and lit his pipe, the short-stemmed clay that he used while fishing. He waited until it was drawing to his satisfaction, blew a gust of smoke, cleared his throat.

"Lancey."

"Yes?" Lancey straightened, alert for an expected request. Unless something of note roused his interest Hendrick didn't usually clutter his fishing with unnecessary talk.

"You met Dirck's family? The van Zandts?"

"Why, yes, Pa," said Lancey, surprised. He knew that already; while she told Hester about the party, her father had been a silent listener. "His mother and father. His brother."

"It is an old Dutch family," Hendrick said, "but no better than your mother's."

"Nor the Quists!"

"Maybe not. Maybe when the van Quists came to this country the van Zandts were like them. The Delanceys, too. Your mother's branch, not the Tory one. But——"

"But, what, Pa?"

"Today is not the olden times." Hendrick replaced his pipe, removed it without inhaling. "Lancey, do—do you like Dirck?"

"Don't you?"

"Ah, sure, but that is not the same."

"What are you trying to say, Pa?" Lancey was careful not to laugh. It has just occurred to Pa, she thought, that Dirck is interested in his daughter as a woman.

"You are a grown girl now," Hendrick said slowly. "Your mother was no older when we wed." The fisherman shifted his pipe from hand to hand, turned it in his fingers, gazed into the bowl as if seeking inspiration from the glowing tobacco. "I—I would not wish you hurt, Lancey."

"Don't worry, Pa," said Lancey, with quick sympathy. She knew her father would never voice a fear for her virtue, but realized he might need reassurance.

"To marry, Lancey, is a serious matter. To marry above or below the place set by your birth makes all even harder. You are likely to— well, to become as a landed fish, gasping and flopping to get back where you belong."

"I am not marrying anybody," Lancey said. She was startled by Hendrick's expression of her own feeling.

"I know this," said Hendrick, unheeding, "because I did it. Your mother could have done better than a common sailor. Her family said so behind my back, but not always beyond my hearing."

"But you were happy!"

"Aye." A thoughtful nod added weight to the statement. "Against odds. But the odds are even greater for the girl who weds above her position. A man can fight back, win respect, acquire money, office, title by work or brains or chance. A woman—no."

Lancey admitted, and resented, that her father was reiterating her own conclusions. It wasn't fair that a girl could only improve her condition by a marriage resented for that very reason. At least it was true in the world she knew, among the established river gentry. In the frontier settlements west of the Hudson things might be different, but not even a long war of revolt had changed the iron-bound customs of the east-bank landed families.

"Pa," she said, impatiently direct, "I told you not to worry. There is no need. Between Dirck van Zandt and me there is naught but

166

friendship. Marriage has never been mentioned." That much, she thought, is true.

"So." Hendrick managed to make the word both satisfied and questioning.

"Are you afraid I might—lose my head?"

"Or your heart."

"No, Pa. I have a good grip on both, and Dirck is not the man to shake it. When I wed it will be my own choice, and until that time I can wait." Suddenly, she was angry; her speech sharpened. "God and Nicholas! Do you think me the sort that swoons at the first male that bows to me?"

"No, Lancey. But——"

"Dirck took me to his home. Jan Elmendorf got himself thrashed by Justin on my account. Neither happening was my idea, nor should I be held blame for them! I am not Jan's girl, nor Dirck's, nor Justin's!"

"All right," Hendrick said.

His tone mollified her. She saw that her father had restored pipe to mouth, was smoking. Her explanations, then, had calmed his fears. She felt a touch of sympathy for Hendrick; the emotion was a feminine mixture of superiority and pity. He would never know how close she had come to the very thing he dreaded. Even Dirck, though he might suspect, would never know.

"There's the moon," she said, "almost full."

"It's a nice night," said Hendrick. He sounded contented, glad to accept her remark as the end of discussion.

Lancey smiled up at the lop-sided white disk that glowed so luminously. Men, she decided, were not difficult to handle once a girl learned the trick. They believed what they wanted to believe, especially when they had no concrete evidence to the contrary.

Of course, she added righteously, she had told her father nothing but the truth, if not quite the whole truth. His advice had not influenced her judgment; she had decided to avoid Dirck van Zandt before Hendrick spoke. It was strange that the occurrences of the same day definitely changed her relationships with Dirck and Jan Elmendorf.

Neither man was aware of her feelings. Dirck, grimly sheepish in front of Pardon and Justin, had hurried away as soon as they landed at the Quist pier; Jan had sailed again aboard the *Lydia*. She expected objections from both, was ready to over-ride them. Jan, in his stubbornness, might be the more difficult to dismiss. He had no

Eunice Wynbridge to soothe his feelings, and his unwanted intentions were honorable. Fortunately he'd given her a perfect reason to be outraged. His scandal-feeding fight with Justin was unforgivable!

Idly watching the nearest float, Lancey turned her thoughts to Justin Pattison. Wet and miserable as she had been after the resue from the river she'd been aware of Justin's attitude.

Anger, she thought, recalling how Justin glowered at Dirck, is the man's ruling passion. It was, strangely, his most attractive mood, a fact the girl found bewildering. When he was calmly cynical, or mocking she wanted to box his ears, but something within her responded to his wrath.

Even when it smoldered, Lancey decided, and didn't flame into speech. His curt rudeness, his scowling disapproval had betrayed him. Justin could not have been more furious over their mishap if he owned and treasured the *Argo* himself.

Instinctively, she knew and cherished the reason. He liked her. Another man might worry when she risked injury, Justin raged. She was pleased by this, equally pleased because it was a silent admission that he no longer considered her to be Dirck's paramour. His glare had been that of a rival.

Lancey complimented herself on a victory. In spite of a bad beginning, she had managed to win Justin's interest and respect. His strange arrival, his service in the war, his intensity about political affairs, added to his attractiveness.

She must, she resolved, see more of him. From the way he talked Justin Pattison would understand why she resented the van Zandts and their calm assumption of superiority.

The white float, a pale cube on the moon-gilded silver of the river, bobbed and disappeared. Lancey blinked at the spreading ripples, waited until the buoy surfaced.

"Pa."

"I saw it," Hendrick said. "It ain't the first one either." He knocked the dottle from his pipe, strewed it over the boat's side.

Lancey caught the under-current of excitement in her father's calm tone. Their first drift after shad was already showing signs of a good catch. Her own feeling disturbed and puzzled her. It lacked the unalloyed glee of former years. She was glad the net was taking fish, happy for Hendrick's sake, hoped to beat the other fishermen, but where was the zest that had made her pulse race?

"At that rate," she said, whipping enthusiasm into her voice, "we'll fill the boat."

"Touch wood," said Hendrick, tapping a finger on the gunwale. "Never count them till they're landed."

"Are they running big?" Lancey was doggedly following a familiar pattern of conversation. She didn't want her father to guess her detachment. How anybody, especially his daughter, could be casual about the opening of a shad run would completely mystify Hendrick.

"Average. Calico and Tanner had some beauties."

"They don't sell. Anyway, not until their master's people are all fed. But, thanks to me, the others will skim the cream off the trade."

"Lancey, one day won't make that much difference." Hendrick was touched by her genuine distress. They had not discussed the delay enforced by her wetting. "Folks will not lose their appetite for shad in a single meal."

"But everybody and his crony will be on the river tomorrow!" Lancey willingly took blame in order to sound convincing. It was easier than pretending that fishing excited her.

"The idlers, yes. Not the merchants, the innkeepers, the workers or the farmers. They will buy as they always do. You must not feel bad, Lancey. The bright sun today drove the shad deep, under the nets. You'll see that we will do better in the night."

"I hope so."

"You'll see. Let us eat now, while we wait."

Unwrapping the parcel of food, Lancey was grateful that her father had substituted chewing for talk. She didn't want to berate herself too much, but she still couldn't explain her disinterest in an event that had always entranced her. She had fretted through a day of inaction; yearned to be on the water. Now she was here, and the shad were afishing, and her enjoyment was halfhearted.

Whatever has come over me, she asked herself, that has caused such a change? Instead of concentrating happily on the business of fishing, she was restless.

They ate in silence. The fare was simple; bread and cheese washed down with swigs of tea. They passed the stone crock between them as needed, found that its swathing of blanket strips had kept the tea hot. The drink was a luxury that Hester dispensed sparingly, but this night's quart was in honor of the shad.

Lancey, in her vague depression, was surprised to find that she ate as well as ever. Night air and exercise had whetted her hunger; she devoured every morsel.

The tide changed as Hendrick finished his post-prandial pipe. As the net drifted back it seemed to draw Lancey's indifference with it.

She felt the old stirring of excitement, welcomed and nourished it.

"Pa," she said, delighted at the lilt in her voice, "it's time to take a look!" She settled an oar between tholepins with deft eagerness.

"Row to the west end," Hendrick said, "and we'll pull them in." His grin showed in the moonlight, and he sounded younger. "I ain't seen one of my own yet."

"Ready or not," cried Lancey, "here we come!" She started to row, pumping her spirits higher with each thrust and pull of the oars. Every stroke sent them closer to the bright moment of hazard that never failed to elate her. The harvesting of the net drew in success or failure, good catch or poor; it was the best part of fishing.

"Now, Lancey, we ain't racing anybody." In spite of his rebuke Hendrick was on his feet, ready to reach for the net.

Oh, yes, we are, thought Lancey, as she jockeyed the boat into position. They were racing their own ignorance. Until the net was in the box, and the shad counted they would not *know!* She had trained herself to wait with patience, but waiting was nearly finished.

"Steady her now," said Hendrick.

"Steady it is."

Watching the first yards of net, filmy and dripping, fold across the gunwale under Hendrick's capable hands, Lancey wanted to shout with joy. This was the remembered tenter-hook tenseness, the breathless anticipation. She hadn't changed. She *was* a fisherman, after all.

Fisherman, she repeated silently. A girl elsewhere, and a woman at times, but a *fisherman* in this boat when the net was hauled aboard.

The sight of a shad, hanging in the coils of glinting web, swept away her last doubts.

Lancey knew it was shad. No other fish had the same glittering beauty. Night turned the green-metal of the back, the silver scales, into an incredible blue. It was the color of an exploding fireworks rocket, of a lamp shining through a pane of bull's-eye glass. She didn't need Hendrick's gratified comment.

"There's a handsome buck."

"Two feet if he's an inch!"

"I think not."

"At least, Pa!"

"Well, a real pretty silverback, anyhow."

The shad was still flopping on the bottom of the boat when

another, gills caught, dangled from the net. After that they came aboard in a steady, flashing succession of blue-white splashes.

Rowing, while her father gathered net, and deftly untangled fish, Lancey tried to keep count. The growing pile of shad bounced and wriggled in an ever-changing confusion that made the task impossible. When Hendrick straightened, finished, the girl shipped her oars. On her knees, forearm deep in shad like a miser laving himself in silver treasure, Lancey counted again.

"Well, Lancey?"

"I make it—sixty-five, Pa."

"Sixty-five." Hendrick's sigh expressed pleasure. "Not bad for an early night drift." His twinkle acknowledged Lancey's triumphant crow of laughter. "Not bad at all."

He was, Lancey thought with tenderness, the best fisherman on the river, the best father anywhere. She waited, knowing from his manner that he had something more to say.

No lights showed from Poughkeepsie now, but the town atop the bluff was bathed in moonlight. It softened angles, turned window panes to squares of mica, linked separate houses with dark bars of shadow. The moon itself had more reality; the town seemed without substance, a place imagined, formed by fancy out of gray-blue smoke.

A gentle breeze rose from the river, danced along the moon's track. Lancey took off her tricorne, shook her piled hair loose. It fell to her shoulders, and the wind stirred it.

"Pardon tallied fifty-three," Hendrick said. "Nobody did better, Lancey."

"Of course not. They can't best us, Pa."

She wondered, briefly, if Justin would be annoyed at their success. No true fisherman liked to be beaten by another boat. At least he would understand her pride in the catch. Dirck van Zandt, she recalled, caught shad for sport with hook and line. He probably couldn't tell roe from buck.

Her earlier, depressing lack of enthusiasm was completely forgotten.

"Ten Bush," said Hendrick slowly, "would have enjoyed this."

"Yes, Pa."

Both voices were low. They needed no further words. It was the first time that a shad run had started without Ten Bush in the boat.

15

Jaycock's ordinary was throbbing with noise. The heavy rumble of men's voices was punctuated by guffaws, tankards hammered on tables, cries for service. It was a jovial uproar that seemed to shake the whole building.

From where she stood, well back from the blaze in the wide kitchen fireplace, Lancey Quist could see into the inn's common room. Under the swirling haze of tobacco smoke the tables were crowded. Amused, the girl wrinkled her nose as she sniffed air baked to warm staleness, sharp with the odor of fried fish. The brace of shad that sizzled over the flame were browned to an appetizing color, but their steam merely blended with the older scents of the kitchen.

Nell Bogardus, cheeks flushed to rosy wetness by the heat, shook the skillet, set it back in place. Wearily she brushed damp hair from her forehead, glanced at Lancey.

"Shad," said Nell, with bitterness.

"It's only this time of year, Nell."

"Thank God for small favors." Nell cocked her head, listening, as an unseen guest raised his voice in song.

Lancey laughed, recognizing the singer by the bawled words, and off-key tune.

> *Oh, the happy fisher's life!*
> *It is the best of any;*
> *'Tis full of pleasure, free from strife,*
> *And 'tis beloved by many.*

"That's Seth Row," Lancey said. "He always sings that when his net is full."

"It's his gullet that's full now," said Nell, sourly. "Him and the rest. You'd think them blasted fish was real silver, the way those men take on about them!" She bent over the pan, turned the shad.

You couldn't explain, Lancey thought, about a shad run. Either you had the feeling or you didn't. It wasn't just fuller nets meaning fuller purses. For a few weeks, a couple of months, life along the river was changed to something miraculous like the draft of fishes in the Bible. Most of the town's males were infected by the same fever; she'd counted a score of boats on the river that afternoon, and the run was only a couple of days old.

Nell's complaint wasn't finished. She said, "I begged Digmus to hire more help, but he's too pinch-purse."

"This won't last, Nell. They just like to celebrate the beginning."

"Nell!" Digmus Jaycock burst through the smoke curtain that filled the kitchen doorway. The little innkeeper held a cluster of pitchers in each hand, shouted as he bustled past Lancey. "Ain't them shad ready? Master Venick wants his meal!"

"I can't hurry the fire," said Nell, whining, "even if he is new custom."

"A stranger?" Lancey was mildly curious. Jaycock's, below the bluff, drew most of its trade from the waterfront. No sloop had made port; a west banker who crossed on the barge ferry might be buying shad for an inland village.

"Rode in this morning," Nell said, "from upriver."

"Peddler?"

"Not him. Says he's aiming to buy land."

Lancey felt a peculiar sensation on the back of her neck, and turned. Digmus Jaycock, holding a pitcher under a keg tap, was staring at her over the top rims of his square spectacles.

"You still here, Lancey?" The innkeeper's smile looked as oily as his sweat-streaked face. A forefinger pushed the glasses up the bridge of his nose.

"You told me to wait."

"That's right, I did." Jaycock turned the bung's wooden valve, watched beer gush into the pitcher. "Had a notion. Might help Hendrick sell some fish if the price is right."

Frowning, Lancey nodded. Digmus would be sure to reap most of the profit from any transaction, but a sale was a sale. She said, "How many fish, and what's the right price?"

"Two, three dozen. Maybe more. A copper the shad less than today's cost me."

"Not for roe," Lancey said. "The full shilling for roe."

"You got roe?"

"Not many. But we will have. It's early to start cutting the price, Digmus."

"I got to ship them, don't I, Lancey?" The innkeeper drummed his knuckles on the beer cask. "And I'm the one's got the barrels to keep them alive in. This feller lives way out in Pleasant Valley. Sawmill man with a passel of hired hands. He *might* want a weekly shipment as long as they last."

Whatever Digmus was charging the sawyer, Lancey decided, it wasn't a bad offer. She knew from experience that prices would plummet as the shad increased. The prospect of a future, steady sale was tempting.

"Seth or Pardon would snap at it," Jaycock said.

"Hard money, Digmus?"

"Well—if I can get it. State paper for sure." The innkeeper turned off the tap, noticed Nell listening, and roared. "*Nell!* Them fish won't be fit to eat!"

"I'm going," Nell said, tipping the shad out onto a wooden plate. "I'm going." With a spoon she raked two potatoes, jackets black as char, from the embers, juggled them into place beside the fish.

Jaycock's bellow whipped her as she scurried from the kitchen. "And take note whose noggin's dry!" He smiled an apology at Lancey, dropped his voice to its normal tone. "That wench is a slattern. The man paid coin in advance."

"Nell does her best," Lancey said, disapproving of the way he bullied the hired girl. Her curtness wasn't noticed. She watched Digmus blow foam from the beer, drink deeply, set the pitcher aside, and start to fill another.

"Needed that," Jaycock said, wiping his mouth. He belched, spoke hastily. "All right, Lancey. Buck like I said, roe like you did." He held out a hand, palm up. "Agreed?"

"Agreed." Lancey touched his fingers with her own. "Of course, I'll have to ask Pa." Jaycock's nod was as meaningless as her remark. They both knew that Hendrick would agree.

"I'll cart the kegs over in the morning," Jaycock said. He grunted as another song rocked the common room.

This time the crowd was singing in full-throated chorus. Lancey, wincing at the loudness, was pleased by the selection. With more will than harmony the assemblage, beating time with feet and tankards, chanted a brave defiance that recalled the years of war.

> *Raise your bowls of rum and gin*
> *In a toast of rousing din!*
> *Confusion to kings,*

Their paid underlings,
And plague take all of George's kin!
Hey-oh, pass the flask 'round.
Hey-oh, quaff the toast down.

The song was applauded by a concerted shout of laughter.
Through the boisterous mirth Lancey heard Nell Bogardus squeal,
a thin sound like the cry of a startled gull. A moment later the hired
girl's voice, giggle shaken but clear, was raised in protest.

"Now, you stop that, Justin Pattison!"

Justin, thought Lancey, is here. She found herself on the threshold
of the doorway, staring into the common room. Frowning, she wondered if curiosity or jealousy had spurred the unconscious movement.
In any case she was glad she'd changed to clean homespun, donned
shoes and stockings, before coming to the inn.

Oven heat from packed bodies made Lancey gasp. Now she could
see the whole chamber, and at first glance there seemed to be no
unoccupied space. Men lined the walls, sat shoulder to shoulder,
back to back. The bonnets of the few women were a sprinkle of dew-
drops caught in a thick hedge.

Well as she knew the custom of celebrating the shad's return,
Lancey was surprised by the size of the crowd. There must be, she
judged, at least five dozen people, good reason for Nell to be harried,
and Digmus smiling.

Her gaze searched through the haze, seeking Justin. There were
candles on every table, but the light was dim, dammed by the sitters
into separate puddles. She recognized fishermen, carters, warehouse-
men, two shipwrights, a sail-maker. Except for the crews of the
voyaging sloops, all the riverfront trades were represented.

In a corner Seth Row argued, earnestly and drunkenly, with his
wife. Mistress Row was rigid with disapproval. At Seth's elbow Gerritt Kimmee sipped his mug and pretended not to listen. The talk,
loud and incessant, was so general that Lancey found it unintelligible.

"Lancey! Over here!"

Pardon Cash's shout overpowered other noises. Lancey turned,
saw Nell moving away from a table that blocked the cavern of the
empty fireplace. Pardon, half rising to wave and beckon, loomed
higher than the mantel. Justin, seated beside one of the post riders,
glanced toward her. The other man at the table was a stranger.

175

"Sit down, Lancey," called Pardon as she approached. "Where're Hester and Hendrick?"

"Home," she said, taking the stool Pardon vacated. These impromptu gatherings were too raucous for Hendrick, and Hester, of course, was bound by her husband's absence. Smiling, she watched Justin shove closer to make room on his bench for Pardon. "Evening, Justin."

"Hello, Lancey. Well met."

She knew, instantly, that he had been drinking for some time. No thickness of speech betrayed him; his movements were steady, his muscles in control. Justin held his liquor well, but there were tiny indications—the dark eyes seemed all pupil; his grin was recklessly aslant.

"What's your pleasure?" asked Pardon Cash. The big fisherman, too, sounded completely sober. "We're all partial to rum punch, but if you'd like gin or——"

"No," said Lancey, "rum punch is fine." She spoke with polite indifference, still gazing at Justin. Strange, she thought, how the drink made him more human, less detached. She was aware that she wanted to reach out and brush back the lock of hair that had fallen over his forehead.

"You know Albo, of course," Justin said, nodding at the post rider. "This other gentleman is Master Venick."

"Christian Venick." The stranger lisped on the *s*.

"Sir," said Lancey, trying not to stare.

"Mistress Lancey Quist," Justin said.

"Mistress Quist." Again the lisp hissed as Master Venick repeated the name. He was the only man at the table wearing a hat, and he raised two fingers to the prow of his tricorne.

The stranger's teeth, Lancey noted, looked too big for his mouth, pushed his thin lips into a pout. Amber-tinted spectacles hid his eyes, but brows and hair were black. The latter, by its stiff neatness, was a wig. Lancey didn't blame him for that. The poor man had need of any adornment he could use. His face showed the rough, yellow skin of lemon peel.

He was well, but not richly dressed. His broadcloth coat was bottle green, the waistcoat brown homespun. The ruffles of his linen were slightly soiled.

Pardon Cash drained his noggin, dashed the dregs into the fireplace. Reaching for a bottle, he yelled, "Nell!" Pouring, he winked at

Lancey. "You'll have this to sip before she even hears me." His next yell flattened the candleflame. "Nell, fetch another mug!"

"Surely," said Master Venick, turning his head to address Justin, "you know what this news means."

"Too blasted well! That's *seven!*"

"Lucky seven," Pardon Cash said, as he mixed.

"Not yet," said the stranger. "Not in this case."

"It's too close for joking," Justin said.

"Justin, what is?"

"Seven from nine, Lancey, leaves only——" Justin saw she was mystified, interrupted himself with a short laugh. "You haven't heard. Maryland has ratified the Constitution. She's the seventh state."

"You're sure?"

"Albo, here, just brought the news."

"It's true," said the post rider, glumly. Like most public employees he was a Clinton supporter. "The news arrived in New York by sail a couple of days ago. Maryland voted for adoption on April twenty-eighth."

"Massachusetts was number six," Master Venick said, "and consequently, Maryland——"

"I can count," said Justin. "I left Massachusetts because she joined the others."

Lancey could hear the harsh anger in his unraised voice, and once more it drew her, touched some kindred quality within herself. She wished to join forces with Justin, but the stranger's presence made her tentative. A woman kept her place, was forthright only before her friends.

"Seven is still just a hair's breadth more than half thirteen." She spoke slowly, glowed as the speech brought Justin's glance. "New York has not decided, nor Virginia. Of course the smaller, weaker states feel need of an alliance, but——"

"Nothing so small about Pennsylvania," said Pardon Cash. He softened the interruption by placing the drink in front of her. "I've been there."

"Or Massachusetts," said Justin, broodingly. His gaze went through her into the past, seeing not the girl but the hills of his home state.

"We are still the keystone," Lancey said. She was not travelled, but she knew her beliefs for truth. "By position, and wealth. Because of the river. Even the British realized that."

"You forget one thing, Mistress," Master Venick said. "When nine states vote this Constitution into being, it has been adopted. Done. Set up. In force."

"For those nine only!"

"Aye, Justin," said Pardon Cash, "but then it's sail with the tide or be left behind." He was arguing for pleasure; there was more heat in his irrelevant complaint. "Where the devil is that wench with my tankard?"

"It has not come to that yet," Lancey said.

"George Clinton won't let it happen." Albo Bosse shook his head in much the manner of one of his post horses fighting the bit. "He's got the votes pledged to whip it, too!"

The stranger smiled, bent forward. "You are both right. But votes can change. Clinton should never have tried to out-write Alexander Hamilton. That young man has the better wit, the sharper pen. He has drowned the governor and his faction in a flood of letters."

"I've read some," Justin said, "but not all."

"There are more than fifty," said Master Venick, "and I doubt not there'll be more."

Albo said, "What good's a letter if a body can't read?"

Master Venick ignored the remark. "Hamilton has another thing. Money. Gold to put those letters in people's hands. Yes, and enough maybe to cross palms and turn heads."

"True!" Justin drank, clapped his noggin on the table. "It's the same trick his kind always use. Buy and bribe. With the purses at his disposal he'll not have to spend a penny of his own."

"There are—purses—on *our* side, too."

Why did he whisper, Lancey asked herself, covertly watching the stranger. This Master Venick made her uneasy. It wasn't his looks, but his manner. He crouched in his chair, glanced around as he spoke, knifing his meal to cool, but not eating.

"I ain't got a side," said Pardon, with a laugh, "nor much of a purse either."

The post rider, feeling his liquor, hiccoughed. Albo's voice was thick, stubbornly argumentative. "Ought to have a side. Old George is the man to follow. Clinton ain't exactly a—a pauper."

"This," whispered Venick, "has naught to do with Clinton."

"Who then?" asked Justin.

Lancey, listening, noted that the conversation was now between these two. She was puzzled by Justin's quick acceptance of the stranger's attitude. He wasn't sneaky like Venick, but he had lowered his voice, and his attitude excluded Pardon, the post rider, and herself.

Christian Venick shrugged. "A few men who are against this document."

"Men without names?"

Yes, Lancey decided, Justin has talked like this before. He was sparring with the stranger, seeking information, interested. He didn't even notice when Pardon rose, went in search of Nell.

"Men with funds," Venick said.

"To do what?"

"A good question," Albo Bosse said, drunkenly.

Neither man bothered to glance at the post rider. There was, Lancey thought, an invisible chessboard on the littered table between them. Justin, motionless, waited for the next move, the stranger's reply.

"To make the blind see, help the dumb to speak." Venick had merely toyed with his food while he spoke. Now, he began to eat busily, plying both knife and fork.

"Preacher talk," said Justin, scowling.

Venick chewed, swallowed, grunted. He said, "Yes, and out of place in such company." He looked at Albo, bowed to Lancey, piled shad on his knifeblade.

"I must go anyway," said Lancey, annoyed. She thought the man rude, ridiculously mysterious. To her surprise Justin made no attempt to continue the conversation.

"We'll talk again," he said, rising. "I'll see you home, Lancey."

"It's not necessary."

"Oh, yes, it is." His grin was sudden, infectious. "I have need of the air. This place reeks foul enough to breed fever." He picked his hat from the floor, led the way to the door.

Lancey, following, remembered that she hadn't even touched her drink. Glancing back she saw Albo Bosse reach for it. She didn't care. Justin was willing to leave a drinking bout to be her escort.

* * *

The night was soft with spring, bright with stars. After the heat of the tavern, the mild breeze from the water felt refreshing, a light coolness that came at intervals. Beside the man and girl, as they walked, the river ran, wide and silent, bedecked in its finest night attire of silver-flecked black.

At first Lancey was content to stroll in silence. She tried, not hurrying, to match her step to Justin's longer stride. Her vision quickly adjusted to the darkness, but she gazed at the river, sure footed on the familiar path.

Justin, too, in spite of his drinking, moved with easy assurance. He didn't weave or stumble, kept close to the girl without touching. The upper part of his face was shadowed by his hat-brim.

They were well away from Jaycock's, out of earshot, and alone, before Justin spoke. His voice was subdued, suited to the deep quiet that surrounded them.

"Lancey," he said, "will you tell me something?"

"If I can."

"Don't you ever think of the future?"

"The future?" repeated Lancey, playing for time. She was a trifle disappointed by the question. If, as she suspected, Justin sought a learned, impersonal answer, she was not in the mood for such a discussion. She said, "Why, yes. Sometimes. No more or less than everyone."

"I don't mean marriage, home and babies, Lancey."

"No, I know you don't." Her laugh was dryly amused. It was like Justin to dismiss as unimportant the speculation common to all young, unwed females. "I do think of other things, too."

"Such as?"

"Well, by the signs the shad this year will run heavy, and that means we'll fish on the dark flood, and——"

He stopped abruptly, glared down at her. When the girl chuckled his snort recognized that she was teasing. "A fair hit," Justin said, "but too close for jesting. Not much else has been in anyone's thoughts since the first silverback was taken."

"'Tis a seasonal sickness and will pass."

"There's a worse sickness, and it is spreading. The news about Maryland showed that. But nobody at the ordinary seemed to take it seriously."

"With one exception. Your friend, Master Venick."

"No friend of mine," said Justin slowly, "for I never saw him before tonight. If that wasn't the rum punch talking, he has a plan. We could use a plan, Lancey. Any plan."

"You mean—about the Constitution?"

"What else?" Justin slapped fist into palm. "Everybody against it—from Clinton on down—is too cocksure, too certain of victory. It's the Hamilton crowd that is working, talking, writing letters. You don't beat a busy enemy by sitting still."

180

"Justin," said Lancey, putting her hand on his wrist, "why is it your concern?" Her fingertips felt his withdrawal, and she spoke quickly. "I'm not being a giddy schoolgirl. I know that the kind of government we get is important, but what difference will it make to you, personally?"

This was what she really wanted to know, and it gave her voice sincerity. How he answers, she thought, will give me the key to Justin.

"For one thing," he said, "I didn't fight a war to swap King Log for King Stork." He turned her toward the river, gestured at the dark rampart on the opposite bank. "There's a lot of country over yonder, Lancey. A lot, all different. I wore out boots marching through some of it. Jersey, Pennsylvania, Virginia. Counting Massachusetts and York, here, I've been in skirmishes across five of the thirteen states."

Lancey glanced up at him, nodded. They were standing close; she could feel his tall strength against her. His arm was around her, but he was gazing over her head, into the distance.

"And I've seen others," he said. "Connecticut. New Hampshire. Maryland. That makes eight. Besides serving alongside men from most of the others. Well, anybody that says the folks from all those places can be ruled by a single set of rules is talking hogwash."

"They did fight together, Justin."

"Sure they did. To get rid of a ruler, and a set of rules that didn't fit any of them! I'm not a blind fool, Lancey. I know there's got to be some sort of Congress in charge of certain problems—like fighting another war, or treating with the Indians. There's whole passels of border country claimed by two or three states at once, and you've got to have somebody can settle those arguments. But this Constitution they're buying—a pig in a poke if ever there was one—will shackle us worse than the chains we broke!"

Swayed by his conviction, Lancey said, "You figure they'll act the way Parliament did, then. Tax tea, and such like."

"They'll act any way they want once they're in power. And the word to remember is 'they!' The men in favor of this agreement. Rich, mostly. Landowners, slaveholders, merchants. They've the money to elect their friends to office, and pay for troops to keep them there. They'll vote for their own interests, and the devil take the rest of us!"

His vehemence, soft voiced to fit the hush of place and hour, moved her. She had heard the arguments before, but Justin gave them fresh meaning. Her interest in the year's great political question was variable; it was, after all, a strictly masculine subject that could be belabored to boredom. But Justin made it almost as exciting as fishing, a bugle call to battle.

"How can we stop them?" she asked, and felt his arm tighten.

"I don't know, Lancey. But you were right back there in Jaycock's. Our best chance is here in New York. They cannot leave this state like a wedge between New England and the rest. If New York defeats adoption, Virginia may do the same."

"But isn't Virginia——?"

"Washington's state? Yes! That's the trouble. He's been their foremost soldier since the old French wars. They're beholden to him, as we all are, and proud of him besides. The fact that he favors this new government will carry weight."

The general was one of Lancey's heroes, but he was far away. She leaned against Justin's arm, seeking the right words to keep him talking. Always practical, she said, "But if it's this state will tip the scales, then how do we make sure the iron is in the right pan?"

"There are ways," Justin said, grimly. "I'm not sure who started the revolt against Britain. I was just an apprentice lad, following my elders. But I learned who held on, and won. The people, Lancey. The men in the field, and their women-folk behind them. Plain, ordinary men, mostly. Ploughboys, settlers, carpenters, smiths. I'm not taking anything from the gentry that fought with us. They were brave enough. But they weren't the pudding, just the raisins in it."

"You spoke of ways, Justin."

"There is one way to get a hearing, and that's to stand up and holler."

"Oh, there'll be plenty of that done."

"Speechmaking, you mean. The delegates up to the courthouse ranting at each other. That's not the kind of hollering I'm talking about. My kind won't even have a voice in that debate."

"Governor Clinton will be there."

"Clinton!" Justin uttered the name like an oath. "All along this river you think he's the big pumpkin. He's on the right side this time, but he's no friend to the people. He proved that when——"

He checked in mid-sentence; the girl heard his teeth click together. She turned in surprise, let it show in her tone.

"When, Justin?"

"No matter. We'd better move along."

Lancey yielded to the pressure of his arm, was glad that he didn't remove it. She walked inside that protective arc, and found it pleasant. It was, she decided, companionable, comradely. Justin was all male, but a girl didn't have to guard herself every moment. He had other things on his mind besides wenching.

The niceness of the night made her wonder about that. He evidently liked her, talked to her like an equal.

"Well," she said, "we can't settle it tonight anyway."

"No, we can't," said Justin, laughing. He slid his hand up her side, drew her closer. "We can't decide anything, but thanks for letting me rave, Lancey. It does a man good to air his brains now and then."

"Does—a woman good, too," she said, pretending not to notice that his fingers were now lightly curled under the curve of her breast. "Most men don't think we have any."

"Fiddlesticks!"

"About politics, I mean."

"Don't fish for compliments, Lancey." Justin bent to look at her face, grinned. "You know blame well you've more than most girls— more of everything. You're a walking grenade, and a threat to man's peace."

"A grenade?"

"That's right. Dangerous for lads that don't know how to handle gunpowder, but part of a soldier's training." He was walking more slowly; the bantering voice was gay. "As a matter of fact, Lancey——"

Something stirred the darkness on the path ahead of them. Justin stiffened, raised his head. Lancey, annoyed by the interruption, glared at the movement.

A shadow detached itself from others, turned to bulk. They felt the ground quiver under the slow tread of hoofs, heard the jingle of a bridle. Then, it wasn't a shadow but a walking horse. Some trick of starlight magnified its size. The rider in the saddle looked a giant.

"Him again," said Justin.

"Who?" Lancey, whispering, was puzzled.

"Who's there?" called the rider.

Lancey gave a murmur of exasperated recognition. Dirck van Zandt, she thought, certainly managed to appear at the wrong time! The horse, moving closer, seemed to shrink to its proper proportions, and she knew he rode Meda.

"Is that you, Lancey?"

"Yes, Dirck." She made no move to withdraw from Justin's encircling arm. She could tell, without looking, that the tall man beside her was amused, at ease. He waited until the mare shuffled to a halt, and his greeting was coolly casual.

"Evening, van Zandt."

"Oh," Dirck said, "hello, Pattison." He raised a hand to his hat-brim, then sat, gazing down from the saddle. There was no stiffness in his manner, but only the mare, craning her neck, moved.

"What are you doing here?" asked Lancey. She heard herself carefully echoing the casual politeness of the men. Biting her tongue, she resisted an impulse to giggle. They were all acting as if this meeting on the river path were a nightly custom.

"Waiting for you," Dirck said. "Hendrick told me of your errand at the ordinary. Hester wished me to stay till you returned, but I couldn't." He paused, leaving unexpressed his desire to see her alone. "I've been making my farewells."

"Going away?" asked Justin.

"Yes. To New York." Dirck was fully aware of the linked figure the pair made. He kept his voice steady. "Chancellor Livingston wants to examine me on my fitness for the law. Master Kent thinks me ready, and my father wrote the chancellor."

"Naturally," murmured Justin.

Lancey heard the soft criticism. A van Zandt and a Livingston would exchange favors to advance one of themselves. She was, she told herself, pleased by Dirck's impending departure. It confirmed her choice; their paths had crossed by accident, were designed for separate routes.

"I'm sure you'll do very well," she said. "You are riding down?"

"Yes. I'll be away for at least a fortnight. I need Meda with me."

"Safer than sailing, too," Justin said.

The remark was flat, almost toneless, but it chilled Lancey. For one dangerous second she was frightened. Dirck had the wit to know an insult, retort in kind. Justin's speech, with its reference to the capsized skiff, betrayed a hidden anger. She did not want a quarrel between these two.

"Well," she said, before Dirck could speak, "I'm sure Meda will be more trustworthy in a squall than I was." Fairness forced her to take her share of the blame. "Her prattling will not distract you, Dirck."

"Nor her eyes," Justin said.

"Why," said Dirck, almost purring, "you don't do Meda justice, Pattison." He patted the mare's neck. "She's too much of a lady to say so, but she's hurt."

The genial foolery warned Lancey. Unless she did something the situation might flare into violence. Dirck's raillery was mocking Justin's bluntness, daring him to continue. In another minute, she thought with despair, they'll be bridling like schoolboys.

She took a step away from Justin, raised her hand to the rider. Dirck, surprised, closed his gloved fingers around her own. Her voice was clear, pleasant, without pleading.

"I wish you a good journey, Dirck."

"Thank you, Lancey."

"We've delayed you overlong, I fear. And Justin and I are late, too." Lancey drew her hand away, knew by the way Dirck released it that he understood.

"Of course."

Justin raised his hat, bowed. "I've no great liking," he said, "for laws or lawmen, but may you go far in your chosen trade, van Zandt."

"Thanks," said Dirck, showing his teeth. "The same to you, Pattison." He bowed in turn, flourishing his tricorne. "My compliments, Lancey. Farewell until our next meeting." A twitch on the reins set the mare in motion. "May Poseidon keep your net free of any strange, poisonous fish!"

"Goodbye," called Lancey.

Meda danced sideways, but Dirck checked her. They moved away at a slow, sedate walk. The mare picked her way along the rough path; the rider did not look back.

Watching them, Lancey knew her relief by the trembling of her legs. She hadn't realized she was so tense. Thank God, she thought, that Dirck had read the signal in her gesture, had accepted dismissal. Then, she frowned, puzzled by his last remark. Dirck had an annoying habit of larding his speech with bookish expressions.

"Who was that he mentioned, Justin?"

"Poseidon. Neptune. God of the sea." He barked a short laugh. "Hell, I've been called lots worse than a poisonous fish!" He turned toward the girl. "You sorry to see him go, Lancey?"

"Dirck? Why, no. He's just a friend, Justin."

"Your friend riles me. Especially on a horse. Horsemen always make my hackles rise, Lancey. Guess I was a foot soldier too long."

They went on toward the fishing village. Lancey had the feeling that something momentous had been settled. When Justin began to whistle, she joined in happily. Their trilled duet of *Yankee Doodle* seemed to salute their new closeness.

16

"Sixty-eight roe," Hester said, "and forty-three buck."

Lancey, helping her father unfold the net for washing, turned to stare at the fish piled on the pier. The shad, scintillating in the sunshine of the May morning, glittered with the brilliance of many colors, silver, purple, lavender, metallic green, the red of rust.

"Good," said Hendrick with satisfaction. "The roe no longer hold back." He had most of the net gathered between his hands, and he motioned Lancey away with a toss of his head.

Stepping back, shaking the web loose as its length increased, the girl couldn't share her father's feeling. After three weeks, with every netting heavier, the run was approaching its peak, but the price dropped with each passing day. A fine, curved roe, shading six pounds because of the bulge under the dorsal fin, now brought less than the early bucks.

The townfolk of Poughkeepsie, Lancey judged, were already revolting against a surfeit of shad. Customers were increasingly harder to find. She carried her basket farther afield each time she sought a market. The boats of casual fishermen appeared on the river less frequently, and even the fishers-by-trade, like Hendrick, didn't bother to row out in the rain.

As they dipped the net in the cleansing tub, hung it, and rinsed it with buckets of clear spring water, Lancey envied her father's placid contentment. For Hendrick a good catch was its own proof of success. What they didn't sell, and couldn't eat, would fertilize his little vegetable garden. If he paid his debts and had money left over, well and good, but all that was less important than a fine haul of shad.

Other years, she recalled, she had felt the same way, paying no more attention to mounting profits than to the ever stronger odor of rotten fish. During the tag end of the war, when she'd been first grown enough to help on a drift, the troop encampments downriver had supplied an unfailing market. In those days a fat roe had fetched a hatful of Continental paper, worthless except as pipe spills. No wonder Hendrick couldn't take money seriously.

The four springs of peace, too, had accustomed them to profitable seasons. With the river open the sloops returned bringing trade and goods. There had been lumber rafts floating down from the mountains, rebuilding everywhere. A new flood of settlers replaced the departed soldiers, and the dispossessed Tories; the militia hung muskets over mantels, and went back to work.

Lancey sighed, remembering, with a faint regret for a smaller self who had bartered shad for a clutch of eggs, or a crock of butter. Clinton's government had improved New York currency, but the valley farms, so recently stripped to supply an army, once more reckoned wealth in terms of produce. Other places, she had heard and read, suffered during that time, but along the Hudson, barring the normal wants of winter, few went hungry.

Even, she thought, when a boatload of shad brought no more than a stalk of rhubarb. Why, then, was she worrying about this year? The rule was as fixed as the moon's cycle—the more shad, the less coin. Who could change that?

"Justin," said Hester.

Startled, the girl swung around with a swirl of skirt. Hester, bare feet hooked together above the water, sat on the edge of the pier, bleeding roe for dinner. Lancey realized that her stepmother was continuing a conversation, not answering an unspoken question.

"Who told you?" asked Hendrick.

"Pardon."

"I wasn't listening," Lancey said, hoping they hadn't noticed that the name had caught her attention. "What about Justin?"

"Caught himself a mighty sturgeon."

"How mighty, Hester?"

Hester, fish in one hand, knife gleaming in the other, flung her arms wide in the immemorial gesture of fishermen. She said, "Pardon hefted it as bettering four hundred pounds."

Hendrick's sputter of exhaled breath expressed disbelief.

"Pardon," said Lancey, grinning, "strains the truth, too."

"It's big enough," Hester said. "I saw it."

"Sturgeon that size," said Hendrick, shaking his head, "would raise Ned in the net."

"They didn't net him. Justin gaffed him."

"Gaffed him?" Lancey stared at her stepmother.

"Speared him, I ought to say. Justin made himself a three pronged spear. Sort of like a stunted pitchfork, but light, you know, and different looking. Pardon says he stuck the critter neat as any Indian."

"Where was this?"

"West bank, Hendrick. North of the ferry landing, I gather. In the shallows along there. They saw this big fellow sporting around—you know the way them sturgeon leap——"

"I know," said Hendrick, growling.

"Pardon says this one flang hisself out of the water high as a sloop mast."

"Pardon says!"

"Don't be jealous, Pa." Lancey, hugging herself, was delighted by Justin's achievement, and her father's reaction.

"That's right, Hendrick. I'm only telling you what happened. The sturgeon was making such a racket they spotted him a way off. So they rowed over that way, and lit a torch, and Justin speared him by torchlight."

"Another lie," said Hendrick, stubbornly. "Ask Lancey. There was no torch on the river last night."

"They fished by early tide. You and Lancey didn't go out till after midnight." Hester laughed at her husband's face. "Hendrick, I *saw* the sturgeon. You can't know everything that happens on the river!"

"That's right, Pa."

"All right." Hendrick, nodding, replaced scowl with smile. "I believe. Justin did good. I wonder where he learned that trick."

Lancey wondered, too. She'd spent a lot of time with Justin in the past ten days, but he hadn't mentioned making any fish spear. Mostly they'd talked of simple things; how flowering dogwood differed from mountain laurel; why scarlet tanagers vanished after a brief appearance. Lazy talk, as careless as the fleecy clouds drifting across the May blue sky above them, and yet not aimless.

They were, she thought, both trying to learn more about the other. They swapped riverfront childhoods, boy and girl, Connecticut and Hudson, with the shrewd trading of cautious urchins. She knew Justin, an orphan apprentice with a hard master, had found beauty only outside that household of harsh prayers, coarse food, and heavy rod. Sometimes he spoke musingly of Massachusetts, of trout in streams as transparent as glass, of wooded hills aflame with autumn fire, of a mountain called Monadnock.

Having no experience with exiles Lancey did not recognize one when he spoke. She listened, moved because the man was moved, sympathetic to the tone as much as the meaning.

"You two going to sleep now?"

Hester's question ended the girl's reverie. Lancey saw that it was prompted by her father's arm lifted stretch. They had fished through the last hours of night, watched dawn from the boat. She wasn't tired but she looked at Hendrick as he cracked the knuckles of the linked fingers above his head.

"No," Hendrick said, "I want to see Digmus Jaycock. Three sloops came back last evening, too, and maybe the sailors will buy."

"I'm not tired either," said Lancey. "I'll take the basket. It's easiest to sell them fresh, before noon-day dinner."

While Hester packed the shad into the basket among wet leaves and riverweed, Lancey washed her face and hands. There was no sense in doing more. It would be hot walking in the morning warmth, and her bare feet would get dustier. Until work was finished, when she could bathe and change clothes, there was no losing the scent of fish.

"You want the barrow, Hendrick?"

"Maybe, Hester. If I can borrow Jaycock's cob and cart I'll peddle the town in style."

Handing the laden basket to her stepdaughter, Hester said: "I sent the girls down to Conrad at the horse-ferry. He might sell some to crossing passengers. We could row them down there easy."

"Good plan," said Lancey, thinking how hard they were trying. "Not much fishing around that ferry. The noise of the horses scare them away."

Hendrick chuckled, grinned at his wife. "Conrad will want a share. Charge me a copper the fish most likely."

"And all the roe he can eat," said Hester, broad face reflecting her husband's grin. She had no delusions about her son's greed. "It'll be worth it if he puts his mind to it. Our Conrad could sell kindling to the Devil."

"He may yet," Lancey said, "if he gets the notion." She turned away, laughing, with the basket balanced by its handle across her forearm. The laughter sounded false. There were times, she thought, when they could all use a pinch of Conrad's shrewdness.

As she left the yard, swinging the basket with the ease of long practice, she heard Hendrick's comment. Her father was evidently impressed by Justin's feat.

"You know, a sturgeon that big ought to fetch a fine, round sum."

"Happen," said Hester, dryly, "somebody is giving a banquet."

Lancey, striding across the hot stones of the shingle, hoped that

Hendrick's opinion proved truer than her stepmother's scepticism. Sturgeon was rarer than shad, a relief to jaded palates. With money clinking in his pocket Justin might be less bitter about the niggardly payment for fishermen's labor. She recalled his words.

"Less each day! And the lot of you acting as if it *had* to happen. Letting every man-Jack and horse groom set his own price! You all catch more shad, and more shad, and more, until you're bumping into each other in the alleys trying to give them away!"

"But, Justin," she had said in protest, "it's always been that way."

"That doesn't make it right, Lancey! Great God Jehovah! A shad run's your best time of year, soon over, and you don't get a fraction of its worth! Because you fight each other instead of the buyers. Yesterday Pardon sold a dozen fish to a man Seth Row was haggling with by chopping a shilling off his asking. Did it laughing, too, and bragged about it after."

"Seth would do the same to him."

"Sure he would! What else am I saying? You've got to join together, not fight each other!"

Ridiculous, Lancey decided, as she had while he spoke. Justin didn't understand a fisherman's glee when his boat beat all others. You couldn't control that, or the number of shad, or what buyers wanted to pay. The axiom repeated itself in her mind: the more shad, the less coin.

She climbed the bluff now by the nearest path, and turned south. It was cooler under the trees, though the green May apple underfoot was splashed with patches of sunlight that had filtered through the branches. Lancey knew she sought the shade less than the clearing where she and Justin had held that conversation.

"Well," she said, aloud, as if answering a squirrel who chattered at her, "it's not far out of the way, and I just want to see it again."

That afternoon, Lancey thought, was when I learned to know Justin best. She bit her lip, aware there was so much more to know, so much left unsaid. He had been vehement only about that single topic. The long years of war he ignored, and, to her surprise, he had avoided any discussion of the coming convention.

His attitude about the latter still puzzled her. When she mentioned the Constitution, he had glanced at her with quick, narrow-eyed speculation. Lancey, expecting heated argument, had been awarded a grin, a sudden shrug, and an evasive reply.

Almost, she recalled, as if he possessed some secret, too rare to share, too deep for my understanding. She was not unfamiliar with masculine condescension, but it seemed strange from Justin.

"A man, isn't he?" Lancey asked herself, then blushed at another memory.

They had ended that afternoon with a kiss, a long, lingering kiss as exploratory as their talk. It had been a very satisfactory ending. Her lips had parted willingly under his mouth; her body had strained against him in the tight embrace. Yet, in spite of trembling limbs and racing pulse, there had been naught of wantonness.

When they drew apart, Lancey recalled, breathless and stirred, neither had sought a second kiss. Turning, they had come away, along the very track she was now walking, in a hand-clasped, dreamy silence.

Retracing their steps, Lancey made the inevitable comparison. Justin had kissed her once; Dirck van Zandt——

"God and Nicholas," she said, flustered into speech by the fact, "I couldn't count them!"

There was, she admitted, a similarity in their kissing, and a very great difference. Both men gave pleasure with skilled assurance. Justin, she guessed, no less than Dirck, had practiced the art before. Neither grabbed like a lout, but Justin didn't try to butter her with a honeyed tongue; his smile had been tender, not gay.

Dirck made a game of love-making. Justin wasn't as easy to cipher, but he wasn't playing a game. He seemed to know the value of patience, savoring each slow stage of their growing love. She dreamed of that single kiss, anticipated the next, with joyful pride. She couldn't even think about Dirck without feeling guilty and sinful.

Yes, she decided righteously, she'd chosen properly in discarding mere carnal pleasure for a deeper emotion. Dirck wanted to get her in bed, but she didn't know half of Justin's urges.

Ahead, the trees thinned as she neared the clearing. The straight trunks stood, clear and dark against the daylight, like the struts of her fan when she held it before a flame. Lancey's step quickened as she hurried forward to the edge of the woods.

The glade was nature made, a tree hedged semi-circle of ground that fronted on the river. New grass, bright green and calf high, glistened in the morning sunshine, but was shouldered aside in places by outcroppings of rock ledge. These were the peaks of the bluff beneath; they thrust their humps, slate gray and stone blue, through the fresh stalks like a school of sporting fish. The river edge of the clearing was all stone, a craggy shelf some two score yards in length.

As Lancey stepped from the underbrush, she stopped, checked by a flash of startled disappointment. The clearing was not empty. Two men, backs to her, were sitting on a rock, gazing down at the river.

Then, she recognized Justin's tallness. Her hand rose to wave, her lips parted to call, but again she paused. The other man's bottle-green coat, sere and dusty compared to the grass, touched a chord in her memory. Justin's companion was Christian Venick.

Her hand stayed motionless, no words came from her throat, but a sound must have betrayed her. The men rose, turning with quick furtiveness. The movement, the tense instant before they spoke, reminded Lancey of a cornered mouse.

"Who's there?" Venick's voice was sharp, querulous.

"Lancey!" Justin called, in recognition. A wave of his hand signalled her to stay where she was.

The girl resented the gesture, resented the stranger's presence in the clearing. This Master Venick, she knew, was still at Jaycock's Ordinary, though she had not met him again. Her dislike was not due to his lisp, or hinting talk. He shouldn't be here, with Justin, in their private meeting place.

Whispering, the men exchanged swift sentences. Across the clearing Lancey was reminded of angry, darting wasps. She hesitated, tempted to leave, but curious. Why was Justin gossiping with Christian Venick?

Then, Venick turned away, and Justin, smiling, came toward her through the grass. He trotted, elbows tight against his sides, at the military pace she recalled from the troop encampments. She waited, watching him approach, searching his face for any shadow of annoyance.

"Morning, Lancey," cried Justin, cheerfully, as he drew near, "I was hoping you'd come by."

"Oh, were you?" The question sounded so callow that Lancey flushed. Her pleasure needn't make her simper! She glanced past Justin to where Venick was already edging into the fringe of trees. Even his walk, she thought, was strange, a sliding gait that seemed ready to explode into flight.

"You and Hendrick make a good drift?"

Her gaze met Justin's. The scarred eyebrow, she thought, never looked more quizzical. He was still smiling, but the dark eyes seemed wary. She shook away the feeling with a toss of her head.

"Fair enough, Justin. I heard about your sturgeon."

"Bull luck. Couldn't miss."

"Justin," she said, with a nod at the now empty clearing, "what was he doing here?"

"Venick? Why?"

"Well, no reason, but——" She paused to let him interrupt, continued when he didn't. "I just thought of this clearing as off the beaten track."

"He was strolling, out for a morning walk. Stumbled in here and found me waiting. We passed the time of day."

Lancey found the explanation a shade too long, a trifle glib. It wasn't like Justin to be unnecessarily wordy. Somehow she was reminded of their first encounter, the night she'd caught him at her father's boat. She said, laughing, "You certainly had your heads together."

"Did we?" asked Justin. "Well, Venick's a man with some opinions worth listening to."

"Venick?"

He frowned at the surprise in her tone. "Yes, Lancey. You shouldn't judge a horse by its color. Venick's all right when it comes to making sense."

"About what?"

"Several things," Justin said, laughing. "The taste of sturgeon. The price of farm land. What New York paper is worth in New Hampshire. And who's the prettiest wench around Poughkeepsie!"

"Who'd he vote for—Nell Bogardus?"

"Nay, I'm the one favored Nell."

This cool mockery was more like Justin, and Lancey felt suddenly that all was well again. His pretended gravity made her chuckle, and she responded to it with exaggerated disdain. Flouncing away from him, she spoke with prim hauteur.

"Favor in return for favors, no doubt."

"In a fashion." Justin waited, grinned when she looked at him. "Twice now she has added my score short by several drams. Such a bar maid is a pearl without price."

"Your wily tongue befuddled the girl."

"I must remember that." Justin reached to help her with the basket. "It is no small gift, and may come in handy with other females I encounter."

"Then come along, and help me talk housewives into buying shad."

They left the glade, swinging the basket between them, linked by it and by a shared well-being. As they walked among the trees, Lancey, in spite of laughter and gaiety, was stirred by a flicker of uneasiness. She was glad she'd met Justin, delighted that his mood was light, happy in his company.

But, she thought, he didn't really tell her anything about Master Venick. Once more he had neatly evaded more questions by shifting the subject.

The girl berated herself for such pettiness. She couldn't expect a man like Justin, trained in self sufficiency, molded by lonely trials, to become effusive overnight. It wasn't that he didn't trust her; he wasn't used to trusting anybody. He'd kept his own counsel too long to prate it easily, even to a loved one.

She understood the feeling. She had no intention of telling Justin all that had passed between herself and Dirck. Why, then, should she be bothered by Justin's evasions? She resented the fact that she was.

"Tell me about the sturgeon?" asked Lancey, forcing the uneasiness away.

"Not much to tell, Lancey. That fish was drunk or crazy, having a high old time coming upriver. Any brains he had were addled from slapping back into the water after leaping out of it. He came straight for the torch and—*zing!*"

Justin raised a fist beside his head, snapped it down as if casting an imaginary javelin.

"Didn't he struggle?"

"Like a bagged wildcat. But the spear went deep and mortal. Pardon was there to help, and between us we boated him."

"Have you sold him?"

"Pardon took him down to town first thing. He hadn't come back when I left."

"But, Justin, he was your fish!"

"It's Pardon's boat, and we're partners now that my debt's paid. Anyway, I can trust Pardon to get the most out of that sturgeon, brag or booty. He's better at both than I am."

That was true enough, Lancey admitted, but few fishermen would let another tell the tale of a prize catch. Justin, of course, for all his skill, wasn't really a fisher-by-trade. She wondered how long he would be content on the river.

"Justin, if your debt is paid, will you be leaving?"

"Leaving?"

"I mean, well, you have your things from von Beck's——"

"Such as they are. I've no reason to leave, Lancey, and several to stay."

"Such as the shad," she said lightly, glowing at his decision.

They left the woods at a stone-fenced mowing that bordered the Post Road. The grass of this field was thick with clover, scenting the warm air, but not yet ripe for haying. Higher overhead now, the sun was a gold coin heating itself to an ever-brighter polish.

Lancey's bare feet felt the sun dried crumbs of the roadbed beneath them. Each trudged in a wheel rut; the ridge between was too narrow to walk abreast. Lancey carried the basket. It was her task. Justin's bootheels raised the larger puffs of tan dust.

Southward, ahead of them, the road stretched for a curveless mile, crooked as a dropped string but always visible. Lancey thought it resembled a forest brook running between tree-lined banks. The rich dark mud of thaw-time had been parched and thinned to trampled dirt.

"Yonder comes travellers," said Justin, nodding down the road.

A dust cloud seemed to form far in front of them. It billowed high, spread, rolled toward them like a bowled ball. Lancey could see the dark smudges of figures inside the tan veil of the cloud, and then two riders above its outer edges.

"We'd better give way," she said. She stepped from the rut and onto the grass beside the road. Justin, across the way, drew aside, removed his hat and mopped his face.

The dust fell back, and the figures emerged from it. There was a covered chaise in the middle of the road, and an out-rider on each flank. The horse in the shafts, a shiny-coated black colt, trotted with frisky, high-stepping ease. Both riders held their mounts to a lope that kept pace with the colt.

With a gasp Lancey recognized the near rider. Tappen Platt, on a gray cob that matched his jacket, rode as if glued to the saddle. The girl's head swung as she glanced at the other horseman, saw Schuyler Davis atop a tall chestnut. Then, turning back to the chaise, Lancey froze. A glimpse of bonnet and cloak were enough. She was certain the driver was Eunice Wynbridge.

Lancey wanted to run, knew it would be ridiculous, scampering flight. She braced herself, legs wide, toes digging into the soft earth. Every detail of her appearance flashed through her mind; bare legs, patched and stained dress, sweating face, tangled hair.

"Oh, no," she whispered in horror. She could not have looked worse. The shad in her basket seemed to double their odor.

For an instant she hoped they'd sweep by, not noticing her except as a roadside waif. A moment later Tappen Platt's grin flashed and he shouted, an unintelligible whoop of joy.

It drew the others' attention. Schuyler Davis glanced, blinked, stared. Eunice Wynbridge's face, even as it became visible, displayed wide-eyed surprise. Then, the cool, even features were contorted by a spasm of devilish glee. As her hands drew the reins tight Eunice was composed again.

She drove well, Lancey noted, and wished that the colt would bolt. Chaise and horses slowed, came to a halt beside her. She could see Justin across the back of the black colt. He was puzzled, frowning.

"Mistress Lancey," cried Tappen Platt, his gray cob curvetting as he doffed his hat, "well met!" His florid cheeks darkened with silent laughter. "I'd not hoped to see you so soon."

"Nor I, you, Master Platt."

Schuyler Davis, bowing, said, "Your servant, Mistress."

His grave tone nearly undid Lancey. She bowed her thanks, knowing he meant to be kind, unable to bear kindness at the moment. She wanted to rage, curse, hurl a clod at Tappen Platt's pug-nose. His amusement, she knew, wouldn't fluster her if that damned Eunice was absent.

Eunice Wynbridge's laugh was soft delight. "Ah, yes," she said, "the fisherman's daughter. And have you fish for sale today, my dear?"

Don't blush, Lancey ordered herself, don't give her any satisfaction. Her voice tried to match the other girl's cool politeness.

"Today and every day, Mistress Wynbridge. These are shad."

"Shaaad!" Tappen Platt bawled, in imitation of a town street peddler. "Fresh caught shaaad!" He brought his fist to his mouth, thumb stiff, and bleated like a fishmonger's horn.

"Friends of yours, Lancey?" As he spoke Justin walked across the road in front of the colt. He stood beside Lancey, hands on hips.

"Hardly," said Eunice Wynbridge.

"As you say," Lancey said. "Hardly."

Schuyler Davis said, "Eunice speaks for herself, Lancey. And Tappen would jest at a funeral. Wouldn't you, Tappen?"

"Have," said Tappen Platt cheerfully.

"We waste time," said the girl in the chaise. "I would like to buy your shad, my dear. It is so much nicer to deal with a person one knows."

196

"How many?" Lancey gazed blandly at the other girl. You know me all right, she thought, and I know you.

"Why, the whole basket, my dear." Eunice fumbled in a purse, clinked coins in her hand. She leaned sideways from the chaise, arm extended. "I do hope this will be enough money."

"Shad are selling," said Tappen Platt, "at about——"

"Tappen," interrupted Schuyler Davis, "hush up." He was watching Lancey and Justin.

Lancey couldn't move. She wasn't sure whether Eunice wanted her to refuse the sale, or would get more pleasure out of tossing alms to the beggar girl. Justin moved from beside her, reached out his palm.

Eunice, frowning, said, "Is this—gentleman—your partner, my dear? A swain, perhaps?"

"You may give him the money," Lancey said.

"Of course. You know best."

Justin took the coins, glanced at them, returned to Lancey. He showed his palm. The girl saw the glint of gold and silver, dark coppers. Her anger blurred the sizes of coins, and she couldn't figure.

"Justin?"

"Roughly," he whispered, "five dollars."

All right, Lancey decided, if she wants to throw her money away! She was suddenly reckless, intoxicated with the thought of more than double price for her shad. She walked toward the chaise with slow, dragging steps. Her shoulders were slumped, and she gazed at the ground.

"It's very generous, ma'am," she said humbly, stressing the title as she stopped beside the vehicle's dashboard. Her anger had changed to grim purpose.

"Thank you," Eunice said, "but charity should be. I'm sure my little pittance is well deserved." The rich girl was enjoying herself. "Now, if you'll just place the basket here beside my feet——"

"The basket, ma'am?" Lancey raised her head. The hazel eyes flashed as she laughed in Eunice's face. "But I never sell the basket. You only bought the shad, Mistress Wynbridge, and here they are!"

She tilted the basket, shook it empty. Fish and weeds tumbled, in slimy cascade, into the bottom of the chaise. Shad slithered across Eunice's shoes, bounced against her skirt. One fat silverback, as if sporting, seemed to try a leap for the lady's lap.

"You——!" Eunice Wynbridge squealed as she recoiled.

Lancey whirled, slapping the empty basket across the black colt's rump. The horse whinnied, reared in fright. Before his front hoofs returned to the roadbed, Lancey was running. She darted up the bank, legs flashing, raced for the trees.

She heard the quick rattle of sound as the colt bolted: hoofbeats, the whir of wheels, a cry from Eunice. Tappen Platt's bellow was choked with laughter. Lancey glanced over her shoulder, saw him spur the gray cob in pursuit. The chaise, swaying, was already yards down the road, dragging a cloak of dust behind it.

Runaway, thought Lancey, and stopped. She wasn't sorry, but she was suddenly ashamed. Her only answer to Eunice Wynbridge's barbed patronizing had been a gamin trick, a guilty child's flight. If the rich girl were injured, Lancey would be to blame.

Justin, poised for battle, was watching Schuyler Davis control his startled chestnut. The tall man quieted his horse, sat, laughing, in the saddle. He spoke to Justin, turned to gaze at Lancey.

She felt she'd forfeited his good opinion. Her action, however provoked, now seemed a crude jape. But Schuyler Davis raised his tricorne in salute, heeled the chestnut, and cantered after his companion.

Lancey leaned against a tree, and waited for Justin. She stared, unseeing, at the ground in gloomy disgust. Eunice Wynbridge had treated her like a gypsy peddler, and she herself had proved the treatment correct. How Dirck van Zandt would laugh when he heard! She winced at the thought, hearing amused contempt.

Folding her fingers over the coins, Justin spoke with bitter sympathy.

"Feller on the chestnut says not to worry. That wench can handle the colt, Lancey. Too bad."

"I—I don't want her hurt, Justin."

"That kind are bound to get hurt someday." He gazed down the road broodingly. His voice was low, but bitter. "I heard her. She and all her kind are going to get their carriages upset sure as Judgment. Upset and smashed to splinters."

Lancey wasn't sure what he meant, but knew he was on her side. She reached out and pressed his arm. Justin, after all, was worth a dozen Eunice Wynbridges!

17

THE GREAT SINGLE TAKING OF SHAD THAT ASTOUNDED TOWN AND RIVER-front happened on a balmy night in late May. That catch was as much a surprise to the netters as it was to the captured fish.

There were signs, omens that any good fisherman could read, but these promised only successful drifts, not opulence. A series of hot days had warmed the whole valley; a warmth retained after sunset. The moon was full, and the water, even at darkest floodtide, was temptingly mild. Lancey Quist, who bathed in it that evening, found it refreshing but without chill.

The girl swam, in the half-light of dusk, from her favorite beach, a little cove sheltered by trees and cliffs. Time and place were chosen with care; she wanted no one to catch her in the short, threadbare shift she wore while swimming.

When she came out she tossed aside the wet garment, and let the air dry her skin. Her strip of sacking-towel was used on the sodden mass of her hair. Lancey rubbed scalp and tresses briskly, enjoying the contrast between that exercise and the soft touch of evaporation on her flesh. She felt clean, very alive, almost weightless, as if she had washed away cares and pounds as well as the day's dust.

"No bones," she said, stretching. "No bones at all!"

It was, she noticed, a fine evening, hushed and expectant. The birds were still, and the insects fiddling. Beside her the quiet flowing river lapped gently at the beach, drawing attention to the fact that the faded color of its current made the hour visible. The water had lost the brilliance of daylight, but had not yet reached the shade worn at night. Overhead the early moon waited, pegged against the darkening sky like an unlit lamp.

Lancey dressed before she tried to comb her hair. She enjoyed the freedom of nakedness, but donning fresh clothes was almost as good. Hester had laundered shift and petticoats to a crispness that deserved the velvet gown instead of sprigged dimity.

She bit her lip as she raked the snarled tangles of her hair into a semblance of order. The russet velvet had disappeared long since, and her stepmother would answer no questions about it. Some dresses, she knew, were unlucky, and mayhap this one was forever ruined.

Returning home, through shadows that thickened between tree trunks, Lancey skipped more than she walked. The night, by all the signs, would prove perfect for fishing, but she was glad she wasn't going out.

It gave her a festive, holiday feeling that not even the sharp tang of dead fish that clung to the Quist yard could dampen. Thanks to Justin, she thought, I won't have to touch a shad this night.

She paused by the empty drying poles to wonder at herself. Never before had she missed a night's drift when the roe were running heavy. Strangely, she hadn't objected, but had grabbed at the chance with delight.

It's Justin, Lancey decided with a shrug. She couldn't very well refuse the chance he had created.

Hendrick had told them at the supper table. "Pardon's asked me to partner him tonight. Share and share. Seems Justin has other plans. So, you can have a rest, Lancey."

Lancey smiled in anticipation, convinced that Justin's plans centered on herself. Since the encounter with Eunice Wynbridge they'd had few opportunities to be alone. That, she admitted, was the reason for the bath, the clean petticoats, and the sprigged dimity. If Justin intended to come acalling, in the manner custom required, she wished to look her best.

She went into the house, sniffing at its warmth. Door and window were wide open, but the embers in the fireplace sent too much heat into the room. The candlelight didn't show that they'd supped on fried shad, but her nose reminded her.

The two little girls were almost ready for bed. Hester, unruffled, was gravely listening to familiar objections.

"But, Ma, it's still light outside!"

"That's right, Rhoda," said Hester, "and you'll be asleep before it's dark."

"*I* won't," said Hannah, sleepily. "Rhoda's bigger but she can't stay awake like *I* can!"

"I can, too, can't I, Lancey?"

"Why don't you go to bed and see?" Lancey ignored Hester's wink of approval. "It's easy to stay awake down here by the candles."

"That's just what they'll do," said Hester, sending the smaller girl toward the ladder with a gentle spank. "Go on, now. Last one up is a rotten egg."

Small Hannah scampered aloft willingly enough, but her sister followed more slowly. Rhoda scowled back as she climbed with the puzzled expression of a buyer sold an unwanted article by unfathomable means.

Laughing, Lancey shoved her bundle of discarded clothes into the settle chest, hung her towel before the fireplace. "Pa gone so early?" she asked.

"Yes," Hester said, "he wanted to take his net down to Pardon's. You know Hendrick. He's afraid Pardon's net ain't stained dark enough for moonlight."

"They'll get along. They know each other's ways."

"Fishermen!" Hester's face, pink in the glow from the embers, sagged wearily. She raised a hand as if to shield her forehead.

"What's the matter, Hester?"

"Nothing, girl. Not really. But, God, am I tired of fish! Cooking them, smelling them, eating them!" She sensed Lancey's stunned gaping, looked up to grin, lowering her voice. "Don't fret, girl. I get this way every year."

"I—I never heard you say——"

"And you won't, in front of Hendrick, or the children. Up till now I did my spouting only when alone. But, this year, you're different, Lancey. I can talk to you now."

So, Lancey thought, Hester has noticed a difference, too. She perched herself on the edge of the table. She said, "You mean I've grown up!"

"Partly. You ain't much older, but you've changed. Couple of months ago you wouldn't have dreamed of sitting here, looking pretty enough to nibble, and to hell with fishing!"

"Well," said Lancey, aware she was turning rosy, "if Pa needed me——"

"I know." Hester leaned back in her chair, sighed. "You're pulling oar for Ten Bush. But every drift now brings in more shad than we can sell, smoke or eat. The run doesn't even show a sign of slackening."

"It won't last much longer." Lancey felt disloyal, but she understood her stepmother's attitude. Hester, after all, had the cleaning and the cooking, but none of the fun of fishing. It was true, too, that a moonlight night had other uses.

Hester rubbed her face with her palm, and seemed to erase all haggardness. She said, cheerily: "You needn't pity me, Lancey. I made my bed, and Hendrick's the man I want sharing it. A butcher's wife must hate the reek of meat, and a brewer's gets tired of beer. I just wanted to speak my piece, and now I feel better."

"I'll confess," said Lancey, "that you can get your fill of smelling fish." She realized as she spoke that she was voicing a long suppressed complaint.

"Don't worry, girl. He'll never notice."

"Who won't?"

"Whoever it is you're expecting. You didn't get all decked out like that just for me."

"Decked out!" Lancey's indignation was spoiled by her chuckle. She thrust her bare feet toward Hester, wriggled her toes. "Why, I haven't even donned shoes and stockings." She cocked her head, considered. "Do you think I should, Hester?"

"This a may-I-pay or a stop-by?"

"What?"

"Did the feller ask you, 'may I pay my respects'? Or do you just figure he'll stop-by?"

"Oh." Lancey threw back her head, and chortled. "Well, since it's Justin, I think I'd call it a guess-maybe."

"In that case," said Hester, practically, "no shoes and stockings. You're at home, and it ain't Sunday."

Lancey wasn't sure her stepmother was right, but it didn't really matter. Justin knew she normally went barefoot and a change might give his visit undue importance. She was gazing, dreamily, at the shimmering orange-red mound of embers when Hester spoke again.

"What makes you think Justin's coming, Lancey?"

"Well," said Lancey, startled by the questioning of a certainty, "why else would he ask Pardon to fish without him?"

"Hendrick thinks he had business down to Jaycock's."

"Even so. That shouldn't take all evening."

"You never can tell," Hester said, "about a man. There's some make a business of tippling, and spend whole days over it. Others get in a tavern, and the liquor oils their tongues, and they talk the hours away. They don't say much of anything, but they forget how to tell time."

"You think Justin's like that?"

"They all are when they get to arguing. You know Justin. Mention that Constitution and he's off and running like a gun shy hound."

There was an undercurrent of seriousness in Hester's banter. Frowning, Lancey said, "You don't sound overfond of Justin."

"Now, don't go putting words in my mouth, girl. I've nothing against the man. Take away Hendrick and a score of years, and I might amble down the lane with him myself." She twinkled at Lancey's sudden impassiveness. "But I'd know where I was going, girl, and how far."

"You talk as if I was a—a ninny!"

Hester leaned forward, placed two fingers on the girl's knee. "No, Lancey. You're old enough, and canny enough, to do your own choosing. Justin or anybody, it ain't my place to pick faults. I do like him; did from the first. But he's got a—a *man* hardness like a swinging sword. A flash to make the heart jump; a swish that's almost a song."

"Yes," said Lancey. She was listening without thought, enthralled by her stepmother's eloquence.

"And he was born to trouble as the sparks fly upward. Sparks cause fire, and fire burns. The female who wants Justin Pattison had better remember that."

"It might be worth it, Hester."

"That little thought," said Hester, "is what hooks most of us." She stood up, smoothed her skirt over her hips. "Why don't you tell me I talk too much?"

Outside the door behind Lancey a toe scuffed a stone, rolled it. The girl whirled from the table at the sound. He did come, she thought. She beamed at Hester as knuckles tapped twice on the door jamb.

"Ahoy, inside. It's me."

"Oh, my," said Hester.

Lancey's jaw dropped as Jan Elmendorf filled the doorway. She was standing in front of both candle and fireplace, and the stocky sailor couldn't see her obvious dismay. Jan hesitated on the threshold; his smile and voice were tentative.

"Evening, Hester. Lancey."

"Hello, Jan," Hester said, "come in." She spoke quickly to distract the man from her stepdaughter's silence. The big woman was feminine enough to be amused by the appearance of the wrong suitor. "You've been a stranger lately."

Jan, stepping forward, paused. He shuffled his extended foot on the floor, took off his hat, turned it in his hands. "The—the *Lydia* has kept me jumping," he said, at last. "Full hold every voyage." He cleared his throat. "I'm mate now."

"That's nice," Hester said.

"Congratulations," said Lancey. He was, she noted, wearing a suit so new the breeches still showed the tailor's folds. His tricorne, matching black, looked fresh from the hatter's. Only the knit stockings and sturdy shoes remained from the once familiar Jan. This, she thought, was a courting call all right, but not the one she'd expected.

Aware of her scrutiny, Jan straightened. He stopped fumbling with his hat, raised it against his chest. Stiffly posed, he asked: "Do you like the new clothes? I got everything down to New York."

"Take you for a sloop captain at least," Hester said. She glanced anxiously at Lancey.

"You look fine," Lancey said. When he beamed, pleasure increasing the scrubbed-polish shine of his face, she saw that he bore no marks from the fight with Justin. She'd vowed to tongue lash him for that, but didn't have the heart. Poor Jan, she thought, puffed as a pouter pigeon, and about as interesting.

"You look fine, too, Lancey."

"Thank you, Jan."

"Er—younguns well, Hester?"

"Sprightly." Hester was trying not to smile. Jan's manners, as modish and new as his suit, fitted him as badly.

"And Hendrick?"

"Same as ever."

"That's good."

Lancey knew that the stiff conversation could drag on interminably. Someone, probably Captain Benjamin, had instructed Jan in courtship behavior, and he was doggedly following the drill. Hester, who had once checked his bloody nose, was to be addressed as a chaperone. Convention also demanded that Lancey, who had done the nose smiting, act like a flattered idiot. It was ridiculous!

"Jan," she said, "it's too hot in here. Let's walk down to the pier." She wanted him away from the house. If Justin was coming, he might arrive any minute, and there was bad blood between the two.

The suggestion brought a visible struggle to Jan's countenance. He showed relief and uncertainty, glanced at Hester seeking reassurance.

"Go ahead," Hester said, "before you start bowing and making a leg. My knees're too old to curtsy."

Jan reddened, almost dropped his hat when Lancey laughed. Touched by his confusion she put her hand on his wrist, drew him to the door. "No matter what anybody told you," she said, gaily, "rules don't hold among friends, Jan."

He gave her such a glazed look of dumb gratitude that she wanted to hit him.

The moon-drenched night silenced them both. Lancey was content to gaze, awed by the silvery beauty that turned darkness to blue-black, and the river to mirror glass. Jan, walking beside her, seemed depressed. Twice he sighed, and when he spoke his tone was sullen.

"What'd I do wrong, Lancey?"

"Jan, you didn't do anything wrong."

"It's how you're supposed to act. Cap'n Benjamin had a book that says so. Before you ask for a lady's hand. You dress in your best, and you visit her at home, and——" His voice choked with disappointment. "I—I thought maybe I'd been asking you wrong. That you'd be pleased."

Lancey dug her fingernails into her palms. She faced Jan squarely, wanting to ease his pain, afraid to sympathize. This time, she decided, it must be ended.

"Jan, I'm the one that's wrong. Wrong for you. I do not love you. I will never be your wife."

"There's someone else?"

"You have no right——"

"Is there?"

His hand clamped on her shoulder, shook her.

"Is there, Lancey?"

"Yes!" Lancey punched his forearm, twisted from his grip. She was angry now, ready to say anything that would send Jan away. "Yes, since that's what you want to hear! Yes, yes, yes!"

"Not Justin," said Jan, hoarsely. "Not him!"

There was such hate in the words, in his glare, that Lancey stepped back, tensed to fight or flee. She wasn't afraid of Jan, but she'd never seen him so enraged. She said, "That's my affair!"

"Listen." Jan reached for her again, but this time she fended him away. "Listen, Lancey, for your own good keep away from Justin."

"I'll take no orders from you, Master Mate!"

He grunted, then shrugged. "You'd be wise to heed, Lancey. That —feller is a troublemaker. Nobody knows much about him, where he's from or why he come here, but——"

"He fought in the war!"

"So did a lot of others, but I never heard they was all angels. Take my word that Justin's brewing something wicked. There's a man staying up at Jaycock's, a stranger——"

"Venick?" asked Lancey, in spite of herself. Jan's ranting was, of course, just an outburst of jealousy, but his mention of the stranger whetted her curiosity.

"You know him?"

"I've met him."

"Well," Jan said, with quiet seriousness, "he's another one who's up to no good. Cut from the same bolt as Justin is Master Christian Venick. They're as thick as—as thieves, and maybe that's just what they are!"

"You'd better not let Justin hear you call him that." Lancey sounded more assured than she felt. Borrowing a boat wasn't real thievery, but soldiers were notoriously light fingered when in need. "He whipped you once."

"Not easy," said Jan, "and mayhap not for keeps. But I ain't talking about that. Why is he playing crony-crony with this Venick in such a sneaky way?"

"Who says he is?"

"I says! They got their heads together this minute, whispering in a corner of Jaycock's common room. Yes, and Digmus hisself serving them."

"Well, after all, it is an ordinary. What's sneaky about two men supping together?"

"Ah!" Jan's satisfied exclamation ruffled the girl's hair. "That's the point. If it's all honest talk why do they have to skulk around corners, and meet behind wood piles? I've seen them do both, Lancey. Aye, with these eyes! And then, they separate and head for Jaycock's on different tacks, like foxes at a hen-coop."

"I—I don't believe it," said Lancey, lying. Jan's vehemence carried conviction; truth rang in every syllable. He spoke without the glibness of rehearsed falsehood, flatly, definitely. She remembered Venick with Justin in the clearing above the river.

"You'd better. I made it my business to watch them, these past days. Soon as the *Lydia* was berthed I began to smell something. Venick's open handed buying drinks, but he only bought me one! Digmus Jaycock steered Venick off me. I fronted Digmus about it, and he gave me a story about not wanting trouble, and the man being friendly with Justin."

"Digmus could be lying."

"He ain't, not about that. If you ask me Digmus is in it, too."

"In what, Jan?"

"Skulduggery. Robbery. Something underhand. Maybe they knew each other somewheres else that got too warm for them."

"No," said Lancey, glad to find a definite denial. "I was there the night Venick first came. I'd swear Justin never knew him before. Besides, Digmus wouldn't——"

"Digmus Jaycock'd sell his soul for a shilling, Lancey, and you know it!"

"Soul, perhaps. Neck, no." The picture of the innkeeper plotting robbery was too much for Lancey. She began to laugh at the absurdity; Jaycock had the courage of a minnow. The laughter helped persuade her that all Jan's suspicions were ridiculous. There was probably a simple, innocent explanation for Justin's attachment to Christian Venick.

"What're you laughing at?" asked Jan, growling.

"You, Jan. You're seeing goblins behind every bush. Venick's naught but a man trying to buy favor from newly met folks."

"And Justin?"

Lancey paused, thinking. It was not like Justin to become any man's toady for a free bottle. She said, "He is a close-mouthed man, who doesn't babble all he knows."

"That I believe!"

"You twist everything to suit your purpose, Jan. There is no reason why Justin must excuse himself to every tosspot who beards him in a tavern." Her defense sounded spurious; Justin had been evasive with her. Sharpening her tone, she stamped a foot. "And if he avoids you, he has cause! You picked that fight!"

Jan shifted his feet, lost his air of determined righteousness. "Now, Lancey," he said, "you know how those things happen. We were arguing and drinking and——"

"Don't lie." Sure of his guilt, Lancey relished the chance to rebuke Jan. His suspicions about Justin deserved no consideration because he'd already forfeited her esteem. "You deliberately provoked Justin. Who gave you the right to make me the cause of a tavern brawl?"

"Nobody said——"

"You dolt! I'm not a fool, Jan. Nor are the folk who heard you! You have no claim on me, but you try to bully any man who bows in passing!" Lancey was merciless, glorying in the justice of her attitude. "You deserved to be thrashed!"

"I heard you watched," said Jan, muttering. "There was plenty made sure I heard."

"And tonight," said Lancey, brutally, "you come acourting mouthing treacle from a printed book, and dressed up like Cornbury's ghost!" The gibe was cruel; Jan's sedate attire deserved no mention of a long-dead English governor whose foppishness was still a riverfront legend after almost a century.

"Lancey!"

"Well, it's the last time, Jan." Turning away, Lancey gazed out across the river. The lanterns on the bows of the fishing boats bobbed with the drift; the lights reflected in the water flickered like fireflies.

"But, Lancey, I——"

"The last time," repeated Lancey, with cold formality. "Your attentions are unwelcome, Master Elmendorf. If you respect my wishes you will discontinue them." The phrases were too tame for her taste. "God and Nicholas, Jan. Go away and stay away."

"What?" said Jan, in stunned disbelief. "Just because I lost my temper and flogged at that—that feller?"

Oh, no, thought Lancey, hearing his tone. No matter how she insulted and berated Jan, he always was deaf to dismissal! Didn't he have any pride? Didn't he even listen?

"I mean it, Jan. You lose that temper and start flogging much too easily."

"Now, I don't know," said a merry voice, "that it's so much worse than dumping fish in a chaise."

They both jumped, startled. Jan swore as he turned. Lancey, whirling, couldn't believe that the figure standing so close was real. He had his hat in his hand, grinning at them. The moonlight tinted the ruffles of his linen and powdered the straw-colored hair.

"Dirck!"

"Your obedient, Mistress," said Dirck, bowing. "My compliments, Master Elmendorf."

"I—I didn't hear you come," said Lancey. She was still dumbfounded. It was really too much that both Dirck and Jan should appear on a night when she expected Justin. "Where's Meda?"

"In a stall enjoying a well-earned rest. I walked in compliment to the night, Lancey."

"How long," asked Jan, "you been standing there?" He sounded gruff, but uncertain.

"Just arrived. What were you talking about that was so fascinating? All I heard was about temper and flogging. When's the fight?"

It was, Lancey decided, done with grace and ease. You had to admire the way Dirck van Zandt managed to draw the sting out of a situation. Neither she nor Jan had been whispering and Dirck had keen ears, but his statement was blandly convincing. She saw the sailor's shoulders relax, heard the relief in his voice.

"The fight's been long since, Master van Zandt. But Lancey was keelhauling me for it just the same."

"The woman's privilege," Dirck said, "that never changes."

Jan laughed and Lancey frowned. She was annoyed that Jan, who hated Justin, yielded so swiftly to Dirck's friendliness. At least Justin wasn't swayed by the old habit that treasured a patroon's smile.

"When did you get back, Dirck?"

"Last night, Lancey. I haven't been home though. Master Kent wanted a full report on the chancellor."

"But, surely," said Lancey desperately, "your family must be anxious about you. I mean, are you a lawyer now?" She was casting frantically for some means of clearing the yard for Justin. He'd made it possible for her to be free, and it looked as if she was holding a levee!

"If answering questions makes me a lawyer."

"Well," said Jan, impressed, "a lawyer, eh."

"Yes," said Dirck, "but there's more important news, Lancey. I met a man in a tavern down there who owns and skippers a Bermudas boat. Seems that he hailed Ten Bush's whaler off the Florida coast."

"The *Aunt Namina?*" Jan asked.

"That's right. Heading south under full sail with no time for anything but a passing shout. Still, all hands aboard are reported alive and well."

"Thank you," said Lancey. She was truly grateful, suspected that Dirck had taken a good deal of trouble. Why, she thought, I wasn't sure he even knew the name of Ten Bush's ship. He must have asked in every seaman's grog shop before he found the right man. Such a message seldom came upriver once a whaler had cleared the mouth of the Hudson.

"How far back was this?"

"Last month sometime," said Dirck, answering Jan's question. "The man wasn't sure of the date." He smiled at Lancey. "I thought you'd like to know."

The girl hesitated, returned the smile. She was sure the news was trustworthy, whatever Dirck's motives in fetching it. Ten Bush's well-being, she told herself, is more important than your meeting with Justin! She said, "Pa will be glad to hear, Dirck."

"Yes," said Dirck abstractedly. He was staring past Lancey at the river, and he pointed with his tricorne. "What the devil's going on out there?"

Jan and Lancey turned as one. Far upriver the bright pinpoints of light from the lanterns had stopped bobbing, were no longer spaced at intervals across the width of the stream. Now they seemed to be converging. One lamp stayed fixed; the others darted toward it. Even as the trio watched the scattered sparkles began to form a cluster.

Staring, Lancey felt a chill of fear. There was always the possibility of accident, and most of the fishermen, including her father, couldn't swim. On a calm night, with the river as placid as the moon, her fear was ridiculous. Unable to identify boats at that distance, she counted lanterns, naming each for an owner; Row, Kimmee, Cash, Calico. Though the Quist boat was moored beside the pier a yard away, there were more than four lights.

"Seven," said Jan aloud.

"Yes," Lancey said, noting by the tide's change that the nets should be gathered.

"Is that right?" Dirck asked.

"Can't tell," Lancey said, still gazing upriver. "There are the four regulars, but we don't know how many others were fetched out by the fine night." The lights were bunched in a ragged circle, like a distant conclave of torches. She listened, but the gentle breeze was from the south, and no shouts reached her.

"It ain't trouble, Lancey," said Jan. "They ain't got that look."

"Fetch Hester anyway."

Jan went without argument, but the girl was grateful for his comment. With all his faults he was riverwise, a sailor, sloop trained and able. As she walked out to the end of the pier, Dirck followed. He stood at her elbow.

"What's happening, Lancey?"

"I don't know," she said, genuinely puzzled. Then, she stiffened as twin lights moved out from the eastern bank, appearing suddenly, edging with slow steadiness toward mid-river.

Dirck said, "That's the ferry barge."

"Yes. But—look, it's not acrossing. The ferry's heading for the others."

The ferry lanterns, higher and brighter than the rest, stopped outside the ring of yellow specks. As Hester and Jan stepped onto the pier, Lancey squinted. She could imagine fishermen and bargemen calling to each other, but was it imagination that made those lights grow larger?

"What's happening?" asked Hester, calmly.

"I think," said Lancey, "they're heading downriver, coming back here."

Dirck said, "They are."

"Ferry and all," Jan said.

They stood, grouped by curiosity and common interest, in watchful silence. Even Dirck ván Zandt was gripped by the ancient patience, as old as fishing, that is part of awaiting the return of men in boats. The beams of the lanterns blossomed; hulls jelled from darkness, became visible. They saw the white splashes where oarblades scooped out water. The boats were separate now, but coming on as a fleet. They heard the men calling to each other, the first shouts.

"All right," said Hester. "They're excited, but they don't sound worried. Nobody's hurt."

Lancey, turning to nod to her stepmother, blinked. There were lighted lanterns, a couple of torches, bunched at the shore end of the pier. For an instant she thought her eyes had held the impression of the boat lamps, then she realized that the riverfront folk were out in force. Somehow, the excitement of the fishermen had reached their families, drawn them from their homes to the Quist landing.

She saw Seth Row's wife, the Kimmee children, Digmus Jaycock. A shouted chant slapped out from the approaching boats.

"Pardon and Hendrick! Pardon and Hendrick!"

"What's that?" called Hester.

Jan Elmendorf bellowed through cupped hands. "What is it? What's going on?"

The lead boat drew away from the others. Calico and Tanner, faces shining like coal as they glanced over their shoulders, were rowing at top speed. It was Calico who, without losing the stroke, raised his voice to answer.

"There ain't never been such a drift!"

Tanner's laugh boomed. He sounded as if he was singing. "It's like the sea of Galilee!"

The slaves let their boat run. Calico shipped his oars, stood up. His shout was joyous, a trumpet of triumph. "We all done holy! But Pardon and Hendrick got nigh six hundred shad!"

"Lost count," called Tanner.

A throaty cheer came from the assembled crowd. It overpowered the tumult of the fishermen.

"Jove," said Dirck. "Six hundred."

Jan said, "That's a lot of fish!"

"Yes," Hester said, dryly, "pressed down and running over."

At the edge of the throng, taller than most, stood Justin Pattison. The flame of a nearby torch cast a wavering pattern, glow and shadow, across his long face, but Lancey saw that the dark eyes gazed at the group on the pier. Jan must have felt it for he straightened to glare. Dirck glanced from Justin to Lancey, grinned.

"I'd call that a full net, Lancey," he said.

"Enough and to spare," said Lancey, and giggled. "It must be the moonlight."

18

THE THREE BOATMATES, TWO MEN AND A GIRL, SAT IN THE DORY and listened while the boy on the wharf, with shrill scorn, gave voice to their secret thoughts. Not one of them glanced at the small figure standing, arms akimbo in strangely adult stance, high above them. Pardon Cash, head bent, watched his fingers as they clenched and unclenched around the handle of the oar he'd rigged as tiller. Face impassive, Justin Pattison gazed at his partner. Lancey Quist peered at both men through lowered eyelashes.

"What do you think I am?" cried Conrad Quist, in outrage. "There's no sense trying to sell that stinking shad! Nobody wants it! You can't give it away! If there's anybody left in this whole, blasted county that won't gag at the sight of one, he'll catch his own. And only addlepated fishermen would bother to do that! I wouldn't make a wooden copper on your whole boatload!" Then he ripped out a round oath for emphasis.

"Pa," said Lancey, listlessly, "would wash your mouth out for that, Conrad." Her stepbrother's tirade roused no anger. They all knew there was too much truth in what he said.

Here, in the lee of the horse-ferry wharf, with the wind cut off and the mid-afternoon sunshine glaring from the steel bright water of the shallows, the heat gripped them with shimmering tentacles. It hadn't been so bad when the dory was under sail, but without the breeze it was broiling. The canvas over the fish had dried from the last sluicing, and the shad stink was sharper.

"Go ahead and carry tales." Conrad was unimpressed. "And carry them fish to Pa, too, before the ferry comes back. The smell of them might turn the horses' stomachs. They just ain't salable, Lancey."

That too, she thought, was very near the truth. They had been cruising since early morning, and they'd ranged from above Kingston almost as far south as the old lines at West Point. Pardon had fitted a mast to his dory, and they'd cast off in high spirits, stimulated by last night's luck. She had even, she recalled, felt sorry for Hester and Hendrick trying to peddle half the catch around Poughkeepsie.

"I'll wager you ain't sold a dozen!" Conrad's jeer was a high-pitched cackle.

Working down here, Lancey decided, hadn't improved the boy any. It had been her suggestion to come here, after they had tied up at every landing, plodded inland to half the west bank farms. But Conrad was wrong. They had, in nine hours, sold fourteen roe.

"Where," asked Justin, "did a nice family like the Quists get a changeling little horn toad like you?"

The mildness of the question wasn't meant to deceive anyone. Pardon Cash, not raising his head, smiled faintly. Lancey looked at Justin, noted the knotted jaw muscles that betrayed hidden anger. He has, she thought, been getting quieter and more furious with every futile hour.

Conrad, flushed with truculence, glared. His voice lost its shrillness; he spoke with cold deliberation.

"And who in hell are you?"

"Nobody you want to know," Justin said, "and vice-versa. Let's shove off, Pardon."

Her stepbrother, Lancey realized with slight surprise, had never met Justin. The boy's visits home had been few, and brief, since Ten Bush departed. She didn't suppose that either wished to be introduced.

"Wait a minute," Conrad said, "I want to talk to you, Lancey."

"Talk," she said, gazing up at him with distaste. Conrad at the moment was as irritating as the heat.

"Not here. Come ashore."

"We have to get back."

"A minute." Conrad was coaxing; he smiled, beckoned. "Please, Lancey, I've got something for Pa 'n' Ma, and as long as you stopped by——"

"Go on, Lancey," said Pardon, "we ain't going no place important now." The big fisherman's narrowed eyes glittered with the same hard brightness the sunshine made on his earring. His grin was savage; he showed his missing teeth heedlessly.

Lancey swallowed, remembering Pardon's boisterous pride in the great haul of shad. He had toasted Hendrick, the dory, the river, his friends, as long as gin and rum had lasted. Dawn had found him fresh, and clear eyed, but now he looked as if he suffered from the aftermath of a drinking bout.

214

"Come on, Lancey," pleaded Conrad.

"Anything," Justin said, with the same quietness, "that will stop his blasted tongue."

Climbing onto the wharf, finding the rough-hewn, weathered timbers hot to the touch, Lancey was discouraged. Justin's black mood, she thought, might make him calm, but it made everyone else wretched. She was the one with her nose out of joint. Her amusement at her overabundance of callers on the previous night had vanished with the realization that Justin, far from being upset, hadn't seemed to mind at all.

"Lancey. Who's he?"

Startled, she pulled back from the hiss of Conrad's whisper. She said, "What?"

"Him." The boy shrugged a shoulder toward the dory. "Old long face there with the blaze in his mane."

"That's Justin Pattison. You've heard us speak of him."

"Talks Massachusetts."

"Why," said Lancey, staring at her stepbrother, "I suppose he does. Some anyway." She liked Justin's manner of speaking, but hadn't given it much thought. "But how would you know?"

Conrad's sneer was smugly confident. "I got ears, Lancey. We get all kinds crossing here. Lots more custom than Poughkeepsie. Maybe even more than Fishkill. Pays to listen. He's Massachusetts all right."

"Swill," said Lancey, inelegantly. "You probably heard us mention it. It's no secret."

"Ain't, eh?"

"No." She was getting very tired of Conrad's attitude. "God and Nicholas! Stop acting as if you know it all!"

"I know what I know."

"You're a horse-stall sweep who's getting too big for his breeches! The way you talked to us just now makes me ashamed your name is Quist! Now, fetch whatever you've got for Pa and Hester, and——"

"That was just bait, Lancey."

"Bait?" She glared at him, feeling the heat more as her anger mounted.

"Sure, I wanted a word with you in private." He saw the purpose in her eyes, and dodged. Her slap, swung with full force, missed him by inches. As he skipped away, fright squeezed his face back to its proper age. "Now, wait, Lancey, wait! I only wanted to help!"

"I ought to box your ears lobeless!" She hesitated, wavering between pursuit, and return to the boat.

Conrad noticed the hesitancy. His composure returned. Leering at her, he raised a hand to his lips, spoke across the knuckles. "Mind my words, Lancey. Don't trust that Justin! He——"

Her movement interrupted him. Conrad whirled, raced away, bare heels flashing. Lancey had taken one step; she stared after him, frowning. First Jan, and now Conrad, warned her about Justin. Consider the source, she said silently. A jealous rival, and an unbearable boy! Such testimony made her like Justin all the more.

She went back to the dory in better spirits. Not even the two men's silent gloom infected her. There was no use weeping over spoiled shad, and she would tell them so at the proper time. They cast off, rowed out of the shallows, raised the sail.

"Home?" asked Lancey, as the scrap of canvas filled, and the dory began to move northward.

"Aye," said Pardon Cash.

Justin said, "Home to more shad."

"Now, look," Lancey said, smiling at them, "it's not as bad as all that. After all, Pardon, you and Pa set a mark for others to go after. It's not your fault that it happened toward the end of the run when folks wouldn't buy."

"I know, Lancey, but——"

"But," continued Justin, harshly, "it didn't help none to be treated like lunatic beggars!"

Lancey stared at him, at the ridged muscles pallid through the dark skin around his mouth. She was puzzled and anxious, too disturbed to notice that this time his wrath failed to kindle her interest. She said, "If you're letting what Conrad said upset you——"

"A whelp in need of the switch!"

The contemptuous tone stung, though Lancey agreed with the sentiment. Conrad, after all, was her stepbrother, and his misbehavior or chastisement was a family matter. Feeling her resentment was unreasonable, she forced herself to speak calmly.

"Justin," she said, "you can't blame people for not buying something they don't want."

"Of course you can't," Pardon agreed.

"You're both wrong." Justin shook his head as if impatience pestered like a fly. "That isn't what riles me. I blame them for their attitude. For not seeing what's happening, and not giving a damn if it does!"

Pardon caught Lancey's glance, shrugged. He said, "It's his riddle not mine."

216

"Look," Justin said, "we were offering fresh fish. We set a low price to start, and lowered it fast. But it never occurred to anyone that it wasn't just a matter of buying and selling. Somebody had to get a boat, row out, cast net, catch shad, and keep them fresh enough to offer. We'd been to some trouble before we arrived at their back doors!"

Frowning, Lancey nodded. There was no refuting Justin's statements, but she thought them about as infuriating as the multiplication table or the tides. Six times six was thirty-six; floodtide followed ebb. What made Justin so angry?

Pardon said, "Well, hell, it's our trade, ain't it?"

"They didn't even think of that!" Justin said. "And another thing. Those shad were good eating." He gestured toward the lumpy canvas that covered the cargo. "But nobody cared that hours of heat might turn them into garbage!"

It was a waste, thought Lancey, wincing. She couldn't think of any remark cheering enough to lighten that fact. The greatest haul of fish in riverfront memory had ended in failure. Gazing over the gunwale at the rippling water her depression was deepened by the dory's speed. Heavy laden, and not designed for sailing, the little boat pushed upriver with sluggish awkwardness.

"Garbage," said Pardon Cash, and spat through the gap in his teeth.

"We just couldn't sell them," Lancey said.

"Sometimes," said Justin, "you have to make people see things." She raised her head, and he thought she'd never looked more womanly, in spite of her shining face, wet with sweat, burnished by heat. For a moment, while the hazel-eyed gaze questioned, Justin was tempted to tell her everything. Then, Pardon's voice recalled him to caution.

"How do you do that?"

"Ask Lancey," said Justin, smiling at her with sudden tenderness. "When a high-busted wench behind a high-stepping colt tried to ride down our Lancey the other day, Lancey knew what to do."

"Well," Lancey said, laughing, "that's one way of getting rid of fish." She was pleased by Justin's change of humor, but slightly piqued. Somehow men seemed to regard her exploit as a great joke; she recalled Dirck van Zandt's amusement. Eunice Wynbridge, she thought grimly, knew better. Her conduct may have been outrageous, but it wasn't meant to be funny.

"Wonder how Hendrick made out." As he spoke Pardon glanced at the shore, adjusted sheet and tiller.

Lancey checked a landmark on the east bank, said, "We'll know soon enough."

"We know now," Justin said. "Poughkeepsie isn't hungry enough to eat more shad. With Seth Row selling, and Gerritt too, there's too much for the travellers at the inns. Tanner told me that the Livingston hands even feed roe to their cats."

Pardon nodded in gloomy agreement. "That's about it," he said. "I'll eat all over fourteen that Hendrick sold."

"You'll go hungry." Lancey ducked under the sail as Pardon tacked toward the east bank. She crawled forward, crouched in the bow, shaded her eyes with a palm.

The fishing village, dead ahead, was closer than she expected, its houses, tinder-box size, strung along the water's edge as if they had slid down from the bluff behind them. A twisting vine of smoke rose from the Quist yard, and the girl wondered if her stepmother was laundering in the heat of the day. The river was bare of shipping; no sail or oarblade moved within her range of vision. Atop its bluff Poughkeepsie slumbered in the sunshine, and the barge moored at the ferry landing looked deserted and forgotten.

The smoke column drew her attention again, and now she could see movement, the orange of flames, the dark figures of people. Lancey narrowed her eyes, staring. She could think of no reason why a crowd was gathered in the Quist yard, but suddenly the whole scene came into focus. The fire was safely contained in a square of stones, and a dozen men milled around it.

"Justin," she called, "come and look. Something's going on."

He crawled forward to join her, grunted as he gazed. Hendrick's unmistakable stocky build walked out on the pier. He waved, and Lancey raised a hand in reply.

"What is it?" asked Pardon, his view cut off by the sail.

"I think it's a party," Justin said.

"Yes." Lancey recognized the festive air of the milling men, Hester presiding over the fire. "They're cooking, and eating."

"Shad."

As the dory drew closer Lancey was able to separate the crowd into individuals. The Kimmees were there, the Rows, Digmus Jaycock, but these neighbors seemed outnumbered by better-dressed strangers. A rank of saddled horses was hitched behind the Quist yard, and the gleam of a coaly bay coat gave the girl a needed hint.

218

Her glance searched through the vari-colored riding coats, found Dirck van Zandt. He was standing in a group, talking, gesturing with a hand that cupped a noggin. Schuyler Davis loomed beside Dirck, and even as she watched Tappen Platt rode his gray cob into the yard. She heard the cheer that greeted him, saw Tappen toss a sack to Schuyler. A moment later two flustered, squawking pullets were spilled from the sack.

"Fish fry for the gentry?" Justin murmured his question.

Lancey felt his resentment, and shared it. She was not sure what was happening, but the horsemen were evidently enjoying themselves. She knew most of them by sight as younger members of patroon families. In typical fashion they were carousing away a hot afternoon.

"What's Pa thinking of?" Lancey asked.

Justin said, "Probably he had no choice."

"What do you mean?"

"Those empty heads have fat purses. If they pay for the shad they eat——" He shrugged, scowling at the crowd. "You can thank your friend Dirck for this, Lancey."

Behind them Pardon Cash growled and muttered as he steered the dory closer to the shore. The final tack brought them almost within mooring distance, and when the sail rattled down they coasted.

Hendrick caught Justin's tossed line, snubbed it fast. His voice was as cheery as his beaming face.

"How'd you three make out?"

"We didn't," said Pardon, glowering at the listening crowd.

The noise, Lancey noted, had died down, and everybody was turned toward the dory. Dirck, smiling, strolled onto the pier behind Hendrick, and Hester bustled forward through the throng. Her cheeks were rose bright from the glow of the cookfire, but she looked happy.

"We sold fourteen," Lancey said, annoyed that she sounded defensive.

"Fourteen!"

She didn't place the speaker, but Tappen Platt's laugh led the derisive titter that came from the horsemen. Dirck frowned, glanced over his shoulder. There was no quelling his friends. The trio in the dory stood in rigid silence while amused voices mocked and boasted.

"Thunderation, I sold more'n that myself!"

"That's no brag!"

"Tappen got rid of *two* dozen."

"Twenty-eight, to be exact."

"But Dirck's Meda got back first."

"Great sport, wasn't it?"

Lancey couldn't believe her ears. Why in the world would these gentlemen jockeys bother to sell Hendrick's shad? That they seemed to have succeeded was even more fantastic. She and Pardon and Justin knew how difficult it was to find buyers.

"What're they rattling about, Hendrick?" asked Pardon.

"It's true," Hendrick said. "It was Dirck's idea. These young men made up a—a wager about it, and each took a number of fish. They rode back into Pleasant Valley, rode far and wide."

Hester said, "And they sold a couple of hundred shad." She nodded vigorously, as if to emphasize her words. "Some for Seth, and Gerritt even. We're eating up the rest."

"You had to get well away from the riverfront," Dirck van Zandt said. "The farmers were willing enough to buy once you could reach them."

"We took anything," Tappen Platt said. "Anything we could carry on a horse. Pullets, eggs, a comb of honey."

"Schuyler even swapped a trout for a roe."

"I happen," said Schuyler Davis, "to like trout."

"We share and share, of course," Hendrick told Pardon Cash. "There's a brass kettle, and a fist full of nails, some seed, a twist of wool yarn——"

"Oh, come ashore and see," interrupted Hester.

"There's some money, too," Dirck said, "but mostly we did better at barter."

"Dirck," called a voice, "does Tappen win or not?"

"Unless one of you questions it."

"*I* question it. He made three trips and he got back last."

"You," said Schuyler Davis, "could have ridden out again. There was no rule against it."

During the babble of friendly argument the trio climbed stiffly from the dory. Hester hurried back to the shad grilling over the fire; Hendrick led the way to where the results of the day's trading were piled against the side of the house. Lancey couldn't deny that the horsemen had done well.

"I'll get Seth and Gerritt," said Hendrick, glancing around, "and we'll take turns picking. Most of this is ours, Pardon, but they did put in a few fish." He chuckled, reached to move a crock of butter out of the sunshine. "They didn't think Dirck's friends could do it. I didn't myself, but he talked me around."

Dirck could, thought Lancey grimly. Her father's enthusiasm left her unmoved. She didn't blame Hendrick and Hester for their unabashed delight, but she felt closer to Justin and Pardon. They hadn't ridden out on a larking gamble. They had merely fretted and sweated through a depressing day. And nobody really gave a tinker's dam!

Amazingly, Pardon took a deep breath and grinned. He said: "And here I was worrying because a dory full of shad was spoiling fast. I even offered to eat all over fourteen you sold!" Pardon's guffaw was a release from tension. He clapped Hendrick on the shoulder. "We'll have to bury our lot, Hendrick."

"That doesn't matter," said Hendrick.

No, Lancey decided, it didn't matter any longer. Even with that much wastage, Dirck's scheme, and his fast-riding friends, had made the record catch a profitable one. The best thing to do was to follow Pardon's example, and accept the result with good grace.

She hadn't managed to do it when Seth Row and Gerritt Kimmee joined them. The two neighbor fishermen greeted Pardon with diffidence.

"Too bad you wasn't here, Pardon," said Seth Row.

"Pardon and me were partners," Hendrick said, "and he shares even. We'll choose turns by lot, and——"

"You can leave me out," Justin said.

The harsh flatness of the statement startled the group of fishermen. It was, Lancey realized, the first time Justin had spoken since their landing. She was glad that he wouldn't compromise, that he refused to forget the dismal sail in the dory.

"Now, wait a second," said Pardon. His protest was echoed by Hendrick.

"Now, wait, Justin——"

"I didn't net those shad," Justin said, "the way you and Pardon did, Hendrick. And I didn't peddle many either. None that brought in this pile of loot. I'll share, thirds, in the sale of fourteen roe, but I don't take charity."

"You think I do?" Pardon's roar overpowered the chattering horsemen. Several turned to stare.

"That's between you and Hendrick."

"I agree with Justin," said Lancey. "The shad we set out to sell are still in the dory. Pardon shares because he was in on the catch. We weren't."

"Lancey!" There was hurt and bewilderment in Hendrick's tone. "What kind of talk is that? There is enough, and more, for all. Wouldn't Hester and I have expected our part of the money you made today? Wasn't it understood that we were all selling the same catch?"

"Aye," said Pardon, "that's true enough. I thought you had the worse chance, Hendrick."

"I would have if it wasn't for Dirck and——"

"That's another reason," said Justin. "I take no favors from Master van Zandt."

Lancey was tempted to say the same, but, turning, saw Dirck was within earshot. He smiled at her, stepped closer. He spoke with amused tolerance.

"Nor need you, Master Pattison. Very little of that pile is mine, nor was any of it gathered as a favor to you. There was a chance to provide some sport for my friends, and their horses. They had all heard of the record catch, and naturally it added spice to the occasion." He gazed at Lancey, tried to convince with sincerity. "I cannot regret that Hendrick profited by our efforts."

Justin said, "I prefer not to."

Neither man spoke loudly, but the tension between them spread across the yard. Lancey saw that most of the horsemen were listening. Hester, frowning and troubled, had stepped back from the fire to peer toward the argument. Even Digmus Jaycock had turned from the beer keg to hear. In the corner near the horses Schuyler Davis and Tappen Platt were murmuring insults at each other as they tried to get the indignant pullets back in the sack.

"That is your privilege," Dirck said. He was aware of the other's height, that Lancey had drawn close to Justin. The look on the girl's face angered Dirck. "The fox who called the grapes sour at least didn't try to spoil everyone else's enjoyment of them."

"That's not fair," cried Lancey. "He's not—*we're* not trying to spoil anything for anybody!" She was furious at Dirck. He dared to rebuke Justin after sneaking behind their backs, and peddling shad on horseback.

"Then," said Dirck, with cool insolence, "my compliments on your excellent success without trying."

Lancey flushed, then paled as she admitted the truth in the remark. The misery in her father's face, the worry in Hester's, the embarrassed awkwardness of fishermen and riders had not been present before Justin spoke. Pardon Cash had a hangdog look; nobody cried out that the truth was unjust! Why had the crowd forced Justin to speak by jeering at their failure?

At that moment a chicken broke loose from Tappen Platt. It fled, in darts and swoops, across the yard, fluttering, squawking, scampering. Men dodged from its path, ducked away from its awkward attempts to fly. The tension broke in laughter as Tappen, a comical caricature of the bird, raced whooping in pursuit.

Twice, the man grabbed and missed. At last, heedless of everything but the elusive pullet, Tappen flung himself in a headlong dive. He caught one yellow-clawed leg, but his momentum carried him, rolling, to crash against Justin Pattison's knees.

Justin, standing very straight, barely wavered at the impact. He kept his gaze on Dirck van Zandt, and he was not smiling.

"Sorry," panted Tappen, grinning up from the dust.

Without glancing at him, Justin stooped, and clutched. He lifted Tappen, and flung him aside, handling the man like a sack of laundry.

Tappen hit the ground hard, and lay stunned. The pullet broke loose, and darted away. Its squawks sounded doubly raucous in the sudden hush.

For a heartbeat no one moved. Then, Schuyler Davis stepped forward, chin raised, eyes grave. He looked from Justin to his fallen friend, and back. Schuyler said, almost mildly, "You might pick on someone your size."

As if moved by an unseen breeze the horsemen shifted positions as they ranked themselves behind Schuyler Davis. With a grunt Pardon Cash flanked his partner.

Lancey opened her mouth, but Dirck van Zandt spoke first. "No," he said. "No, Schuyler, there'll be no brawling. Let's not wreck what we've done."

"My dear Dirck," Schuyler said, "I do not brawl. But if this fellow has any gentlemanly pretensions, I will gladly have my seconds call on——"

Tappen Platt sat up and swore. He rose shakily, pushing away Dirck's helping hand. "Schuyler," he said, "if there's any quarrel it's mine. I'm the one went boots over buttocks." He turned to face Justin. "Sir, I bumped you most rudely. My apologies for that. I offer them with the expectation of a proper reply."

It sounded, Lancey thought, all stiffly formal but it was dangerous. Tappen waited, dignified in spite of dusty clothes. Justin, unafraid, curled his lips in the familiar, reckless grin that chilled her. She saw Digmus Jaycock grab Justin's elbow, lean close. The innkeeper's face worked, but his whisper was so quick that Lancey wasn't sure she heard.

"You blasted fool! You'll queer Venick's plan!"

Justin's grin stiffened, broadened; his eyelids drooped. Lancey saw the dark eyes glint as he glanced about for listeners. She was carefully gazing at the ground when he spoke.

"My apologies are certainly in order. I acted without thinking. A wrestler's trick triggered by our sudden collision. Your servant, sir. I am truly sorry."

"So," said Hendrick with gusty relief. "Well done by both parties. Now, it is forgotten. Hester, our friends are not eating!"

"Well," cried Hester, "it's ready. I ain't spoon-feeding grown men!"

Lancey noticed that the innkeeper brought Tappen Platt a tankard of beer. Jaycock's square spectacles never once turned in Justin's direction.

19

IN THE FIRST WEEKS OF JUNE THE SHAD RUN SLACKENED; THE dwindling number of fish gave warning that the yearly migration was over. At the same time delegates to New York's Constitutional Convention began to arrive in Poughkeepsie.

Lancey Quist found this combination of facts amusing. It was, she thought, almost as if the political meeting was planned as a substitute entertainment. There was no doubt now of the convention's importance. South Carolina, a faraway state that in Lancey's mind consisted of Charleston and palmetto trees, had ratified the new document on the twenty-third of May. With the realization that eight states had signed, that only one more was needed for adoption, the citizens of the state of New York in general, and the township of Poughkeepsie in particular, decided they had been chosen by destiny.

This decision ignored two other conventions; New Hampshire to the north, powerful Virginia in the south. In the opinion of the town, both would be wise if they waited to profit by New York's example.

Even Justin Pattison, the most vocal and violent of the riverfront men, agreed. "New York's the most important," he told Lancey, "and what's decided here should decide the others!"

"You sound," said Lancey, amused, "as if you'd been born on the river."

"God forbid. I might have been taught to touch my forelock to an old Dutch name on a thousand acre grant."

The girl frowned, finding the complaint wearisome after so much repetition. This might have been true once, she thought, but it wasn't any longer. There was a squirt of acid in her reply.

"Do you think Pa does? Or Pardon?"

"No," he said, blinking, "the rivermen are the best of the lot. They're the ones——"

"Yes?" she asked, when he didn't finish.

They were sitting in their favorite clearing, gazing down at the river. Justin plucked a blade of grass, chewed it. He glanced sideways

225

at the girl, shrugged. "They're the only ones," he said, "with any gumption."

That was not, Lancey thought, what he started to say. Angrily, she recognized another evasion. He must think she was blind or stupid! Ever since Digmus Jaycock's whispered warning she'd been aware of Justin's changed manner of living. He fished less and less, frequented the ordinary more. Jan was right; Justin for some reason was in league with Christian Venick.

Anger hardened into resolution. She had picked this man over all others because they thought alike. She was tired of mystery. How could she offer loyalty and faithfulness if Justin refused to give her the chance?

"Justin," she said, facing him, "what are you and Venick up to?"

"Venick?"

"Venick."

"Now, what makes you think——"

"Oh, please," Lancey said, "*please*, Justin. If you answer one more question with a question, I'll scream." She saw his face go wooden, but there was no stopping now. "You and Digmus Jaycock and Venick are mixed up in something. It's obvious. Why can't you trust me?"

"If it's that obvious, you've been spying."

"It didn't take any spying. You see less of Pardon, less of me, than you do of them!"

"I can't spend all my time with you!"

"Nobody——" She heard her voice rise, caught her breath to check the words of rage that might end everything. For an instant, while she linked her fingers tightly, she wondered at her discretion. When before had she tried to avoid an open quarrel? But she could not gain his confidence by recrimination. She said, "Nobody is asking that, Justin, but I would like all your trust."

"Lancey," he said, troubled, "it's better you don't know——"

"Because what you plan is—dishonest?"

"No! What do you think I am?"

"I am trying," she said, "to get that straight."

Justin looked at her. He rose, walked a few restless paces, back and forth, as if seeking to arrange his thoughts through motion. Lancey watched him, meeting his eyes calmly. She could hear the murmur of the river below, and the birds chirping in the trees that hedged the clearing.

"All right," Justin said, squatting beside her, "I cannot tell you Venick's plan because it is not my secret, and I pledged myself. He

226

knew my name from old friends who are now in the Vermont Republic, but I joined in willingly. Jaycock seems to know Venick from other days, and is well paid for his trouble."

Lancey nodded, afraid to speak or speculate lest she lose a single syllable.

"You must take my word, Lancey, that there is nothing dishonorable in the plan."

"Of course," she said.

"Thank you. Now, I can prove that my trust is as great as yours, because I am placing my freedom, and perhaps even my life, in your hands."

She said, "You are a fugitive."

"Yes. You have heard of Shays' Rebellion? Over in Massachusetts."

"It was in the town paper."

"There was a great deal that wasn't printed anywhere, Lancey, and a lot of it was truth. We weren't just a band of troublemakers, hotheads, outlaws like some said, or soldiers who wanted to put the army in power. Dan Shays wasn't like that, nor Luke Day, nor Adam Wheeler, nor Eli Parsons. They were the leaders, and the rest of us felt pretty much as they did. If we were wrong it was wrong law that made us so, and we rose in arms because there was no other way.

"Shays was captain because he'd been one—and a good one—during the war. I never happened to serve with him, then, but I'm proud I followed him when I did. He was big framed, red faced and honest, with no lack of courage.

"We were west-country men, remember, from the Berkshires, and the Hampshires, and the valley of the Connecticut. We'd gone to war, willingly, when Boston found the king's rule too heavy to bear, but the shoe was on another foot once Boston ruled the state. The lawyers, and the merchants, the ship owners, the office holders gave lip service to liberty, but made sure they lined their pockets.

"Men who had fought, and maybe shed blood, for independence came back to Massachusetts and misery. They'd been paid in worthless paper. Their farms had been neglected; their families were in want. And they found they were being taxed out of the little they had left.

"I was no farmer, had neither family nor property, but right is right, Lancey. I sided with my comrades.

"There was a spate of talk about how we expected to be treated like heroes. Rubbish! Those men wanted to keep their land, that's all, to make a living and feed their children. But their taxes wouldn't let them!

"And they acted mighty patient for hotheads. Do you recall when the trouble broke out?"

"I think so," Lancey said. "It was the winter before last, wasn't it?" She was listening with parted lips, thrilled to discover that Justin could still excite her with a tale.

"Earlier," said Justin. "Fall of '86, and winter of '87. The war had been over for about three years, but things were getting worse, not better. The courts haled men up for land taxes, took away the land, threw debtors into gaol. Courts with highly paid judges, where legal action cost a small fortune.

"The whole of Massachusetts wasn't blind. There were resolutions passed in Boston, in the State Senate, in the Court of Common Pleas. But nothing was *done!* Not until we did it.

"We started closing courts that autumn. We closed them before they could take any more land away, and we did it with muskets to prevent argument. Maybe a judge or two was hooted at, or a tax collector pummeled, but mostly nobody was hurt. When the Supreme Court tried to sit at Springfield we raised a rumpus until it adjourned.

"That's when old Bowdoin decided to send troops against us. The governor picked Ben Lincoln to lead them, for God's sake! Lincoln, who'd lost his sword at Charleston, and only got Cornwallis's at the surrender because General Washington was generous.

"Still, he had over four thousand men, and I don't think we had that many musket balls. We needed powder and shot and we decided to go for the arsenal in Springfield."

"Where you'd lived," said Lancey, recalling earlier conversations.

"That's right. Before the war, and after. If there was any town I called home that was the one.

"We figured General Sheppard, who commanded the arsenal, would fight. Shays led part of us into the town on one side to draw his fire. Luke Day was to come in from the other side and attack Sheppard in the rear. Luke had a good half of our force hid out in an apple orchard.

"Sheppard hit us about as we expected, only sooner and harder. He ripped us with a volley, and drove us, but we didn't break. We pulled back, waiting for Luke Day, and the rest of the boys. They didn't come, and they didn't come.

"Dan Shays grabbed my shoulder. What with cold and fury his

face was purple. 'Justin,' he says, 'you know this place. Find Luke and tell him to high-tail in here!'

"I took out for that apple orchard, skirting the fight, cutting through the town. Springfield seemed quiet and deserted as I drew away from the rattle of the muskets. There was snow on the eaves, and the streets were silent and empty. I went cross lots, and by back alleys, trying to avoid drifts and run on the hard packed snow.

"Then, as I came out the head of a lane, I ran into a squad of armed citizens hurrying to join Sheppard. There were plenty in Springfield against us, and one of these happened to be the son of my old master.

"'Say,' he yells, 'that's Justin Pattison. He's one of them.'

"I never had liked that lad, but I never liked him less.

"'Surrender!' shouts another.

"Well, of course, I pulled foot, with the six of them after me, guns popping. Nothing hit me, but we were so close those balls went by like flung gravel. I half turned, running, and fired my musket from the hip. Young Eph fell and the rest scattered.

"There was no one in the orchard when I got there. Luke Day was gone, and everyone else. They'd heard, they said, we'd been chased out of Springfield, and that Ben Lincoln was coming. By the time I caught Luke Day's bunch, heel-and-toeing it down the pike, it was true enough. All of it, though we didn't know it then.

"We camped, after Dan Shays rejoined us, in a snow-covered field near Petersham. It was a glum camp of bitter cold and discouraged men. Ben Lincoln's four thousand found us there, came at us without warning, and smashed us. Some escaped, Dan Shays, Luke, Adam and myself among them. The rest were hunted down like rabbits trapped in the high snow."

Justin glanced around the sun-bright glen, and shivered. Lancey reached, clasped his hand.

"That's about it," Justin said, "except that I was a long time getting over the wound I took at Petersham, and it was a longer before it was safe to travel. You see, the friends that hid me got word that young Eph died, amputated, and they'd hang me higher than Haaman back in Springfield."

"Justin!"

"So help me God, Lancey, I wasn't even aiming. I just wanted to fright them."

"But they would hang you," Lancey said, "higher than Huddleston." She recalled Poughkeepsie's most famous hanging, when, eight years before, the whole town had watched the execution of a British spy. Gallows and death throes were vivid in her memory.

And they would do that, Lancey thought, to Justin. Her hand gripped his tighter, holding him safe from such an end.

"That's why," Justin said, "I've no use for your Governor Clinton. He didn't have to call out his militia."

"Clinton?" Lancey said, confused. Then, she realized that Justin was still talking about Shays' Rebellion.

"Supposed to be for the poor man!" Justin's voice was tight with bitterness. "Well, we were poor enough, and whipped, but he marched an army to the border in case any of us might try to sneak into his precious state! Yes, and he put prices on our heads."

"I remember," said Lancey. "That was printed in the *Country Journal.* One hundred fifty pounds for Daniel Shays. A hundred for Luke Day, and some others."

"Blood money. The damned Pharisee!"

"Well, maybe he didn't know all the ins and outs of——"

"What was there to know? Dan Shays fought all over this state! Ticonderoga, Saratoga, Stony Point! But George Clinton wanted to clap him in irons for something he did in Massachusetts."

"He escaped, didn't he?"

"Yes, he's safe in the Vermont Republic now." Justin shrugged, stared moodily at the ground. "But that isn't the worst of it, Lancey. In Massachusetts they used what we'd done as an argument in favor of this Constitution. So such an outrage could never happen again, they said. And folks listened, and voted to ratify."

Lancey saw the pain in the dark eyes. Why, she thought, he's as hurt as a small boy. Justin, the cool fighter, the wrathful veteran, the unbowed rebel! His weakness surprised and touched her in a way that his bitterness had never done. Tears blurred her vision, and pity softened her voice.

"That isn't your fault, Justin."

"It's always a fault to lose."

"No," she said, "you've lost other times. In the war. But you fought again, and again, until we won."

"We won a war, Lancey, and every day it becomes less a victory. First we fought for our rights as English citizens. Then, because we couldn't get them otherwise, we fought to be free and independent states. And now we seem determined, state by state, to trade both freedom and independence for a government that grants only the rights it wishes!"

"New York won't."

"I wish I was sure of that!"

That shook her because she had never heard him admit the possibility of defeat. For all his warnings, his disdain of George Clinton, his scorn for riverfront lethargy and the county's respect for landlords, Justin had always argued with passionate conviction. The Constitution must *not* become the law of the land. It could be prevented if New York stood firm.

Justin smiled at her concern, at the moisture brimming her eyes. It was a smile that combined affection and disillusion. He said, "I have staked everything, Lancey, on one last desperate gamble, but if it fails——"

Now that, Lancey thought, is mere foolish talk. How could Justin, a fisherman spectator, stake everything on a gamble that could influence the outcome of the convention? No matter what was decided in the courthouse they would all go on living.

"I don't understand," she said, honestly.

"No, of course, you don't."

"Do you mean that——?"

"You must not ask my meaning, Lancey. You must trust me, as I have trusted you."

"Oh, I do, *I do!*"

Her cry was completely sincere. Justin had done what she asked, revealed more of himself than she had expected. She knew his past, and the knowledge dissolved her suspicions. He had followed Daniel Shays; he would not let Christian Venick involve him in anything unworthy. Lancey admitted she disliked Venick without cause. Only a man could judge the worth of another man's plan.

"Young Eph," he said. "It was fair fight, Lancey."

"Of course it was."

"You—you're not upset?"

She shook her head, tossing her hair. The stranger killed in the fight at Springfield meant no more than the redcoat soldiers that he had slain in war. If men fought with muskets some would be killed. Lancey had no scruples about that. She knew Justin; he was no more a murderer than he was a thief, though she had once caught him trying to steal a boat.

"Anyway," she said, with inspiration, "you didn't do it. You said 'amputated,' and the surgeon's to blame."

"Well, now," said Justin, "I can't rightly claim that. 'Twas my shot made him need a surgeon, though some of them are too quick at lopping off limbs."

For some reason, Lancey thought, maybe because there was bad blood between himself and the dead man, Justin needed reassurance. She leaned forward and cupped her hands under his chin. Their faces were very close. His scarred eyebrow twitched as he raised it.

"That's over and forgotten, Justin."

"Not back in Massachusetts."

"You're not there, you're here. And I can prove it."

Lancey kissed him with deft thoroughness. It was a kiss intended to bring solace, and it succeeded only too well. Justin's arms went around her shoulders, drew her close; his lips murmured against her mouth.

"Lancey, Lancey."

"Dear Justin."

"Oh, I love you, Lancey."

She had thought there'd been enough of talk, but he had said the one extra thing she wanted to hear. He'd never said it before, and even now he spoke with strained gruffness. It was, she decided, a proof of his sincerity, far different from the glib phrases of Dirck van Zandt.

"I love you, too," whispered Lancey. She made the statement firmly, feeling it disloyal to think of one man while kissing another. She ran her fingers through Justin's hair, held his head close as they kissed again.

This was a long, lingering kiss that left them both stirred and breathless. Justin gazed down at the girl lying back in his arms. Her face was flushed, her smile tremulous. The hazel eyes had never seemed so vivid, wide with excitement, bright with anticipation. Lancey's rapid breathing fluttered the bodice of her dress, and his hand went toward that movement almost involuntarily.

She gasped at his caress, closed her eyes. His very deftness was at once stimulating and weakening. She drew herself toward him, blindly seeking another kiss.

They lay side by side in the long grass, resting a moment, mutually accepting a respite from passion. Lancey opened her eyes. The sky overhead was very blue. Around her, close, was the perfume of spring, the sun warmed scents of earth, and grass, and clover. Justin's arm pillowed her head; his muscular length pressed against her from ankle to shoulder.

"Justin," she said, softly, looking at him.

He smiled, reached to complete the disarray of her bodice. She's lovely, he thought, and willing. The warm, soft roundness of her flesh was disturbingly smooth after the roughness of the homespun.

Lancey trembled under his palm, reached to clutch his hand. She held it still, tight against her.

"Justin, we—we mustn't."

"No?"

"No. Please. I——"

"Lancey."

"Oh, God, Justin, don't."

"We'll be wed, Lancey."

"Wed?"

"Yes, I—I'm asking you to marry me."

His face was very close. The so blue sky beyond it was very far away. Justin wished to marry her, had asked. He wasn't like Dirck, but she couldn't think clearly. Her senses seemed to be shouting to her to accept, and she couldn't think for the tumult.

"Don't you trust me, Lancey?"

That was it, Lancey thought. She had asked for his trust; she couldn't in turn refuse her own.

"Yes," she said. "Yes, Justin."

He leaned to kiss her. As they kissed Lancey let go of his hand, put her arms around him.

It was her gesture of trust.

20

THE MORE IMPORTANT DELEGATES TO THE CONVENTION, THE FACTION leaders, arrived in Poughkeepsie on the sixteenth of June, the eve of the meeting. They sailed upriver from New York aboard the sloop flotilla, and the townsfolk lined the roadway from the landing to watch them disembark.

Lancey Quist, standing with her family, was impressed by the size of the crowd. Town and countryside had turned out in force. Shops were shuttered and farm chores skimped; only the inns were open for business. Even Hendrick and the other fishermen neglected their trade to welcome the distinguished visitors. The first sight of the sails flashing from the south brought chattering excitement from the packed ranks of onlookers.

The girl barely gave the maneuvering sloops a glance. Her gaze scanned the throng in search of Justin Pattison.

Her cheeks burned at the memory of their lovemaking in the clearing. She was, to her surprise and relief, still a maiden, but that was not due to her own scruples. She had permitted Justin liberties that no other man had been allowed. Lancey's knees felt watery as she recalled the caresses, her mounting passion, her readiness to submit to the final, expected act.

Once more, she thought, her body had betrayed her by its heated desires, but her decision had been deliberate, her surrender complete. She had been willing to let Justin win her; it was his choice alone that had saved her.

Lancey remembered that without disappointment. Her enjoyment had been intense enough to dispel any momentary feeling of incompletion. Justin had been tender, thoughtful, skillful. How right she had been to trust him!

His reasons had been valid and worthy. He'd mentioned her youth and innocence, the uncertainty of immediate marriage, his love, the wedded bliss in their future. Her respect and devotion, Lancey decided, had been increased by Justin's behavior. She recognized, too,

234

an unmentioned taboo. For safety and reputation a girl had better wait until her wedding night. Anything else was dangerous, might mark her as a sinful strumpet. There was, she knew, many a slip between the banns and the blanket.

In all honesty, she thought, I don't deserve Justin. Any other man would have taken advantage of her.

Hester, holding a daughter by each hand, nudged Lancey. "There's Dirck," she said, nodding.

A group of horsemen were walking their mounts toward the landing, leading saddled, riderless horses. Lancey saw Dirck in their midst, riding Meda, flanked by his father and brother. Tappen Platt rode beside Schuyler Davis. The riders were dressed in their best, as splendidly groomed as the shining horses.

"The gentry," said Lancey, using Justin's scornful tone.

Hendrick turned in surprise. He was enjoying the crowd, the air of excitement, the holiday occasion. The riders had brought a good natured murmur of admiration from nearby spectators, and Lancey's remark jarred him. He said, "Dirck is our friend, too, Lancey."

"Too?"

"Aye," Hendrick said, slowly, "as well as Justin. There was no cause for Justin to resent what Dirck did for us about the shad. There is no reason for you to take sides."

"No reason, Pa?" Lancey stared at her father. Of all the people assembled here, she thought, I have the best reason for taking sides in any quarrel between those two men!

"Lancey didn't mean that, Hendrick." Behind her husband's shoulder Hester shook her head at the girl. "That group *is* gentry, and here to welcome Alexander Hamilton."

"How do you know?"

"It's no secret," Hester said. "Everybody knows. Seth Row's wife told me. The van Zandts, and the rest are against George Clinton, and for adoption."

"All the gentry are," Lancey said, "except the Livingstons."

Hendrick scowled, shrugged. "It is right that Dirck stands with his family. We are still beholden to him."

"Of course," said Hester, forestalling her stepdaughter's speech. Again, she gave Lancey an almost imperceptible headshake. "We like them both, don't we, Lancey?"

Swallowing her retort, Lancey nodded. Hester's twinkle mocked male blindness, and female weakness. The girl colored, glanced away, wondering how much her stepmother guessed. She had, Lancey thought, liked them both indeed, but her choice was Justin.

They had reached their understanding in the clearing, but she didn't dare risk a repetition of the circumstances. Their meetings, since then, had been within sight, if not earshot, of others. They had spoken of love, and held hands, but there had been no opportunity for ardent courting. Justin seemed busier than ever with Venick, but she no longer questioned that.

Lancey's searching gaze was without anxiety. She merely wished to look at Justin. If, as she suspected, his secret business concerned the convention she might see him even less once it opened.

He wasn't present, she decided, at least in the part of the gathering she could see. Other familiar faces drew her attention: the Rows, Digmus Jaycock, Nell Bogardus. She saw Pardon Cash, hatless, towering above a distant group, and stared for a full minute at the men surrounding the big fisherman. There was no one who resembled Justin.

A roar rose from the landing, a shouted name that was tossed along the long lines hedging the roadway. Men were disembarking from a sloop. Lancey recognized one stalwart figure before his name reached her.

"Clinton," said Hendrick.

"Clinton," Hester said.

Around her, Lancey heard the name mentioned, repeated, bellowed, cheered. It climbed the slope of the bluff with the gunfire crackle of branches breaking before a high wind.

"It's Clinton."

"There's Clinton."

"Clinton."

Poughkeepsie, in spite of its east-bank position, claimed the governor as its own. Many who cheered had crossed the river from Clinton's native Ulster County, but even these did not outshout the townsfolk. They all knew him, had seen him as recently as six months ago. He was valley born, river bred, one of themselves.

Lancey yelled with the rest, her voice lost in the general acclaim. She felt no disloyalty to Justin, thought he would understand. This was, after all, the man who had led the state for as long as she could remember—the first, the only, non-royal governor.

Whatever his faults, she decided, he deserved the praise and the applause. His had been one of the early voices raised against the Tory landlords, among the first to cry for independence. If, in the long struggle to keep the British from control of the Hudson, George Clinton had been a more willing than able general, he had proved his courage and his energy. The redcoats had driven him, and beaten him, but they had never crushed him. With Washington's help, he had managed, except for the raid that razed Kingston, to hold on to the upper river.

George Clinton, grinning, raised his hat to the cheers, and the sunshine turned his hair to the silver of birchbark. He was a big man, six foot four, heavy in shoulders and chest, with a paunch of middle age bulging his waistcoat. There was more of the farmer than lawyer about him, a broad-faced genial farmer, with a large nose, and very shrewd eyes.

He waved and climbed into a carriage, and the crowd cheered the group with him. These were Poughkeepsie men, Clinton men —Melancthon Smith, Zephaniah Platt, Gilbert Livingston. The elegant young fellow with the quiet smile was the governor's nephew, DeWitt, General James Clinton's boy.

By craning her neck Lancey could see Dirck van Zandt. He was waving his arm and shouting. So were Tappen and Schuyler. Beekman van Zandt and some of the other older men sat their horses silently, but even they were smiling.

The gentry, she thought, didn't mind cheering a man allied to the Livingstons. Then she admitted that the sneer did not apply to Dirck. He'd cheer a man he meant to fight as readily as he'd laugh at a girl he wished to kiss.

"Eunice Wynbridge for instance," muttered Lancey.

"What?" Hannah grabbed at her stepsister's hand. "What, Lancey?"

"Nothing, dear."

As the governor's carriage ascended the slope, headed for the Clear Everett house, the cheers died down behind it like the settling dust. The first part of the show was over, but there was more to come. The folks who had shouted for George Clinton wanted to be sure that his political rival had heard.

Dirck van Zandt wheeled his coaly bay mare across the roadway; the other horsemen followed. They blocked the view of the landing, but Lancey could see that Captain Benjamin's *Lydia* was alongside her mooring. Down there, at the foot of the hill, people were jostling each other, pointing.

"Told you," Hester said, "they'd come to meet Hamilton."

"What's he look like?" asked Hendrick.

"They say he's on the small side."

"And young," Lancey said. "Thirty. Thirty-one. Something like that."

"I wouldn't call that so young!"

"Depends, Pa." Lancey sounded thoughtful. "He was a colonel when the war ended, but nobody knew much about him." She was quoting Justin and Dirck, things she had read. "He's fast become the governor's chief rival. 'Course it didn't hurt that he'd been General Washington's aide."

"Didn't hurt none either," Hester said, "that he married a Schuyler!"

The crowd made the same comments, showed the same curiosity. Few had seen this stranger who favored the Constitution. Rumor said that he wrote the arguments that those who could read had passed on to the rest, arguments that made sense, that a man could follow. This Hamilton, if he *did* write them, was a mighty sharp young man.

Then, as the little cavalcade swung about, the crowd fell silent. There were strangers riding with the others now, and one of them was Alexander Hamilton.

Lancey knew him at once. The quiet crowd, she judged, felt the same instant recognition. There was more to it than his age, his bearing, or the manner in which he edged his horse into the lead position. The act was done with ease and graciousness, with the unthinking arrogance of one who assumed command by right. But there was more to it than that.

He rode into Poughkeepsie like a conqueror, and the watching people recognized him.

"Good looking, ain't he?" said Hester.

Nodding uncertainly, Lancey stared at the man. Why, she thought, he isn't so small! Then, she saw that he wasn't tall either. His slenderness and posture made the most of every inch. Hamilton's clothes, rich black, seemed to have been molded on his figure, as neatly fitted as a handmade glove. He rode well, but not with casual grace as Dirck rode. This was a man who had trained himself to control an animal.

"Yes," she said, "he's good looking." He reminded Lancey of Eunice Wynbridge. His was a more masculine face, but the even features had the same chill, contained expression. This was, she admitted, an unfair comparison because Hamilton was being stared at by hundreds of unfriendly eyes. Lancey was sure he was aware of that fact, ignoring it.

The horsemen came up the slope in a rough wedge with Hamilton riding point. There was no sound from the crowd. In the stillness Lancey could hear the clop-clop of the hoofbeats, the jingle of bridle chains. Hamilton held his steed to a walk, and his head turned as he surveyed the packed ranks on either side of the road.

He was almost in front of Lancey when the first hiss broke the quiet.

It was a sudden, startling noise, alien to the county, but it ended in a long-drawn, high-pitched catcall. The more familiar yowl of disapproval made Lancey quiver. She stared toward its source.

There, easily found by the disturbance as people drew away from him, was Justin. Hands on hips, chin raised, his throat worked as he finished the catcall with a flourish. Then, he stood motionless, grinning.

Hamilton's horse shied, was instantly checked. Other animals danced nervously, but none reared or bolted.

Oh, no, thought Lancey in dismay.

Another catcall wailed lower down the slope. A third sounded from another quarter. Others followed in a lunatic series of echoes; single men, always, scattered through the throng. There were hisses, hoots, caterwaulings.

Lancey, eyes darting, identified several yowlers. They were riverfront roughs, Jaycock's custom. Yes, she thought, and Venick's hirelings, led by Justin.

Alexander Hamilton laughed, turned his head, still laughing, and said something to Dirck van Zandt. The younger man's scowl vanished, he nodded.

Hamilton's laughter, Lancey saw, made his face more youthful, animated. The cool dark eyes warmed with humor. She knew then that he had magnetism, and no fear. Men would follow him, she thought, because of that. He might never be a beloved leader, like George Clinton, but he could inspire a devoted loyalty in a select few.

Without haste, enjoying himself, Hamilton spurred his horse to a canter. Taking cue and pace from their leader the others followed. They rode away with the amiable chatter of a returning hunt on a deserted country lane.

The crowd, Lancey noted, was shocked, scandalized. Disapproval sharpened the murmuring voices. As the ranks dissolved, spread into the roadway, separated into groups for the walk homeward, faces were dark with indignation.

Hendrick Quist, surprisingly, expressed the general feeling in a sentence.

239

"That was childish," he said, "and inhospitable to a stranger guest."
Lancey bit her tongue and said nothing.

* * *

From the day of its opening the Constitutional Convention was
dominated by the personality of Alexander Hamilton. Neither the
hostile majority of delegates, nor the town of Poughkeepsie, realized
this at first.

The town was proud that the governor had been chosen to preside.
It was the logical choice, but George Clinton wasn't proud. He was
aware that the position stilled his tongue; he grew more choleric with
every speech. Clinton sat like a wrathful judge who watched the jury
being swayed by the wrong lawyer.

Melancthon Smith, the right lawyer, attacked the proposed document with eloquence and skill. Poughkeepsie bragged of Smith's ora-
tory, repeated his arguments. Yet, even when it crowed the loudest,
the town was concerned with the reaction of a single member of
Smith's audience.

How did Hamilton like them apples?

There was room in the small courthouse for only the most influen-
tial spectators. These crowded the gallery, jammed the doorways.
Outside, under the windows opened to the fine June weather, the
overflow clustered in ever-changing, never-diminishing groups. After
every session the few who knew what had happened spread the news.
These unofficial town criers became, depending on their social circle,
the toasts of taverns, or the pets of parlors.

Thus, the details filtered down to the populace. The debate was
reenacted; the arguments repeated and misquoted. Who said what,
did what, wore what, was a topic that engrossed every supper table,
atop the bluff or along the waterfront.

It was, Lancey Quist thought, very like the early days of a shad
run. Most of the town, the workers, the sailors, the shopkeepers, went
about their business, but shared the excitement of the participants.
They asked eager questions, and wanted a tasty morsel for their
nightly fare.

By the end of the week even the riverfront had learned one fact.
Melancthon Smith's apples didn't bother Alexander Hamilton. That
quiet-voiced young man ate them core and seed.

Lancey was disturbed by the effect this might have on Justin. She
had seen him only once since the performance at the landing, and
their conversation had not been pleasant.

"That hooting, Justin. You don't call that your desperate gamble, do you?"

"That," said Justin, laughing, "was just a sample. To let Hamilton know he wouldn't have things his own way."

"He knew that without your antics."

"Oh? You think we should have cheered him?"

"I think he's still laughing."

"He won't laugh next time."

"Next time?"

"You tend to your fishing, Lancey. It's no concern of yours!"

He had stamped away, leaving her flushed with anger. She wondered, later, why she hadn't shouted after him. From the moment they met she'd fought with Justin, and now, when she loved him, she was afraid to open her mouth. This was a new experience for Lancey.

Next morning she swallowed her pride, and went looking for him. She found Pardon Cash alone on his pier, mending net.

"Justin," said the big fisherman, "has sort of retired from fishing, Lancey."

The girl sensed the hurt hidden in the casual tone. She said, "It's just during the convention, Pardon."

"Tell the fish."

"You—you're still partners?"

"Aye. Far as I know. I don't split with a messmate easy, Lancey. But Justin—well, he's got some notions I can't go along with."

"You mean—with Venick?"

The wide shoulders shrugged; Pardon's face might have been a weathered figurehead. "Ain't for me to say. You better ask Justin about that."

Stalking home, Lancey tried to remember the last time Pardon had refused to tell her anything. She was too depressed to go to Jaycock's. If Justin was there, he was likely to think she was spying. Love, she decided, had a deal of misery mixed in with the joy. That, of course, was only to be expected. She was, she told herself, Lancey Quist in love with a real man, not some silly goose mooning over a dream beau.

Meda whinnied a greeting as she entered the Quist yard. Dirck van Zandt was sunning himself on the doorstep. The two little girls listened with rapt absorption while he talked to their parents. Hendrick was outside the house, Hester within.

"—and much as they hate him," Dirck said, "they listen. When Hamilton rises to speak you can hear a fly stamp his feet in that room. Hello, Lancey."

"Hello," she said, defensive and annoyed. He was an enemy, for Hamilton and against Justin. She found even his smiling twinkle a deliberate goad intended to hurt.

"Hendrick says he can spare you."

"Sure," agreed Hendrick.

"Spare me for what?" Lancey wished to know what she refused. She was certainly not going anywhere alone with Dirck van Zandt. He only had one thing on his mind! She'd made her choice, picked the better man, a more moral man, a fine——

"Well," said Dirck, interrupting her thoughts, "I can get you into the convention if you'd like to see it."

"*You can?*"

Her startled delight made Dirck grin. He'd been counting on her curiosity, her enthusiasm, that zest for new experience that was so characteristic. The selling of the shad had gone wrong; Lancey had joined forces with Justin Pattison. It would take some effort to correct that mistake.

Dirck did not underestimate Justin. The New Englander was taller, had brains, a fine record as a soldier, that damned white lock of hair. He was, in short, a formidable rival.

"Yes," Dirck said, slowly, "this is evidently van Zandt day. Places are being held for all of us. My father and mother. My brother. You will be most welcome, Lancey."

She stared, fully realizing the implications. This was no jest, a sudden impulse to enliven a party by producing a strange girl. Dirck was deliberately planning to display her with the members of his family before the gentry of Poughkeepsie.

"Dirck," she said, "I—I'm not sure——"

"My parents send their compliments, Lancey. They wished me to say they would be pleased to have your company." There was no need, Dirck thought, to mention the hour-long arguments that had produced that invitation. Then, as he saw her expression, he was aware that she knew. He said, "God's truth, Lancey."

"Lancey," said Rhoda Quist gazing at her stepsister with interest, "close your mouth."

"Face'll freeze that way," Hannah quoted her mother.

"God and Nicholas!"

Lancey's exclamation, low but desperate, brought both children to their feet. Her stepsisters knew it meant trouble when Lancey sounded like that. Only Dirck's arms, quickly encircling, kept them from flight.

"Don't mind them, Lancey."

"Mind? Who? I wasn't."

Stunned, she gazed down at him. Dirck smiled back from his perch on the threshold. He was sitting jauntily, ankles crossed, with Rhoda leaning against a shoulder and Hannah almost in his lap. Lancey didn't notice the little girls. She was hardly aware that he wore blue coat and fawn breeches, that his linen was spotless, his boots gleaming with polish.

His eyes, she thought, are the startling blue of sunshine on the river. She probed them for hidden motives, perplexed by a vague recollection that they had beguiled her long ago.

Dirck van Zandt felt uneasy under the steady gaze. He was anxious, nervous. This was Lancey, with whom every cast and wile had failed. Damn the wench! Couldn't she tell that he'd changed? He wanted her more than ever, but he would not cheat. He spoke with teasing banter, daring her to think him insincere.

"We won't go near the river this time."

"We'd better not," said Lancey, and grinned. She, too, remembered their duckings. He was, she knew, gambling that she would not be outraged by the memory. It was a compliment and she accepted it as such. "Those who drown go down three——"

Then, dismay contorted her face and Dirck thought he had lost. "Oh, Dirck!"

Her wail startled Hendrick across the width of the yard. Rhoda and Hannah gaped in slack-jawed fascination.

"What's the matter?"

"I—I can't go, Dirck!"

"Don't you want to?"

"Of course, I do! But—the convention and all—all those people——" Lancey ran her palms down the front of her sleeveless homespun. She kicked a bare foot forward, wrung her hands. There was no avoiding the bitter truth. She could not face Dirck's mother, that flint-eyed little matron, in faded dimity.

"I don't understand, Lancey."

"I—of course you don't, but—I just don't——"

"What's the matter," said Hester, looming broad in the doorway behind Dirck, "with the russet velvet?"

"The—the russet—*Hester!*"

"It's hanging in here waiting for you. Good as new."

243

Dirck barely managed to draw Rhoda aside in time, as Lancey hurdled past them into the house. He glimpsed a flash of more bare leg than he was meant to see, grinned his appreciation at the sky. Some day, he thought, if I get my way, she'll have gowns aplenty to choose from.

"Come away, younguns," he said, rising. "We'll talk to your Pa while the ladies make medicine."

Dancing around her stepmother, Lancey bounced like a ravenous puppy. Hester, holding the gown high, pivoted to keep it out of reach. Broad grin and beaming eyes mocked the older woman's stern commands.

"Stay back, Lancey. Keep your paws off!"

"But, Hester——"

"You ain't touching this dress, till you're clean. You're not taking no fish smell to the courthouse!"

Nodding, Lancey locked her hands behind her back. She couldn't believe her eyes. In the shaft of sunlight that streamed through the open door, the velvet gown was vividly beautiful. It was, she thought, even finer than she'd remembered, restored to an elegance beyond her dreams. The sodden, bedraggled cloth she'd last seen now had a nap as silky as fine fur.

"Hester, how in the world did you——?"

"I didn't," Hester said. "I know when a task's beyond me. I took it to Calico's wife."

"Calico's wife?"

"Uh-huh. Name's Fidelia. She's Miz Livingston's personal slave. Has charge of her whole wardrobe. Fidelia knows tricks about female finery." Hester regarded the velvet with critical approval. "It took time and patience, Lancey, and lots of both. Whole vats of steam, and brush strokes by the hundred, I guess. Whatever she did, it worked."

"God bless Fidelia."

Hester glanced at the fireplace. "I've water hot, and as soon as you're scrubbed——" She interrupted herself as Lancey yanked the homespun skirt over her head. "Lancey, the door! Dirck's out there!"

He's seen me in less, thought Lancey gaily, but paused until she heard the double slam of the Dutch door. She was peeling down her petticoats when she remembered Justin.

The exuberance drained out of her, and she stood motionless, clad only in her shift, underskirts forming a pool around her ankles. Lancey bit her lip, frowning, horrified by her own fickleness. Dirck's invitation had simply erased Justin from her mind. Yet she had accepted Justin's proposal of marriage, promised to wed him. She was, if secretly and unofficially, an affianced girl!

Justin, she knew, would not approve of her attending the convention with Dirck. There wasn't the slightest chance that Justin wouldn't learn about it. Even if he didn't see her the gossip would be all over Poughkeepsie by morning.

Dirck, she judged, had planned it that way. She didn't doubt that he'd waged a mighty struggle to obtain his parents' consent. Her public appearance at such a function as a family guest had, in the customs of the county, a single explanation. It was a silent announcement of open courtship.

She had never really expected Dirck van Zandt to make such an announcement, and the victory made her glow with pleasure. But, if she went, she sailed under false colors by admitting his courtship was welcome.

An engaged woman had made her choice. Lancey had chosen Justin. To go with Dirck was to reject Justin. To refuse to go would insult Dirck's hard-won offer.

Damn and blast, said Lancey silently, it was all as tangled as a fish net in a gale!

Hester, pouring hot water from kettle to basin, turned, puzzled by the long silence.

"What's the matter, Lancey?"

The girl stared at her stepmother. There was no use seeking advice. Two things repeated themselves in Lancey's mind. The convention was the biggest happening that had ever taken place in Poughkeepsie. The red dress, lost and ruined, had been found and restored.

"I was wondering," said Lancey, making her decision, "how to arrange my hair."

21

"AS IT IS ESSENTIAL TO LIBERTY THAT THE GOVERNMENT IN GENERAL should have a common interest with the people, so it is particularly essential that the branch of it under consideration should have an immediate dependence on and an immediate sympathy with the people."

Alexander Hamilton, speaking about the proposed House of Representatives, was using his voice the way a virtuoso handles his instrument. The assemblage, delegates, officials and spectators, listened in silence, almost without movement. Every gaze in the crowded confines of the courthouse was fixed on the slender, erect figure of the speaker. For an age of bombast Hamilton's delivery was simple; he seemingly disdained oratorical flourishes in order to present his ideas with clarity.

Listening, Lancey Quist realized she was witnessing something extraordinary, perhaps momentous. The girl lacked the words and experience to recognize a great artistic performance, but she instinctively knew that this was a rare occasion, when a man and an historic moment blended in perfect harmony.

He might have been born, she thought, for this cause and this convention. She wondered pensively what this man's future could hold that would ever equal these days of triumphant power.

Whoever won or lost, however the country was formed or governed, surely no man, not even Alexander Hamilton, could hope to reach brilliant perfection more than once in a lifetime. Here was a dominant will that held its audience enthralled. It was a triumph of personality over prejudice, of an eloquent conviction that convinced.

Lancey's judgment was formed by her own feelings. Hamilton spoke with such careful, precise language that even she could follow his discourse. He was untiring, patient, unruffled, bolstering each argument with explanatory detail, answering every objection point by point. She had heard someone say he was calmly logical; she knew, somehow, that he made no mistakes.

246

She forgot that he was for ratification, against Clinton, against Justin and her own inclinations. He made no impassioned pleas, and the girl found his manner too cold to be attractive. Yet when Hamilton reached a conclusion, she nodded in agreement.

This man, said Lancey silently, left you with nothing else to do!

After Hamilton finished and sat down, Lancey sighed. A stir and rustle vibrated through the room. Men shook themselves as if awakening from a coma. For the first time Lancey noticed that the hour was late; shadows were thickening in the corners. The rays of sunshine that came through the western windows had a strangely diluted radiance.

"That," whispered Dirck van Zandt, leaning close, "was a speech!"

She nodded, aware now that her feet hurt, and her calves trembled from standing for so long. The gallery was crowded and Dirck's mother had the only available seat. Lancey didn't mind. Far across the hall, with another party, Eunice Wynbridge sat in comfort, but her glare made Lancey's aching muscles a pleasure.

Down on the convention floor someone called out a motion for adjournment. The formality seemed unnecessary. People were gathering hats and wraps, rising. Even George Clinton, scowling and impatient, held his gavel poised to end the session.

"It's over," Lancey said.

"For today." Dirck kept his voice low. "Nobody wants to try to answer Hamilton without a night's preparation."

Mrs. van Zandt turned to peer at Lancey from under the rim of her bonnet. She said, "I hope you enjoyed the proceedings, Mistress Quist."

"Oh, yes, thank you."

"And understood them."

Neither the chill tone, nor the sniff that accompanied it, bothered Lancey. She merely smiled with polite diffidence. Dirck's mother had greeted her with a stiff formality that hid defeat and disapproval. Beekman van Zandt's surreptitious wink and the younger Beekman's broad grin had told the girl all she needed to know. Amelia van Zandt had, for once, been routed by her men folk. She didn't like it, but she had cried truce.

"Not completely," Lancey said frankly. "This was all very new to me, ma'am."

Mrs. van Zandt squinted, munched her lips as if tasting the girl's remark. "Well," she said, "that's honest." She gazed around, noted the convention was adjourned, frowned at the press jamming the doorways. Gathering gloves and umbrella, she hesitated, decided to be gracious. She said, "You looked very nice anyway, my dear."

"Stunning," said her husband. He patted Dirck's arm, made no attempt to lower his voice. "Good stock, son. Long in the flanks for all her size. She'll breed."

Young Beekman muffled a guffaw, and pushed a path toward the stairway. Lancey, face scarlet, quickly followed on Dirck's arm. She didn't dare glance at him, could feel suppressed laughter quivering his sleeve. Behind them Mrs. van Zandt's voice clanged like a dropped handbell.

"Really, Beekman!"

"Well, dammit, Amelia," said Master van Zandt, "my grandfather was a cooper, and yours was a piddling *brewmeister!*"

"Oh, my," murmured Lancey, half-expecting the roof to collapse. Dirck squeezed her hand. He said, "You're a success." He was feeling gay, delighted with the day's results. Lancey's success and Hamilton's were strangely connected in Dirck's mind, and he considered this a good omen. After today, he thought, neither ratification nor my courtship can fail.

"Good stock," said Lancey gruffly, and giggled. She, too, was pleased by her reception, but she felt uneasy when she recalled her promise to Justin. It wasn't exactly fair to lead Dirck on, to let him, and his family, think she was still free to choose.

She decided to cross that bridge when she must. So far Dirck had only requested her company; he might never propose. Lancey dismissed her uneasiness resolutely as they edged slowly toward the exit.

Outside the courthouse the sunset sky had a foreboding look. There was no breeze, but to the west, over the river, the afternoon's sultriness seemed to have congealed, turned haze to an inky murkiness that was spreading. Distant clouds were massing into thunderheads; no valley resident could fail to read the signs. A storm was brewing. One of those violent, clamorous, lightning-lashed storms that periodically minimized the majesty of the Hudson.

Lancey noticed these portents, noticed also that few of the convention crowd seemed disturbed. People loitered, mingled with friends who had failed to gain admission. Men stood in groups, discussing the speeches; women exchanged gossip and criticized other women's apparel. The horses, saddle and carriage, hitched in long rows that hedged all four arms of the crossroad, were more restless than their masters.

"Going to storm," Dirck said, "but I'll have you snug at home before it hits." He was turning to speak to his brother, but never completed the movement.

Somewhere close a musket blasted. The sound of the gunshot froze the crowd to momentary stillness; the flash from the muzzle, a mica-speck in the darkening daylight, drew every gaze.

Across the road, at the corner of the old Dutch cemetery, a knot of men twisted and turned in sudden motion. A tall figure broke free, scrambled up the roadbank, ran, darting among the gravestones, through the burying ground. Another, trying to follow, was knocked sprawling. One man, square built, stepped aside, dropped to a knee, leveled a musket at the fleeing figure.

Lancey's heart lurched as she recognized the fugitive. It was Justin!

Before the marksman could fire, a big man, moving fast, lashed out a kick snapping the gun upright, so that it spat its flame at the sky.

"That's Pardon Cash," said Dirck.

"Yes." Lancey hoisted her skirts and ran. Fast as she sprinted, Dirck was beside her in five strides. His arm went around her as supporting prop and she was grateful. Petticoats, and shoes, were hampering.

They were the first to reach the struggle, and as they did it ceased. Lancey saw that other fishermen besides Pardon were involved. Seth Row was helping a fallen stranger to his feet. Gerritt Kimmee was arguing with Phineas Child.

The sight of Master Child sent a chill down the girl's spine. He was a deputy sheriff and his presence meant that Justin had escaped the law. She noticed that the younger of the two strangers, the apple-cheeked lad that Seth Row was dusting, held two fingers against a bleeding mouth.

"Pardon," she said, "what's happened?"

Now holding the musket the big fisherman spat through the gap in his front teeth. The squat stranger answered in the nasal twang of New England.

"Fine town, Poughkeepsie. Helping murderers to bolt."

"Murderers?" Dirck sounded puzzled.

"You boys oughtn't to have done that," said Phineas Child. "The man was a prisoner."

"Now, look," Pardon Cash said, "keep your dander dampened, Phineas. You're a Poughkeepsie law officer. Justin's been here several months, and, far as I know, he hasn't done anything that broke any of the laws around these parts."

"Justin?" Dirck asked. "Justin Pattison?"

Pardon Cash nodded, said: "That's right. These strangers come along and make certain claims, but there's no telling how true they might be."

"True as true," said the stranger. "The man's wanted for a killing, and there's a thirty-pound reward for his capture."

"This," Phineas Child said, "is Sheriff Aaron Nichols of Springfield in Massachusetts. And the other's his helper, Samuel Hart."

Young Samuel Hart bowed, spreading his fingers to display a bloody smile. Sheriff Nichols ignored the introductions. He glared at Pardon Cash, reached for his musket. The crowd from the convention had gathered, was asking excited questions, but neither the fisherman nor the officer paid any attention.

"Sorry," Pardon said, "but Massachusetts law ain't New York law. Justin's our friend, and we couldn't rightly let you cart him off to gaol." He relinquished the gun.

"Back home," Nichols said, "you'd all go in his place."

Seth Row said, "This ain't back home, mister."

"Now, now," spluttered Phineas Child. "These here officers, Sheriff Nichols and Master Hart, showed proper and right credentials. They are what they say they are. They asked for assistance and I gave it as was only decent. You fellers shouldn't act like they misbehaved."

"If you're so sot on defending Justin Pattison," said Nichols sourly, "why'd one of you send word he was in these parts?"

"Send word?"

"Yeah!" The Massachusetts sheriff's nod was emphatic. "Party by the name of Quist."

"Quist." Lancey whispered the name with disbelief. Since the first mention of Springfield she'd realized that Justin was in serious trouble; the backwash of Shays' Rebellion had somehow followed him here to the banks of the Hudson. She knew the matter was serious, but couldn't believe that the sheriff had correct information. "Did you say—Quist?"

"That's right, Mistress." Aaron Nichols glowered at her. "Most of us back home was willing to let bygones be bygones. What's over and done should lie fallow. But when a feller riding through—Philadelphia to Boston—asks around about is there any reward for Justin—well, there was no holding Eph Cutting's folks. Eph's the one Justin killed."

"This feller," Dirck said, automatically mimicking Nichols' tone, "wasn't named Quist?"

"No, no. He'd been asked that by said Quist. Over here on your river."

No Poughkeepsie man as much as glanced at Lancey. Dirck's hand came to rest on her shoulder as if casually. Even Phineas Child's face reflected the impassive expression of the three fishermen. The crowd, trying to listen and question at the same time, milled in restless bewilderment.

"Conrad," said Lancey with horror.

Dirck's fingers tightened; Pardon Cash spoke rapidly. "That's neither here nor there," the big fisherman said. "You might easily be mistaken about the looks or size of——"

Sheriff Nichols interrupted. "I've known Justin Pattison," he said, "since he was no taller than your breeches' knee buckles. We had the right man. Thanks to you and your friends he's loose again. But I know my duty and I want him taken."

"Of course," Phineas Child said. "Of course. We'll get the town sheriff. The deputies. Form a posse. With thirty pounds' reward there'll be plenty to lend a hand. He can't cross the river, and he can't go far afoot."

The Massachusetts man's glance flashed from Pardon to Seth Row to Gerritt Kimmee. He said, "You'd better send a few armed men among the fishermen, just to make *sure* he can't cross the river."

Phineas Child started giving orders. There was a scurrying, a gabble of excited voices. Someone ran for the town sheriff. Others, joyous at the prospect of a man hunt, hurried to get their guns. Aaron Nichols, leaning on his musket, told young Hart to patch his mouth, and watched the preparations. Anger made him hold himself as rigid as his gun barrel.

The trio of fishermen drew apart. Lancey and Dirck joined them. The girl clutched Pardon's wrist.

"Pardon, tell us the whole story."

"They caught him at Jaycock's," said Pardon. "The two New Englanders and Phineas was together, armed, and Justin never had a chance. If Gerritt, here, hadn't been in the ordinary having his tipple, we wouldn't know about it yet."

Gerritt Kimmee nodded; he swabbed his lips with a palm before he spoke. "I saw them come in. Justin was sitting with Digmus and Venick, but he saw them, too. He said something, low like, to Venick, and stood up. That sheriff one, Nichols, he called Justin by name, and Justin went along with them as meek as a lamb."

"Yes," said Lancey. She knew Justin's meekness, the false quiet that waited for the proper moment to explode into action.

"Well," Pardon Cash said, "it took Gerritt a few minutes to get hold of Seth and me. That's how we didn't catch up with them until they reached the graveyard here. Naturally, we wasn't going to let no outsiders take another fisherman to gaol. They'd been right canny, sneaking around the town to avoid folks, but we were waiting for them. Phineas tried to argue with us, but Justin suddenly took things in his own hands."

"Aye," said Seth Row, "he even caught *me* by surprise. They'd just mentioned that somebody named——" He glanced at Lancey, swallowed, continued. "Somebody named Quist was in line for the reward, when Justin jumped. After that I was busy."

"Can he get away?" asked Dirck.

"I don't know." Pardon sounded dubious. "They'll be watching all of us. There'll be constables asquatting on every boat in the village, and they'll send horsemen to the ferries. If he's penned this side of the river they'll run him down sooner or later." He cocked his head, scanned the bruised clouds in the purpling western sky. "And from the looks of things this ain't going to be any night to be out in."

"Even," said Gerritt Kimmee, "for a murderer."

"Justin's no murderer!"

Lancey might have saved herself the indignant cry. Only Dirck's hand, again tightening on her shoulder, showed that it had been heard.

Seth and Gerritt shrugged in unison. Pardon Cash smiled without humor. "We ain't asking," he said. "He rowed with us, Lancey. Cast net and made drift. That's enough for us. But the man sounded certain sure."

Seth Row said, "Thirty pounds is a lot of money."

There was, Lancey realized, no sense in arguing about Justin's innocence at the moment. A glance at the thinning crowd, the purposefulness of the men that gathered around Phineas Child, convinced her that time was precious. Sheriff Nichols, grim and laconic, was making sure that the hunt was organized with efficient speed. Even while she watched a rider pelted down the Filkintown Road toward the ferry, and another swung his horse into the Post Road, heading south. From the steps of the courthouse people, delegates and guests, gazed at this bustle with idle interest.

"Justin will be all right," Lancey said. "He can take care of himself. Come, Dirck." She didn't care if they thought her heartless; she even

252

tried to make her voice gay. The important thing was to get Dirck alone, to enlist his help. Justin needed her, and Lancey's whole body burned with the determination to save him.

He was, she told herself, the man she loved, yet it never occurred to her that Dirck might refuse his aid. She was sure she could rely on Dirck.

As they moved away from the fishermen Lancey's voice was quick and low. She spoke for Dirck's ears alone, rapid, clipped speech without tremor or hesitation.

"Dirck. Dirck, I think I know where he'll hide!"

"Justin?"

"Yes. It's a place we both know. We must find him, Dirck. He'll need help to get away."

"You want him to, Lancey."

"Oh, yes. Yes!"

Dirck's step didn't falter. He walked beside her, head tilted, as if listening to a girl's chatter. Lancey's whisper was vibrant with emotion.

"Justin's not a murderer, Dirck. It happened in Shays' Rebellion. They shot at him, and he fired back. He didn't mean to kill the lad. It was fair fight."

"You know this?"

"He told me! We can't let them catch him and hang him, Dirck! We can't!"

"No," said Dirck, "I guess we can't."

Something in his voice, a false note, a shade of strain, made Lancey pause, gaze at him more closely. Dirck, she recalled, had taken her to the convention, had not expected the day to end with a burst of activity. She was filled with sympathy and understanding, sadly aware that she had spoiled his outing. He didn't know that she was pledged to help Justin because he was her future husband.

"Dirck," she said lamely, hoping that he would contradict her, "there's no reason why you should get mixed up in Justin's troubles. Your mother and father——"

"Can find their way home," finished Dirck. He smiled at her, steered her toward the place where they had left the mare. If this, thought Dirck, is more than Lancey helping a friend, it is time I knew it. He forced himself to keep his voice calm and steady.

"Just tell me where to go, Lancey, and what you'd like me to do."

They found Meda, and mounted in silence. This time, as Lancey placed her foot in Dirck's locked hands, was hoisted to the pillion rigged behind the saddle, she gave no thought to arranging the velvet skirt. The only thing in her mind was reaching the clearing as quickly as possible. That, she was sure, was where Justin would go to ground. He would be certain that she'd come there!

Riding south, along the Post Road, Lancey twisted her lips in a wry smile, stung by the difference between this ride and the one they had taken, only a few hours previously, on the way to the convention. Then, Meda had walked, stepping delicately as if fearing to rumple Lancey's gown; now the mare cantered. Then, she and Dirck had bandied light-hearted conversation; now they travelled in silence.

She was again riding behind Dirck, with her arms around his waist, but she tried not to remember that she'd enjoyed the warmth of his nearness, the play of his muscular back. Now, such a feeling was unfair to a harried Justin.

To their right, over the river, the sky had turned livid, a bilious color shot with streaks of blackness that had run, like wet bad dye, from the dark curtain behind them. Meda went at a ground-eating pace, hoofbeats as regular as a clock pendulum, but they rode through a half-light, hushed atmosphere that gave the journey an unbelievable quality. There was no one else on the road, in the world, besides themselves, and the man they were trying to save.

"Conrad," said Lancey, once, against Dirck's collar.

Dirck said, "You don't know that. It's a guess."

"No. I know. Somebody crossed on the horse-ferry who spoke Massachusetts. That was all he needed. Conrad would do anything for money."

"He's only a boy."

"He's a—a scavenger! Conrad hardly even knew Justin. All he was interested in was the pounds he might bring."

Dirck shrugged, warned by her bitterness that this was no time for discussion. He heeled the mare from canter to fast gallop, too conscious of Lancey's clasp about his middle, wanting the whole business finished as soon as possible.

He was riding to the rescue of his rival, and he knew it, but he made no effort to think clearly. Lancey wanted him to do this. Until it was done he could not demand why, or place his own qualities in the scale opposite those of Justin Pattison.

The damned nuisance, he said silently, has hamstrung me by getting himself in jeopardy!

Lancey prodded him, showed the place where they should leave the road. As they climbed the slope, weaving between the trees,

Dirck slowed Meda to a walk. They moved, now, through an eerie forest; in the vague luminescence of the gathering storm the tree trunks were witch fingers poised around them, ready to clutch. The light, filtered through foliage, was bad, shadowy, an unreal reflection that lacked substance. Around them no leaf stirred; the only sounds were those of their own passage.

They came out into the clearing, and could see the sky. Dirck took one look, and grunted. It was gray with threat, darkening and ominous.

"Justin," called Lancey. "Justin?"

"He's not here," Dirck said. "Nobody's here." The clearing, in the weird glow as daylight retreated before the dark of evening and tempest, seemed a magic glen, an evil fairy circle.

"Justin," cried Lancey again.

Far to the north lightning flickered. No thunder reached them, and the sky, after that brief spasm of lurid glare, appeared even darker.

"He may be miles away, Lancey."

"No. He'll come here! I'm sure he will!"

She was more than sure; she was positive. This was their meeting place, the scene of their lovemaking, where they had exchanged the words that bound them to each other. Justin would not flee without seeing her, and, with pursuit spreading, this was the only safe rendezvous. He needed help, and she had come to give it.

"We'll have to wait," she said.

Reluctantly, Dirck dismounted, tied the mare. The clearing didn't strike him as an attractive spot in which to endure a brawling thunderstorm. Already the encircling trees had lost identity, were blended into a solid black wall. The open space looked sere and lonely, a bare patch of ground that nobody had ever visited.

Dirck raised his arms to the girl. "We can't wait long," he said. The distant lightning flickered again, visually supporting his statement.

Lancey slid down from the horse, was caught. She stood for an instant, holding Dirck for balance, and the breathless calm made her nervous. In spite of her worry about Justin she was glad that Dirck was with her. She spoke softly, with a rare timidity.

"We must wait till he comes, Dirck."

"How can you be sure he will?"

"Because—" said Lancey, and paused. She had rehearsed the speech mentally, but now felt oddly reluctant to speak it. Still Dirck deserved to know how things stood between herself and Justin. She said, "Because he's asked me to marry him, and—and I said I would."

She braced herself, awaiting anger or cold silence. Lancey was surprised at the strength of her concern for Dirck. If I truly love Justin, she thought, nothing else should matter.

Dirck laughed. His hands slid up her arms to grasp her shoulders, but he shook her only once, and gently.

"Now why in the hell," he said, "did you do a fool thing like that?"

"Why—why——"

Sputtering, Lancey was unable to answer. His laughter, the amused question, had shocked her speechless. Didn't Dirck believe her? I love Justin, she thought in silent protest. I *do!* Her inarticulate stupidity angered her, and she tried to twist from Dirck's grasp.

Holding her fast, Dirck said: "You'll have to change your mind, Lancey. You can't marry Justin."

"I—can't——" His coolness fanned Lancey's anger. She welcomed the feeling because it loosed her tongue. "Who says I can't?"

"I do. You're going to marry me."

"I'll do exactly as I——" She stiffened as his meaning penetrated. His face was very close to her staring eyes.

"Exactly as you please," Dirck said. "Fine! That means we'll be wed!" He drew her close, and kissed her.

Oh, no, thought Lancey, that's all over. She tried, vainly, to turn her head, to keep her lips tightly closed. Instead, her arms slid around him, and her body pressed against him. Even as she returned Dirck's kiss, enjoying it, she deplored her conduct. You carnal wench, Lancey's mind exclaimed. You sinful, lecherous, fickle harlot! Is it Justin one day, Dirck the next, any man whose kisses give you pleasure?

"Please, Dirck."

"I love you, Lancey."

"Me or—or *this?*"

"You *and* this, Lancey. I think—I hope—you love me."

"I—I don't know," she whispered, trying to tell the truth. She was clinging to him, but only because she needed support. "I'm—I thought I loved Justin."

Lightning curled its white whip through the sky, cracked it. The report was earsplitting, a sharp blast that seemed to shake the earth.

It startled them both, drove Lancey deeper into Dirck's embrace. She flinched, hiding her face against his coat. Thunder had never frightened her before, but this was like a judgment from Heaven.

"It's all right, Lancey. It's all right."

"Dirck."

"It isn't even close yet." He was holding the girl with one arm,

256

reaching for Meda's bridle with the other. The mare didn't like the thunder either. Two skittish females, Dirck thought, with exasperated affection.

Dirck neither saw nor heard Justin until he was wrenched away from Lancey. Even then he had no chance to dodge or guard before a hard fist smashed into his face.

22

"JUSTIN!"

Lancey's cry was almost a frightened scream. His sudden appearance, the outburst of violence, seemed a terrifying aspect of the thunder and lightning. The mare whinnied shrilly, reared, but the girl's first concern was Dirck. He was lying, crumpled, where the vicious blow had driven him. In the thickening gloom Lancey could not see his face.

"Dirck," she said, and started toward him.

"Oh, no!" Justin barred her way. "Let him lie there! It's only your sex keeps me from stretching you alongside him!"

The fierceness of his voice held her more than the threat. She stared at him, uncomprehending, but fear left her and was replaced by anger. She said: "He's hurt. You'd no need to strike him."

"And you in his arms," Justin said. He was coldly raging, speaking thickly, but with care. "How many times in one day can a wench betray a man?"

"You're easily betrayed! Dirck kissed me, yes, but——"

"He's welcome to your kisses!"

Another flash of lightning brightened the clearing, and Lancey glimpsed Justin's scowl. In spite of herself she shivered. She had never seen this man, couldn't possibly love him. He had a right to blame her, perhaps, but not like this.

"I'm sorry, Justin." Lancey sounded contrite. "I honestly thought I loved you, but——"

"Liar!"

"I'm trying to explain!"

"You're good at that," Justin said, sneering. "You have a way with fine sounding phrases. And all the while you'd sell a man behind his back."

"Sell? What are you talking about?"

"Have you been so busy with your fancy friend that you don't know a sheriff's come from Springfield?"

258

"Of course, I know. We saw you break away from them. That's why Dirck brought me here. To help you, Justin."

"Help me? After it was you who sent them word?"

"Me?" Lancey shook her head as if to clear her hearing. "*I* sent them word?"

"Oh, stop it, Lancey, you sicken me. Aaron Nichols had your name. 'Quist,' he said. 'You can thank a party called Quist for this, Justin,' he said."

"And you thought that I——?" Lancey didn't bother to finish the question. She was outraged and furious. If he could think *that* of me, she decided, his love was small indeed. Blood drained from her cheeks, came back with tingling heat.

"Who else here knew my story?"

Justin's bitterness was equaled in Lancey's reply. "No one knew maybe," she said, coldly, "not even Conrad. He merely cast his net in hope of gain."

"Conrad?"

"My brother. The tender at the horse-ferry. Conrad Quist. He has the name, too." Her voice rose as she flared out at him. "Blast your mistrust, Justin! I'm ashamed I ever said I loved you!"

"Your brother," said Justin. He glanced at Dirck. "But you and van Zandt——"

Following his glance, Lancey saw that Dirck had rolled over, was sitting up. She tried to push past Justin, but he caught her wrist.

"Lancey, wait!"

"Let me go!"

"It was a natural mistake."

"If you thought that," she said, "why did you come here to our clearing?" Lancey made no effort to free her arm. She didn't look at Justin, watched Dirck slowly rise to his feet. His sluggish movements made her weak with sudden tenderness.

"Venick was to meet me here," muttered Justin. He was too skilled a fighter to miss Dirck's revival, and he swung Lancey out of the way. "You want more, van Zandt?"

The girl recognized the savage pleasure in Justin's tone. He wronged me, she thought, but he would welcome Dirck as a whipping boy. Fear clogged her throat. Justin was the bigger man, and she had seen him fight.

Dirck, hatless and swaying, straightened his coat. He said, "A coward's blow, Pattison, while I wasn't looking."

"You're looking now."

259

"Yes, and at a bully." Dirck sounded calm, spoke with deliberate contempt. "You evidently mistreat girls, too."

Justin growled, let go of Lancey, and crouched. His remark was drowned by a closer clap of thunder; Lancey stepped between them as the lightning flared.

"Get back, Lancey."

Both men spoke at once. The girl shook her head, held a fluttering hand toward each. "No," she said, firmly, "I'll not have it! I brought Dirck here to help you, Justin. You owe him an apology and——"

"I'll see him damned first," interrupted Justin.

Dirck said: "No apology is acceptable. He struck me. Under other circumstances I'd demand a gentleman's satisfaction, but as it is——" Dirck shrugged out of his coat. "I'll have to settle it by thrashing him."

"Dirck," cried Lancey, in panic, "he's much bigger and stouter, and he nearly crippled Jan Elmendorf——"

"For God's sake, Lancey!"

The horrified bellow that exploded from Dirck stunned Lancey into silence. She had never heard Dirck give way to such uncontrolled fury. Justin's laugh stung her to the realization that she'd said the wrong thing. Desperate, aware she'd blundered, that she had broken some male code that she didn't understand, the girl turned to Justin.

"You know I'm right. You'll be taking a cowardly advantage——"

"Lancey," said Dirck, "will you *please* hold your tongue!"

"No, I won't! I——"

"Put your coat back on, van Zandt." Justin ignored Lancey. "You mentioned a gentleman's satisfaction. It will give me great pleasure to supply the same."

"Here?"

"And now."

"May I ask how, with what weapons?"

They were talking so quietly, with such an odd formal air, that Lancey's head turned as she glanced, puzzled, from one to the other. To hear them, she thought, you'd almost believe the quarrel was mended. A chill lump of dread seemed to be forming in the pit of her stomach.

"Pistols," Justin said. He gestured toward the woods behind Dirck. "And witnesses enough so nobody'll accuse me of murder this time."

Dirck turned, and then Lancey, too, saw the yellow lights bobbing among the trees. She blinked as lightning turned the clearing to white radiance, but the lights were still there when darkness returned. As Dirck donned his coat she knew them for lanterns. Thunder rumbled, and she judged the lightning was closer. It was coming at shorter intervals, now.

"Friends of yours?" asked Dirck.

"I think so."

Dirck bowed, picked up his hat, and went to soothe the mare. Meda wasn't very happy, but she quieted under her master's stroke and murmur. Lancey hesitated, but Justin was gazing at the glowing squares; she walked over to join Dirck.

"Dirck," she said, whispering, "what did he mean by murder?"

"There's no question of that," Dirck said impatiently. "He just likes to wind his own horn."

The lights bobbed into the clearing, and by their glow Lancey saw the faces and figures of two men. She recognized Venick and Digmus Jaycock before the latter spoke.

"Justin?"

"Over here," called Justin, "and fetch those lamps. It's as dark as pitch."

The men started forward, dodged wildly as lightning startled them. Venick's shout barely beat the following thunderclap.

"Who's that with you?"

"It's all right," Justin said. "It's just Dirck van Zandt and Lancey Quist."

"You haven't told them——"

"I've told them nothing, Venick. Did you bring the pistols I asked for?"

"Yes," said Digmus Jaycock, "my own brace." The innkeeper held his light high, peered toward Dirck and Lancey. "I suppose it's safe to talk?" He barely waited for Justin's nod. "Pistols won't help you much, Justin. They're searching the riverfront for you. There's men at my place, and at Pardon's."

Venick said, "You won't be much good to us caught or running."

"I'm not running," Justin said. "I'll hide out until the day of the vote, and lead the lads as we planned. But first there's a little matter to be decided between Master van Zandt and myself."

"At your convenience," said Dirck, with cold politeness, "though the storm will be upon us any minute." Even as he finished thunder and lightning, roar and streak, crashed above the clearing.

Lancey, trembling from the noise, aquiver from the growing dread within her, watched Jaycock take a pair of pistols from under his coat, give them to Justin. Strangely, she heard the click of the steel as he snapped each lock to examine the priming in the pans; it was a thin, metallic sound compared to the deep growl of the thunder. She clutched Dirck's arm as Justin led the others toward them.

The curved gunbutts gleamed in the pale diffused beams. They hung across Justin's forearm, thought Lancey, like the sleek, drooping heads of slain brown birds. Colder pinpoints of light glittered on the steel hammers, seemed reflected in Justin's dark eyes. His face looked as white and hard as the edges of the flints in their cocks.

"My apologies," said Justin, "that these pieces are not proper for the occasion. But they are twins, both loaded, and you may take your choice."

"Thank you," Dirck said, and took one. He hefted the weapon's weight without glancing at it.

"What is this foolery?" asked Venick, lisping.

"A duel?" Jaycock winced at the lightning, competed with the thunder. "A duel, Justin?"

"No," said Lancey. "No! Dirck. Justin. You mustn't." Her dread hardened to certainty. She had never known a duellist, or anyone who had witnessed a duel; differences on the riverfront were settled by brawls. She'd heard of the formal ritual by which men killed according to a code, but it was remote from her life. Not Dirck, she thought, aghast. Not Justin.

"Jaycock can act for me," said Justin, levelly. "You seem to have brought *your* second."

Dirck smiled down at Lancey's hand on his arm, shrugged. He said, "As you wish."

"No, Dirck, please." Lancey, horrified, was pleading. "Justin, this is madness!"

"The girl's right," Venick said, "in more ways than one. This could double your troubles, Justin."

Justin stared at him, coldly determined. He said: "You give the word, Venick. Gold or no gold the riverfront men won't follow *you*, and you know it. Unless I lead them there'll be no rising."

"This conversation is beyond me," said Dirck, "but I don't think that you'll be able to lead anything." He smiled blandly, and yawned.

"Ten yards apart." Justin was clipped and brisk. "A lantern at our feet to mark position. Venick calls the preliminary commands, but we fire at the first lightning flash after that." As if drawn by his words, lightning crackled, luridly brightening sky and clearing.

"Agreed," said Dirck. Gently he withdrew his arm from Lancey's fingers. "Stay with Meda, will you, Lancey? She's a mite restless."

"Dirck, wait!"

He laughed, touched her cheek with his knuckles. "I'll be right back, Lancey."

"Why don't you tell the wench," said Justin as he moved away, "that this has nothing to do with her?"

"Nothing to——"

"That's right, Lancey," said Dirck, cheerfully. "Nothing at all." He took a lamp from Jaycock and walked off, swinging it.

That, the girl recalled, was part of their stupid code. Jan had fought with Justin under the same pretense. They had some fool notion that the lie protected a girl's honor. Honor! What did honor have to do with making a corpse of a lover?

The two figures, with their blobs of horn-dimmed candlelight, moved apart. Their shapes were dim, almost lost in the darkness, but the lights made identification possible. There, on the right, stockings showed Justin's walk. To her left, where the black boots flashed as they turned, was Dirck.

Lightning blinded Lancey; thunder smothered her scream. She couldn't stand this! This duel was to the death, and when Justin fought he never lost! One thought shrieked in her brain, through the tumult of her heartbeats, the uproar of the coming storm.

She loved Dirck van Zandt!

Dirck, cried Lancey silently. Dirck must not be hurt, killed. She started to run forward, but hands gripped her, held her fast.

"Whoa," said Digmus Jaycock in her ear, "you could get hurted, Lancey!"

From the darkness close by came the voice of Christian Venick.

"Are you ready, gentlemen?"

"Ready," said Dirck.

"Yes," Justin said.

The glow to her right made knitted stockings visible. Lancey turned to her left, where polished leather was streaked with light. Those shining lines wavered as her eyes blurred.

"Cock your pieces," Venick called. "Present them."

Dear God, prayed Lancey. Dear God, not Dirck. Neither, please, but not Dirck!

Lancey could hear the wind rising, stirring the woods. So far it was only bending the tree-tops, but the girl felt as if it blew through her, chill and keen.

Digmus Jaycock's breathing was heavy, as rasping as if he snored.

The wait seemed endless; the very air was charged with electricity. Lancey's tension increased with each slow, passing moment. Where was the lightning? It had flashed with increasing frequency as the storm closed; now, it was taking minutes. Where *was* it?

Jagged and brilliant, the lightning cast its thin tracery across the sky. For a glaring instant it froze the clearing into a cold, blue-white stillness.

Everything was outlined starkly, black shapes in lurid brilliance. Lancey saw the grass, the trees, the outcropping rocks, Venick close, Justin and Dirck more distant and separate, against the glittering background. Both duellists stood with arms raised, pistols aimed, as rigid as signposts.

Then, with a crack that ripped, shuddering, through the atmosphere, the light was snuffed out.

"Lord Jesus," said Digmus Jaycock, "that hit close."

Ears ringing, Lancey didn't hear the gunshots. Orange jets of flame stabbed the darkness as the pistols fired.

"Dirck?" Her shriek was shrill against the hollow rustle of the wind. "*Dirck?*"

"Still here," said Dirck, subdued but gay. "A clean miss. But who threw the thunderbolt?"

Thank God, thought Lancey, as her heart leaped in her chest. The night tilted, closed in, began to spin. I must not faint, she told herself. She dug her fingernails into her palms, bit her tongue, tightened every muscle. She would *not* faint. She would not!

Justin's voice was dry, unamused. He said, "Here, too, and we'll have to try again."

Digmus Jaycock swore. "Again?" cried Venick. "Are you daft, Justin?"

"We burned powder," Justin said, "nothing else. That leaves us where we started." His voice rose to question. "You agree, van Zandt?"

"Naturally," said Dirck, after a tiny pause. "Your servant, Master Pattison."

"Reload the pistols, Digmus."

"No!" Lancey glanced from one lantern to the other. The wind, rushing now, seemed to mimic her note of hysteria. She knew she couldn't stand a repetition of the duel, another tortured wait for the shots, and the result. By God's mercy Dirck lived, and Justin, and they must not tempt fate again! "No," she cried, and the word came bursting from her throat in an ever-higher succession of explosions. "No, no, no, no!"

264

Jaycock let go of the girl with startled haste. She heard Dirck's voice, but her own shrieking made his cry seem thin and distant.

Then, earth and sky were shattered by a tremendous, deafening thunderclap, and lightning turned everything to one vast, blinding glare!

Lancey flung her hands over her ears, shaken by the force of the blast, unable to see or think. For an instant she quailed in panic, helpless before the storm's fury. Darkness came again, seemed blacker than before.

The rain, so long delayed, gave a quick spatter of warning, and came lashing down in torrents.

Meda whinnied in fright, and the girl whirled to calm the mare. She was holding the bridle when Dirck shouted.

"Venick! Jaycock! Give me a hand here!"

"Justin's down," Jaycock said, darting away.

Struck by lightning, Lancey thought. She ran toward the figure stretched beside an overturned lantern. The rain slashed at her face, plucked at her skirts. Through the turmoil of the tempest she could hear Dirck swearing.

"Venick! Damn it, Venick, where are you?"

Jaycock called, "Venick!"

Stumbling, Lancey dropped on her knees beside Justin. She stared up at Dirck, gasped. "The lightning——"

"Lightning nothing," Dirck said, with a snort. "He's been shot. The stubborn idiot just wouldn't admit I'd hit him."

Cradling his head on her lap, Lancey Quist bent over Justin to shield his face from the downpour.

* * *

Slowly, leaning into the rain that the wind whipped in flurries from the surface of the river, the bedraggled little procession descended the slope toward the fishing village. Even the horse, plodding under a double burden, slipped in the muddy slick of the narrow path.

"Easy, Meda," said Dirck van Zandt. "Easy, girl."

He walked in front, leading the mare, picking their way by instinct in the darkness. Only one lantern cast any light, and its candle was guttering. Digmus Jaycock carried the lamp to guide his own steps.

"Dirck," said Lancey, low and worried. "He's slumped again."

"He lost a lot of blood," said Dirck, glancing over his shoulder. Atop the pillion Lancey's face was vague blur, half hidden behind

Justin's bowed shoulders. Lancey, thought Dirck, will hold him in the saddle. She had wept over Justin's wound, torn a lawn petticoat into shreds for bandages.

"I got to get back to the inn," said Jaycock, sniffling.

"You stay with us," said Dirck, with finality. "We need you to help carry Justin." He was irritated and worried. Lancey's solicitude for the wounded man might be only pity, but Dirck knew the adage about that emotion's kinship to love.

"Yes, Digmus," Lancey said, "it was bad enough that Venick ran off in the darkness."

"Damned coward," mumbled the innkeeper.

"I'd call him worse," said Dirck. And Justin, too, he thought grimly. Justin had forced the duel, and now he was a wounded warrior. Lancey would have to nurse him for several days. Dirck, grinding his teeth, swore he'd not lose Lancey whatever happened.

"We're getting close," Lancey said.

"If you take Justin to Hendrick's," complained Jaycock, "he'll be captured for sure."

"Stop your whining," said Dirck.

"I'm taking him home," Lancey said, "where he'll have care. That's all that matters now."

She was wet and miserable, but determined to be calm. The moment of panic when she first saw the blood from Justin's side had been Lancey's worst experience. She blamed herself for what had happened. If she had not led Justin to believe her promises, mistaken sympathy and lovemaking for love, he would not have been racked by jealousy, would not have challenged Dirck.

Justin, the girl thought, the competent, the indomitable, has lost everything. He was wounded, hunted by the law, beaten in combat by the type of man he despised. If she could do anything to ease his humiliation, she would certainly do it.

The worst of the storm had gone racketting down the valley, but the rain continued. Southward over the Highlands, the thunder was now a dull and distant rumble. As the path neared the foot of the bluff they could see the river, swollen and angry, running with the sluggish gray current of dirty sludge.

"We're getting close," Dirck said. "There's a light in Hendrick's. You go ahead, Jaycock, with the lantern, and find out who's there."

"Don't forget to come back," said Justin in a weak, but mocking voice.

"Justin!"

266

Lancey's cry was as astonished as the stares of the men. Dirck nearly dropped the mare's reins. He didn't know much about gunshot wounds, but Justin's collapse had worried him. The man had muttered incoherently, had seemed dazed and barely conscious when they hoisted him on the horse.

"You all right, lad?" asked Jaycock.

"No," Justin said, "but I'll do. I've had worse wounds. The grogginess—I must have hit my head when I tumbled."

"You did." Lancey had noticed the bruise on his temple, but it seemed petty compared to the bleeding hole in his side. She wondered if his rational talk was pretense, a fever symptom, really delirium. "You hurry ahead, Digmus. Don't try to talk, Justin."

"I need to, Lancey," Justin said. "Where's van Zandt?"

"Here."

"Is the ball still in me?"

"No," said Dirck, "it passed straight through the flesh of your side." He was impressed by the wounded man's interest. "Far as I could tell there're no bones broken."

"Then, that's all right. From the way it feels, there's nothing to worry about unless it mortifies."

"Justin," said Lancey, outraged by his calm diagnosis, "you bled like—by the gallon!"

"My eye," Justin said, "no matter how it looked. I always bleed buckets, Lancey. Had an army surgeon once tell me it was healthy." His chuckle was genuinely amused. "This is a fleabite compared to what hit me at Monmouth or Petersham."

The hero, thought Dirck bitterly. This Justin couldn't behave like a normal human, but had to remind everybody of his honorable scars.

Lancey felt both relieved and annoyed. Justin's attitude, if true, made light of his danger, but also of her worry. She decided he was being brave. At any rate she wasn't going to take *his* word about the seriousness of his wound.

Peering ahead, the girl saw that they were now close to her home. Light streamed from the open Dutch door, promised warmth and shelter.

Hendrick, waiting beside Jaycock in the Quist yard, wasted no time with questions. Lancey jumped down from the pillion, watched the three men carefully ease Justin out of the saddle. He made neither protest nor comment at the prospect of being carried.

The girl, hurrying ahead of the shuffling men, found her stepmother busily wadding the settle with bedding. Hester stared, raised her voice in a wail.

"Lancey, your dress! Not again!"

Lancey, flinging her cloak aside, glanced down at the rain-soaked dress. Why, she thought, I knew it was clinging and drenched, but paid no attention. Too much had happened for the russet gown to be important.

"Hester," she said. "Justin's hurt."

"I know. Shot. Digmus said."

"He may need a doctor."

"Pardon will know. I sent Jan to fetch him."

"Jan?" Lancey whirled, startled. "Jan Elmendorf?"

"Yes," said Hester, nodding, "he's been here all evening, waiting to capture Justin if he came."

"But, then—Jan hates Justin. He'll go for the sheriff and——"

"Not Jan. He wants to hale Justin to gaol all by himself." Hester turned as the men edged their burden through the doorway. "Put him over here on the settle, Hendrick."

Justin grunted in pain, and Dirck's voice ripped out angrily. "For God's sake, Jaycock, watch what you're doing. You nearly dropped him."

"Steady," Hendrick said. "Steady now."

As they placed the wounded man on the pile of bedclothes, Hester bustled forward. She said, "We'd better get those wet clothes off him before he takes a chill."

Lancey gazed at Justin, frowned. His face, shining wet from the rain, showed the tautness of strain. Though his cheeks were flushed, his brow was pallid. The dark eyes looked hot with fever. They rolled as he glanced around the room, then narrowed.

"Wait a minute," Justin said, "where's Venick?"

Trying to ease his jacket off, Hester paused at the sharpness of the question. She said, "Who?"

"Venick's gone," said Lancey. "He ran off while we were trying to bandage you. Just disappeared."

"But he can't." Justin pushed Hester's hands away, struggled to sit up. "We have to change plans, but I'll be fit in a couple of days."

"What plans?" asked Dirck.

Justin ignored him, pointed a finger at Digmus Jaycock. "Catch him, Digmus. Tell him there's nothing to worry about. He can't pull foot on us now."

The little innkeeper paled, wet his lips, blurted a sentence. "Don't be a fool, Justin."

"What?"

"What I said. Venick dassn't risk using you now. With sheriffs and what-not after you. He'll keep running till he's safe. He must have thought you were bound to be captured with a pistol ball in you."

Nobody else in the room moved. They were all watching the speakers, the angry wounded man and the frightened tavern owner.

Justin said, "But I'm *not* captured!"

"He couldn't chance it," Jaycock said. "Him being a Tory and all——"

"Tory?" Justin's interruption crackled through the room. "*Tory?*"

The name, Lancey thought, sounded like an epithet, brought a prickle of gooseflesh to the nape of her neck. She glanced at the others, saw a reaction on every face. Dirck's mouth was tight; Hendrick was glaring. Even Hester had stiffened to her full height. The bitterness of civil strife had been neither forgotten nor forgiven.

"Venick was a Tory?"

Jaycock flinched at Dirck's tone, managed a nod. The fury in Justin's voice made Lancey jump.

"But I took his money! *Tory money!* I've got every riverfront rough between Rhinebeck and Fallkill primed with it, ready to march on the convention with muskets!"

"What?" Dirck whirled on Justin.

"We planned to riot," Justin said. "To demonstrate! To show the convention delegates that they'd better not vote for the Constitution! But, God Almighty, if he bought us with Tory money——"

"This is true, Digmus?" Hendrick's voice was a deep growl.

"Yes," said Jaycock, in a whisper. "Venick came down from Canada. He swore the governor, Sir Guy Carleton, had no finger in his scheme, but Tories supplied the cash all right." He swallowed, took defiant courage from their disapproving silence. "Where's the harm in taking good coin? Justin wanted to raise a rumpus anyway. Why should he care who provided the money?"

"It's the difference," Justin said, "between Dan Shays and Benedict Arnold, you mealy-mouthed, whining son of a sloat!" He sank back on the settle, stared at the ceiling.

There goes, Lancey thought, that last desperate gamble he mentioned. She felt, strangely, no pity for Justin's defeat, but a faint contempt. Rioting like a pack of schoolboys insisting on a holiday!

"Well," roared Pardon Cash as he stamped into the room, "I

thought the convention was up at the courthouse. Clear the decks here! A lad's been shot, needs care!"

Lancey busied herself helping Hester remove Justin's shirt. When she glanced around, Dirck was gone.

23

AMAZINGLY, IT WAS JAN ELMENDORF WHO PROVIDED THE MEANS for Justin Pattison's escape. He hated Justin no less, but he had his reasons.

On the morning after the duel Lancey found Jan lounging in the Quist yard when she emerged. The girl was feeling seedy, and sure she looked worse. For all that Pardon Cash, after washing the wound with hot gin, had declared that Justin had suffered no more than a graze, Lancey had nursed a restless patient almost till dawn. Even when he dozed she'd stayed awake, trying to make sense of her battered emotions.

She'd been so sure that she loved Justin; now she was twice as sure it was Dirck. Lancey only half recalled that Dirck had mentioned marriage, and declared his love, while they were alone in the clearing. What with storm, and duel, her fear and hysterics, everything that had happened seemed to be part of a fantastic nightmare.

The sight of Jan's sullen face and stolid build was like a bracing plunge in cold water. At least, she thought, I've not changed my opinion of *him!*

"You clear out of here, Jan Elmendorf," she shouted. She was sure she knew why he was there, and it spoiled the fineness of the day, dimmed the brilliance of the freshly washed blue of the·June sky. "You're not taking anybody to gaol from this house!"

"Shhh," hissed Jan, glancing around, "somebody might hear, Lancey."

"Let them hear!"

"You don't mean that." Jan faced her squarely, hands on his hips, chin thrust forward. "Dirck van Zandt says you'd never forgive me if I was to deliver Justin to the authorities."

"Oh? When was this?"

"Last night. I was here when Dirck came out, and Digmus Jaycock He invited me down to the ordinary for a nip." Jan's eyes brightened,

271

and he grinned. "Say, can that Dirck drink! He must have drained three bottles of Jaycock's best claret."

"I'm not surprised," said Lancey. She noticed Jan's familiar use of Dirck's name, and smiled inwardly. Charms them with claret, she thought, every time.

"Well, anyway, he said you'd never forgive me. Said you'd cherish Justin in—in durance's bile, and hate me till your dying day."

"He was right."

"That's what I thought. And Dirck said that if I helped Justin get away, you'd always remember it."

"Right, again," said Lancey, a trifle nettled by Dirck's choice of words. Jan was trouble enough without encouragement.

"So I've a plan, Lancey. The *Lydia* sails again in three, four days. Of course he——" Jan nodded toward the Quist home—"he couldn't come aboard at Poughkeepsie. But we could pick him up from a small boat on the river."

"What about Captain Benjamin?"

"He said it was all right after Dirck explained about Shays' Rebellion. Of course he charged Dirck double passage."

"Charged Dirck?"

"Dirck paid in advance."

Lancey wasn't sure she could trust Jan, but she agreed to ask Justin. In spite of his vaunted powers of recovery it was obvious that he was in no condition to ride or walk; even the climb from rowboat to sloop deck might be too much for him. She was surprised by Justin's instant enthusiasm.

"It's the perfect plan, Lancey. Even if the Springfield men return home, the Poughkeepsie sheriff will be looking for me. I can rest on the voyage and walk ashore when we reach New York."

"But—four days—your wound——"

"There's no point in coddling myself. Besides, I'm anxious to get away as fast as I can."

"Why?" asked Lancey, and then blushed.

"Yes," said Justin, gazing at her, "there's that, Lancey." He was pale under his tan, but the dark eyes were still defiant. "I fought that duel to kill Dirck van Zandt. He proved the better marksman, and I lost. But if I stayed around here——"

"You'd try again?"

"I might."

They were alone in the Quist downstairs room. Sunlight streamed through the open top of the Dutch door, and Lancey could hear the

272

piping of Hester's daughters playing outside. She gazed at the floor, counted the cracks that joined the wide boards between her feet and the fireplace. Her voice was very low.

"Where are you going, Justin?"

"West," he said at once. "Kentucky maybe. Or the Ohio valley. The country the Pennsylvania riflemen talked about. Out there they'd consider Shays' Rebellion just a market-day fracas that got out of hand."

There was farewell in his statement, and they both knew it.

* * *

The river changed from ebbtide to flood, signalling the transition to the discerning eye by movement and color. As always, on a day of June sunshine, the water's blue seemed to laugh at the rival blue of the sky. The bright sun of late morning turned the lazily moving puff-clouds to masses of whipped cream against a single shade, but it touched the wavelets with a golden wand that brought sparkle and variety. Here the current matched the canopy above it, there the river ran darker; one cove cupped an eddy pale as sapphire, another gleamed like polished marble with wind-stirred ripples for veins. Even the high, tree-covered banks, gay with the green of early summer, appeared to have been designed as a setting for the stream that flowed between them.

Lancey Quist, dangling her bare legs from the end of her father's pier, gazed at all this beauty and yawned in boredom. She had seen the Hudson's every mood, found nothing surprising about its present loveliness.

Northward, upriver at a point above the town of Poughkeepsie, a lone fishing boat drifted. Distance dwarfed the craft to thimble size, but Lancey knew it was Pardon Cash's dory, with Hendrick aboard as the big fisherman's partner.

No other vessel moved within the range of Lancey's vision. Even the ferry barge had not made a crossing for the past hour.

The girl felt lost, and a little lonely. All the sounds she heard were familiar, nature formed: the soft lapping of water against the piles, a twittering bird, the whisper of foliage to a passing breeze. The house behind her was empty. Hester had taken the children visiting. A fish net hung, drying, on its rack, but Lancey considered this poor company.

It looks listless, she thought, and empty, the way I feel.

Justin was gone, safely away in the early dawn. There had been no trouble. Everything had gone according to plan; the transfer from rowboat to sloop had been made without a hitch. By now the *Lydia* was farther down the river than Lancey had ever sailed.

Lancey, brooding, tried to summon a tear for Justin's departure, and failed. The few days of nursing him had settled that question forever. Justin had wasted no time mourning his losses. In fact, Lancey decided, his farewells had been jarringly cheerful.

"By this time," Lancey said, aloud, "he's probably arguing Jan Elmendorf into a mutiny against Captain Benjamin."

The thought produced a grin. Poor Jan was certainly susceptible to argument. Dirck van Zandt had persuaded him to help a man he hated. She expected no trouble when Jan returned to find that he'd removed the wrong rival. The sailor was awed and impressed by Dirck. Lancey suspected that the shooting of Justin had won Jan's steadfast friendship.

"And just where," she asked the west bank opposite, "is that glib-tongued Master van Zandt?"

She had seen Dirck only once since the night of the duel. Two days ago he had galloped Meda into the Quist yard, shouted his news from the saddle.

"Lancey, Hendrick, Hester! The word's just arrived. New Hampshire ratified!"

Lancey recalled their stupefied questions, her own utter disbelief.

"Are you sure, Dirck?"

"When?"

"I—I don't believe it."

"It's true!" Dirck had sounded positive, as well as angry. "New Hampshire voted to adopt the Constitution on the twenty-first of June! New Hampshire, for God's sake!"

"But—but doesn't that mean——"

"Yes, Lancey! That makes New Hampshire number nine. The ninth state! It's the law of the land now, no matter what we decide here in Poughkeepsie!"

"What's the convention going to do?"

"I don't know. Everybody's in an uproar. Clinton's off in one corner swearing that it doesn't make any difference, and Hamilton, smiling and quiet, is in another knowing blame well it does. The town is worse than the delegates. There hasn't been so much talk since the courthouse burned down! I've got to get back!"

Dirck had wheeled the mare, and raced away. Leaving me, Lancey remembered, without a single affectionate word, in worse condition than the town.

For Poughkeepsie was still suffering from shock and outrage. Lancey, hurrying to join the crowd around the courthouse, had shared the local feeling. After all the excitement, the anger, the fierce debate, another state had cast the deciding vote. Overnight Poughkeepsie had toppled from its eminent position, had ceased to be the most important town in the independent states.

Some took the news in glum silence; others were loudly indignant. The townsfolk had considered the convention a personal possession that combined the best, most dignified qualities of county fair and republican forum. Now that possession had diminished in importance, was no longer *the* great contest, and people felt they'd been swindled.

Digmus Jaycock was among the angriest. The little innkeeper had hammered fist in palm, and shouted.

"That piddling New Hampshire! They done this on purpose! Ain't they always tried to get the best of us in New York? They set up those Hampshire Grants years back just to spite us! On land that's rightly ours! And, look what happened. Now it's the Vermont Republic, ain't even part of the country!"

Lancey, listening, had suspected that Jaycock's anger was intended to quiet any rumors about his loyalty or friendliness to Tories.

The delegates to the convention had, after the first flurry of excitement, acted with more deliberation. Lancey had managed to catch glimpses of both leaders. George Clinton's bulldog look refused to admit even a minor defeat. Young Alexander Hamilton, dapper and cool, walked like a man now sure of victory.

They will argue for weeks, Lancey guessed, before a vote is taken.

The sunshine was making her drowsy, and she yawned again. As far as she was concerned the convention, like the shad run, was over.

"Except," muttered Lancey, "you can depend on the fish coming back next year, but you never know what men will do."

This remark pulled her mind from sleepy lethargy. Lancey, head lowered, stared at the river beneath her feet, as if seeking the answer to her puzzle in the depths of the blue water. Dirck van Zandt was a man. Did she know, for sure, what he would do?

His absence was beginning to worry her. Perhaps he regretted the proposal made in the clearing, or, more likely, never meant the words to be taken seriously. Dirck had certainly, she recalled, taken her acceptance for granted. Maybe the mixture of gathering tempest, her nearness, the mention of her betrothal to Justin had goaded Dirck to speak of marriage.

"Fighting fire with fire," said Lancey, miserably.

Dirck was clever, guileful, wily. Nobody else could have talked Jan and Justin into the same sloop, neatly removing both by one voyage. From the first she had hesitated to trust Dirck. If his offer of marriage was merely part of a devious scheme Lancey thought she would die.

She loved him.

That was the bald and simple truth. Whatever happened Lancey knew she could never escape again.

"*Lancey!*"

The hail was quite close, and she glanced up, startled. She recognized the little boat at once, rose to her feet. The *Argo* carried her spritsail like a banner. Lancey's heart leaped in reply. Dirck, grinning at the tiller, held something aloft and yelled.

"Betrothal gift!"

Betrothal, thought Lancey. Her hand flashed high in a wave that was half-salute, half-triumph.

Sunshine gleamed on fresh red paint, glittered on polished steel. Lancey gaped, staring, suddenly weak with elation. She gave a gasp of delight.

The gift Dirck flourished was a pair of brand-new red skates!

"Red skates!" called Lancey. "You fool! It's summer!" Nothing could have pleased her more. The skates were at once a reminder of the past, a promise for the future.

She stood there watching Dirck as he brought the *Argo* toward her.